WOVEN IN DARKNESS

WOVEN SAGA #1

LUCY HOLDEN

FEHU PRESS

For Brigitte
Who has been there through every chapter of this book with an infinite supply of bubbles, love, patience and encouragement.

WOVEN IN DARKNESS

LUCY HOLDEN

THE NIGHTGARDEN SAGA PRECEDES THIS BOOK, BUT IS NOT
REQUIRED READING FOR THIS SERIES.

NIGHT GARDEN SAGA IN ORDER:

THE WOVEN WORLD

A NOTE TO THE READER

Indigo is the ephemeral stuff of this world. To Work, or Weave it, is what you and I might call 'magic'.

A full glossary of terms regarding the people, places, institutions and lore of the Woven World can be found in the endnotes at the back of this book.

No world is simple. And if it was, what would be the point in writing about it?

I hope you get lost in this one.

Lucy.

PROLOGUE

HIRAETH

*M*y first memory is of Hiraeth Forest.

The letters of my name are carved here, on the smooth trunk of the fountain tree: *Zaria*. I was a child when I carved them. I wonder sometimes if it was my way of telling the world that I existed. That I was more than the slave braid around my neck or a bag of coin that filled every year on the same date. More than the caretaker of four other children, all of us thrown together by a fate none of us can recall.

The people of the Seam won't enter Hiraeth. They are afraid of the whispering trees and strange shadows, of the dark creatures that find their way here from distant worlds. But Hiraeth is where the Seam Guards found us all those years ago. I belong here just as much as any of the dark creatures. Perhaps I am a dark creature myself, and the whispers are trying to call me home.

The fountain tree is an old yew, with ancient prop roots that twine about a smooth marble bowl. Calling it the *fountain tree* is a childhood habit and not strictly correct. The fountain doesn't have taps, and no water comes from it. Curled writing in a long-forgotten language carved on the underside of the bowl denotes it as a silverscye, a doorway leading to the pathways through the Interweave.

The Pathfinder is late. The pale winter sky is deepening to indigo, and night will soon be here. Even I am not Fool enough to be in Hiraeth after dark.

I am more afraid today than I have ever been, and I have lived a life in which fear is ever present.

Yesterday, for the first time in fifteen years, the five bags of coin that came with our slave braids did not fill.

I know this because every year, on the same date, I pick the lock to Hodda's office and creep in at dawn to check if the bags are full or not. So long as that annual coin appeared, none of us could be sold. But today it did not. The bags are empty. And that means we are Hodda's to sell.

Body and soul, as the words of the slave trade go.

Never has it felt lonelier to be the eldest of our small family of five, and never has a secret weighed more. Normally I would share it with Doron, my brother, who is only a year younger than I. He is no longer a child, has been fighting in the ring for coin almost as long as I have been coming to Hiraeth to trade in Darkwine. Between us we have raised our three younger siblings, holding the two girls, Shimi and Neoma, between us when they cried at night for the mothers they never knew; carrying the baby, Levin, until he was old enough to walk alone. Doron and I have never needed to speak of the life we can't remember. We both recall well enough standing amid these trees on a dark, cold night, with no memory and only each other to rely on. Whatever came before that moment has never been my concern. It's what comes next that haunts me.

We're bound in the way survivors are, quietly and with unquestioning loyalty. I've bandaged Doron's broken bones just as he has my wounds after Hodda's beatings. Throughout it all, we've planned and schemed for only one goal: freedom.

The breeze is picking up, though the silverscye is not yet

whispering. I know I shouldn't be here so late. Doron would say I shouldn't be here at all, or at least, not alone. But I need time to think. To plan. To decide how best to proceed. And for perhaps the first time, how much I should tell my siblings.

I've been training for the Braid Race almost since the day we arrived in the Seam.

If I win, my braid will be unwoven.

If I lose, I will die.

But there's little point in dwelling on that.

Win the Braid Race and my freedom with it. Use the prize money to buy my siblings from Hodda. Find a way to get their braids unwoven.

Four steps to freedom. A mantra that has sustained me through beatings and poverty for as long as I can recall. A plan so deeply ingrained in my being that I have neither questioned it nor allowed myself to consider the possibility it might fail.

A plan that could never be executed, so long as those bags filled.

I've always known Hodda would never give us up so long as he received that annual payment. Why would he? We're free labor, to be used as he sees fit in his Dark and Disorderly House.

But now the bags are empty, the Braid Race is a matter of days away, and I have no idea how to tell Doron, or the others, about the future we face. Either I win that Race and we have a chance, or the threads that have bound our lives together for fifteen years are about to be brutally severed, our destinies cast to the winds of fate.

Hodda might hold the ring on which the ends of our five braids are knotted, but he has never truly owned us—until now. If he unties those knots, exchanges them for coin, and says the words, whatever plan I have will at best become infinitely more difficult. At worst, my siblings will be lost to me forever, along with my slim chance at freedom.

Doron has come with me to the Braid Race every year,

although we've never allowed our younger siblings to attend. He and I have leaped to our feet and cheered the winners with savage triumph, hearts aching with longing and hope as we watched them be unbraided by the Astrian Weaver.

But unlike the other slaves, who leave soon after that glorious moment, Doron and I have always stayed, standing silent witness as the other competitors die, one by one. Some choose to take their own life right there on the track, their lifeblood running quietly into the dust, rather than face the wrath of their masters.

I've remained silent about the bags of coin because I need to be certain the person on that track, possibly facing that same choice, is me.

I can face the Race itself. I can face the savage consequences should I lose.

I can't face watching Doron or any of my siblings take my place.

And the only way to ensure they do not is by keeping my knowledge of the empty bags to myself.

The Pathfinder once told me the gloaming is when the fabric between the worlds is thinnest. It's also when I feel most alone. I harness my horse Teddy to the carrick, keeping one eye on the silverscye. I might be at peace in Hiraeth Forest, but I'm no Fool. The Seam may not be the shining world of Astria, but neither is it the Foolish world, where knowledge of Weaving has been lost entirely. The Seam lies between, a fold stitched into the Interweave long ago to protect Astria. On the Astrian side of the silverscye lies the world of the Indigold nobility, a place of wonders I can barely begin to imagine. One where even the lowliest Indigold peasant can earn their needle and learn to Work as their gifts dictate. Sometimes I dare to dream of what that might feel like, to hold a needle in my own hand and know how to make it Work. It is a private dream, one I never speak of.

No slave is permitted to hold a needle.

The Seamish side of the silverscye is another world entirely, one of poverty and desperation. Centuries of interbreeding with monsters and Fools has created the Seamish race, who don't hold needles and wouldn't know how to Work them even if they did. A world of Astrian exiles, most enslaved as I and my siblings are, whom the Seamish themselves despise. They call us Weorpan: the unwanted.

Perhaps everyone has a darkness inside of them. Amid the squalor of the Seam, many look to the gleaming world of Astria for solace, believing happiness lies on the other side of the silverscye. But I don't think the darkness inside me is something that can be discarded in the pathways of the Interweave. Instead I focus on freedom. That is a goal I can understand, a hunger I can believe might one day be satisfied.

The darkness I keep to myself.

And besides, the Seam is where Anahita's Gold pierced the Interweave long ago. Hiraeth Forest is where the fold between the worlds is at its most porous. Dark Rips appear here for no reason at all, and creatures dark as Anahita herself with them.

In the Seam, the darkness never really left.

The shadows are growing, and the heady scent of Darkwine wreathes about me.

The Pathfinder is coming.

CHAPTER 1

STRANGER

"*Y*ou're a long way from home, little criminal."

The silverscye is still closed, and that voice doesn't belong to the Pathfinder. The braid around my neck prickles with an odd, unfamiliar awareness.

I mentally calculate the distance between my horse and me.

"You wouldn't make it before I reached you." The stranger stepping out of the trees barely five paces away is one of the tallest men I've ever seen, and I stand barely two inches under six feet myself. Despite the cold, he's wearing only a loose white linen shirt, open at the neck and rolled to the elbows. His hands are thrust into the pockets of his dark breeches, which are topped by gleaming black boots. His small smile doesn't quite touch his eyes, which are quite the strangest I've ever seen. A deep, shadowy indigo, they're rimmed in smoky black and shot through with silver.

"You're not from here." I know it as surely as I do that he is dangerous. Not just because he is a stranger in Hiraeth at dusk, although that alone is cause enough for alarm. Despite his casual appearance, every inch of his body, from the loose, rangy shoulders to the corded muscle in his forearms, suggests a lethal, coiled power. I could run, but he's right: he'd reach me before I made it to Teddy and the carrick.

Besides, running would mean missing the Pathfinder and his Darkwine delivery. Darkwine means coin, and given today's events, coin matters more than a stranger in the woods, no matter how dangerous he looks.

"You should leave." I face him squarely. The scent of Darkwine twines about me, thick and seductive. "The silverscye will open soon, and the Pathfinder doesn't like surprises."

His dark, straight eyebrows rise, a hint of amusement lighting the sloping eyes beneath. "I think perhaps it is you who should consider leaving." The growing shadows lend his face a timeless quality, his dark blond hair seeming to glow with light of its own. It hangs loose against a strong jaw and skin the color of burnt sienna. Facing him is mesmerizing, like looking into a summer sunfall. "Tonight isn't the time for your illegal Darkwine activities."

"I'm not here illegally." *Well, not entirely.* "I'm here to collect Darkwine for the Paladin abbey."

"Ah." His smile twists into something much harder, his eyes darkening like Hiraeth's night shadows. "Our noble Paladins seem to have forgotten that their role is to protect a fountain and mix a sacred drink. They grow increasingly bold in their dark experiments. Although using a slave from a Disorderly House is a new low, even for them."

Icy contempt drips from every word.

He has clearly never met Leo. Thinking of the hapless Paladin Divine who is too afraid to come to Hiraeth to collect his own Darkwine, I suppress a smile. A less likely manipulator of innocents would be difficult to imagine.

"How do you know I'm from a Disorderly House?" His presumption annoys me more than his manner intimidates me. My eyes are the deep amethyst of Darkwine itself, and since childhood people have taken me either for an addict or the child of one. Men tend to draw the conclusion that I make my coin on my back. I try to counter those assumptions by making myself as unappealing to men as possible, from my loose tunic and trousers to the tightly plaited hair coiled neatly behind my head.

"You're a slave." The stranger tilts his head, implying an immutable fact. "It would be something of a miracle if you weren't in a Disorderly House."

A faint crack echoes in the distance. The air seems almost to quiver, and an ugly, sulfuric scent fills the clearing. I spin around, every sense alert. The sky is no longer pale but a sickening rust color, and a restless wind is picking up. Somewhere in Hiraeth, a Dark Rip has opened.

"You need to leave." The stranger's eyes on the tree line behind me are grim and distant. "Hiraeth isn't safe tonight."

I open my mouth to tell him this is hardly the first time I've heard a Rip open in the forest, then think better of it. The Pathfinder is undoubtedly close. If I can just get this man to leave, I can pick up the Darkwine I need, then get out of here.

"Of course." I bend my head obediently and move toward Teddy. I make a show of tightening the harness, but my other eye is on the silverscye, where I can see the faintest shadow appear.

"Don't linger." The stranger's voice is abrupt, and when I turn, he's regarding me through narrow eyes, as if he knows exactly what is going through my mind. "It isn't safe."

I nod, gathering Teddy's reins. When I glance back a moment later, the clearing is empty, the tall stranger gone as if he'd never been. In the distance beyond the trees, the sky is swirling with the fierce winds that always accompany a Rip.

For what it's worth, I know he was right: Hiraeth isn't safe for anyone when a Dark Rip opens. But today is not a normal day, and a Dark Rip, even one so close, seems far less dangerous than the future looming in the empty bags on Hodda's desk.

"Zaria."

For the second time, I swing around, knife at the ready, but this time it is Doron's lithe figure coming out of the trees, and I relax, at least a little.

"What are you doing here?" I smile, but my heart is racing. I've never been any good at lying, and Doron knows me better than anyone. I've been avoiding him since yesterday morning. "I thought you were fighting in the ring tonight."

"And I thought you said the Darkwine wasn't due until tomorrow." Doron is six feet of lean, honed muscle, hardened by the fighting ring. His skin is raw umber to my dark ocher. Our brother Levin, conversely, is pale as the winter sky. None of us look at all alike. Nor do we know our ages, but I estimate I was about five the night we were found, and Doron somewhere around a year younger than that. If that makes me approaching twenty, then Doron is at least eighteen. I tend to forget how much he has grown until I catch sight of him unawares, like now. Then I notice the rather grim light in his eyes, the tension in his angular face.

"You've been avoiding me." Doron has a harelip scar that runs a jagged path up one side of his face. Longer than a normal harelip, it's laced with the same silver as his eyes, which glitter now as he stares at me. He's the quietest of us all and rarely speaks unless it's necessary. He and I have never had a real argument, or not one that I can recall, and that makes the intensity in his face now even more disturbing.

I look away from him, unwilling to lie, but even less inclined to explain why he is correct. "You shouldn't have come." I nod at the ugly orange sky. "There's a Rip in the forest, and the Pathfinder is late."

"There are often Rips. And the Pathfinder will come soon enough." There's an odd certainty in Doron's tone. As if to affirm his words, the first whispers rustle the leaves about us. In contrast to the vicious winds that accompany a Rip, the silverscye breezes are light and restless, carrying mercurial snatches of strange voices. Usually I find a certain thrill in the moments before the silverscye opens, as if hearing the echoes of other worlds somehow brings them closer. Bound as I am, even the illusion of escape has an almost mystical draw for me.

But today the restless whispers, combined with Doron's tightly controlled tension, trigger a feeling of unease that grows rapidly worse when Levin's sturdy figure emerges from the trees a moment later.

"We need to hurry." His blue eyes, normally sparkling with good humor, are shadowed with caution and move warily around the clearing. "The Seam Guard are close by, and that was definitely a Rip opening up."

"Yes, Levin." I know I sound impatient, but I'm growing more unsettled by the minute and with every whisper that comes from the silverscye. "There's obviously a Rip. What isn't so obvious is what the two of you are doing here." The surreptitious glance they exchange, and Doron's unsmiling face, shifts my internal danger gauge to high alert.

"What's going on?" I look between them. Levin drops his eyes almost immediately, glancing sideways at Doron.

Doron stares directly at me. "We know the bags didn't fill."

The leaves overhead dance, and behind me I hear the low, dull roar as the silverscye begins to open. I nod slowly, trying to ignore the hard lump in my chest. "I was going to tell you."

"When?" Doron asks flatly. "Before you entered the Braid Race or after?"

"I don't know." I want to say more, but the words won't come. I can barely name my fears myself, let alone explain them.

I didn't tell you because I'm afraid of what you might do. I can face the Race myself, but I can't face losing any of you.

Even the thought of saying something so blatantly coercive turns my stomach. I've never imposed my fears on my siblings, and today is not the time to alter that.

"Did it ever occur to you that the rest of us have a right to know?" Doron's low tone is relentless. "That we also have decisions to make?"

"What decisions?" Fear, thick and cold, rises in my throat. "We have a plan, Doron. We've always had a plan. Nothing has changed." But even as I say it, I hear the pleading note in my voice and see the hard, unforgiving light in Doron's eyes.

"Everything has changed." Doron pulls a bag from his shoulder and nods at the silverscye behind me. "When the Pathfinder leaves, I'm going with him."

CHAPTER 2

PATHFINDER

The marble softens, then begins to ripple, shimmering with the coming silver. The ripples form an oval that gradually grows brighter, like moonlight on water. Strange whispers fill the air around us in a muted roar, then fall abruptly silent as the marble fades completely, revealing a gleaming oval swirl of indigo, gold and aqua. The silverscye is open.

The Pathfinder's silver comes through in a stream of shiny bubbles that hang on the air above the bowl. It isn't the silver I'm watching, though.

It's Doron.

The fixed, determined expression on his face terrifies me.

Levin, who has always hated tension between any of us, is standing by the carrick, stroking Teddy. The horse is as unsettled as the woods around us. Night is growing, and the wind caused by the Dark Rip hasn't calmed. If anything, it is growing stronger, whipping the whispers from the silverscye and causing the Pathfinder's silver to tremble uneasily on the air.

"Slaves can't go through the silverscye." It's the first thing that comes to mind, but I know as soon as the words are out they're the wrong ones. Doron's intelligence is often masked by silence, but that doesn't mean it isn't sharp. Telling him something he not only already knows but has clearly considered is the fastest way to alienate him. Going by his clenched fists, I've clearly succeeded in doing just that.

"Doron." I reach for his arm, but he twists away, the silver in his eyes and scar glittering fiercely. All five of us bear marks of Astria. Like all Weorpan, we are Indigold, not Seamish, even if we can't carry needles and are bound to servitude by our braids.

Doron's silver is one of the more obvious marks. It made him an object of deep suspicion right up until the day he stepped into the fighting ring and put a stop to the insults with his body. It's not hard now for me to see behind his anger to the boy he once was, confused and scared by the hatred and suspicion that saw him repeatedly knocked to the ground, simply for existing.

"I found a way to get through." Doron's mouth is set into a hard, implacable line.

I know that look.

"You found a way." I repeat his words slowly, trying to work out what possible way he can have found that we haven't, at some point, discussed.

We're standing on either side of the fountain tree now, the silver forming and reforming as the Pathfinder takes shape.

"Is it a way that gets the braid off your neck, once you're in Astria?" My fear comes out sounding like anger, but I'm powerless to stop it. The truth is that I'm terrified.

"It will take a year," Doron says quietly. "But yes, at the end of that year, the braid will be unwoven." He glances at Levin, who has dropped any pretense of tending Teddy, his eyes now moving warily between us instead. "You know I can't join the Paladins," Doron says. "They only take perfection, like our golden boy Levin, here." His mouth twists in a sharp smile that doesn't reach his eyes. He taps his scar. "And we both know they'll never accept someone with a scar full of Pathfinder's silver."

"You don't know that's what it is," I begin, then stop when I see his impatience.

"It doesn't matter whether it is or isn't. The Paladins only care about what it might be." He pauses, then takes a deep breath. "I'm going to the Drop."

His words fall into the space between us at the same time that the bubbles finally join into one mass. The mass forms a figure that shifts from silver to man, and then the Pathfinder is standing before us.

His appearance never reforms in the same way twice, though he always has the thin, sharp features of his kind, with narrow eyes that shine like the first stars.

"I can't linger." Never known for flowery manners, the Pathfinder's greeting is nonetheless unusually cursory. He glances around warily. "There was strange movement in the pathways. An unfamiliar presence. I don't like it." He looks at Doron, then me, with a derisive smile. "You're just telling her now, I take it."

I barely hear a word over the roaring in my ears.

The Pathfinder curls his fingers toward the silverscye. There is the familiar thick, heady smell, followed by a steady torrent of Darkwine that the Pathfinder directs neatly into the leather flagons that appear from beneath his cloak.

"The Drop." I focus on Doron, trying to ignore the Pathfinder's sly eyes. "You want to be a Stitched Man?" The Stitched Men are the hardest of the Seam Guards, sailing their ships over the Drop and into the dark realms of the Interweave itself. They navigate the mysterious pathways and tangled threads which bind one world to another, their arcane stitches keeping the fabric between the worlds secure, and chaos at bay. To be a Stitched Man is an honorable path. One that can bring great fortune.

And one from which few return.

"I already look the part, at least." Doron touches his scar again. He doesn't quite smile, but at least the hard anger has left his eyes.

"The Seam Guards will help, once Doron is through." Levin, sensing the slight shift in tone, interrupts.

My fists tighten involuntarily. It's beginning to make sense. The boys from the local Seam Guard taught Doron everything he knows about fighting. In their own way, they've been there for all of us over the years. But that does little to reassure me now. And I find the gleam of hero worship in Levin's eyes even more terrifying than Doron's determination.

Will he be next?

Clearly my concerns must show in my face, because Levin turns away, catching flagons from the Pathfinder and tying them to the carrick.

"I still don't understand how you can get through the silver-scye in a slave braid." I have to raise my voice to be heard over the rising wind, and the light is fading fast. A storm must be coming.

The Pathfinder shoots me a sly smile. "Somebody owed somebody else a favor."

My heart stops. *A Shadow Bargain?*

A Shadow Bargain is always one favor for another of equal, but not necessarily the same, value. It sounds fine until one considers the mother who saves her child from death, only to watch her grandchild die instead.

"Not mine," Doron says hastily, seeing my face. "The Seam Guard organized it." I close my eyes in relief. The words binding a Shadow Bargain are specific: *Take what you want, and pay for it.* Only nobody ever knows what the payment will be, when it will come due, nor even which member of the family will be called to pay. At least Doron hasn't bound us all to an unknown debt.

But that doesn't lessen the devastation I feel.

"Together." I struggle to get the word out. "We always promised each other we would leave together, or not at all."

"No." Doron's composure cracks, and I catch a glimpse of the emotion he's battling to hide. "That was your promise to us, Zaria. You said that so long as one of us remained enslaved, you would never be free. Maybe you meant it as a comfort, and maybe when we were children, it was. But we're not children anymore."

A branch whips across my face, and I almost welcome the stinging cut, the taste of blood. The pain is infinitely more bearable than Doron's words.

"That promise doesn't give you the right to hide the truth from us. And it doesn't give you the right to stop us trying for freedom, for ourselves or to help each other."

Part of me understands his logic and wonders if he might be right. But another part of me, the part that has spent all the years I can recall making decisions to keep the others safe, is screaming that this is a rushed decision, and a rash one. Doron's words demand that I unpick a lifetime of planning in a split second. Worse, that I go to the Race facing not only death, but the far darker prospect of leaving my younger siblings utterly alone, with neither Doron nor myself to rely on.

The wind is really picking up, and the Pathfinder's eyes dart around warily as he fills the last of the flagons. "I'm not staying around while you two argue," he says. "Make your choice."

"It isn't fair to ask him to stay," Levin says, behind me. "It isn't fair on any of us." His young face is set in unusually stubborn lines.

I'm not ready for this.

These conversations are supposed to happen after the Race. Not now. Not when we're poised on the brink of change. All I've ever wanted is for my siblings to choose their own futures. Everything I've done has been to ensure they have the best chance to do that. I always thought they understood that is what my promise meant. I certainly thought Doron knew. I've never tried to explain myself. And now isn't the time for those explanations.

Or for such momentous decisions.

"I have to go," Doron says roughly. Pain and determination war on his face, a battle that breaks my heart to watch. "I must, Zaria. The Race is two days away. If you win it, I know you will do all you can to help us. But we no longer have the security of the coin bags. If you lose, it isn't only your life that will end on that track. Hodda won't ever trust any of us again. We'll be sold, and whatever choices we might have now will be gone. I might make my fortune with the Stitched Men." He twists his head curtly, cutting off my objections before they find voice. "If I do, I can try to buy freedom for the others. If I go, I can at least offer them another chance, no matter how small." He shakes his head. "I can't just stand aside and watch you, Zaria," he says hoarsely. "I can't watch you die out there for us and do nothing at all."

There is an odd thud somewhere in the distance. Doron looks around, frowning. "That voice." He takes a couple of steps away from the fountain. "Can you hear it, whispering?"

"There are always whispers from the silverscye," I say impatiently. "Doron—"

But my brother holds up a hand, shaking his head. "This is different." He glances at me, frowning. "Can't you hear it? Calling for help?"

I pause, listening, and for the briefest moment I think I do hear something. A girl, perhaps, calling out; but it's a wisp on the air, nothing more, and I have other concerns.

An acrid stench of sulfur crosses the clearing. Unease grips my stomach, the whisper forgotten. "We need to leave, Doron."

"Finally, something on which we agree." The Pathfinder turns to the silverscye. "It isn't safe here tonight. You!" he calls to Doron. "Say your goodbyes, boy." Moving to hold the marble edge of the fountain, the Pathfinder's form shimmers as he begins murmuring the low words that open the pathways. Doron turns between him and the direction the strange whispers, indecision writ large on his face.

I've never begged any of my siblings for anything. From the day we found ourselves in Hiraeth, I've known they are my responsibility. I'm the eldest, and I've done what I can to keep them safe, whether it meant doing their chores when they were sick or physically standing between them and Hodda's willow stick. What I've never done is inflict my own emotional fears or doubts on them.

Until now.

"Please don't do this, Doron." I hold his eyes with my own, letting him see the loneliness and fear I've always kept hidden. "Please don't leave them alone. If I die in that Race, they'll have nobody else."

We stare at one another amid the rising wind, and I see it, the moment his defenses crumble under the weight of my plea. I see the heaviness I have always carried settle on his shoulders, and the defeat in his face as he slowly nods.

Dark, corrosive shame grips a part of me I have spent my entire life trying to preserve, the fragile honor that is all a slave has in the face of the darkness binding them. In forcing Doron to stay I have compromised it forever, and that shame, I know with dark certainty, will never leave me.

"Come!" roars the Pathfinder, but instead of taking his hand, Doron twists away, his face empty and desolate.

The Pathfinder looks at me. "Fool," he hisses.

There is a swirl of silver, then the silverscye closes, and the Pathfinder is gone.

CHAPTER 3

DARK RIP

I want to take it back.

I want to reopen the silverscye and thrust Doron into the future he'd chosen for himself, instead of holding him captive to my own fears.

"Doron." I turn toward him, hand outstretched, but my brother is no longer looking at me. He's staring toward the trees at the edge of the clearing with a fixed, distant expression, as if part of him is already somewhere else. "Doron!" This time I have to shout over the howling winds.

They should have quieted now the silverscye is closed.

But instead of fading, the winds are a dark screech that seems to shake the sky itself, bending the ancient trees until their boughs split under the strain. The ugly orange hue of earlier has returned, shadowing the clearing in an unnatural light that has nothing to do with our world.

"Zaria!" Levin is battling a terrified Teddy as the horse strains against the harness, wanting only to escape whatever is coming. "It's a Dark Rip! We have to go!"

I know what it is. I know we need to leave. But Doron is

walking across the clearing with a slow, deliberate gait, almost as if he's under some kind of Weaving.

"Doron!" I scream his name over the wind. He turns his head to me as he reaches the first trees.

"Can't you hear it?" I see his mouth move rather than hear him over the deafening cacophony all around. "Someone is in there." He gestures toward the bending trees. "She needs help, Zaria." But whatever I might have heard earlier is gone. I can't hear anything but the rising wind and my own internal screams of fear.

"We have to leave!" I lunge forward in horror as Doron turns toward the trees, desperate to reach him, cut through whatever dark voice is calling him from within that unseen void. The air at the edge of the clearing is rippling uneasily, and Doron is walking straight toward it.

"Doron!" I'm running across the clearing, Levin thundering directly behind me in the carrick, but even as I scream Doron's name, I know, with a terrible certainty, that we're too late.

The Dark Rip splits the air directly in front of him, a vicious tear in the fabric of our world. I've never seen a Dark Rip up close, and the reality is more terrifying than even my darkest dreams. The elliptical shape of a serpent's pupil, it ripples like a fathomless black sea, stretching into a long, terrible tunnel with no discernible end. It has a grasping pull that sucks the air from all around and freezes me in place, so that I'm utterly incapable of moving.

Deep in the black tunnel, something is moving.

It's no more than a small dot at first. Powerless to move, I watch as the dot grows larger. Something is coming slowly toward us, distorted by the rippling air as if it is swimming underwater. As it comes nearer, the shape becomes more distinct. It is an enormous boar, standing half as tall as the oaks bending in the breeze, with tusks the length of a man's arm. As it comes closer to the elliptical gash where the Rip opens into our world, I realize there is someone mounted atop the boar, a man with white-blond hair and a narrow, determined face.

He seems not to notice Doron at all, though my brother is standing, as paralyzed as I, barely paces from the dark opening. The man's eyes are fixed somewhere over Doron's head.

They're fixed directly on me.

Unable to move, I watch helplessly as the man's arm slowly raises, the orange light glinting off a small metallic object in his hand. There's a sound like a crack of thunder and a sudden, searing pain in my arm. Then the boar is bursting out of the rippling darkness, breaking whatever it is that has held us all immobile. Time begins to move once again—and so do I.

"Doron!" My scream comes out as a strangled gasp, all that is left after the strange vacuum in which we've been held. I twist to leap aboard the carrick, just as Levin is about to jump down from it to help his brother.

"No!" I catch Levin's arm and haul him back into the carrick as he struggles against me.

"Let me go," he cries hoarsely, reaching for Doron, his face anguished. "Let me go, Zaria!"

But I know there is nothing he can do. Doron is directly in front of the Dark Rip, while we are barely halfway across the clearing. The man on the boar is raising his arm again.

This time, the weapon in his hand is pointing directly at Levin.

Seeing the direction of the man's arm, Doron turns toward us, his eyes filling with a growing horror I know all too well.

"*Run!*"

I know Doron is roaring at us, but I can't hear him, only see his mouth move as he gestures for us to flee. One hand grasps his knife, a pitifully small object compared to the monstrous beast bearing down upon him. The acrid stench of sulfur burns the air about us. Doron is running toward us now, stumbling in his haste, not, I know, in any real attempt to outrun the boar, but in a desperate effort to put himself between it and Levin.

Doron glances over his shoulder. The boar is almost upon him. He turns back toward me, his eyes stark with terror, and I know what he is asking.

Time slows once more, this time in my mind.

Doron is too far away for either of us to help him. We can't possibly reach him before the boar does. Levin is struggling against me, fighting to run to Doron's aid, and it's all I can do to hold him in one arm and Teddy's reins with the other hand. The Rip's acrid stench reaches for us, and it seems I can taste Dark-wine on my tongue, as if death itself is coming for me. In that moment of terrible decision, I almost wish for it.

There's an odd movement nearby, and I realize with a disjointed shock that the stranger who called me criminal earlier is back in the clearing. Where he came from, I couldn't say, but in some peculiar way he seems to belong here. Any trace of his initial smile is utterly gone, his face twisted and fierce as he faces down the boar and rider thundering toward us.

"Go," says the stranger curtly. He makes an abrupt gesture with one hand, and Teddy spins on the spot as if he has been physically picked up and turned around, taking the carrick and us with him.

The boar rider's small weapon cracks the air again. Just as we spin away from the Rip, something hard thuds into Doron's body with a vicious, heavy finality.

"No!" Levin cries hoarsely in my ear, his arms outstretched toward Doron. "You can't leave him; we have to help . . ."

The tall stranger facing down the oncoming boar turns briefly our way. He thrusts one hand toward us, and Teddy leaps forward, racing toward the woods. In the moment before the stranger turns back to the boar, a savagery as fathomless as the Rip itself gleams deep in his eyes.

"No," Levin says again, but his voice breaks, for even as he speaks, the boar is leaping over Doron's falling body. Our brother tumbles away from our view, sucked into the Rip's terrible, infinite blackness.

Then we are at the edge of the clearing and the boar has veered off into the trees, racing away from us.

As we plunge into the forest, I glance back.

The tall stranger who came to our defense is standing directly in front of the Rip, facing it down as if he and the darkness are ancient foes. Raising one arm, he draws it down in a masterful gesture of finality.

As abruptly as it opened, the Dark Rip closes.

Doron is gone.

Night falls across Hiraeth, and I drive the panicked horse through the trees, tears drying where they fall on my face.

CHAPTER 4

DARKWINE

"*Y*ou left him!" Levin's voice is rough with fury and pain. "I wanted to save him, and you made me leave."

Teddy's harness is half off, and we're thundering through the trees at a breakneck pace. I couldn't answer Levin even if I wanted to—and I don't.

"Doron wanted to leave." Levin's words are shameful stones cast with unerring accuracy. They land in the depths of my soul and settle, changing my internal landscape forever. "It was you who made him stay. I heard you. I heard what you said, Zaria." Emotion splinters his voice. "It's your fault. All of this is your fault." He lapses into dry, shuddering sobs against which I have neither defense nor argument.

I drive Teddy as fast as I dare, only reining him in when we reach the edge of Hiraeth. Levin leaps from the carrick before it stops moving, running into Lostport's maze of alleys without so much as a backward glance. I can't bring myself to call out to him.

I know that every word he said is true.

The flagons of Darkwine Levin tied to the carrick back in

Hiraeth are somehow still attached. After what they have cost us all, I feel like pouring them into the gutters. Instead, more from habit than any real decision, I turn Teddy toward the dockside cellar I use for storage. If Doron and Levin know about the coin bags failing to fill, then Shimi and Neoma, our sisters, do too. They both adore Doron. I doubt either of them will ever forgive me for tonight's work.

I doubt I will ever forgive myself.

I drive through Lostport with my head down, letting Teddy pick his own path through the familiar streets to the dock. I glance at the entrance of the Paladin abbey as I pass. There's no sign of Levin, but I know he's in there. He's been talking to Leo for months now. I've been telling myself that it's just a boy's natural curiosity about alchemy, but after tonight's events I need to face the fact that Levin is likely seeking his own pathway to freedom.

Doron was right when he said Levin is a perfect Candidate for the order. The Paladins prize physical perfection, both in their alchemists and those chosen for their military arm, the Blades. Trials for the latter are held on the same day as the Braid Race and offer an alternate route to freedom with far better odds, since multiple Candidates can qualify. Slave braids are unwoven after completion of the first year.

Candidate year, however, is notoriously cruel. Few slaves survive it, and even if they do, they must commit to the Blades for life in order to be unwoven.

The price for failure in the trials is the same as in the Race: death.

None of these options are new to me. We've discussed them all many times: the Stitched Men, the Blades. But they've always seemed nebulous propositions, hovering on the distant horizon of an unthinkable world in which I somehow failed to save us all and my brothers are left with no other options.

They don't belong to the here and now, in the world where Levin is barely fourteen, and Doron—

Dark eyes filled with fear as he tumbles slowly backward into blackness . . .

—Doron is gone forever, because of me.

My right arm hangs uselessly at my side, wounded by the small metallic weapon used by the boar rider who came from the Rip. Blood drips down the side of the carrick. I welcome the pain. I wish it was worse.

I wish it was me who fell into that Rip.

I drive past Disorderly Houses already filling with the Indigold nobles who visit the Seam during Race week. They come for the high stakes, the thrill of betting their coin against death itself. I used to wonder if any of the Indigold ever stop to think of what kind of life could be miserable enough to induce an entire field of slaves to risk certain death for only one slim chance at freedom. Years of watching the Indigold nobility get high on Darkwine and death during Race week, however, has brought me to the conclusion that they rarely think of us at all, except as entertainment.

I despise them for that.

Streets teeming with drunken revelry give way to the darker, mist-covered alleys of the docks. I turn the carrick down a twisting series of ever narrowing paths, watching carefully behind me, until I reach the dockside cellar I use for storage.

I wasn't lying when I told the stranger I was collecting Darkwine for the Paladins. What I didn't mention is that I take a profitable cut of the product, which I then trade throughout the Seam. The Paladins are responsible for mixing the dark, potent distillation used in the Coronastrian Tapest's Cupbearing ceremonies. In Astria, where the alchemy is more complex, that distillation is known as the Divine drink, hence the title given to the Paladin alchemists who mix it: Divines. Since Leo would likely poison us all by accident if he tried to do it himself, I mix it for him, just as I do the sweeter, though no less potent, aphrodisiac favored by men in the Disorderly Houses. I never make the heady mix that offers Darkwine dreams to the addict or the dying. In its most lethal, pure form, Darkwine is certain death. More than one addict has died from their desire for ever more exotic dreams. The heavy brew brought by the Pathfinder requires careful management.

Leo's incompetence has been my good fortune. He's terrified of Hiraeth and almost comically incompetent at his job— undoubtedly why the Paladins shipped him off to the outpost of the Seam. Our arrangement suits us both.

I unload the Darkwine with my good arm, trying not to think of the pain in the other one. It's dull and steady, a red pulse that is almost blinding when I move the wrong way. Every movement is a dark reminder that I'm still here, while Doron is gone. I wonder why I'm even bothering with the Darkwine. We've been saving the coin we make from trading for the day freedom came. Now freedom seems more distant than it ever has, and far less important without Doron to share it with.

Besides, the Race is only two days away. It's likely I won't live long enough to ever see the dockside cellar again.

I leave just enough Darkwine on the carrick for both the Paladin Abbey and Hodda, then close the door. I'm shivering as I climb back into the carrick, more from pain, grief, and the aftermath of shock than cold. The braid around my neck prickles, yet another painful reminder of all that has been lost. I urge Teddy into a smart pace. I need to outrun the memory of Doron's face and get back before my absence is noted. I barrel out of the alley, taking the corner on one wheel in my haste.

Too late, I realize there's somebody in my path.

I haul on Teddy's reins, and the horse rears in shock. The carrick tips, throwing me onto the cobblestones. I land painfully on my injured arm in time to watch a panicked Teddy race down the alley, dragging the upturned carrick behind him.

Darkwine from the spilled flagons hangs in a heady cloud on the air.

"Dreaver's Tells," I gasp.

"These docks do seem to bear them a remarkable resemblance, I'll grant you that."

I last heard that voice snarling at me to leave Hiraeth. Hearing it again plunges my body straight back into the horrific scene I so recently left. The tall stranger, by contrast, seems entirely unaffected by the drama of the night's events. "Andras." His tone is dry, almost bordering on the amused, as he turns to someone behind him. "Fetch the horse."

I open my mouth to protest that I don't need anyone chasing after my horse, then close it abruptly as I find myself suddenly upright once more.

"Careful." The man's eyes gleam even in the darkness, and I can't help but remember the savagery I saw in them back in the forest. "That was quite a fall you took." Perhaps intending to steady me, the man grasps my wounded arm. I twist away, unable to entirely stifle a groan of pain. His hand drops immediately. "I beg your pardon," he says icily, stepping back. "I meant no offense."

I shake my head, in too much agony to contradict him. The pain, which I've mentally overridden until now, has suddenly become unbearable. I clutch my arm, trying to breathe, willing myself to control it.

"You're hurt." The man's voice alters. It isn't kind exactly, but nor is it the barely restrained ferocity he showed in Hiraeth. "Show me."

I turn away instinctively. Kindness isn't something to be trusted in the Seam. Certainly not from a stranger who I last saw standing before a Dark Rip as my brother tumbled into it.

"Don't be a Fool." He reaches out again, thankfully for my uninjured arm this time. "I won't hurt you." He slips the linen shirt from my shoulder with a gentleness at odds with his grim tone. I shiver, less from his touch than from an instinctive expectation of pain. It doesn't come, though. The man's hand pauses for a moment as the zumi on my back is exposed, but to my relief, he makes no comment. Fresh blood is seeping from what seems a frustratingly small wound in relation to the excruciating pain it's causing. I wince as he twists my arm to examine it.

"Hold still." The note of command in his voice makes it clear he's unaccustomed to his orders being disobeyed, and the iron strength in the hand holding me suggests that fighting him off would be no easy matter.

I feel a warmth in my arm, at once both invigorating and soothing. Light falls in a glittering stream from the man's hand, like the stars on a moon-dark night, twisting around and into the wound. I can almost feel the broken pieces of my body healing as the starlight stream enters them, stitching together what has been blasted apart.

Stitching.

I stare at the bent head with slowly dawning fascination. "You're a Weaver," I say.

CHAPTER 5

WEAVER

*T*he starlight stream coming from the stranger's hand feels nothing like the clumsy ministrations of the Seamish salvers. Nor even like the finer, more skillful Work of Feivel, the Weaver at the Coronastrian Tapest who taught us our letters as children. Of course, Feivel doesn't have his Weaver's needle anymore. He lost it during the War and uses one made for him by an Indigold needlemaker in Astria.

My thoughts are roaming off in a thousand directions at once, my mind overwhelmed by the events of the day. It takes a moment for me to realize why I'm thinking of the kindly Feivel.

"You don't have a needle." The words are out of my mouth before I think to stop them.

The stranger doesn't look up from my arm, but I sense his smile. He twists his hand so the starlight narrows into a fine thread, then disappears altogether. "What an observant little criminal you are."

"Stop calling me that." I tug away from him, pulling the shirt protectively back up over my exposed skin. I hate anyone seeing the zumi on my back. It's an explosion of deep amethyst lotuses, shot through with a dagger that runs the length of my spine, a serpent twined about the hilt. Like so many other things in my life, I don't know where it came from, nor what it means. In the Seam it has only ever been another way in which I am different, a mark of the world that exiled me and thus something to hide.

"Why didn't you help Doron?" I can't hide the anger in my voice, and I don't want to. Even saying his name hurts. The thought that he might have been saved, and wasn't, makes me furious.

The Weaver's eyes narrow slightly. "He shouldn't have been there." The savage light from the forest might be gone, but the colors in the depths of his eyes still shift disconcertingly, like a distant fire burning against a night sky. "None of you should. I told you it wasn't safe in Hiraeth."

"That isn't what I asked." I swallow through the ache in my throat. "You closed that Rip; I saw you do it. If you can do that, you could have saved my brother." I think of Feivel's lessons, and my heart leaps with a sudden thrill of hope. "You still could save him. If you're a Weaver, you can go into the Interweave."

He gives a curt shake of his head. "The Seam Guard tell me your brother was bound for the Stitched Men. His fate is their responsibility now. I do not interfere with Indigold affairs." The finality in his tone warns against pursuing the matter further. "And given what came out of that Rip," he adds, a rather menacing shadow crossing his eyes, "it would seem that I have savagery enough to manage here."

His eyes come to rest on my braid. It prickles with a strange awareness when he does. It's been doing that, I realize, ever since I met him in Hiraeth this afternoon. In all the years I've worn the braid, I've never once felt its presence against my skin unless Hodda is twisting the braid knot on his ring, and even then, only when he touches it deliberately. Now the braid seems to spark against my skin as soon as the strange Weaver is nearby, just as the scent of Darkwine seems to linger in the air around him.

It's unsettling and, after what already feels like the longest day of my life, one too many things to try to process.

"That zumi on your back." He's studying me with disquieting scrutiny. "Who made it?" When I don't immediately answer, his fingers skim the underside of my jaw, tilting my face up more by suggestion than force. He doesn't so much look as he does absorb me, as if comprehending in an instant the entirety of who, or what, I am. "You don't know." It isn't a question, and I don't bother answering. His fingers drift down to hover just over the braid at my neck. "Shadow Woven," he murmurs, almost to himself. "Then you also don't know who ordered your enslavement, nor who Wove the braid."

"Now who's observant?" My challenge raises no more than a faint flicker of amusement in his otherwise unyielding expression. Goaded, I go on: "You could always unweave it for me."

I know even as I say the words that it's a futile request. I didn't always listen well to Feivel's lessons, but even I know that a Weaver can't simply unweave a slave braid. There are rules. Even, it would seem, in the golden land of Astria.

The Weaver doesn't seem remotely put out by my remark, however. His hard mouth twists into something akin to a smile. "Such matters are for Indigold lords and their council." He steps back, though his eyes remain on my face, still studying me.

Frustrated and tired, I shake my head. "You won't find my brother. You won't unweave my braid. It seems that you can't help me at all."

Silver gleams deep in his eyes. "I thought I just did."

"You know that isn't what I meant."

Rather than answer, the stranger twists his hand, and the spilled flagons rise to hover in the air before him. Another curl of his fingers, and a stream of Darkwine pours into them, seemingly from nowhere.

I'm fascinated despite myself. I've seen Indigold Work with their needles before, but the Indigold are merely students of the

Weavers, the extraordinary immortals born with needles of their own who can create wonders from the threads of life itself.

The Indigold nobles who visit the Seam say that Astria's golden needle was lost during the Battle of the Tower, and that now another Weaver can never be born.

They also say that battle saved the world from darkness— but at what cost? Watching the stranger's elegant hands Weave Darkwine through the air, it seems tragic that such wonders should be lost to the world.

Or perhaps, I think with a strange twist of longing and melancholy, *the tragedy is that tonight aside, it is unlikely I will ever know such wonders at all.*

Teddy's hooves clatter on the cobblestones nearby, and the man called Andras hands me the reins. "Your horse is fine." Very white teeth flash against midnight-dark skin as he grins at me. Gold hoops gleam in his ears, and in contrast to his friend's casual attire, his robes are bright brocade, richly embroidered with gold thread. "But your worthy beast did mention he didn't like what he saw in Hiraeth earlier. I doubt he will go easily into the woods, the next time you wish to make your little trades."

I find his comments deeply unsettling, particularly when Teddy nudges his new friend with almost slavish devotion. "I'm perfectly able to take care of my horse, thank you."

The Weaver, ignoring my words, rests his hand on Teddy's head and studies me for a long, disquieting moment, his face thoughtful. "Andras," he says lightly, "I suspect our stay in the Seam may be of a somewhat longer duration than anticipated."

Andras casts him a curious sidelong glance. "Surely a Hiraeth beast is a matter easily managed in a night, Harken?"

Harken. There's a certain stark solitude to the name. *It suits him,* I find myself thinking.

"Ah." Harken's eyes narrow. "The beast, perhaps, yes. But a pistol-weaving Fool is another matter entirely."

"A Fool?" My eyes widen as I look between them. "How can you be sure?"

"I know a wound made by powder and shot when I see it." Harken is still staring at me. "How often is it, Andras, that a Fool finds their way through a Dark Rip by accident? Particularly a Fool carrying a pistol and riding atop an otherworldly beast?"

"Rare as Anahita's Gold." Andras's hand slips unconsciously to the curved knives tucked into his belt. "I take it tonight's work will not be left to my wranglers, then?"

"Perhaps not, old friend." Harken drums long fingers against his leg. "We might safely send wranglers for the beast. The Fool, however, will warrant somewhat . . . closer inspection." His smile has a distinctly sinister edge.

"Wranglers?" I look between the two men. "What are wranglers?"

"More monsters, little criminal," says Harken, in a deceptively cheerful tone. "Rather more obedient ones than those you met tonight, however."

He steps away, his amused expression almost more insulting than the fact that Teddy seems to like him as much as Andras, nudging at his side for treats as if they have been acquainted for years.

"Just try to drive more safely, in future." He nods at my arm. "And do your best not to antagonize any other dark creatures in the woods. You're fortunate that weapon didn't strike a few inches to the side." Distant fire flares in his eyes again. Closing one hand around the reins, he hands me into the carrick with the other. "You should stay away from Hiraeth." The sinister half smile still hovers on his lips. "There are easier methods of procuring Darkwine than Pathfinders, my little criminal."

His words recall the specter of Doron's face. Grief tears through me, cavernous as the Rip itself. I briefly close my eyes, trying to will it away. "If you won't help, then what is it that you do, exactly?" Pain makes my voice hard.

His eyes sharpen. "Very rarely, it seems, what others consider to be the right thing."

He holds my eyes, but whatever answer I seek in his remains hidden in their mercurial depths, just another dark mystery in a long day full of them. Too tired for any more games, I click to Teddy and make my way down the alley.

I'm almost at the end of it when I remember that Harken never explained how he healed my arm without using a Weaver's needle.

I turn back to ask him, but the two men are gone, leaving only shadows and mist in the street.

CHAPTER 6

KRAKEN

I slip in the back door of the Dark and Disorderly, avoiding the front entrance with its two lamps and the wooden sign that has dangled from one rusted hook for as long as I can recall. The back entrance is by the stables and rarely visited by clients. Unfortunately, tonight is the exception. As I creep through the kitchen and toward the stairs, I almost collide with an Indigold nobleman coming from the water closet at the end of the corridor.

"Ha!" His hand closes around my arm. I wince instinctively before realizing the pain there is quite gone, thanks to Harken.

No thanks to Harken for anything else, I think, not without an edge of resentment.

"Why such a frown?" The Indigold man stands the same height as me. He has dark hair and mean, calculating eyes the murky brown of a still pond, currently staring at my mouth. "Lips like that must earn your master a fortune. But if you want Indigold coin, you should learn to smile."

I duck my head to avoid his scrutiny. "I'm not for sale."

As I say the words that have shielded me from unwanted

advances throughout my years at Hodda's, I'm hit by the sickening realization that they're no longer true.

The man smiles unpleasantly. "Everything in the Seam has a price." He plants his hands to either side of me on the wall. "Even covered in filth from the stable," he says, his eyes like hands on my flesh, "I'd tumble you."

With the experience of long practice, I twist free of his grasp and flee upstairs, his mocking laughter following me, though at least he himself doesn't.

I enter the small attic room I share with Shimi and Neoma to find them both crowded in front of the chipped, tarnished mirror, readying themselves to go downstairs. I feel an almost passionate rush of relief at the familiar sight.

They don't know about Doron, then. Or about the empty bags of coin. They couldn't look so excited if they did.

My sisters and I have always lived in different worlds. For me, the Dark and Disorderly is a cage from which I escape at every opportunity and have been plotting to leave behind for as long as I can recall.

For my sisters, though, it's the only home they've ever known. Each, in their own way, has made it their own.

Shimi has been sewing gowns for the older working girls since she was barely old enough to hold a measuring tape. Neoma, who was clearly born with the Sight, has read cards and palms for clients in the front salon for almost as long.

Different though we might be, we are still family, or as close to one as any of us have. I know I should tell them about Doron. The longer I wait, the worse it will be.

Just as I open my mouth, Shimi stands up, and I see what she is wearing.

It isn't the aqua silk sheath that makes my mouth snap closed in shock, though even I know that color has been somewhat out of vogue since the War. Aqua and gold are the colors of the Waterlands, of the disgraced and now dead Kraken King, Roark.

Nor am I much concerned with the depth of the cleavage on display, or the split at the side that travels the entire length of her thigh. Shimi has always favored daring styles. Diminutive in size she might be, but her curvaceous figure never goes unnoticed.

What shocks me is that the split is on the right side, exposing the zumi that Shimi has, every day until now, done everything she can to conceal.

With good reason.

Wrought in vivid gold and aqua detail, covering the entirety of Shimi's upper thigh, the zumi is an extraordinarily lifelike image—of a kraken.

The symbol of Roark, the king whose six decades of corrupt rule and cruel ambitions very nearly destroyed Astria.

And now, less than twenty years since the Kraken was defeated in the final Battle of the Tower, Shimi is displaying her zumi as if it were the greatest of trophies.

"Guess who's downstairs?" The low excitement in Shimi's voice stalls my questions.

"Who?" My voice sounds hollow to my ears, but Shimi, entirely absorbed with her own reflection, doesn't seem to notice.

"Caspian." She says the name in a tone that suggests I should recognize it. When I look blank, she sniffs impatiently, leaning in to add a smoky outline to her copper eyes. "Caspian. Lord Carliss of Caeruleis. Heir to the Kraken King himself," she says irritably, when the first two titles don't catch my attention.

"Ah." I strive to keep an even tone. *That explains the outfit.*

"And with him is Foley, Lord Ormond of Dencover." When this doesn't make an impression either, Shimi scowls. "Honestly. Don't you pay attention to anything? Foley's father is the Astrian Comitas. Head of the Council of Twelve. He's basically the king," she adds, when I don't react. "Well, the closest thing to it, anyway, now that Astria doesn't have kings."

"Oh." I try to think of something to say that won't anger her or betray what happened in Hiraeth. No matter what it will cost me later when they learn of my subterfuge, I know there is nothing to be gained by delivering the news of Doron's fate now. "You both look very beautiful."

That much, at least, is true. Shimi's face glows like fresh honeycomb, her almond-shaped eyes gleaming, silky russet hair as perfectly dressed as ever. If my face sometimes receives unwanted comments, Shimi's can stop a room. A face reader from Basetana once told her that the slight drop at the center of her top lip is called a "pearl in the sea" and considered a mark of great beauty. Shimi has long mastered the art of highlighting it, tonight in some deep, lush shade that looks like crushed berries.

In contrast to Shimi's tawny sensuality, Neoma's face is much finer, her pale aqua eyes distant and often unfocused. Usually bound in a big knot on her head, or at least contained in a braid, tonight her blonde hair snakes about her face in a wild mass of ringlets. Neoma's hair has always been extraordinary, with an otherworldly quality that makes it seem to move on its own.

It slowly dawns on me that there is nothing accidental about the way Neoma's hair is dressed tonight, nor the shimmering gold, backless gown which couldn't be less like Neoma's retiring personality. It's clear both are Shimi's doing. Even I know that the symbol of Dencover is the Serpent Queen, a woman with snakes surrounding her face. And the Dencover color, of course, is gold.

Neoma is barely seventeen, Shimi a year younger again. Both have been safe from the Indigold clients, protected by those bags of coin, just as I have. Never once have I seen them dress for the salon as if they were for sale.

Until now.

I was wrong. My heart sinks. *They already know about the coin bags.* Whether or not they also know what has happened to

Doron, I'm uncertain. What I do know is that for the second time today, I'm about to have a conversation I've long danced around.

I know that Shimi has always secretly dreamed that a visiting Indigold lord would be her ticket to freedom. Every working girl in the Seam has heard stories of slaves who are bought by Indigold noblemen and subsequently freed. The fact that not a single one of those girls has ever so much as sent a message to confirm their miraculous liberation doesn't stop the stories being repeated, over and again, with ever more exaggerated detail. I've never believed any of them. And somehow, I always thought I'd free us all before it became truly necessary to talk Shimi out of doing anything stupid.

But now here we are.

And by the gleam in Shimi's eyes, she has already made her mind up about what her own future will hold. My eyes shift to Neoma's pale figure. *And Neoma's, too.*

Perhaps, had it been Shimi alone, I might have been able to leave it be. Shimi is a survivor, and I know how stubborn she can be when her mind is decided. But Neoma is a different matter. Fragile, often utterly removed from reality except for when she is busy reading palms in the salon, she has always been the one who needs the most care of any of us. The thought of her in the hands of some coarse Indigold brute like the one I just encountered downstairs makes my stomach turn.

I know I must tread carefully. But I can't simply stand by and watch them do this.

"You know neither the Comitas or his son have the authority to undo a Shadow Braid," I say quietly. "It takes a petition to the council, now that there is no king. And even when Astria had a king, they were crowned by winning the Maverick's Race, not by inheritance. The Kraken King's son is no royal heir. He can't free you. Neither of those lords you are dressing to seduce have the power to unweave your braid, Shimi, even if they wanted to."

Shimi swings around fiercely. "They both sit on the Council of Twelve. They might not be able to free us themselves, but they will bring us one step closer to those who can. Much closer than anything here in the Seam." She turns back to the mirror, meeting my eyes in the reflection, her own shimmering with an unsettling light. "We know about the bags of coin," she says sharply. "And we know what happened to Doron. Levin told us." Her lips tighten, and I realize that what I took for excitement is, in fact, a hard, brittle shield over her grief. "He thought you might not." The betrayal in her eyes breaks me. "It seems he was right."

Just as with Levin earlier, I know there are no words that can mend that look in her eyes. I glance at Neoma, bracing for her accusations, but she is staring blankly into the mirror.

Oddly blankly. Even for her.

Gripped by a terrible suspicion, I look at her more closely. Sure enough, I see the telltale stain of Darkwine on her mouth. My eyes, wide with horror, move back to Shimi.

"Don't judge me," Shimi says fiercely. "Don't you dare judge me, Zaria. And don't you dare interfere. You've done enough damage already."

CHAPTER 7

LORDS

"*I*t's about time." Hodda, his eyes already amethyst rimmed and bleary, glares at me in the corridor when I finally come downstairs, now in the plain black dress I wear in the salon. "I thought you'd fallen into a Rip." My heart stops until I realize it's his poor attempt at a joke. Filling his cup liberally from the Darkwine flagon on my tray, he goes back into the salon, his squat, coarse face wearing the obsequious smile he reserves for clients.

At least Levin hasn't told him yet.

The salon is a fug of noise, heat, and smoke. At the center of the room is a round table at which several Indigold lords are engaged in a card game. My stomach clenches when I see Shimi's tiny form held lazily across the knees of the man who accosted me in the corridor, his fingers idly stroking the kraken zumi on her thigh. His coat is the same aqua as Shimi's dress.

Caspian, I think, with a surge of disgust.

Neoma, her eyes animated by the Sight, is leaning across the table, reading the palm of another man. Her abilities, I think bitterly, are no doubt exaggerated by the Darkwine with which Shimi has dosed her. She certainly appears to have charmed the

Indigold whose palm she's reading. He is short and stocky, with black hair slicked straight back from a flat, brutish face. Clad head to toe in gold brocade, he can only be Foley, the Lord of Dencover.

"She's my good luck charm, this one, with her serpent hair." Tipping a cup of Darkwine down his throat, he pulls Neoma between his legs, kneading her slender arm with pudgy fingers. "Tells me I'll win coin to spare on the Race. I've a good mind to buy her and take her with me back to Astria for the Revels." His loud, braying tone smacks of arrogance and entitlement. "They say this year's Maverick's Race will be the richest yet. Lands, a title, and more coin than a man can carry. Should make for the Dreaver's own Season of Revels." This time when he drinks, he spills Darkwine on Neoma's dress.

"My Aunt Sereia tells me that one of the entrants in this year's Braid Race is an outsider." Caspian throws the dice with a lazy flick of his wrist. "An Indigold, exiled as a child with his parents. She says he's son of Astrian nobility. He wears a hereditary braid, presumably a punishment for his parents choosing the wrong side in the War." He shakes his head, mouth twisting in disapproval. "He's one of ours, though, not some peasant slave from the Seamish gutters. He's bound to win, given the half-bred Weorpan who make up most of the field." I grit my teeth at the insult, though Shimi, coiled docilely in his lap, doesn't react at all. "If he wins it," Caspian says musingly, "and he's any good, it might be worth spending a few coins to take him back to Astria. We could set him up to win the Maverick's Race." He winks at Foley. "Another estate never goes to waste."

"Well, if your Aunt Sereia likes this outsider's chances, then so do I. The Dreaver knows talent in the Seam is rare as Anahita's Gold." Foley's hands roam Neoma's flesh distractedly. "And Sereia's the Paladin Weaver, after all. A quiet word in her ear should guarantee the outcome you want in the Braid Race." He clinks his cup to Caspian's. "It's not like there's anyone here likely to stop her," he adds contemptuously.

It's just a game to them.

After all that has been lost today, it's crippling to hear the outcome of the Braid Race discussed with such easy contempt.

They think nothing of bribery and corruption to achieve their ends, and for what? Not to save a life, but to make a larger pile of coin. Impotent fury races through me like liquid fire.

"Careful, Foley." Caspian is watching me, his eyes sharp with interest. Too late, I realize some of my emotion must have registered in my expression. "People might think you were planning something."

Shimi flashes me a furious look. I turn away quickly, but not before Caspian notices Shimi looking at me. It seems to pique his interest. "You know," he says, slipping his hand around the inside of Shimi's thigh, his eyes on my face to gauge my reaction as I pour Darkwine, "I think I like your idea of buying slaves, Foley. It's always nice to bring a souvenir back from one's travels. You," he calls to me. "Bring us wine."

I grip the tray. In my current state I might as easily put a knife through Caspian's throat as pour him more of the Darkwine currently slipping down it.

"Here, child." Mallory, one of the older, kinder ladies of the house, takes my tray. "Let me serve our guests. You should go upstairs and rest."

Caspian's arm shoots out, roughly pulling me back when I would turn away. "I told the girl to serve us," he snaps at Mallory, eyes flashing with spite. "If I wanted the opinion of an old whore, I would have asked for it."

"Of course, lord." Mallory hands me the tray, her eyes flickering briefly to mine in a silent warning. It's a shorthand we've all known since childhood: the many ways to manage the moods of men.

"Who would pay good coin for something so old and used

up, anyway?" Though the insult is to Mallory, I know it's me Caspian's trying to taunt. I poor the drinks, keeping my head down.

"If I were you," says a gruff voice from a chair in a dark corner of the salon, far away from the gilt-edged sofas and marble tables at which the Indigold lords sit, "I'd shut my mouth and play my hand instead."

"Ho!" Caspian says, as the rest of his cohort hoot in anticipation of the coming argument. "Brave words, friend."

"I'm not your damned friend." Garrick, the tough, grizzled old Seam Guard in the corner, pushes back his chair. Garrick is one of Mallory's most faithful customers and one of my earliest memories. He's been training me for the Braid Race since I was old enough to hold Teddy's reins.

Garrick is also the man I trust most in this world.

It was he who found me and my siblings on that long-ago night in Hiraeth Forest. Rather than putting a knife across our throats, as many would have, given the dark origins suggested by Shadow Braids and Woven bags of gold, he chose instead to save us. Garrick says little, but has seen a lot. Seam Guards are renowned for their fighting prowess, and the golden scar on his face marks him as a Stitched Man, one of the few to have done duty at the Drop itself.

I feel a savage stab of satisfaction when I see Caspian's smile falter. "The woman you just insulted is a friend of mine," Garrick growls. "You'll apologize to her. Then you'll shut your mouths, drink your wine—and fuck off."

"And where is it exactly you think we should go, old man?" Caspian is still trying for the upper hand, but the fragility of his bravado is plain to anyone with eyes.

Garrick doesn't so much as blink. "You can go to the Savage bloody Court, for all I care. Arrogant little pricks like you could do with a lesson or two in manners."

"The Savage Court!" Foley gives a bray of scornful laughter, though Caspian, I note, doesn't share it. "It's so-called king isn't so savage these days. Harken stays hidden in those mists of his most of the time, from what I can tell."

Harken?

My heart thuds queerly, my arm tingling with the memory of a starlight touch, there and gone.

Harken is the Savage King?

I see him standing before the Dark Rip, his face a twisted mask.

Yes. I know it with an odd certainty, and yet still it seems impossible.

"Oh, you think him tamed, is that it?" It's Garrick's turn to laugh. His voice jolts me back to the salon, though it seems as if all the pieces of the room have rearranged themselves in the moment it has taken me to make sense of their words.

"Well," Garrick goes on, "you can think Harken is hidden away in his mists, if you like. But if I were you, I wouldn't fuck around by saying that name too loudly, unless you like the idea of finding out the truth for yourself." Grinning coldly, he pulls Mallory into the protective circle of one heavily muscled arm, his rough hand stroking her hair reassuringly. "What say you take me upstairs, sweetling," he says softly, "and I'll see you safe the rest of the night."

My heart twists. Whatever Indigold lords like Foley might say about talent, in the Seam, it's simple kindness that is more rare, and infinitely more treasured, than even Anahita's Gold.

Throwing Hodda a bag of coin heavy enough to make a satisfying thunk, Garrick pauses in front of the Indigold table. "I've paid for your wine," he says in a low, menacing growl. "Drink it, and fuck off, before things get unpleasant."

I wait until the awkward silence has passed and conversation resumed before slipping into the corridor, where a grim-faced Garrick is waiting for me.

"I heard about Doron," he says without preamble.

I realize with a hollow jolt that it was likely Garrick and his men who helped Doron plan his escape.

And I ruined it. I push away the memory of Doron's terrified face with an effort. *Not here,* I think. Not now.

It's a mark of Garrick's honor that he doesn't berate me for what he surely knows is my mistake. He puts a large hand on my shoulder. It's the most physical affection Garrick has ever shown me, and unexpected tears threaten my eyes. But I haven't lived in a Disorderly House my whole life without learning to at least control my emotions, if not hide them entirely. He releases me and turns away.

"Garrick."

He pauses, raising his eyebrows.

"The Savage King. Harken." Saying the name aloud feels dangerous, like entering an unknown world. "Who is he, exactly?"

"Now," Garrick says slowly, his eyes narrowing, "what would you be after, asking me a question like that?"

In the brief silence that follows, I think of a dozen answers, but don't dare try any of them. If there's one person who can see through subterfuge, it's Garrick.

"He's someone best forgotten, is who he is." Garrick's tone is grim, even for him. "And he certainly ain't someone you want to be on first-name terms with." His scrutiny is sharp enough that I drop my own gaze. "He was created to guard the Woven Court during the War. He's guarded it ever since, so well there ain't no Woven Court to speak of anymore. They call it the Savage Court now, and he its king." His mouth tightens. "The Savage King doesn't seek company," he says tersely, "and those who find his usually regret it. We clear?"

I nod, my face coloring.

"Clear."

CHAPTER 8

HODDA

I stand in the corridor for some time after Garrick leaves, trying to reconcile the memory of Harken's intoxicating starlight touch with Garrick's grim warning. I know little about the Woven Court, although the old people in the Seam remember the years before the War, when Weavers still came to visit the Seam with their Indigold apprentices. Back then, they say, every Indigold, whether blacksmith, lawyer, Seer, or salver, was trained under a Weaver master. The Weavers brought the Indigold here to teach them service, helping the less fortunate in the Seam by salving, repairing stonework, or improving the fields. Feivel once told me that although the Indigold called them masters, it was the Weavers who had always served the Indigold, rather than the other way around. But whatever wisdom and good the Weavers may once have brought has been lost to the Seam for many years now. Apart from Feivel, who no longer has his Weaver's needle, and now Harken, the only times I've ever seen a Weaver is on the day of the Braid Race, when the winner's slave braid is unwoven, and even then, only from a distance.

I saw the fierce flashes in Harken's eyes, the way he closed down the Dark Rip. I even heard him speak of darkness and savagery. Yet still it is hard for me to imagine him heartlessly closing the Woven Court to the Weavers, who, at least before the War, had only ever brought harmony and joy to the world.

When I finally return to the salon, Hodda is sitting at the Indigold table. His squashed face wears a satisfied look that I don't like at all.

"Come on, Foley." Caspian stands up and sweeps the coin on the table into his purse. "Let's get out of here." He turns to Hodda. "We'll be back tomorrow to collect the goods we paid a deposit on." He nods at Shimi and Neoma without looking at them. "Make sure they aren't damaged between now and the time we take their braid knots from that ring you hold." Seeing me, Caspian lingers for a moment, pulling Shimi in for a last, almost vicious kiss, staring at me over her shoulder as he does. Then, smiling coldly, he leaves, ushered out by a nodding, obsequious Hodda.

The door is barely closed when Shimi turns to me, her eyes blazing fiercely. "We got them," she breathes, all trace of the girlish flirt of a second ago utterly gone. "We did it, Zaria." She turns to Hodda as he locks the door. "They offered a good price, didn't they?" Her smile is suddenly soft and warm, the hard triumph in her eyes replaced by the sweet docility Hodda always seems to fall for. "Please say you'll take it, Hodda?"

"Well, well." Hodda's meaty face wears the self-satisfied expression of a man who feels he's fought for a good deal and won. He raises a warning finger, his customary meanness returning. "But don't think I can't change my mind, because I can. You'll still find yourselves on your backs upstairs, if I choose it."

Shimi hangs her head in feigned submission, but the satisfied gleam in her downcast eyes is not dissimilar to Hodda's own. She shoots me a hard look as she turns to the stairs. I can read her meaning clear enough: *Don't do anything to ruin it.*

"Not you." I turn to find any trace of Hodda's former geniality gone. He points to his office. "I'm a long way from done with you."

I follow Hodda into the dark, windowless room he uses for counting coin, twisting my hair into the tightest knot I can as I go. The first time Hodda beat me, when I had been in his house only a matter of days, he had shorn my mahogany curls to the skull, telling me hair like mine was wasted on a slave when it could fetch a high price at market. Since then, I've taken great care never to wear my hair loose again. Binding it tightly has in some ways become a reassuring ritual. Hiding my hair feels like keeping part of myself private, untouched by Hodda's pernicious reach.

And I have a bad feeling about this particular summons.

The air is still and musty. A lone candle flickers on the desk. Its dim light is nonetheless sufficient to highlight the quivering rage on Hodda's face.

Far worse, it also reveals Levin, sporting a bloody nose and closing eye, standing in one corner. By the way he's clutching his neck, I can tell Hodda has been using Levin's knot on his ring as a tool of torture. While I'm accustomed to him twisting mine on a daily basis, he generally reserves the use of it on my siblings for the very worst of crimes.

My bad feeling becomes a whole lot worse. Then Hodda throws the Master's Ring onto the table, and my stomach falls away altogether.

Four of the braid knots gleam softly in the low light, the same pearlescent, shadowy silver they have always been.

The fifth, however, looks as if it has been through a fire. It is a charred, deathly black and gives off the same terrifying sulfuric smell as the Dark Rip into which Doron fell. Simply looking at it fills my heart with dread.

Knowing my own traitorous face too well, I keep my eyes down.

"Fifteen years I've fed and clothed the ungrateful lot of you. Given you a roof over your head. A safe place to sleep." Hodda begins on the familiar refrain.

And been paid good coin to do so, I think savagely. But there's no point in bringing up the bags of coin. Somewhere in between the day we were taken into the Dark and Disorderly and now, Hodda has ceased to think of the bags as payment for us and instead simply as his right.

"Could have been the best house in all Lostport," he moans. "But who wants to come to a house full of sniveling brats, eh? You tell me that. Not to mention brats that have all got the Dreaver's mark on them." Coming around the desk, he rips the gown from my torso, exposing both the ink on my back and my bared breasts to the room. Levin lunges forward, but Hodda twists his knot on the Master's Ring, and Levin sinks to his knees, clutching the braid around his neck and gasping for air, his eyes wide with fear and horror. Levin has never seen Hodda's rage up close. Doron and I have always stood between our younger siblings and Hodda's worse tempers. Watching Levin's horror now hurts me far more than any of Hodda's humiliating tortures ever have.

"The Dreaver's ink, is what that is." Hodda traces the intricate pattern on my back with the willow stick. It takes all my self-control not to wince at the smooth, insidious touch. "Just like the scar on your brother's face, or the mark of the Kraken itself on your sister. I never should have taken in such a cursed lot." He raises the willow stick and brings it down with stinging force, hard enough to draw a stripe of blood directly across the ink on my back. "And this is how you repay me." He grunts as the thin whipping stick cuts another line in my flesh. "By helping Doron, the only one who earns me good coin, to escape to the Drop. Don't bother denying it!" The next blow lands with even more force, driven by the rage in his voice. "Do you think me some Fool, to be taken in by your Stitched Man and his tales about Dark Rips? Do you think that I don't notice your coming and going, the deals you do behind my back?" He drops an empty lockbox onto the desk in front of me, it's cover brutally bashed open. I stare at it in mute disbelief, hope leaching slowly away.

"Of course I know," Hodda hisses in my ear. "I've always known. I tolerated your scheming for the bags of coin. For the Darkwine you brought and the fights Doron won. But now there's no more coin, and no more Doron. You conspired with that Stitched Man to send him into Astria, just to spite me."

I barely hear him. I'm staring at the empty lockbox. The coin that was in that box was the result of fifteen years of careful hoarding. Fifteen years of secrecy and danger, all for the dream I have held on to since the night I found myself in Hiraeth with four children and no recollection of how any of us had come to be there: to free us all.

From the slave braids that bind us. From the endless, grinding poverty of our existence. But most of all, from the crippling fear that one, or all of us, will be sold, the only family I have ever known broken apart, cast aside on the winds.

And now we are here, facing all of that and worse—and I no longer have coin enough to even enter the Braid Race.

From somewhere beyond me, I hear someone start to laugh. It isn't until I see the expression on Hodda's face that I realize the laughter is coming from me. The empty lockbox has ripped away the last threads holding my heart together.

"You truly believe that, don't you?" I stand up despite the whip and stare at Hodda, less afraid of him than I've ever been, even though his hand hovers over the braid knot. "You truly believe we would lie about losing our brother to a Dark Rip just to spite you. It never even occurred to you what that black braid end might mean."

Hodda's eyes flicker down to the Master's Ring and back up to me, narrowing suspiciously. "It's a trick of the Stitched Men, that's what that braid is." But I can hear the uncertainty in his tone, and by the way his eyes shift to Levin, it's clear my brother told him the same thing. Then his eyes harden. "Rip or Drop," he hisses. "Either way, makes no difference to me. Gone is gone. But you'll pay for it, both Levin and you. There'll be no more hiding him behind you, not now. Levin will take Doron's place in the fighting ring." He points a thick finger directly into my face. "And you will start earning on your back."

His eyes squint nastily.

"After you heal, that is. And after the beating I give you tonight, it will be a time before you'll be fit to so much as walk to a bed, let alone lie on one."

He twists the braid knot, and I fall to the floor. He wields the willow stick in earnest now, landing blow after blow across my back. Some of his blows land on the places Harken recently healed with his starlight thread, and those don't seem to hurt so much. That moment in the alleyway seems like another world, as do all my dreams and plans now.

For the first time since Hiraeth, I allow myself to truly see Doron's face. Not the expression he wore as he fell into the Dark Rip, but the defeated, shattered face he had when he turned away from the silverscye, and the future that might have saved him.

The future he lost because of me.

Seeing his face helps me welcome the stinging blows. They feel real. They feel like justice.

"You bastard." Levin's hoarse cry is cut short by a vicious sideways blow from the willow stick. His whole body convulses as Hodda twists his braid knot on the ring, causing Levin to turn purple as he struggles for breath.

"Leave him!" I mean to scream, but my voice comes out a rasped whisper, barely there, and I realize with a kind of detached surprise just how badly I have been beaten. "You have what you want. Leave Levin alone."

"Always their protector," Hodda taunts me. "But there's no helping him now. By the time I'm done, neither of you will be fit to crawl downstairs the day of the Race, let alone enter the damned thing. You're mine—and mine you'll stay, until I say otherwise." He brings the stick down again and throws one of the empty bags of coin onto the ground before me. "The coin has run out, girl," he hisses. "And so has your time. You're living on my time now, and by the Dreaver himself, I intend to see you don't ever forget it."

He twists the braid knot on the ring, and at last, the longest day of my life fades to merciful black.

CHAPTER 9

GARRICK

I dream of Darkwine.

Not the sweet, amethyst-colored dilution the Paladins mix for the Tapest. Not the heavier aphrodisiac drunk by men in the Disorderly Houses. Not even the thick, heady brew that offers Darkwine dreams to the addict and the dying.

I dream of pure, lethal Darkwine straight from the berry, a distillation that means certain death for any who drink it.

It runs through my uneasy rest in a dark, seductive ribbon, like it had from Harken's hand into the flasks. In my dream, the slow-moving ribbon twines about different faces: Doron's, leaden with defeat as he turns away from the silverscye; Levin's, grief ravaged and accusing; Shimi's, fierce with suppressed tension; Neoma's, vacant and detached, gone somewhere far inside herself.

And drifting somewhere amid that lethal Darkwine river, Harken's indigo eyes follow me, a hint of silver gleaming at their core, like distant lightning amid the darkest part of the forest.

I wake on the stone floor of the stable, almost longing for the oblivion of a Darkwine death. *Perhaps*, I think dully, staring at a dung beetle barely inches from my face, *I will ask him for that, the Savage King. If ever I meet him again.*

It must be midafternoon, because I can smell Mallory's lunchtime soup and the cry of the flower sellers, who always wait until the hours before dusk to begin plying their trade. I can see little reason to move. Dried blood has stuck the remains of my tunic to my body, and I can barely see out of either of my eyes. Even the slightest movement breaks open one of the hundreds of open cuts left by Hodda's willow stick. Part of me wonders if I am dying already.

"You're awake." Garrick is kneeling beside me in the thin layer of straw. "Mallory wanted to take you upstairs, but I knew you wouldn't want your sisters to see."

I close my eyes briefly in relief. "Levin?" My voice is barely a whisper.

"Mallory's with him." Garrick holds his water flask to my mouth, and I drink gratefully, wincing as the water runs into my cuts. "Best you leave your brother be," he says gruffly. "For a time."

I know he's right. And it's always been Doron that Levin has turned to, not me.

They all turned to Doron.

It's never really bothered me before. Over the years we all developed different roles. I earned coin for our future, made plans, and took the brunt of Hodda's rage. Doron fought in the ring for the coin that kept Hodda happy and took care of the younger ones when I couldn't. I might have taken beatings so they didn't have to, but it was Doron who wiped their tears and heard their stories.

Now not only am I the reason that Levin has lost Doron, I also failed to protect Levin from Hodda's wrath. No wonder he doesn't want to see me. I doubt any of them will.

I don't blame them.

I swallow more water, wincing as I slowly push myself to

sitting. Garrick steadies me with one large hand. He offers me a crust of bread rather than pity. I'm grateful. We both know pity is wasted.

"I'll take that Darkwine to Hodda." Garrick nods at the flagons by the wall, the ones Harken filled in the alley. It seems like a lifetime ago. "Best you stay out of sight. And you need to get this lot to the abbey. Feivel's got a Cupbearing ceremony over at the tapest this afternoon. Dreaver knows it ain't safe to trust that Fool of a Paladin to mix it for him, so best you see to that while you're there." Garrick's scowl almost makes me smile. Almost.

Garrick turns his back as I wash gingerly from the pail of water he brought. It isn't his fault we wound up in Hodda's dubious care, but I know he blames himself for it nonetheless, and never more than at times like these.

"There's somewhere else you need to be, too." A small leather bag thuds into the wall in front of me and falls to the stone below. "I heard about Hodda taking your coin," he says gruffly. "You'll need this if you're going to register."

I take the clean linen he's hung over the stable door, eyeing the coin on the floor. "I don't think there's much point," I say quietly. "I wasn't good enough for the Race even before Hodda's beating. I'm certainly not now."

"And you're going to let a few cuts make that choice?" Garrick's voice is unexpectedly harsh. I turn in surprise, my linen shirt hanging loose over my trousers. Even the touch of the material on my skin hurts, and blood is already soaking through it where old cuts have opened. "Hodda ain't going to sell you to some fine Indigold lord, Zaria." He looks at me grimly. "He'll have you on your back within the week. I ain't letting that happen. You've been good enough to win that damned Race for years. Even cut up as you are. I'd bet my last coin on it." He nods at the leather bag with the glimmer of a smile. "I *am* betting my last coin on it."

I swallow over the lump in my throat. "Hodda—" I begin.

Garrick's eyes narrow. "I'll take care of Hodda." Uncorking a flagon, he passes it to me. "Smell that."

I do, and my eyes widen.

"Hey?" Garrick nods, grinning at my expression. "Don't know where the Pathfinder got this batch, but your average Paladin's pale brew, it ain't. Few glasses of this and Hodda should be dead to the world." His grin fades. "Or just dead," he says rather grimly. "Either way, he won't stop you entering that race, lass. You've my word on that."

I'm fairly certain the strength of the Darkwine has nothing to do with the Pathfinder and everything to do with the indigo eyes that haunted my dreams, but after Garrick's warnings about Harken, I decide it's best not to mention that particular encounter.

"Are you sure?" I'm not certain exactly what I'm asking about: the coin, my abilities, or poisoning Hodda. *All of it, I guess.*

Garrick meets my eyes. "As sure as I've ever been about anything, lass," he says quietly. "And if there are any of those coins left when you're done, give them to your sisters."

I turn away abruptly to hide the sudden tears pricking my eyes. There's never been time for tears in the Seam, and there isn't now.

On the long-ago night he found us in Hiraeth, Garrick took us to the tapest. Most in the Seam would have killed us. Shadow Braids hide the identity and motivation of those who Wove them. Though not unheard of, they are unusual. Most slaves in the Seam are either common criminals, or they wear hereditary braids so old their origins have been long forgotten. Five abandoned Weorpan children, bound by Shadow Braids and standing beside Woven bags of gold, suggest dark origins. None would have missed us, or blamed Garrick if he'd taken a knife to us and the gold for himself.

He took us to Feivel instead.

The two of them went door to door, trying to find someone who would take us in. Hodda was the only one who agreed.

Shadow Bargains cannot be altered, nor undone. The moment Hodda accepted that ring and the bags of coin, our fates were tied to his. By the time Garrick and Feivel learned what manner of man he was, they'd also learned that any intervention on their part had brutal consequences for us. So long as Hodda holds the ring, he can torture us with impunity.

I've never blamed either Feivel or Garrick for bringing us to Hodda. I know the five of us would have been dead that night had it not been for their mercy. And both have done all they can to help us since. It's more kindness than most slaves in the Seam ever know.

"Go see Feivel, then register." The straw rustles as Garrick turns to leave. "Stay away from here until late, give me time to get the Darkwine down Hodda's throat. Then get what sleep you can. I'll meet you at the circus tomorrow." The rustling stops as Garrick pauses at the stable door.

"I'll stay for the Race." Garrick grips the doorframe with one big hand. "But when it's done, I'm leaving for the Drop. We've been ordered to take a ship into the Interweave, to look for Doron."

My heart misses a beat. The Interweave is as much of a mystery to me as it is to most, but the memory of the Rip that took Doron will live inside me forever. I can't bear to even think about Garrick sailing into the dark, chaotic realms beyond that tunnel.

My fault, I think dully. *This is all my fault.*

"An' there's something else." Garrick spits sideways and looks away from me. "Wiley and the boys," he says gruffly. "They're coming with me. You should know that I didn't ask it of them. They all offered."

I can't speak. While Garrick trained me for the Race every

spare minute he had, Wiley and the boys from the Seam Guard taught Doron the skills that made him so lethal in the ring. That they would now put their own lives at risk by sailing into the Interweave to search for him touches me almost more than I can bear.

"If Doron can be found," Garrick says, his grip on the frame tightening briefly, "then we'll find him. I promise you that, lass."

I watch him stride away, through a mist of tears that I don't dare allow to fall.

CHAPTER 10

CUPBEARING

*I*t's late afternoon by the time I'm standing in the alchemy room of the Paladins' abbey. I lift the cup and hold it to the light, gauging the mix through the thick glass panels on each side.

"I think that's it." I turn to Leo. "Don't you?"

"Oh, I couldn't say." Leo looks up from the book he's studying and smiles shyly. He's thin, with limp dark hair, sloping shoulders, slightly knock knees, and a lazy eye that makes it hard to know which way to look when he's speaking. It's surprising that the Paladins ever took him, given the importance they place on physical perfection. That said, being a Paladin Divine in Lostport is as close to unofficial exile as it's possible for any Indigold to get.

"You know," Leo says as I turn to leave, "it's my Uncle Saxan who oversees the Paladin Candidate trials."

Well, that explains how he got a job. I'm unclear why he's telling me this now.

"Yes." Leo looks even more nervous than normal. "He's First Blade. Head of the military arm of the Paladins," he adds. Leo touches the alchemy tool roll on the table beside him in an unconscious, rather nervous gesture. Every Paladin carries one, but I don't think I've ever seen Leo use anything out of his other than the small herb knife Feivel gifted him. He uses it in the garden they tend together, a rare show of alliance between the Tapest and the Abbey. Once united under the Coronastrian faith, the War placed a bitter divide between the Astars who use the Divine Cups in their tapests and the Paladins in the abbeys who mix them, though I never did enough lessons with Feivel to understand the origins of the split.

Leo has a talent for gardening, Feivel once told me, rather sadly. *It's a pity the Divines are forced to practice alchemy above all else.* The tool roll always sits on the table beside Leo's books, bound and still like a silent reprimand. Once, when he put the small herb knife away in it, I glimpsed a name stenciled on the inside: *Jaxan.* Given the similarity to his uncle's name, I imagine Jaxan is Leo's father, but not voicing curiosity about such matters is one of the strange diplomacies of the Seam. If Leo was the pride of his family, he'd be presiding over an abbey in Astria, not leaving his tool roll untouched while he reads books and tends an herb garden in the Seam.

"I'm certain," Leo goes on shyly, "that if I ask, Uncle Saxan will ensure that Levin makes it into Candidate year."

Even if I wanted Levin to enter the trials, which I absolutely do not, given his current battered state, there isn't a chance he'd pass the Paladin's requirement for physical perfection. I'm about to say this when Leo surprises me by saying, "And I know the Paladins would take you also. I can help you hide the wounds on your face." He gives me a shy smile. "I think," he says softly, "that it would be hard to find anyone more perfect than you."

"That's very kind of you, Leo." Distinctly uncomfortable, I pretend not to see the faint color on his cheeks. "But Levin is . . . unwell, at the moment. And I can't leave my brother and sisters to go with the Paladins."

"You're not going to enter that horrible Race, are you?" He

looks terrified at the thought, his amethyst-stained hands trembling. "You could die, Zaria." He says it with a faint air of surprise, as if the idea has only just occurred to him. I almost laugh. *The ignorance of the Indigold never fails to astound me.*

"Thank you for the Darkwine." I back toward the stairs, then run up them before he can say anything to embarrass either of us further. Strictly speaking, I don't need his Darkwine, but it's a game we all play. I pretend that I don't have Darkwine other than what is in his cellar, and Leo pretends not to notice when I drive past with flagons full of the stuff.

I leave through the abbey's gleaming entrance, made of deep indigo flamestone inlaid with the Indigold Cup symbol, which the Paladins take as their own: a silver cup with a serpent twined about the stem. The Coronastrian tapest opposite is noticeably less glamorous. Its roof is crumbling, canvas covering the places where it has collapsed entirely. The once-gleaming star over the entrance is rusted and cracked. Of the six golden lines that are overlaid to create the twelve-pointed star known as the Astris, the central one has been burned to a blackened stump. It happened to a lot of tapests after the War apparently, something to do with the Coronastrians being blamed for losing Astria's golden needle.

I watch the Cupbearing ceremony from the back benches in the tapest. I've always liked the peace in here, the stone and wood worn smooth with age, redolent with the aromatic scent of the incense used by astrids for hundreds of years. Sometimes it seems as if I can feel the tears and prayers of all those who have sat on these benches before me. I find a strange comfort in their imagined presence.

The proud Seamish parents hold their newborn infant before the twelve-pointed Astris. Feivel lifts the glass cup in which I'd mixed Darkwine and well water, and the two Cupbearers each sip from it in turn. Then Feivel holds it to the baby's lips. "You are revealed," he says solemnly, touching the baby with his makeshift needle. "You are awoken."

The baby screams and the parents beam, shaking Feivel by the hand. I try to imagine a real Indigold Cupbearing in Astria, one where they mix the Darkwine with genuine Paladin's Water, not just well water from the back of the abbey. In Astria, when the baby drinks, a Weaver touches the Cup with their needle, and the baby's innate gifts are revealed. Nineteen years after that, when the baby is an adult and ready for their own needle to be made, they drink from the Cup once again, this time with a needlemaker present. The needlemaker reads the sediment, then uses it to create the needle that the person will hold for the rest of their life. Oddly, of all the lessons Feivel has tried to teach me, that is the one I've never had any trouble remembering. I need only close my eyes to envisage a needle in my own hand, created from the very threads of my own soul. I can almost feel it there, a needle of my own.

Revealed and awoken.

Of all the wonders of Astria, it is the needle that holds the most tantalizing allure for me. In the streets of the Seam, orphans often wave sticks in the air, pretending to Work as the Indigold do. Even as a child, I never played those games. It felt like a betrayal of a treasured dream, a passive acceptance that my hand would never hold a needle. Some deeply personal part of me has always refused to relinquish that dream.

Dreams are dangerous for slaves. But they are also all we have. Instead of wielding a stick, I would close my eyes and imagine my palm tingling as my own needle found its home.

Perhaps, I think now, closing my eyes and slipping into my old childish game, *Shimi could have been a Dress Weaver's apprentice. Neoma might have gone to the Isle of Nine, to be trained as a Seer by the priestesses there. Levin has always been talented with herbs. He might have studied horticulture, or even become a salver, mixing cures for the ill. And Doron . . .*

But there the game ends. My eyes fly open, unwilling to relive yet again the haunting memory of my brother tumbling into the fathomless depths.

I think of Harken drawing his hand down to close the Rip and reach instinctively to touch the place on my skin he healed with the starlight stream from his hand. To my surprise, I discover that despite Hodda's whip having cut everywhere else it landed, the parts where Harken healed me are entirely free of either marks or pain. Even now those parts of my skin tingle faintly to the touch, as if a residue of whatever Weaving he used remains in my body.

His words echo in my mind: *"It seems I have savagery enough to manage here . . ."*

How, I wonder, *does he deal with savagery exactly? And how long will it keep him in the Seam for?*

Then I remember Garrick's warnings and mentally chide myself for wasting my energy even thinking about such matters. My life is already filled with savagery. And besides, Harken has made it perfectly clear that he doesn't consider braids, nor the unweaving of them, to be his business. In fact, in the brief time we met, I was left with the distinct impression that Harken considers his world to be one of monsters and Dark Rips—and anything beyond that to be of no concern to him at all.

I'm not certain why I should find that sad.

CHAPTER 11

TAPEST

"*Z*aria!"

I look up to discover the Cupbearing has ended and Feivel's rotund figure is bustling toward me. Grief twists his already ravaged face.

"I cannot tell you how sorry I am to hear about poor Doron." The scar across his face is a dark, sinuous gash, shot with gold like a living thing. Today it glitters more than normal, as it always does when he is agitated. Garrick once told me that only the most powerful Weaving could have made such a terrible scar. It slashes his face from one temple to the opposite jaw, winding down around his neck. When we were small children, Feivel used to joke he had a slave braid, just like us.

In a way, I suppose, it's true enough. Feivel is a Weaver, but he lost the needle he was born with during the War. A Weaver's memories are held in their needle. The Seam is perhaps the only life Feivel has left to him, having lost so much of his own.

"Thank you." I allow him to take my hands.

"Great Weaver," he mutters under his breath, studying my face. Feivel's eyes are a rather startling deep, Darkwine purple shot through with gold, another souvenir of whatever dark

Weaving caused his scar. They glisten with emotion as he scrutinizes me. I gently slide my hands from his, turning away. I've never been comfortable with overt displays of emotion, even from Feivel.

"You're still entering the Race." It isn't a question, and his voice is resigned rather than censorious. Like Garrick, Feivel understands the hard reality of the Seam.

I nod. "Yes." I glance outside. The gloaming has fallen, coating the Seam in dull shadow. "I was waiting for dusk to go and register."

"I'll be there, tomorrow," Feivel says quietly. "Garrick and I both will. We'll stay—" He breaks off, but I know what he meant to say.

We'll stay until it's finished. Until you win, or you die.

Despite being a Weaver, Feivel wears the plain robes of a Coronastrian Astrid. The cord of twelve knots encircles his waist, at the end of which hangs a simple twelve-pointed Astris. Feivel works each of the knots through his fingers in a repetitive rhythm, as he often does when considering what to say. Even in the Seam, every child knows the twelve words taught by Weaver and Astrid alike, one for each of the knots. *Joy*, I recite mentally, watching his fingers. *Kindness. Patience. Love. Harmony. Clarity. Compassion. Purity. Understanding. Forgiveness. Bliss. Serenity.*

I take comfort from the familiar ritual. From the knowledge that a world once existed in which those qualities must have mattered. Even if that world is fading now, after the War, still, for me, the familiar words shine a light against the dark, corrosive fear of death.

"I've always thought," Feivel says, his kind eyes resting on me, "that there are a great many similarities between the Darkberry fruit and fear."

I look at him rather uncertainly. I'm never too sure where Feivel's odd thoughts will take me.

"Darkberries are a strange, powerful fruit," he says. "Incredibly dangerous. But they also have a consciousness, containing within them the Indigo threads of life itself." He smiles when I look surprised. "Like fear, a lone Darkberry can kill, and usually does. If it doesn't kill, it can wipe all sentient thought from a mind, leaving it an empty vessel, the body it inhabits no more than meat." His smile fades, and his strange eyes rest on mine. "But Darkberry is also the most powerful medicine there is," he says quietly. "Taken at the right time, in the right circumstances, there is no poison or illness in a body that Darkberry cannot cure." He takes my hand again, pressing it reassuringly. "Be afraid, tomorrow," he says. "But let your fear lend you wings. Let it serve you, not kill you."

I nod, swallowing an unexpected lump in my throat. Feivel still holds my hand, as if there's something else he wishes to say.

"Zaria." He says my name reluctantly, as if second-guessing what he is about to say. "Garrick mentioned—he said you may have met the Lord of the Woven Court. Harken," Feivel adds delicately.

"Oh." I withdraw my hands, not wanting to lie, but also not keen to discuss the encounter.

"I advise caution in any dealings with him." Feivel's face is unusually grim.

"So Garrick said." I look at him curiously. "Why?" I ask bluntly. "What is it that he did, to make you all fear him so much?"

"He killed people." Feivel's answer is so flat and hard it takes me by surprise. "During the War. He didn't fight for the Kraken army, of course, but nor did he support the Northern Alliance— or not until the very end, and even then, only reluctantly."

"It was a war." I frown, confused. "People die."

"You don't understand." Feivel is shaking his head. "Harken killed any he decided were guilty, irrespective of their allegiance. He made neither allies nor friends, on either side. He dispensed whatever justice he saw fit, when and how he decided to deliver it, and to Indigold and Weavers from both sides. I'm not denying there were Weavers who did wrong." He inclines his head sadly. "There were Kraken Weavers who did terrible things, who broke every one of the twelve principles. They deserved to be punished. But such punishment should rightly have been delivered in the Woven Court, by their peers. Not summarily, by Harken.

"Among the many Weavers Harken killed," he says quietly, "was a Paladin Weaver."

I'm puzzled. "I thought Weavers were immortal."

"Weavers can be unwoven." Feivel's mouth is rather grim. "There are kind ways that might be done. Cutting the threads that bind their immortal soul to flesh, for example."

"Harken didn't do that," I guess.

"No." A dark shadow crosses Feivel's face. "Harken unthreaded the Paladin Weaver. It is a brutal, cruel end, one so painful the Weaver goes mad with agony long before it is over, without the mercy of falling into unconsciousness. Harken cleaved the man through and drew forth every thread of his immortal soul." Feivel's lips tighten. "If that wasn't bad enough, Harken didn't just unthread him. He Wove the threads of the man's soul around his body, binding him to consciousness, and to eternal agony. Then he hung the body over the gates of the Paladins' abbey." He nods grimly when my eyes widen. "The body hung there until long after the end of the War, the man's still-conscious eyes staring in stark agony at the Paladins who passed beneath it every day. None were powerful enough to undo Harken's Weaving, nor even to ease the man's distress."

The gruesome image hangs in the dim light, silencing whatever I might have said.

"That is the origin of Harken being called Savage," Feivel says quietly. "But it isn't the only reason."

I stare at him, wondering what on earth could possibly be worse than what he just described.

"Eventually the body on the gates disappeared." He meets my eyes. "But so did Harken. He never reopened the Woven Court after the War ended, even to those Weavers who had created him and entrusted him to guard their world." Feivel's eyes are distant, looking into a past I know he can no longer clearly see. "Far worse," he says, "he bound the priestesses of the Isle of Nine behind those same mists, along with the Woven Tower, inside of which, many believe, lies the golden needle of the Coronastrian Tapest that was used to defeat the Kraken in the final battle.

"It was bad enough that Harken should brutally murder Weavers," Feivel goes on, "his own people. Even worse that he should deprive the surviving Weavers of their home in the Woven Court, and Astria the wisdom of the Lotus Palaces, which have been the center of history, law, culture, and knowledge for Indigold and Weaver alike for centuries.

"But worst of all, with the loss of the Isle, and the golden needle, went any chance Astria might have had to create more Weavers. The Great Ceremony needs all three: the priestesses, the isle itself, and the golden needle. When Harken took the Woven Court into the mists, he not only stole Astria's past." Feivel meets my eyes, his own dark with pain and shadow. "He stole any chance we had to build a future."

CHAPTER 12

CIRCUS

I leave the tapest and walk through the dark alleys toward the circus where the Race is held, turning all Feivel said over in my mind.

The circus is a large, ancient space on the edge of town. Its oval track is surrounded by rising stands of old, crumbling stone, a remnant from the glory days before the Seam was Woven, when Lostport was still part of Astria. The circus was old even when the Seam was created. In the centuries since, it was sparsely maintained by the occasional visits from Weavers and their Indigold apprentices. Now, however, with none in the Seam who know the secrets of such stonework, it is rapidly deteriorating.

Is this what Harken has condemned Astria to? I look around at the ruins that characterize the Seam. *A future of brutality, crumbling stone, and gray despair?*

Tugging my scarf up to hide the worst of my scars, I take my place in the line before the small, barred booth where the registrar sits. Nearby stand a group of visiting Indigold nobles, their richly embroidered coats and gleaming buttons in stark contrast to the dull wools and mean tunics of the slaves. A bookmaker in their midst casts an experienced eye over each entrant that steps up to the booth. The nobles drink Darkwine in silver cups, laughing as they discuss the odds given to each.

To my left, the registrar for the Paladin Candidate trials stands not in a booth, but out in the open, scroll in hand. He's taller than any Indigold I've ever seen, seven feet at least, with shoulders the width of a carrick and blond hair so white it shines in the gloaming. He's wearing indigo Paladin's robes embossed with the familiar cup and serpent. He takes names gravely, as if doing so is a sacred rite. There is a quiet dignity to his demeanor.

I see the lone blade on his sleeve and realize, with a start, that this must be Leo's Uncle Saxan, the First Blade. A more unlikely family connection is hard to envisage. In comparison to Leo's rather pathetic appearance, this man looks like the living embodiment of the Paladin's quest for perfection. My heart twists at the thought of a Paladin like this man, but even worse, a Weaver, being tortured as Feivel had described.

"Name." The registrar's bored voice jolts me back to the present.

"Zaria."

"Master?" He barely looks up from the quill and parchment before him.

"Hodda, of the Dark and Disorderly House." I'm aware of the cluster of nearby Indigold, laughing scornfully as they take in my bloodstained shirt and slow, careful movements.

Laugh away, I think savagely. If I win tomorrow, it won't matter. If I lose, I might just be able to throw my knife hard enough to take one of them with me before I die.

"Slave braid?"

"First generation." I pull my scarf aside to show him.

The Paladin in the booth raises his eyebrows. "A Shadow Braid. No wonder you're racing."

I shrug, all the answer I have to that remark. He hands me

the pass with the number seven on it. As I turn away, I hear the bookmaker call my odds: a hundred to one. I smile darkly and resist the urge to give the Indigold vultures a jaunty wave.

I'm heading back to the alleys when a small group of Indigold catch my eye. They're standing beneath a large oak, at a good distance from the bustle and lights of the registry. It's not only the furtive way they are talking, their heads close to one another, but the fact that I recognize three of the faces. Two belong to Caspian and Foley, which is cause enough for concern. But the third face sends a cold shock through my entire body, closely followed by an almost blinding surge of rage.

It's the same hard-faced man I last saw in Hiraeth Forest, riding a boar out of the Dark Rip that took my brother.

Sudden fury makes me reckless. I edge around the crowds, pretending to study my pass, until I'm within hearing distance of their conversation. Sliding into the shadow of a nearby wall, I lean down on the pretext of adjusting the leather strap on my sandal.

"Arkady is a friend." The woman speaking has her back to me as she nods at the boar rider. She wears Paladin's robes and has rich auburn hair that falls to her waist in a straight, gleaming sheet. "He will be racing tomorrow, and I intend to ensure he wins." Her voice is clear and cold.

"Sereia, favorite aunt of mine." Caspian's tone is heavily laced with irony. "You read our minds. Foley and I had intended to ask you for a little help to achieve exactly that end."

"A little is all it takes." Foley puts his arm about Arkady and smiles ingratiatingly. "And besides, the Paladins seek perfection, do they not? Look at the face on this one. Blond haired, blue eyed, and just as handsome as that block of a Blade you have running the trials. How in the Dreaver's Tells did you end up in the cursed Seam, wearing a braid, Arkady?"

I sense an edge of envy in Foley's voice. His own diminutive height would barely reach the Blade's chest and is a far cry from the physical perfection he describes.

"My mother was exiled to the Foolish world." Arkady speaks quietly, with little expression. "As punishment for being a Kraken spy."

"A Kraken spy!" Foley gives a low whistle. "She was lucky to escape Astria with her life."

Sereia makes a sound almost like a hiss. "Far too many good people died at the hands of the Savage King. Condemned by Harken for nothing more than loyalty to my father, the king." Her voice is bitter and hard as cut glass. "That Woven abomination will pay for his rough justice, one day." She glances around cautiously and lowers her voice. "Arkady's is a hereditary braid, and the lord who Wove it is long dead. Arkady has to win that Race, or enter Astria as a slave. I won't see a loyal Kraken servant so debased. I intend to ensure he enters Astria as a member of the Indigold nobility."

Her tone is as much command as commentary. Caspian and Foley appear suitably impressed, and Arkady sufficiently grateful. Sereia looks between them all and gives a curt, decisive nod. "Good. Then I shall leave him in your hands, for now. Take care of him." She pauses. "He may prove useful to us all." She turns without explaining further, and I catch sight of her face for the first time: a pale, perfect oval with deep emerald eyes.

Beautiful, I think. *And utterly venal.*

I stay down as she passes, my heart thudding with sick tension. There was a sinister note to her final words that makes me think Sereia has plans for Arkady that extend beyond a favor to an old ally.

The heady scent of Darkwine floats across the ground, making me slightly dizzy as I come upright. The Indigold nobility are clearly getting an early start on the festivities.

"Taken a liking to racing, my little criminal?" I turn, startled. I didn't hear anyone come up behind me, and I'm good at sensing the presence of others. Harken's eyes gleam beneath a low-brimmed hat, flashing with their strange light.

"I'm not little." After what I've just heard, I'm in no mood for games. "And I'm certainly not yours." Knowing what I do now of Harken's past, it's all I can do to look at him.

Harken's glimmer of a smile is as mercurial as it is deeply unsettling. As I turn to continue walking, my scarf falls down, revealing the cuts on my face.

His smile disappears. "Who did this?" His eyes travel the cuts along my throat. He slips my shirt off one shoulder before I can move away, audibly sucking in his breath at the sight of my bloodied body.

"It doesn't matter." I twist out of his grasp, pulling the shirt up over my shoulder. I need to leave.

"You can't race like that." His voice is flat and hard. I wonder why he would care.

"I'll be fine." I meet his eyes, and my own slide away. Without really knowing why, I say, "It helped. What you did to my arm. I mean, it is helping. I'm healing faster than normal."

"Normal." He repeats the word slowly, a dangerous light in his eyes. "Then it's a normal occurrence, a beating such as this?"

I tilt my head in an equivocal gesture. "Ish. It's normal-ish."

"Normal-ish." His eyes soften slightly, though his mouth is still a hard line. "I'm not sure I'm familiar with the term."

"It's pointless, anyway." I'm unable to keep the bitterness from my tone. "The Race is fixed. I just heard one of the Paladins promising someone they would win."

"Yes." His voice has a hard, cold edge. "I, too, heard that little exchange."

I think of what Harken did to the Paladin Weaver. *No wonder Sereia hates him,* I think. *She was probably related to the Weaver Harken unthreaded.* That should make me pity her and loathe Harken.

I don't quite know what it says about me that it doesn't.

CHAPTER 13

GAMES

"*Y*ou should still race."

Harken's finger slips under my chin, tilting my face toward him. "You outran that Fool once before. I believe you may well do so again." He draws me closer, slipping my shirt aside as he turns my back to him. "And I can help you to heal," he murmurs. "A little faster than normal-ish, at least."

I tense instinctively. I know I should run. It is dangerous to even speak with someone capable of the things Feivel described.

But then I think of Sereia, promising Arkady he will win.

You want to beat him? I tell myself. *Then you take whatever help you can get, no matter who delivers it. And it isn't like Harken is the first monster you've met.* I see Hodda, his hand over the braid knot, narrow eyes filled with spite. *Nor*, I think grimly, *even close to being the worst.*

I shiver at the first starlight touch on my shoulder, closing my eyes. Knowing what to expect makes me more aware of the actual sensation, the effervescent thread winding into my body. Knowing the nature of the man controlling it is something else. I push those thoughts aside.

I win, I think, *or I die*. It truly is that simple.

The starlight travels along the fiery paths made by Hodda's stick and beyond, wending into places inside where old, long-forgotten wounds lie still, drawing the dull stagnation from them and replacing it with vibrant life. It's only when Harken touches my face that I shy away.

"No." I shake my head, catching his hand in my own. "Hodda will know if you heal my face."

Something cold and hard flashes in his eyes. "Perhaps," he murmurs, "I should meet with this Hodda of yours."

A dark part of me considers this. But even if he means it, and even if I could trust him, swapping one master for another is not freedom. And emotional bondage, it seems to me, is an even worse form of slavery than the braid I wear.

I step away and pull my scarf around me, suddenly aware of the chill on the air. "Not unless you want to buy all four of us, and take us with you."

His eyebrows rise in surprise. "You have more siblings? I thought it was just the three of you."

Or two, since you won't help me find Doron. But I can't say that aloud. To say it would make it true.

"Yes. Well," I correct myself, "they're not my siblings, exactly. But we've been together since they were babies."

"Winning won't free them, though." He scrutinizes me curiously. "Only you."

"If I win, I can buy their freedom. Then I will find a way to get their braids off." Perhaps because of what I just heard Sereia promise, my plan has never sounded so pathetically hopeless to my own ears.

"Why bind your fate to theirs?" Harken studies me as if searching for some hidden meaning. "Why not take the coin from your win and leave them to make their own way?"

"Because the only true freedom for me will come when I know they, too, are free to decide their own destiny." I wince at the memory of Doron's face. "They're my family. My responsibility. I'm bound to them whether I choose it or not. We are all freed," I say, almost to myself, "or none of us are."

How many times, I wonder, *have I said those words?* And look where they have brought me—to almost certain death, and whispers in the shadows with the Savage King himself.

I feel an irrational urge to laugh at the absurdity and horror of it all. That, or burst into tears and flee into the night.

"Then you still plan to race, despite what you overheard?" Harken is watching me with an expression I can't quite read.

"Of course I will race." I think of Shimi and Neoma, of Levin. "It's a chance," I say dully. "Even if it's a bad one."

His eyes flicker briefly toward the trees, where only moments ago Sereia promised to help Arkady steal the Race. Hard silver gleams in the indigo depths, and I suddenly realize why Harken seems so interested in whether or not I will compete.

"You don't want them to win." It's beginning to make sense. "That's why you helped me. You want me to beat them."

"Must everything be a transaction?" His half smile gleams in the darkness, though it doesn't touch his eyes.

I shrug. "For a slave in the Seam, yes." The cautious part of me knows I should leave it at that. But caution hasn't served me lately. "Why is Arkady still alive?" I step close enough to see a muscle flicker in his jaw, the infinitesimal narrowing of his eyes. Not wishing to betray all I know, I choose my words carefully. "You said you had savagery enough to manage here. Isn't Arkady the savagery that you stayed to manage?"

Harken's strange smile hovers still, though shadows chase through his eyes. "Let us say that I believe Arkady to be a part of the game. Not its master."

The game. The urge to laugh leaves me entirely. *That's all this is to him. And me just another piece in it. That's all any of us are to Astria.*

I shake my head, suddenly exhausted. "I'm right, though." I know it. "You want me to beat Arkady because you don't like him, or those who support him."

"I don't like them, little criminal, that much is true." He raises his head, and even in the shadows, I can see that his smile has quite gone. "I don't like them at all."

I'm turning to leave when he says abruptly, "It's what you might call a compromise." When I don't respond, his mouth hardens. "Leaving Arkady alive. It's a compromise."

A compromise that might well be about to cost me my life.

"Compromise is just a polite name for a bad bargain." I don't bother to hide my contempt. "And I never make bad bargains."

I expect him to disappear with his customary mercurial swiftness.

Instead, when I turn back, he is still watching me go, a slight frown on his face.

CHAPTER 14

SIGHT

I wake on Race morning to a bright, clear dawn. Even lying in our small attic, I can feel the palpable current of excitement running through Lostport, evident in the Race flags hung outside the Disorderly Houses, the shuttered shops that closed for the festivities, and the sheer quantities of Darkwine being consumed from first light.

I creep downstairs to find Hodda still fast asleep, sprawled facedown on his bed fully clothed. The flagon beside him is empty. Given the strength of the Darkwine in that flagon, he won't wake before late afternoon. I'm rather disappointed that he will wake at all.

I spend the morning engaged in all my usual dull tasks of cleaning and preparation, nervous enough that the mindless labor is a welcome distraction. Levin finds me before the sun is high. He moves stiffly so as not to reopen his wounds, and his face is a bloody mess despite obvious efforts, by Mallory, I imagine, to help him heal. I think of Harken's silvery touch with a wave of impotent frustration.

A few moments of his time are all it would take to heal Levin.

But I know that whatever odd dynamic has developed between us, it won't extend to Levin or anyone else.

"You're racing, then." It isn't a question. Levin's voice rasps with pain and exhaustion. I nod, unable to think of anything to say that can take away the empty, flat expression in his eyes.

I am the cause of that emptiness. I force myself to face it. *I did this to him. To all of them.*

"Then I wish you luck, Zaria." Levin puts out his hand in an oddly formal gesture. I stare at it. Barely days ago, he would have embraced me without a moment's hesitation, blue eyes shining. Levin might be stubborn, but he has always been the sunniest of us all, the first to offer a kind word for Mallory, a tisane for one of the girls, and a ready smile to all. Overnight, it seems, in place of that cheerful boy is this dead-eyed young man with swollen, bloody lips that look like they will never smile again and a stiff, outstretched hand.

I take it anyway, covering it with both of my own. "I'm sorry about the trials."

We both know he has no chance of entering if he can't so much as stand upright without holding the stable wall. Levin nods curtly. His hand slides from mine. I watch him walk slowly, painfully up the stairs and hear the door close behind him with a soft click of finality. I won't see Levin again today, I know.

My heart thuds sickly in my throat. *I may never see Levin again.*

Competitors are expected at the circus by early afternoon. I go back to my room, where Shimi is brushing Neoma's hair on the bed. The two girls are rather less ebullient than after their perceived triumph in the salon. They both adore Levin. And he hasn't hidden in the stable, as I and Doron always have, nor bandaged the worst of his cuts so they can't see. Levin's beating is probably the first time, I think, that they've really understood what Hodda is capable of.

I sigh inwardly. That knowledge will only make Shimi more determined. Despair overwhelms me again, as it has every moment since the Dark Rip. In my mind, I see lifeless bodies lying on the track, their lifeblood running into the dust.

Don't think about it. Not now.

"You can't race," Shimi says flatly, looking at my face. "Hodda beat you within an inch of your life. You were barely moving when I saw you last. You can't compete like that."

Earlier, I debated whether seeing them this morning was a good idea. But I can't leave without saying anything at all. I don't know how today ends, although I do know the odds aren't good. *A hundred to one, to be exact.* I fight the slightly hysterical urge to laugh that seems ever present lately.

"I'm going to watch it, anyway." I turn away from her sharp eyes and reach for the bag containing the last of the coin Garrick gave me. I throw it to Shimi. "Garrick wanted you to have this."

"Why?" Shimi eyes me suspiciously.

"Because he's going to the Drop, and she's entering the Race."

Both of us turn to Neoma, startled. "I can just tell," she says softly. Her pale face colors slightly, but her eyes on mine are steady enough. I'm still trying to work out how to answer her when Shimi rounds on me.

"Are you insane?" She leaps up, copper eyes hard and brilliant. "You'll hang, if you don't die in the Race itself. Which you will, after the beating you took!" Her voice rises with every word.

"Be quiet, Shimi." Neoma's voice is oddly clear. Shimi, taken aback, subsides. Neoma reaches for my hand. Her touch is cool but oddly penetrating.

It feels not unlike Harken's.

Since the Rip, every thought seems to lead back to him.

Neoma's eyes become distant, as they always do with the

Sight, then suddenly brighten. "You are strong." She looks up in surprise. "Truly strong, Zaria. He healed you. He made you . . . better than you were."

"Who healed her?" Shimi looks between us, frowning. "Look at her face, Neoma. There's nothing healed about those wounds."

Neoma waves her away impatiently. "The mists." She frowns, as if trying to peer through something. "You have to see past the mists, Zaria. See the truth." Through the tiny window high in the wall of our room, a thin ray of sunlight falls directly where she stands. For a brief, poignant moment, Neoma is bathed in golden light, like a distant, ethereal angel.

Then her eyes dull, and she drops my hand. I kiss her cheek, but she is still and unresponsive, as always, after the Sight.

I glance at Shimi. In the golden light her eyes are brilliant, her beautiful face smooth as polished glass. "Don't," she says, backing away when I would have approached her. "Don't, Zaria."

I can't tell if it is a plea or a warning, but I know better than to push her. I look at them both, thinking that this is how I will remember them, bathed in winter sunlight.

"Goodbye," I say.

There isn't anything else to be said.

CHAPTER 15

RACEMASTER

"*R*eady?" Garrick greets me at the entrance.

"Ready." There isn't a great deal to say.

I wear a leather belt around my waist, the knife Garrick gave me years ago thrust through it on one side. It's almost a sword, and more than many competitors have.

We enter the mounting yard, where the competitors mill around in varying states of nervous tension. The Race is capped at thirty entries, and every place is taken this year. The Indigold nobles lean on the stone walls watching us, laughing as they drink Darkwine from silver hip flasks, their faces flushed. Off to one side, Arkady is engaged in deep conversation with Caspian. I keep my eyes down, trying not to let anger take me. Foley and Sereia join them, together with a third man wearing Paladin's robes. He has a politician's wide smile and thick black hair and shakes the hands of all those in the small group, including Arkady, with hearty laughter.

"That weak bastard is Gareth, the Paladin Consul," Garrick says in my ear. "He's Racemaster, but it's that Kraken snake Sereia he answers to. Don't let 'em see you lookin'," he growls, turning me away. He grips my arms. "Don't get distracted."

I nod, my skin prickling with tension. Even my slave braid feels odd, as if it's writhing on my skin. It almost feels like a stranger on my body. *Perhaps it senses how close we both are to freedom.*

"Zaria." I turn, startled, to meet Feivel's anxious eyes, gold flashes of alarm touching the vivid purple depths. Despite knowing he would be here today, I'm still touched to see him. "Apparently the Paladin Divine from Astria considers the Race beneath his dignity." Feivel lowers his voice. "Which means he will be represented by the unfortunate Leo," he murmurs, casting his eyes skyward in exasperation.

Garrick gives me the ghost of a wink. "Then I'd stay well clear of the Race Cup, if I were you."

The Race Cup is given to each competitor at the start line. In the dark humor of the Seam, the slaves refer to it as the "last cup."

If Leo is mixing it, the joke will likely be on them.

There it is again, the nervous urge to laugh hysterically. I swallow hard. My hands are shaking.

The Racemaster, Gareth, calls us to the center. I try not to think of him shaking Arkady's hand.

"For those who don't know," says Gareth, his voice carrying clearly across the ground, "carricks and horses are all provided by the Paladins and allocated at random when you pull a number from the Cup." He holds up a gleaming silver chalice with a flamestone serpent twined about it. "As for the rules, well." He tilts his head and smiles as the Indigold boys hoot raucously. "There aren't many, if I'm honest." This receives another burst of wild cheers and catcalls. "Yes, yes." Gareth holds up his hand, grinning boyishly, his hair attractively tousled. "But there are some, so listen up, you pack of reprobates."

His jocular tone is entirely for the benefit of the watching Indigold. The slaves are pale and silent.

There is nothing amusing about this race for us. There is only the waiting carricks and horses, and a track that leads to death.

"Number one," Gareth is saying, "the race is three full circuits. Nobody can win who does not complete all three, staying on the designated track for the entirety of each. Number two: while all means necessary may be used to upend or otherwise disable your opponents"—he pauses, waiting for the Indigolds' raucous war cries to die down—"it is entirely forbidden to Weave or Work in any way at all to gain advantage. Let me be very clear about this," he says sternly. "This race is about skill, speed, and fighting prowess. If I see the faintest flash of a needle, or suspect collaboration with any in the stands to Weave or Work, I will not hesitate to eliminate the competitor."

Unless the collaboration is done by the Paladin Weaver, that is. I clench my fists in resentment.

From the corner of my eye I see Caspian and Foley smirking into their cups. Caspian catches me staring and raises his cup in ironic salute, his grin growing darker. I glare at him.

"Don' look," growls Garrick. Turning away, I draw a deep breath and focus on the Racemaster.

"Finally," Gareth is saying, "rule number three: the race ends when a competitor completes the third circuit, leaps to the platform, and grasps the Cup with both hands." He holds up a finger. "Both hands, mind. Not one. Not an arm, or with legs. Both hands, clearly visible, on the Cup." He holds it up again to demonstrate. "And now, with all that said . . ." He thrusts the Cup high in the air. "Only one can be freed!"

He roars the words. The Indigold roar with him. Many of the slaves echo the words. But their voices are hollow, and they say the words like a mantra, their fearful eyes as desperate as they are determined.

I know they are thinking, as I am, of the many corpses carried out of this circus after every race.

But just like me, they have decided the risk is worth it.

What price hope? I think, looking around at the pale, set faces.

I take my number and make my way to the corresponding horse and carrick. There is nothing to choose between them, no one animal more spirited than the next. The carricks are all built for the race, with no seat, but strong footboards for us to brace ourselves against as we stand. Ugly iron protrusions from the wheel hubs will enable a good driver to spike the wheels of another opponent. Some drivers, Arkady included, carry long whips, and all wear some form of blade.

Garrick has always advised against a whip. "Gets in the way," he's taught me. "Better to make friends with your horse than whip it."

I approach my gentle-eyed mare. "Hey, girl." I rub her nose. "Ready to have some fun?" The mare whickers. She also looks at me slightly askance, as if she knows all too well how terrified I truly am. I rest my hand on her neck and close my eyes, allowing my senses to flow into hers. The mare trembles softly, then goes very still. I feel it, the moment we truly meet, the shock of her awareness touching my own. "That's it," I murmur, swinging myself up into the carrick, letting my hand trail to her hindquarters, then straight onto the reins, maintaining the connection. "We can do this, can't we?"

The slave on the next carrick casts me a curious look, and I know a moment of panic. *Is it Weaving, or Work, what I can do with animals?* I hardly know, having grown all my life in the Seam. I know it's unusual, the way I can sense animals. *Will I be disqualified before I even begin? Surely I can't be eliminated for something I don't even understand?*

Nobody says anything, and I shake off my doubts. My entry number puts me seventh from the inside rail. There are ten between me and Arkady, and a dozen more beyond him. Arkady's blade is no knife but a long, lethal sword. *A gift from his new Indigold friends, no doubt,* I think bitterly.

"Here comes that bloody Paladin with his cup of poison." Garrick scowls. "Don't drink it, now, mind."

The other slaves are all gulping the Darkwine, grasping for any courage they can find, even from a bottle.

"Only one can be freed." Leo says the traditional words as he hands me the Cup, but his hand shakes, and his eyes, as he watches me sip, are dark with fear. "Good luck," he whispers. I'm glad he's too nervous to notice me toss the contents of the Cup down my sleeve. At least I learned something from a lifetime in Hodda's damned salon.

"Right." Garrick's large hand covers my own on the reins, his steady brown eyes on mine. "Remember your training. Forget them Indigold bastards in the stands. You're going to race, and you're going to win. You hear me?" I nod, unable to speak. "Then go," Garrick growls, "and get that bloody braid off your neck, lass. The boys and me are all with you." He raises an arm, and through slightly blurred vision, I see Wiley and his grizzled pack of Seam Guards rise in a roar, waving madly. Going by their enthusiasm, they've definitely had more than a bottle or two of Drop ale.

Gareth mounts the stand, the Cup gleaming beside him.

"Here we go, lass." Garrick's grim eyes meet mine. He squeezes my hand one last time. "Show the bastards what you can do."

Gareth raises his arm, and silence falls across the circus.

His arm drops.

CHAPTER 16

SLAVES

*T*he mare lurches into flight, snorting with fear and excitement.

The line spreads across the circus track, dirt churning from hooves, drivers urging their horses forward with whip and word. At first, it's fairly even, as everyone finds their pace, but by the first turn the carnage has begun.

From the corner of my eye I see one of the carricks on the inside of the track cartwheel into the air, pulling the squealing horse over on its side. The driver, thrown free, lies facedown on the ground. Paladins run to cut the horse free and carry the driver's body from the track. He's not the only one. By the time the first circuit is done, the least experienced drivers have toppled their carricks or overturned them trying to avoid those who have fallen.

But not Arkady, I think grimly, rounding the end turn to head into the second lap. I'm positioned halfway down the group of carricks that are still upright, while Arkady is almost a full carrick length ahead of the entire field.

Bending forward, I let my senses reach down the reins, both reassuring and encouraging, and the mare leaps forward in response. I weave the carrick around two drivers, edging ahead as we approach the turn. One of the closest yells out as the driver on the inside, driving a black horse hard, deliberately entwines the spike protruding from the hub on his wheel with the spokes on the other. It topples over immediately, spilling the driver onto the track. I have a glimpse of his devastated face as we round the turn.

The carnage on the inside is working to my advantage, giving me a tighter race circuit, but between the ruthless driver cutting them down and Arkady cutting his way through the others on my right, only two carricks now separate me from the driver on the inside, and three from Arkady on my right. The driver closest on my left, thinking to play the same rough game as the one on the inside, leans over to grasp the reins of the slave between them. I want to call out to them to fight Arkady, not each other, but I'm too late. The driver miscalculates, and both carricks veer off, tipping their drivers onto the ground.

Now it is just the driver on the inside track and me, with only two left on the other side between me and Arkady.

I know the inside driver is coming for me. Bloody red lines cover his terrified horse's back where he's whipped it, and I feel a savage flash of rage. Every slave knows the touch of a whip, the humiliation of being bound. That any would stoop to draw blood on another creature gives me the spur of anger I need. Bracing myself against the footboard, I check the tension in the reins, feeling for my knife. It's on my right, and the driver is on my left; he's already drawn his own sword, a long, lethal-looking thing. I allow him to draw closer, see him lean across—

I spin away so my back faces the horse, reins still wrapped around my left arm. As he lunges with his sword, thinking to cut through the reins that a moment ago were right before him, I meet his sword with my own knife. In a real fight, it would have been over in seconds, for my blade is no match for his. But he thought to cut reins, not meet another blade. His eyes widen in surprise, and he rears back. As I spin back to face the front, my left arm steers the mare toward the driver's carrick. In the time it has taken for him to try to attack me, he has lost speed, and I'm just far enough ahead to cut in front of him. The mare grunts as she surges forward, giving me the extra pace I need to gain the inside track.

Now going into the third lap, Arkady and I are neck and neck, Arkady having dispatched the carricks between us so we now race side by side. The driver I've just bested can't find a gap between us. In my peripheral vision I see his carrick hit an unseen obstacle and cartwheel into the air.

Unseen obstacle.

It hits me just as I catch a fleeting glimpse of Sereia in the stands. She's standing very still, her eyes locked on the Race. *That's how she's doing it*, I realize. *By overturning the other carricks.*

Leaning forward, I croon to the mare, urging her on, aware of Arkady, grim faced beside me, wielding the whip relentlessly upon his horse with the same hand about which the reins are wound. The sword in his hand is covered in blood.

His left hand.

Too late, I realize he has been fighting his way toward me with that sword arm from the start of the race, unlike the bulk of the field, who drive as I do, with reins in the left and knife in the right.

No wonder he cut through the field so quickly, I think with rising panic as he comes closer. He'd have dispatched nearly every slave with one cut of that thing.

I can't fight him with my knife. I know it from the deft way he wields the sword as he drives for me. All I have is speed. I lean forward again. *Go*, I will the mare. *Like the wind, now. Go.*

The starlight stream from Harken's hand seems to surge through my veins, dancing in exhilaration down the reins. The mare squeals in surprise and leaps as if struck by lightning herself, surging forward, finding a reserve neither of us knew she had.

I've pulled ahead. I can see the Cup gleaming on the podium in the center of the track.

I've practiced the leap from my carrick to the Cup's wooden frame a thousand times, as well as the final climb of a few feet up to the podium.

But that was leaping at an oak tree in Hiraeth, with Garrick yelling instructions and nobody in my path.

Today it means crossing Arkady's path, and I am not yet far enough ahead to do that. Glancing back, I see his eyes gleam. He knows I can't cross his path to the podium without meeting his bloody sword first—and I have no doubt Sereia will ensure my carrick topples at the crucial moment.

Not today. I grit my teeth. *That can't be how today ends.*

The podium is coming closer.

I gauge the distance between Arkady's horse and my carrick. Carefully, I ease off slightly on the reins, just enough to bring us alongside, as the podium comes into reach.

With one slice, I bring my knife down and cut the reins between me and the mare.

I leap out of the carrick just as it spins wildly off the ground. A second later, and I would have been thrown beyond help. As it is, I land on Arkady's horse's back in an inelegant sprawl. I scramble across, my hands catching the far side of the podium just in time to swing myself off the horse and hang from the frame.

I hear the roar of the crowd in the stands for the first time, though I'm sure they've been screaming all through the race. Arkady, his visor raised now to show a face white with shock and fury, is on the opposite side of the wooden frame, climbing fast, sword in hand.

But I don't have the burden of a sword. And a lifetime of practice in Hiraeth means I climb faster.

My hands reach the podium, my feet scrabbling for a toe hold; but in a last devious trick, there is no final step, and I have to haul myself up using my body weight alone. Every muscle strains, my legs flailing uselessly in the air, and I see triumph dawning on Arkady's face as he pulls himself slowly up.

"No!" The word is a hoarse scream. I close my eyes and simply will my body up, straining every muscle, the cuts on my face and neck that Harken hasn't healed splitting open again so blood runs into my eyes.

But it works.

I'm on the podium, my hands reaching for the Cup—

We grasp it at the same time.

I stare at the handles in dumb shock and look up to find the same expression in Arkady's eyes. We reached for those handles at exactly the same moment, I would swear it. I've no idea how anyone could pick the outcome.

Then Gareth rubs his hands gleefully, Arkady's face settles into a smug smile, and the last glimmer of hope leaves me.

If I had made the podium a moment earlier, taken the Cup clear enough for all to see, perhaps it might have been different.

But a draw?

No.

The race is Arkady's.

CHAPTER 17

CLAIMED

*G*areth lifts the Cup from our hands, and I slump on the podium, my head down, blood and sweat dripping off my fingers.

I know I am dead.

"So very close!" Gareth holds the Cup high, and the Indigold roar. The slaves, though, are no longer cheering. The competitors are sitting on the ground, heads down as I am, waiting to die. Those in the stands watch in grim silence, deprived of even the vicarious thrill in watching one of their own gain liberty. Arkady might wear a slave braid, but he is a stranger to the Seam, and his long sword and short odds mark him as the Indigold favorite. None of us are naive enough to think the Racemaster will rule against him.

"But there is still a clear winner, nonetheless," Gareth goes on. Even with my head down, I see his hand go past me as if in slow motion and reach for Arkady's, raising it high in the air. "Only one can be freed!"

"Only one can be freed!" roar the Indigold in the stands, calling out the words over and over as they applaud. I think I should probably move, though I can't quite imagine why and have no idea to where.

"Perhaps," drawls a sardonic voice, "today might prove the exception."

I freeze. The crowd gasps, momentarily silenced. Then a low murmuring begins, the whispers washing over me like an incoming tide.

Harken is standing in the middle of the track. In stark contrast to the lavish brocade and gold embroidery of the watching Indigold, he wears a simple ruby morning coat open over a linen shirt that hangs open at the neck. His top boots gleam through the dust coating them, his long legs encased in black breeches. In contrast to the unctuous Racemaster on the podium or the plump Indigold in the stands, his six and a half feet seems built like a lethal piece of machinery. Just as his casual manner of dressing doesn't disguise the quality of the cloth, nor can it hide the supple tension of his body, every powerful muscle evident but not obvious.

Especially when he takes a casual step forward and is suddenly standing on the podium beside us.

"Lord Harken." The color drains from Gareth's face. He bows stiffly. "I was not informed you planned to attend."

"I was unaware the Paladins wished to be kept informed of my plans." Harken seems almost amused. Up close, lit by the late afternoon glow, the hard, precise lines of his face are devastatingly beautiful. A trader in Lostport once showed me a rock made of raw amber. *That is what he seems carved from*, I think, *as if he is lit from within.* His mouth is fuller than I thought, the bottom lip slightly heavier than the top. His face isn't as angular as night made it. There is a broad, ancient strength in the deep-set eyes and high cheekbones, a sardonic certainty that has a power of its own. His dusky blond hair hangs to his shoulders like some kind of ragged lion's mane, grazing the edges of the indigo eyes, their mercurial gleam made even more arresting by the sunlight.

Gareth swallows hard, coloring slightly. "Did you come to observe the Race, my lord?"

His visible fear gives me an almost savage thrill.

"No." Harken's one word clearly conveys his contempt for both the Race and its attendees. "I came to claim what is mine by right." His eyes rest briefly on me.

Gareth frowns. "Yours, my lord?" his eyes flicker to either side, as if seeking counsel, but he is quite alone on the podium.

"Those of your order in attendance today are, perhaps, too young to recall the traditions of old." Harken's voice carries clearly over the stands, his contemptuous tone suggesting that age has nothing to do with the Paladins' recollections. There is a sharp twist of his hand, and a moment later, Feivel is standing beside us on the podium. "Feivel," Harken says agreeably. "Perhaps you might enlighten the Paladin Consul as to my meaning."

"This Race is run by the Paladins!" Sereia's shrill voice rings out from the stands. "You have no authority here, Harken."

"This is not your pet council." Harken's voice is coldly dismissive. "And I have authority wherever I choose to exert it." He doesn't address Sereia by name, nor so much as glance at her as he speaks. "Feivel," he says again, nodding his head politely. "Please."

Feivel casts me an apprehensive look. "Enshrined in Race law," he begins, "is the right of the Sav—of the Woven Court," he quickly amends, "to claim a slave of their choosing who might be freed, in addition to the Race winner."

My heart lurches to a leaden standstill, then begins, very slowly, to beat again.

"I've never heard of any such law." Gareth's blustering, however, is rather undermined by his panicked glances toward the stands.

"My dear Lord Consul." Feivel raises a rather dignified

eyebrow. "I may have lost my personal memories when I lost my needle, but I assure you, my knowledge of Astrian law remains quite exhaustive. Rather unsurprising, since, I am told, I wrote many of them myself." He spreads his hands in a self-deprecating manner that makes some of the crowd titter and a few of the slaves' heads rise in slow, half-hearted hope.

"Now that we are clear." Harken touches my shoulder, bringing me dizzily to my feet. His hand closes over the slave braid at my neck. "This one," he says, "will come with me."

The consul's face is a picture of blank amazement. I have a vague impression of the crowd rising to their feet and a final glimpse of Feivel's small figure holding up his arms for calm.

Then a swirling, glittering mist descends, and the circus is gone.

CHAPTER 18

BOUGHT

a strong arm holds me fast. Amid the swirling chaos, my braid seems oddly alive, like a silken river about my neck.

I feel something solid underfoot, and the mist disappears.

I'm standing on the Lostport dock. In front of me is an old fishing trawler, paint peeling from its cracked timbers.

"It's not much," comes Harken's dry voice from behind me. "But it's home."

I stare at the trawler, too stunned to even take it in. "What am I doing here?" My voice is little more than a faint rasp.

"It was an interesting decision, I agree." Harken nods toward the gangway leading onto the trawler. "Why don't you board, and I will tell you all about it."

I glare at him. "I'm not going anywhere near that boat." I glance at the trawler again, this time fully comprehending its derelict state. "And I don't believe for a second that is your home." I look around, half expecting the world to disappear as abruptly as the circus did a moment ago, taking the entirety of Lostport with it this time.

Taking Shimi and Neoma. Levin.

"I told you." I don't even dare to believe, yet, that he might actually free me. And I can't bear to think of disappearing without knowing the fate of my siblings. "There are four of us. I can't leave without them. I won't." I don't hide my desperation.

"Your sisters were bought this morning." Harken's tone is matter-of-fact. "They were gone before the Race even started." He unties the gangway, kicking it into place with one booted foot. "And your brother made it through the trials. He is now officially a Candidate in the Paladins."

Levin? My skepticism must be obvious, because Harken, watching me, goes on: "He fought off two fully armored Paladin Blades while covered in brutal scars, and with no more than a pocket knife." His mouth curls slightly. "The Paladins would never let such perfection go unrewarded."

Despite the contempt in his tone, I think he's telling me the truth.

How could Levin have done that? I wonder, thinking of his stiff gait the last time I saw him. And yet . . . I think of his face as Doron fell away from us. Of his oddly formal manner as he wished me luck. In his own way, I know, Levin is every bit as determined as me, or Doron, or Shimi. And possibly even more stubborn.

If anyone could face down two Blades while barely alive, I think with reluctant admiration, *it's Levin.* I can't be angry that he took the chance he saw. I can only be glad he's alive. For now, at least. I've heard dark tales of Candidate year.

But that leaves Shimi and Neoma, and Harken's blunt words about them: *"Your sisters were bought this morning."*

Caspian's sneer crosses my mind, followed sharply by the memory of Foley's coarse, pawing hands. I shudder.

"They all seemed happy enough with their choices." Harken gestures toward the gangway, indicating that I should board.

I stare at him, aghast. "You have no idea what would make them happy."

"And you do, is that it?" Harken fixes me with a hard eye. "Wasn't it you who told me that you will only know *true freedom* when your siblings, too, are free to decide their own destiny?" He lifts a shoulder. "It seems to me," he says rather dismissively, "that they've all done that. Perhaps you should respect their choices."

"Choices they made out of desperation!" I'm so taken aback I struggle for words. "I wanted freedom for them, not another form of slavery. My way—"

"Your way would have left you dead on that track," Harken interrupts me bluntly. "Or at Hodda's hands." Silver, sudden and dangerous, flashes through his eyes. "He seemed . . . unusually excited at the prospect of torturing you."

"You spoke with Hodda?" I stare at him, trying and failing to imagine that scene.

"I'm not certain that *spoke with* accurately describes our encounter." His mouth twitches. "Hodda appeared to have consumed a rather more concentrated form of Darkwine than might be considered healthy." He raises an eyebrow at me. "I wonder who might have filled his flask with that?" He continues without waiting for an answer. "It was a brief visit. Just long enough to pay the required coin for this." He holds up the end of my slave braid. I've only ever seen it on the Master's Ring, one of five knotted there. Until this moment I've never realized the strange comfort I've taken from the knowledge that whatever happened to the five of us, we were all bound by that same ring, knotted together, side by side. Now the twisted braid end looks terrifyingly alone in Harken's hand. I've been bound by it almost as long as I can recall. I've risked everything in my bid to free myself of it, and now Harken's hand on it is like a strange caress at my neck.

"You bought me?" I can barely breathe. "Why? I thought you were claiming me for the Woven Court. Feivel said on the stand that you would free me."

"Ah." Harken holds up a finger. "I believe the exact words of the law in question is that the Woven Court has the right to claim a slave of their choosing, who *might* be freed. *Might* being the operative word in this case. But more on that later." He sounds almost impatient, glancing at the sky as he speaks as if assessing the weather for sailing, rather than discussing the fact that he quite literally holds my life in his hands.

A life that apparently matters very little to him.

I'm momentarily lost for words. Fear and impotent rage twist sickeningly inside me.

"As for this." Harken glances at the braid end with visible distaste. "In my experience, it is unwise to leave such . . . loose ends, shall we say, to the vagaries of fate." His mouth twists in a sardonic smile that makes me furious.

"Give me that." I reach for the braid, only to find it whisked out of reach.

"I'm afraid I can't." Harken is still half smiling. "Not yet, at least."

"Is my freedom a game to you?" Despair and desolation pile atop the exhaustion I feel in the aftermath of the race. "If you think withholding that vile thing is amusing," I say, anger and helplessness writhing like the braid itself against my skin, "then you either know nothing of what it is to be a slave or you are every bit the savage they call you." Anger and helplessness writhe like the braid itself against my neck.

Harken's eyes flash with a sudden, fierce light. "I assure you I understand slavery better than you ever could." His voice is hard as ice. "And savage though I might be, I do not play games, little criminal. And never with freedom.

"I will explain," he says tersely, "but I would prefer to do it at my leisure, and in more pleasant surroundings." He nods at the gangway. "If you wouldn't mind."

"If I wouldn't mind?" The world around me dims, a strange roaring in my ears. "You healed me," I whisper. "You made me well. You made me think you were kind." When he remains silent and stony faced, my shock turns to hard, hot fury. "I never should have trusted you. Garrick and Feivel were right all along." My voice is shaking. "And *savage* is too kind a word for what you are."

"That much is true." His tone is deceptively light, though his mouth has thinned into a hard line. "And I suggest you would do well to remember it." The braid end swings in his hand as he nods at the gangway. "It's time we were gone."

"You bought me," I say again. My voice cracks on the words, but I force myself to look at him. "You own me."

He meets my eyes. "Body and soul," he says quietly.

Body and soul.

The slave oath, made when coin is paid to transfer the braid. My worst nightmare, and the sentence I have worked my entire life to avoid. The one line even Hodda has never had the right to use.

The braid end twists slowly in Harken's hand, the slave braid curls insidiously about my neck, and something inside me breaks.

"Go to the Tells," I say hollowly.

Without waiting for a response, I turn and walk up the gangway and onto the boat.

CHAPTER 19

NEXUS

I sit up on the bow watching the dying sun, the sea spray cold on my face. I barely notice it.

I won't enter the cabin of the trawler. So long as I sit up here, I'm still in the world I know. Something tells me that the moment I enter that cabin, my life will change forever.

Feeling the strange frisson at my neck, I shudder. *My life has already changed.*

"Would you stop doing that!" I spin around, glaring at Harken, who stands in the cockpit, one arm loosely draped over the tiller. "I can feel it, you know. Every time you touch that damned braid end, I can feel it. Even Hodda had the decency to leave the knots alone, unless he was actually trying to torture us."

Harken's eyes flash with something that almost looks like surprise, though I know it can't be. He's the Savage King. Lord of the Woven Court. He probably taught the Indigold how to Weave the damned braids in the first place.

And now he owns me.

Body and soul.

I want to throw up. I want to run away.

I want to kill him.

Whatever he sees in my eyes seems to have at least some effect. "I apologize." He bows his head in a more awkward gesture than any I've previously seen from him. "How—what do you wish me to do with it?"

"Give it to me," I say promptly.

"I regret that isn't possible at this time." The final rays of the sun gleam from his eyes, making them hard to read. "But I certainly do not wish to plague you with it." Reaching into his shirt, he comes up with a plain man's ring, hanging from a leather cord around his neck. "If I tie it to this, I promise it will be safe—and that I won't touch it again." He pauses, and I realize that in some twisted play on the master and slave arrangement, he's waiting for me to give my consent.

"Do what you wish." I turn away from him.

I feel it, the moment he ties the braid. I've only ever known Hodda's brutish hand on the knot, tightening it viciously as punishment. This is different. I recall the moment before the Race, when the braid seemed to writhe on my skin.

That must have been when he took the braid from Hodda. I feel both furious and strangely fascinated. There is a brief tension as Harken ties the knot about the metal, and then stillness. A moment later, I'm aware of a slow warmth spreading through my body, like a shield against the growing night.

It's him. The braid is resting against his chest. *It's his warmth I can feel.*

Hodda always kept the Master's Ring in a drawer. To have it worn against another's skin makes me want to tear the braid off, taking my skin with it if I must. I grip the wood on the deck and breathe deeply, forcing myself not to claw at it hysterically or to simply leap into the sea itself.

But the slave in me who has survived fifteen of Hodda's whip flatly refuses to give Harken the satisfaction of knowing the control he might wield, just by manipulating that small piece of woven cord.

First, I think coldly, *I need to know why he took me.* It makes no sense, none at all. What could the Savage King possibly need with a slave?

I shiver. Night has fallen, and the sea spray is no longer refreshing but icy on my skin.

"Come."

I leap to my feet, startled to realize Harken is standing right behind me.

"I wish you'd stop doing that," I snap. "At least warn me."

"I shall endeavor to remember that." He gestures toward the cabin below. "But now you must go below deck. We need to pass through the Nexus, and you can't be up here when we do."

"The Nexus?" I swallow uneasily.

Unlike the Drop, which falls directly into the Interweave, or a silverscye, which opens a pathway through the Interweave from one specific point to another, the Nexus is a hub within the Interweave itself. It is a fixed place where pathways from many worlds beyond our own meet. Only those with training, like Stitched Men, Weavers, or Pathfinders, can find and navigate it. The ships on which most Indigold come from Astria to the Seam are manned by all three, though the Indigold themselves can never recall anything of the journey after their arrival. Garrick told me once that memory loss is an oddity of the Interweave. For the unindoctrinated, all recollection of the strange pathways is lost the moment the Interweave is left behind.

I look doubtfully around at the peeling timbers and mean dimensions of our vessel. "You're going to sail—*this*—through the Nexus?"

Harken's mouth quirks at the edges. "I'm not certain that 'sail' is exactly the correct verb, but certainly, yes, the *Hydra* will take us from the Seam, through the Nexus, and into Astria.

Andras!" He turns to the cockpit, and a dark figure comes toward us, materializing into the man I met by the docks. "Please take Zaria below deck."

"Zaria." Andras smiles, his teeth gleaming in the darkness. "How is Teddy, your horse? A noble beast, that one."

"I'm not going below deck." I back away from his proffered hand, my own slipping surreptitiously around to the knife in my belt, remembering too late that I cast it away in the final moments of the Race.

"Well." Harken looks mildly amused. I sense he knows exactly what I was reaching for. "You certainly can't stay up here." He walks around the deck to the cockpit. I follow him at a wary distance.

"Why not?"

He unties the tiller and props one foot on a bench seat as he squints ahead into the darkness, seemingly entirely unbothered by the rising wind that beats against us, churning the water below into a white, roiling mass. "Because if you do," he says, in a tone that implies he is exercising finite patience, "you will be spun off the deck and into the Interweave. From there, you could find yourself anywhere—a mortal street in the Land of Fools or facing demons in one of the worlds through the Dark Rips. Either way, I won't be able to find you, and you won't be able to find your way back."

I glare at him. "Perhaps I would be better off."

"Perhaps." He shrugs, the half smile still on his mouth. "But as one who has followed many such loose threads before, allow me to warn you that there are far darker fates to be found in the Interweave than that offered at the end of a slave braid." He tilts his head. "Particularly one held by me, if I do say it myself. Andras." He nods, and Andras grasps my arm. "Take her below, please. And don't forget the Darkwine."

"Darkwine?" I twist out of Andras's grasp. "You're going to make me drink Darkwine as well?"

"A king is nothing of the kind if he does not care for his subjects," says Harken lightly. "Even a savage one."

"I'm not your subject." I feel my sanity spinning out of my grasp. "I'm your slave."

"Even then." Harken casts me the ghost of a wink. "Trust me when I say this is one journey you won't want to take without Darkwine. And besides." He grins darkly. "I mix a rather better vintage than they do in the Seam."

Given all I know, his amusement at my predicament shouldn't shock me, I suppose. But it does. I thought—naively, in retrospect—that I saw mercy in him.

Clearly, I was entirely mistaken. *Not for the first time lately*, I think bitterly.

I briefly consider refusing to go below. But even the Stitched Men pale when the Nexus is mentioned, and although none have ever described the journey, I figure that in describing the dangers, at least, Harken isn't lying. Shaking off Andras's hand, I go down the ladder ahead of him.

The cabin is as unimpressive as the exterior, one narrow table bound on either side by hard wooden benches. A small sink and cooking stove is on the other wall, with what I assume to be the head and two berths up ahead in the bow. "For a king," I say, looking around, "he doesn't really do luxury, does he?"

Andras grins again. There's an openness to his smile that reminds me oddly of Levin, though Andras's red eyes have a menacing edge more reminiscent of Doron's. Several weapons hang from various parts of his body, which seems almost as powerful as Harken's own. Andras, I suspect, would be utterly deadly in a fight.

He hands me a flagon. "Drink."

I take it but have no intention of drinking. Whatever is coming, I want to be alert for it.

"There's no point in pretending," says Andras, watching me. "And you will thank me for it later, believe me." He watches me for another moment, then raises his eyebrows. "No? Not a wise choice, Zaria."

As if in response to his words, the *Hydra* lists sharply to the right, throwing me hard against the wooden table. I yelp in surprise. Harken's head appears in the hold, his smile quite gone. Andras shrugs. "She doesn't seem to like Darkwine much."

"Dreaver's Tells." Harken lands, catlike, beside me, and suddenly I'm held by the same iron arm that brought me here, the flagon at my lips. Silver fire gleams in his eyes, seeming to enter my veins, removing all thought of resistance. "Drink," he says quietly.

I drink.

The world spins, and all becomes dark.

CHAPTER 20

COURTYARD

*A*t first, I don't realize I'm dreaming.

I'm standing amid the smoking ruins of a courtyard, surrounded by death.

The dead are so many they cover the ground almost entirely. The few still alive seem wounded beyond help. Around the edges of the courtyard, carved archways lead into a series of what must once have been exquisitely beautiful ancient buildings. Amid the destruction are strange snippets of poignant beauty: a blue lotus floating in a pond, a garden of lilies that is perfectly intact.

In the center of the courtyard are the remains of a great fountain tree, twisted and black, no more than a burnt remnant of its former glory. Only the sheer breadth of the trunk betrays the many years it must have stood in this place. Great chunks of marble surround it, broken and shot through with shards of gold that glitter with an oddly sinister light. The marble must once have formed the shape of a twelve-pointed lotus, for the ground around the tree is scorched black in that precise shape, a dead shadow of its former glory. Bodies lie strewn around the periphery, fallen where they died, defending what now lies in ash.

Part of me wonders if this is one of the Darkwine dreams of which

I've only ever heard stories, but another part of me knows instinctively that I'm seeing something that is real enough. Where it is, however, and how I'm seeing it, I've no idea.

I sense rather than smell the acrid smoke lingering in the air, similar to the Rip that swallowed Doron. Even stronger than that is the heavy feel of Darkwine. It clings to the air about me as if it were Darkberry itself on the vine. At first, I think that is impossible. Everybody knows that the only place Darkberry grows is inside the Woven Court.

Then I see Harken.

Initially I don't recognize his tall figure. Dressed in a simple indigo robe, he bears no trace of the Savage King I have met—no sardonic smile or grim, hard-set features. This Harken seems infinitely younger, his face smooth and fresh, almost blazingly beautiful. But it's his expression that is most striking.

He stares at the destruction and carnage around him with a child's shock and terror, his face desolate with loneliness. He glances behind him, and in the distance, I see tall closed gates. Instinctively I know he is locked inside here, trapped behind those gates and amid this terrible wreckage, alone and utterly lost.

He bends to one of the lilies that remain intact, and as he touches it, the flower blooms with vibrant color, a blaze of beauty amid the darkness. He cradles it in one palm, tears rolling down his face.

A sound of pain makes him turn. Beside the charred remains of the lotus fountain stirs the figure of a man, one of those who has clearly fallen in its defense. Harken is at his side in an instant. The man lies facedown, his tunic covered in dirt and ash, his body broken and bloody. Harken touches the shoulder tentatively, and the man moans in response. Harken's face lights up with childlike hope.

The scene is swept away, replaced with a montage that passes like time.

Harken nurses the fallen man back to health. The man is a Weaver, I realize, when I see the needle Harken places lovingly at his side. It is silver, which I know only Weavers use, and elegant, entirely unlike the thicker needles wreathed in indigo I've seen the Indigold use in the Seam.

Harken bathes the broken body, healing the worst wounds.

For what seems to be many days, the man sleeps. While he does, Harken tends the dead, Weaver and Indigold alike, for both seem to have fallen in equal measure.

Carefully he washes the bodies and wraps them in cloth, binding each with flowers he picks himself. He lays them all to rest in the courtyard, pausing to hold his hands over the earth covering them, so the flowers with which they have been buried spring forth as new plants.

Time passes in my dream as Harken buries body after body, pausing in his morbid task only to tend the wounded man, who lies slumped with his back to me, seemingly utterly defeated, uncaring of whether he should live or die.

As time wears on and the bodies slowly disappear, I realize that Harken is burying them around the dead shadow of the old lotus fountain. What at first seemed a random graveyard slowly takes on an exquisite geometry of perfect design, each flower complementing the other.

By the time the wounded man can stand, the courtyard is no longer a scene of devastation, but a serene dedication to beauty and art, marred only by the terrible, blackened scar at its center.

I see Harken bring the wounded Weaver, staggering on trembling legs, out of his bedchamber to see the garden. They stand side by side, their backs to my viewpoint. It's only when I see the shoulders of the wounded man begin to shake that I realize he is crying, great, heaving sobs that bring him to his knees, his face dropping to his hands.

Harken drops beside him, his own face a picture of confusion and worry. The man shakes his head, unable to speak, but when he puts his hand on Harken's shoulder, I understand without words that it is the beauty that has so moved him, beauty he had never thought to know again in this place.

Time moves on.

The man and Harken work side by side, creating a natural wonderland from the destruction all around. I can only see the man from behind, never his face, which is hidden beneath a broad-brimmed hat. As the days pass, his hands darken with the sun, his body growing strong, and gradually, he begins to laugh again.

I see him guiding Harken's hands, teaching him how to use his own raw, incredible power.

It is then I understand that I'm witnessing the first days of Harken's existence, the earliest days after he was Woven into being. Although I see a full-grown man, I understand, though I couldn't have said how, that Harken is as fresh to this world as an innocent newborn. I can sense the wonder felt by the Weaver he has saved, that such power and innocence could exist in one form, such beauty be born amid devastation so great.

Beneath the archways, I see Harken's teacher nurturing small seedlings of a strange tree I have never seen before. The seedlings have smooth trunks with a multitude of prop roots and heart-shaped leaves of deep lapis, veined in vivid carmine. Soft, melodic notes ripple among the leaves, like the echo of a forgotten song.

Finally, as a long summer seems to be drawing to a close, I see Harken and the Weaver standing before the charred wreckage of the fountain tree. This, I sense, from the excitement and trepidation in them both, will be the crowning glory of their Garden of the Fallen, their monument to the dead.

Together, they raise their hands, the Weaver with his silver needle and Harken with no more than long, elegant fingers, twisting and Weaving the air.

The largest of the seedlings drifts across the courtyard to settle amid the blackened stump. Its roots come down, twining in and around the remains of the old, absorbing it as a new tree rises in its place. From the fallen marble new stone is wrought, smooth white with soft hints of starlight, growing like a living thing to become part of the tree. On each petal of the lotus fountain a word appears, etched deep into the marble, the same words I have seen Feivel say as he touches each of the twelve knots on his Coronastrian cord: Joy. Kindness. Patience. Love. Harmony. Clarity. Compassion. Purity. Understanding. Forgiveness. Bliss. Serenity.

As each word appears, the deep lapis leaves grow in a shimmering, heart-shaped crown over the marble, their blazing carmine veins casting a soft glow over the etched writing.

The two Weavers stand side by side, holding their creation together, and then the man beside Harken gives one flick of his needle. Crystal clear water bursts forth from the fountain, tumbling down to fill the lotus-shaped pond made by the smooth prop roots. From there, it flows all through the Garden of the Fallen, turning it to a scented, vibrant sea of light and color, from which soft, harmonic tones come like a gentle auditory breeze.

The pair bring their hands down, and their great Weaving is done.

Harken turns around, facing the closed gates, and I see his face fall once more into desolate lines, sense his dread at the eternity stretching before him, lonely and bewildering. For a moment his eyes rest on my invisible form, almost as if he can sense me.

I feel a strange, prickling sensation, then the garden fades from sight, and all is black once more.

I sleep.

CHAPTER 21

HYDRA

*W*hen I finally wake, it is on a vast sea of silk and billowing cushions, facing a wide, open window. The late afternoon sun dapples light across waves far below my open window, from which small shapes leap. I realize, in wonder, that they are dolphins. A soft, warm breeze stirs the bed coverings. There is no trace of the courtyard I saw in my dream, nor of the dank old fishing trawler I boarded back in Lostport.

The room itself has intricate geometric patterns carved into the walls and a strange, curlicued writing I can't decipher. In the corner, fresh water trickles from a wall fountain over which grow delicate ferns. Oil lamps burn in the sconces on the walls, casting a soft light in the shadows where the sunlight leaves off.

The day had already faded when Harken forced the Dark-wine down my throat, and now it is afternoon again; I've slept an entire day through. My body feels refreshed. Andras was right—I'm grateful I slept through whatever tumultuous passage we have taken, even if my sleep took me on another journey altogether.

I lie in bed for a time, still caught in the vision I saw.

Perhaps it was a Darkwine dream.

I discard the thought almost as soon as I have it. I've witnessed addicts caught in Darkwine dreams, many times, and heard them speak of what they see. At best, they drift on a euphoric sea that grants brief flashes of insight, into themselves or into dimensions beyond their own.

At worse, they thrash in agony, trying to outrun the dark demons haunting the corridors of their mind.

My vision felt real. I remember the prickling sensation that brought me out of it.

I know that feeling. I know exactly what it is.

Tentatively I reach up, touching my braid with one finger. It's the lightest of touches, barely there, but it's enough; like lightning illuminating a dark night, I catch a glimpse of Harken in that garden, staring at the tree he had wrought.

I lie almost frozen in place, my mind twisting and turning to make sense of what I'm seeing.

I've always known there is a connection between braid and braid end, of course; Hodda delighted in torturing me with it on frequent occasion. And sometimes I wondered if the five knots on the ring linked my siblings and me in some odd way, too. More than once, when one of them was in danger, or a state of high emotion, I've felt a prickling of awareness at my neck.

In both cases, however, the sensation was only ever physical. Never once did the braid cause me to glimpse inside the mind of someone else.

But now I'm sure that my vision is exactly that: a link between Harken's mind and my own.

It showed me Harken's days after he was first created, of that much I'm certain. I'd been a silent, invisible witness to his first days walking this earth as the Lord of the Woven Court.

I try to recall all I know about the Woven Court and Harken, but there's no hidden treasure trove of memory to plunder. From my youngest days, my focus has been the Braid Race and training to win it, not Astrian stories. All I know of Harken is what Feivel told me—that he took the Woven Court into the mists, depriving Weavers of their home and Astria of their heritage.

But how Harken came to be Lord of the Woven Court, and for what purpose, I have no real idea. Nor do I understand much about Weavers or how they are created, other than it is a very rare occurrence and happens because of the Great Ceremony.

If I can see into his head, can he see into mine?

The thought startles me into action. I roll out of bed and land on polished floorboards, discovering, to my horror, that I'm quite naked and shuddering to think how I came to be so. Clutching a sheet about my body, I enter a bathroom that is more aptly described as a marble wet room. Water flows from a wall fountain like the one in the bedroom, tumbling into a tub that seems cut into the marble itself, or to grow from it. The marble reminds me of what I saw Harken rebuild in the Garden of the Fallen, soft pearlescent white shot through with something that gleams like starlight. Bathing here feels like being in a forest glade that has somehow grown a bathroom. The water flowing into the tub smells like fresh orange blossom and jasmine.

"It's about time, too." I spin around to find a little creature straightening up from stacking fluffy towels in the corner. "You slept through the night, and half the day again." The creature is no more than four feet tall. It wears a red tunic trimmed in gold thread, tied with a woven cord the same color. Its head is round and lined as a dried prune, its eyes narrow and dull red in color, with a single black pupil, but no iris. A few thin strands of black hair have been carefully combed into place over the otherwise bald pate and stuck down with some kind of glossy substance. "You should bathe," it says, casting me a look that can only be described as disapproving. Taking the edge of the sheet, it tugs me toward the bath.

I pull away from the insistent little fingers. "Who are you?"

I really want to ask what, rather than who, but even new to Astria as I am, I'm pretty sure that would be considered an intrusive question.

"I'm Hegal." The little creature tilts its head at another, very similar creature eyeing us beadily from the corner. "This is Magel." Magel looks much like Hegal in basic appearance, but with long white hair arranged in a messy bun atop its head. Its eyes are the same red, but with a sloped shape. Its legs beneath the scarlet tunic are very thin, almost dainty, with turned-out feet in narrow slippers. In place of a hand, it has two long, smooth digits that look more like glossy black claws, though they seem to move efficiently enough. "Woman." Hegal glares at Magel. "I told you to draw a bath. Not stand there staring—"

"Oh, hush, old man." Something shoots out from beneath her tunic, so fast I barely see it. Hegal yelps and leaps aside, rubbing his backside.

"There's no need for that," he says in an injured tone.

"Then stop showing off like a Fool and leave the girl to bathe in peace." Magel shoos him unceremoniously out of the room and smiles at me, showing a mouthful of very white, gleaming teeth with rather sharp points. "I took your old clothes and washed them for you, although, as I told the master, you really should have new gowns." Shaking her head and muttering under her breath about the idiocy of men who think nothing of a woman's needs, Magel ushers me into the bath.

"Master." I seize on the one thing that makes sense to me amid all of this. "Then you and Hegal are slaves, like me?"

"Slaves?" Magel tugs the sheet from my body with a shocked face. "Of course we're not slaves. The master would never—" She glances at my slave braid and cuts herself off. "We're house demons," she goes on, not looking at me, "and faithful ones, too. We've been with the master from the beginning." She maneuvers me into the tub, dunking my head underwater to preclude any more questions.

House demons? Who in all the Dreaver's dreams thinks keeping demons as house servants is a normal thing to do? Or perhaps they are quite unremarkable in Astria?

I come up for air, look around at the strange, curlicued writing on the walls, and think that question is probably the least important one I should be asking.

"This will be your cabin until we reach the Indigo City." Magel sets about washing me, an experience to which I'm so unaccustomed I can do little other than cower in the bath and submit. "It isn't quite as grand as the Water Palace, mind, but we have to compromise aboard the *Hydra*."

"Compromise," I echo faintly, taking in the silk sheets and luxury of my surroundings.

"Those cuts." She eyes my face critically, clicking her tongue in disapproval. "I could fix them in a moment, but the master said—" Again she stops abruptly. Though her skin is the color of old wood, I would swear she is blushing.

"No, do tell me." I watch Magel closely. "What, exactly, did the master say about my cuts?" I wave pointedly at my slave braid. "You and Hegal might not be slaves, but I most certainly am. He bought me." *Body and soul.* I push the internal whisper away, unable to bear even thinking those cursed words.

"I don't know anything about that." Magel purses her lips. "But if he bought you, then the master has his reasons. And if he wants me to leave the cuts as they are, then there'll be reasons for that, too." Her voice is rather subdued, and she avoids meeting my eyes in the mirror opposite. Obey orders Magel might, but I have the distinct impression she heartily disapproves of them.

Given that Magel has claws rather than hands, her ministrations are surprisingly gentle, and I almost groan in pleasure when she digs into my scalp, untwining my long plait.

"You have the most beautiful hair," she says, in a somewhat unflattering tone of surprise. "Women in the Indigo City would pay all the coin in their vaults for such luscious curls. And those eyes! You will be quite the toast of the Revels, I imagine, when we arrive."

"The Revels?" I spin around in the tub, sloshing water all over the floor. "Do you mean the Maverick's Race? Is that where we're going?" I feel a sudden, sick sense of excitement.

"I shouldn't have mentioned the Revels." Magel is clearly flustered. "You'll have to ask the master about that. He's coming to see you as soon as you're ready to receive him." Backing away from the tub, she hurries for the door, gathering my discarded clothes as she goes. "There's a tray of food"—she gestures to a silver tray on a round ivory-topped table nearby—"and more in the galley, should you wish. The master said to ring the bell when you are ready to see him." Still chattering away to herself, clearly warding off any more uncomfortable questions, Magel leaves. I half expect to hear a key turn in the lock, but there is nothing. Just to check, I wrap myself in a towel and pad across the floor. The handle turns without difficulty. I put my head out into the deserted corridor, then close the door again.

I'm not locked in, then. I'm in some kind of sumptuous Woven palace that can float, on my way to the Revels. Which means we're heading for the Maverick's Race.

The Maverick's Race is an annual event in Astria. For centuries before the War, once every ten years, it was the means by which Astrian kings won their throne. Though Astria has a council now instead of a king, the Race is still held every year.

Its prize is the richest in all Astria. I remember Caspian and Foley's calculating eyes: *Lands, a title, and more coin than a man can carry.*

Not, however, for a slave. That is the origin of the Braid

Race in the Seam, which is always held three months ahead of the Maverick's. The timing is an ancient tradition, the idea being that Astria is so egalitarian that a slave might win their freedom, then go on to win the Crown of Astria itself. It is little more than illusion, of course. But a seductive one. Every slave has dreamed of winning, even if they might never admit it. No braided slave, however, can compete in the Maverick's Race.

And I'm still braided.

Sleep has restored some of my native optimism.

I survived Hodda. I'll survive this, too. And I'll get this braid off my neck somehow.

Magel has laid out a set of loose trousers and shirt made from soft cotton silk, in the russet hues of sunfall. It flows around me as if I'm wearing nothing at all.

I pull my hair back into a tight plait and wind it into a knot at the back of my head. In the mirror, my face is still a brutal mass of livid red wounds.

Good, I think. *Let him see the true face of slavery.*

I pick up the bell and ring it.

CHAPTER 22

ANAHITA

"*A*wake at last," Harken greets me when I open the door to his knock.

"No thanks to you." I glare at him and turn my back, walking over to take a seat at the ivory-topped table. I've already eaten some of the fruit there and drunk all the water from the jug that mercifully refills itself. To my surprise, I don't feel hungry at all, but I do feel like I could drink a river and still come up parched. "I imagine you dosed me with enough Darkwine to take down a horse."

I watch him from the corner of my eye, looking for any sign he might be aware of the connection between our minds, or of the vision I had, but his face is unreadable as ever.

"I only gave you enough to see you through the Nexus." He seems more amused than annoyed by the accusation. "Your long sleep was pure exhaustion, I should imagine. Unsurprising, given the events of the past few days."

I leave that alone. "You don't enslave your demons." I switch direction abruptly. "Why me?"

"Ah." He leans back and clasps his hands behind his head, long booted legs stretched out before him, crossed at the ankle.

"I told you back in the Seam that I wanted a chance to explain at leisure." He gestures to the airy ceiling and dappled waves beyond the open window. "Now that we find ourselves in a more . . . restful environment, let me start by saying that I did not claim you after the Race in order to keep you as my slave."

I freeze, barely daring to breathe. The sun dances in his eyes, creating a mercurial effect that makes it hard for me to read the expression in them.

"Had I simply bought you from Hodda, that Shadow Braid binding you could only be removed with the council's approval." His lips tighten. "And I do not deal with the Indigold Council."

Does that mean he thought of buying me before the Race? For what purpose? I stare at him through narrowed eyes, unsure where this is going.

"I claimed you," he says quietly, "because doing so gives me the official right to free you."

But you haven't. I try not to visibly react. Just the mere prospect of freedom is headier than any Darkwine brew.

"If you plan to free me," I say carefully, "then why haven't you?"

The familiar half smile pulls at the corner of his mouth. "Because I want to make you an offer."

An offer? I stiffen immediately, images of being pawed by the men in Hodda's House passing uneasily through my mind.

"Not that kind of offer." Harken reads my face more easily than I might like. "Let me explain." He draws his legs up abruptly and leans forward, clasping his hands between his knees. "Recently there's been a marked increase in the Dark Rips opening in Hiraeth. More worryingly, they're being opened from the Seamish side of the Interweave." He nods at my surprise. "Exactly. The Rips aren't caused by otherworldly creatures breaking through from other worlds. They're being deliberately opened by someone from our world, who is either very powerful or who possesses a very powerful tool. I want to know who that person is and what they want." He smiles silkily. "I believe that you can help me uncover those answers. As soon as I have them, your braid will be off, and I will pay you handsomely for your trouble. On that you have my word."

He paints an intoxicating picture. Freedom feels tantalizingly close and almost impossible to refuse. I try to stand back objectively, to find the trap I am certain exists in his offer. No matter Harken's seeming sincerity, I haven't lived so long a slave to put any stock in promises.

I try to keep my internal turmoil from showing on my face. "Why do you think I can be of any use in helping you gain answers?"

"Feivel told me your story, or what is known of it." Harken pours himself a cup of wine and sits back in his chair, regarding me with an almost lazy scrutiny, which nonetheless seems to absorb every facet of my being. "It's a unique combination," he says. "A Shadow Braid, the zumi on your back, bags of coin Woven to refill. In the Seam, such mysteries matter little. Even in Astria, a slave's story is of little consequence, no matter how interesting.

"But now I, the Savage King, have publicly claimed you." His tone is heavily laden with irony, his mouth curling in a smile that is part contempt, part self-deprecation. "My disinterest in Indigold matters is notorious, if I do say so myself. My claiming you, and so publicly, will spark intense speculation regarding what I might know about you that others do not. In a matter of days, your curious story will be on every set of lips." His mocking tone implies he is accustomed to others discussing his motives in such a manner, though how he might feel about that is well hidden behind his sardonic mask. "I have just made you the most intriguing scandal in all of Astria." He raises his cup in ironic salute. "More importantly, I have made you a mystery that I hope will prove irresistible to those I seek."

I stare at him, my mind whirling. "You want to use me as

bait." I would laugh, if it wasn't so patently obvious that he's serious. And if I wasn't so concerned about what all this means for my freedom.

"A crude term." Harken tilts his head. "But yes."

"For what?" I ask bluntly. "You already know it was Sereia who brought Arkady through that Rip. We both heard them talking, the night before the Race."

"Ah." Harken slings a booted leg over one knee and regards me with a small smile. "But that's just it, you see. She didn't. I know this, because I know for a fact that she has been nowhere near any of those Rips. I also know a little about Sereia's abilities. I don't think she has either the skill, or a tool powerful enough, to open a Rip as deep and precise as the one through which Arkady came. Whatever plans she might have for Arkady now, I don't believe it was she who plotted to bring him to the Seam. Which begs the question of who did, and what they hope to achieve by it." His eyes narrow slightly. "There is also the small matter of Arkady shooting at you. Perhaps he meant to kill you; perhaps he simply didn't want witnesses to his entry into the Seam. If it's the former, you will be the most effective lure imaginable, both to Arkady and to those helping him."

I stare at him in surprise. "Why in the Tells would he be trying to kill me?"

"I have no idea." Harken gives me a lethal grin. "Fun, isn't it, little criminal?"

I close my eyes and see Doron tumbling into the terrible void. *What if that Rip was meant for me? What if Doron's disappearance is my fault twice over?* Even the thought fills me with sick dread. I open my eyes to find Harken watching me. "Then what is it," I say, "this offer of yours?"

"I want to take you to the Revels." Harken lounges back in the chair, regarding me shrewdly. "Show off that braid, and the zumi on your back, and see what emerges from the dark corners of the Indigold nobility."

"That seems a rather nebulous plan." I frown, trying to work it out. "Is there someone specific you suspect?"

"No." His answer is short and terse. Something flickers in his eyes, a flash of deadly silver, brief but unmistakable.

That's it, I think. *That's what he's not telling me. There's someone, or something, that he wants very badly.*

"I guard the Woven Court." Harken is watching me closely. "It is my responsibility to monitor those who may pose a threat to it." His need to justify his interest only confirms my suspicions. Strangely, I'm almost reassured by understanding his motivation.

I don't mind who, or what, he plans to torture, so long as it results in my freedom. And perhaps, though I barely dare think of it, I might learn something of what happened to Doron.

"You mentioned a tool." It's been playing in my mind since he said it. "What kind of tool can open a Dark Rip?"

From the corner of my mind, I see the tension go out of Harken's face, a return of his customary insouciance, all of which serves to confirm that my suspicion is correct: Harken has a target in mind. *The rest of this is just a sideline.*

"Have you heard of something called Serpent's Gold?" When I shake my head, he says, "More than two thousand years ago, there was a very powerful Weaver named Anahita. She's known to history as the Serpent Queen."

The Serpent Queen is familiar, especially given my recent encounter with the Lord of Dencover, but I'd thought that name no more than a mythical symbol and Anahita's Gold just an expression. "Do you mean that Anahita actually existed?"

"Oh, Anahita was real enough." Harken's tone is grim. "She brought Serpent's Gold, to Astria from another world. Though its origins and working are shrouded in mystery, there's no doubt it has extraordinary properties. The six golden needles of Astria were forged from it, and Anahita herself used it in alchemy, which is why the gold is often referred to by her name.

Eventually there was a war, and Anahita was blown into the Interweave, along with a lot of the Serpent's Gold. It's drifted there ever since, creating holes that the Stitched Men fix."

Harken stands abruptly and moves to the floor-to-ceiling windows, which open onto a small private deck. They currently stand open. He leans on one, his hand gripping the frame. "Serpent's Gold can open Dark Rips, just as it can create holes in the Interweave. But it takes a large amount, and great skill, to create the kind of tool that opened the one through which Arkady came." He glances back at me. "Do you know why Roark became known as the Golden Kraken?"

"No." My life in the Seam didn't leave a lot of time for history lessons, and I was too busy training for the Race to worry about the War that had resulted in my exile.

"Many don't," he says. "Even in Astria, many never knew that Roark's body was possessed by Anahita." He nods at my surprise. "Like Anahita's Gold, it seems her immortal threads never really left the Interweave. She had no body to attach those threads to—until Roark went searching for her." His fingers drum restlessly on the frame. "Roark was obsessed with the power offered by both Anahita and Serpent's Gold, and unlike the others who had been seduced by Anahita's whispers over the centuries, Roark had the resources to indulge his ambitions. He could also shapeshift, as can any Indigold, with practice. In Roark's case his alternate form was a kraken, which was how he became known as the Kraken King. Whether he agreed to let Anahita use his body or not, we'll never know. The end result, though, was that Anahita Wove herself into Roark's kraken form and set about building an army that supported her old ambitions. Her return sparked the five-year War that ended in the Battle of the Tower." He meets my eyes. "Are you with me so far?"

I nod slowly. "I think so."

Harken pushes off from the wall and takes his seat again.

"I'm explaining it so you understand that there are plenty, especially among the Paladins, who still believe Anahita's lies: that given the perfect body and the right alchemy, they, too, can become immortal. They don't say this publicly, of course, and it matters little if they meddle with their potions behind closed doors. But Dark Rips are another matter." His eyes hold mine. "I believe that whoever opened that Rip is likely a Kraken follower who was never caught. Which I find rather interesting," he says silkily, "since it was I who caught most of them."

You didn't just catch them. I clearly recall Feivel's words: *Harken . . . unthreaded the Paladin Weaver.*

I suppress a shudder. "What happens to me, if your plan doesn't work?"

Harken leans forward and clasps his hands, holding my eyes. "The Maverick's Race marks the end of the three-month Season of Revels. Whether I find what I am looking for or not, you have my word that you will be free by the day of the Race."

CHAPTER 23

DEAL

*T*here is a surreal thrill in speaking about freedom in such an easy manner. It's close enough that I can taste it, and that makes me both wary and nervous.

"You say you can free me without consulting the council," I say, watching him. "But you also paid Hodda coin and said the words. You hold my braid. You are my master now, regardless of your intentions. Why are you asking my permission, or offering to make a deal, when you already own me—body and soul?" I put particular emphasis on the last words, not least to remind myself of our respective positions.

"I will unweave that braid right now, if you choose it," Harken answers bluntly. "You can disembark at the nearest port, with as much coin as you ask for. We're currently sailing down the Stitched Sea, just off the coast of the Wolf Weald. Lupa, the Lady of the Weald, is a friend of mine. She will certainly aid you. You can seek out your siblings, do your best to free them."

"But you won't help me with my siblings," I say slowly, thinking of Shimi and Neoma already somewhere in the clutches of Caspian and Foley. Of Levin, even now bound for the brutal Candidate's year.

Of Doron, lost somewhere in a Dark Rip, if he still lives at all.

"No, I won't." His face hardens. "But just to be clear, I won't unweave your siblings as part of our bargain, either. Their fate is not mine to decide, and as I said, I don't interfere in Indigold matters." There is a finality to his words that warns me from pushing the point. "If you choose to disembark, you will have seen the last of me, little criminal. I am not in the habit of taking slaves, nor of stalking young Indigold women, no matter how beautiful."

Having lived my entire life being called Weorpan, and considered a freak, even by the leering men in Hodda's salon, being referred to as both Indigold and beautiful in the same sentence is an odd experience. I tuck the sentence away in my mind, to be taken out at a time when Harken isn't observing every one of my reactions.

"So," I say slowly. "You have made your offer."

Lounging with one arm slung over the back of the chair, long limbs sprawled across it, he regards me with a lazy smile. "Yes."

"Then allow me to counter it."

Harken's eyes narrow slightly, but more with curiosity than wariness, and his smile, if anything, grows a little. "I'm listening."

"I want to compete in the Maverick's Race." I take a deep breath. "And I want to win. I want to win enough money to ensure that nobody can ever touch me or my siblings again." I wait, but Harken doesn't immediately answer. "I'm not asking you to interfere in the Race itself," I add hastily, "but I will need you to pay the entry fee and supply everything I need for the Race, including a place to train. Slaves aren't permitted to enter." The braid feels suddenly heavy around my neck, as it always does when I allow myself to acknowledge it. "So I want your word that I will be freed in time to compete. And I want someone to witness your promise."

Beyond my cabin, the sun is at a midpoint over the horizon, turning the sky a buttery gold and the sea a brilliant turquoise. A lone bird hovers in the distance, wings cupped on invisible winds.

"You remain determined to free your siblings, then." The sun reflects off Harken's eyes, turning them to silver fire.

"I told you back in the Seam: so long as one of them is bound, I will never be free. You think me a Fool," I say, when he doesn't immediately answer. It annoys me that I should care.

"No." One long finger taps against the wooden arm of his chair. "I think you surprising. And very little, in this world or any other, still surprises me."

He stands abruptly. "Very well, then. I accept your counteroffer. You will wear the braid during the Revels and play the part of my slave in public. Of course, you are under no such restrictions out of the public eye. Please consider yourself entirely at ease, here on the *Hydra* and afterward, when we reach my Water Palace in the Indigo City. You will be freed before the Maverick's Race, but I will not promise when, exactly, since that depends on what I discover and how long it takes. In the meantime, though, I will supply all you need to train for the Race and secure your entry. As to the witness." He smiles wryly. "In my experience, a secret, once disclosed, has little chance of remaining thus. I have a witness in mind. One, it could be said, that specializes in secrets." The amused curve of his mouth makes me instantly wary. "They will arrive tomorrow," he goes on. "Will you agree to wait?"

I nod, though not without suspicion.

"I would like to heal those wounds, however." He nods at my face. "Magel gave me a most disapproving glare after sighting them."

"No."

He looks rather taken aback.

"You bought me. Body and soul, remember?"

His face darkens. I'm not above taking a perverse delight in his discomfort. It's my own petty revenge for the horrific moments when I realized I had been traded as livestock. "Well, this is the body you bought," I say. "This is the price of slavery. And won't it better serve your case if I look the part you have asked me to play?"

Harken eyes me narrowly. "I wonder who is playing games now, little criminal." But he doesn't object, instead turning to the door, where he pauses. "This." He raises an uncharacteristically awkward hand to the braid end, then stops abruptly, as if he's just recalled my request for him not to touch it. "I can't unbraid you. But neither do I wish to cause you distress. What would you like me to do with the braid end?"

I have a sudden, visceral urge to tell him about the vision, and the strange link that the braid seems to have forged between us.

We are allies, of sorts, after all.

I discard the thought almost immediately. I'm being used as bait, and despite his promises, I know Harken hasn't been entirely honest with me about who, or what, he's looking for. While I believe he means to honor his promise to me, in the split second that his guard was down, the glimpse I had was of deep, brutal fury, long tempered into lethal intent. *Passion like that doesn't simply fade with time*, I think. The Savage King Feivel described to me, and who Garrick warned me from associating with, is dangerous and vengeful, and that brief glimpse was enough to remind me that he still lives inside Harken. Whatever secret he is guarding may one day prove strong enough even to overthrow Harken's promise to me.

Then again, I think, *I should at least give him the chance to be honest.*

Instead of answering his question, I ask one of my own.

"Earlier, you said you aren't looking for someone, or something, in particular." Harken stiffens. His eyes become flat and opaque, impossible to read. "The more I understand about what you seek, the more I may be of use to you in your search." I nod at the braid end. "If I trust you with that braid end, perhaps you might trust me with the truth?"

"The truth." Harken gives a harsh cough of laughter. "The truth is that I am bound to the Woven Court far more tightly than any slave braid can bind you, Zaria. If you believe nothing else, believe that. I understand your desire for freedom better than most ever will. The rest is Savage business and need not trouble you. Nor do I advise you to seek further answers from other sources." There is a dark warning in the eyes that hold mine. "I have no desire to play the part of master." His mouth twists in distaste. "But anything you need to know about me, I will tell you myself. Should you go seeking information beyond what I willingly offer, I will not hesitate to unweave that braid and remove you from my court." The steel in his eyes leaves me in no doubt that he means every word. "And now that we understand one another—" He holds up the braid end again, his mouth softening. "What do you wish me to do with this?"

If I questioned my motivations before, now I am all too aware of the choice before me. Harken has just made it very clear that I am not to seek further answers beyond what he offers. I'm not adept enough at self-deception to pretend that seeking the insight offered by the braid connection is not a direct contradiction of that request. I am, in essence, using the connection to spy on Harken. I don't feel at all good about that deception. *But then he is using me, too, for whatever revenge it is he seeks.*

Then there is the fact that I may have been Arkady's target. Or that whoever Harken seeks might know what happened to Doron. A lifetime of slavery has taught me that knowledge is power, and it's clear from Harken's words that he intends to control the flow of information, share only what he deems necessary for me to know. The braid connection offers me an advantage that I feel reluctant to relinquish. *Keeping the connection doesn't mean I have to use it.* I push aside my qualms. *It's simply a precaution, in case I suspect Harken is holding back information pertaining to me, or Doron.*

No matter how aligned our interests are now, it's impossible to know what the future might bring.

"Keep it." I nod to the braid end. "Wear it where others can see it, so they know you purchased me." I give him a small smile. "Just try not to touch it. It feels . . . odd, when you do."

He nods slowly. "Very well."

My conscience whispers that the decision has nothing to do with rationality, and everything to do with the illicit thrill of the connection itself.

But I thrust those whispers down deep inside, where they can't be heard. I've always known emotional bondage to be a trap, and love the greatest form of slavery.

Then I wonder why on earth I'm associating Harken with any kind of emotions, when I'm still his slave. *This is a business arrangement,* I remind myself sternly. *He still holds that braid, and your future, in his hands. Never forget that.*

"Until tomorrow, then." Harken's face wears the hint of a frown, as if he's trying and failing to discern my thoughts.

Thank the Great Weaver for that. Somehow, I feel certain that if Harken knew anything of our connection, he would have told me.

That realization does nothing to assuage my guilty conscience at all.

He gives me the glimmer of a smile. "I do believe, little criminal, that we managed to find a compromise." A shadow crosses the sun, momentarily dimming his face. "I hope," he says quietly, "that you do not come to believe it a bad bargain."

Guilt twists uncomfortably inside me. *And I hope that you never know I lied as we made it.*

He turns back to the door, so I can't see his face. "Dawn," he says in a rather abrupt tone, "is especially beautiful."

He leaves as the sun falls behind the horizon. I sit in the tawny shadows, watching night grow over a strange land.

CHAPTER 24

SHADOW

*D*espite having slept so long the previous day, I fall into another dreamless sleep, waking in the predawn, a balmy breeze ruffling the soft silk bed clothes. Pushing them aside, I wash quickly and go out to explore.

I pass through a large salon with a high, curved roof and rich rugs over the wooden floorboards. At one end a fire blazes in an enormous grate. Large, comfortable armchairs by the windows face out onto the ocean, still grainy in the half light. Books line the walls, interspersed by lanterns with intricate wrought iron covers, lit by candles within. Their designs make kaleidoscopes of shadow in the soft light.

I climb the ladder, coming out onto the wooden deck.

The vast expanse of the ship, and its twelve tall masts, is certainly extraordinary, given the meager dimensions of the decrepit trawler I boarded back in Lostport. But it's the world around me that is truly arresting.

The moon setting behind a dark smudge of distant horizon to the west is a great silvery disk that seems to cast sparks from the sea itself as it slowly slips from sight. To the east, the coming sun casts brilliant rays into an indigo sky. The dawn isn't pale and cold as it is back in Lostport, but a symphony of wild color that changes with every moment, gold and rose dancing across the sky. The sea between the falling moon and the coming day shimmers with the shifting color.

The water is a bright aqua, so clear that even from my position on the deck high above I can see straight through it to the mountains and valleys far beneath the surface. Water plants I've never known sway underwater, gleaming with every color of the rainbow. Among the dolphins and fish I know from living in Lostport swim a host of other creatures. Vibrantly colored seahorses gallop proudly across the ocean floor on long, curled tails, chased by an octopus in such brilliant blue hues it almost hurts to look at it. A large creature I took to be a whale suddenly sprouts a pair of iridescent, scaled wings and soars up and out of the water, circling above the *Hydra* before diving straight down into the sea again and disappearing.

The braid at my neck tingles.

"She's a storm dragon." Harken is on deck beside me. The dawn turns his hair into a blazing halo about his face, his eyes more mercurial than ever, the aqua sea finding a reflection in them. He rests one booted foot up on the side timbers, leaning on the top rail as he points at the dark shadow rapidly disappearing beneath the surface. "They're a rarity, even here in Astria." His lips curve in a slow half smile. "And Huxley almost never reveals herself to strangers. You must already have made an impression."

Despite the circumstances that led me here, I feel a sudden shiver of excitement. After a lifetime in the alleys of the Seam, I am finally in Astria. Standing on the deck of a Woven ship, watching a storm dragon disappear into the sea at sunrise.

Harken's hand touches my waist, turning me gently toward the west. "That is the shoreline of the Wolf Weald." He points over my shoulder, his voice close to my ear, and I feel another, darker thrill. His boot remains on the side timbers, his drawn-up knee barely inches from my hip. Not one part of his body touches my own, and yet there's an intimacy in our nearness that sets every nerve in my body alight. "And that"—he nods at the water below—"is the Stitched Sea. We're sailing south, toward the Indigo River. We'll turn inland there tomorrow night and reach the Indigo City by dawn."

"Where's the Drop?"

"South." Harken turns me again, so my back is to his chest. "Sail past the Indigo River," he murmurs, "and further, until the coast of Astria ends. Turn west past the Isle of Jezarah. Keep sailing, and eventually you will reach the Drop."

My heart clenches with a sudden, fierce pain. I wonder if Garrick is there. If he's setting sail into the Interweave, even now.

"I'm expecting the visitor I told you about shortly. Our witness. Don't let them alarm you." Harken's tone is dry. "They're harmless, no matter their appearance."

I don't ask any questions. The dawn is too beautiful for conversation. For a long moment, we simply stand together, watching the day grow.

Harken draws away from me only seconds before I'm startled by an animal rearing up from the water and leaping over the deck. To my utter astonishment, and no matter how improbably, it's a camel. It falls obediently to its knees to enable its rider, an extremely beautiful woman, to dismount.

She's wearing layers of aqua cloth that shimmer in the early morning light, and her hair, beneath a filmy veil of a slightly lighter color, is a deep, rich umber. Despite having emerged from the sea, her clothes are quite dry, as is the camel itself, who wanders off toward the bow of the boat after giving me a disdainful glance.

"A slave," she says by way of greeting, staring at the braid about my neck. "A rather singular amusement, Harken, even for you. I did hear a Breeze that you had been entertaining yourself with a Saber from the Wolf Weald."

Harken stiffens slightly. I make a mental note to discover what a Saber is.

"No?" Very white teeth gleam in a knowing smile as the woman looks between Harken and me. "I do hope I didn't speak out of turn." Her almond-shaped eyes are the strangest I've ever seen, the pupils shaped almost like the Dark Rip in Hiraeth, elliptical slashes of darkness that float on a sea of gold iris, at once utterly compelling and equally unsettling.

"You're early." Harken's tone is laced with amusement.

"I am never early. I am never late." Her brow arches in obvious disdain. "I arrive always at the perfect time. Whether you recognize it as such, Harken, is a matter quite beyond my control."

"Zaria." Folding his arms, Harken nods resignedly at the woman. "This is Gemory."

"The witness," I guess.

"Witness!" Gemory whips out a beautifully painted silk fan and flicks it open, her eyes above it moving between us with avid interest. "I didn't realize you'd summoned me for professional reasons, Harken."

"You say that," says Harken dryly, "as if we are in the habit of meeting for any other reason." Gemory casts her eyes skyward but looks not remotely put out by his rebuke. Harken turns to me. "Gemory is a Shadow."

I exert considerable discipline not to openly gape.

"Ah." Gemory eyes me over her fan. "I detect a degree of suspicion." She drops her eyes briefly to my braid. "We don't create the bargains, child. A Shadow is merely the facilitator." She snaps the fan closed. Her brief smile is as dangerous as it is fleeting. "We do, however, trade in secrets. I assume that is why you require me today." Her eyes shift keenly between us. "To witness a bargain of your own," she says, her eyes flaring with interest. "One you don't even trust to your demon." She taps Harken's arm thoughtfully with her fan. "Interesting."

I try not to stare at Gemory. Though my own braid is Shadow Woven, I have no memory of ever meeting a Shadow. They are spoken of in whispers and regarded with even more suspicion than Pathfinders. All I know is that they can grant any favor, big or small, so long as the person asking willingly accepts the consequences implied by the famous words of the Shadow Bargain: *Take what you want, and pay for it.* Those who make such bargains are bound to silence, and Shadows themselves famously keep their secrets, which adds to their air of mystery.

I realize Gemory is watching me with eyes brimful of mischief. Coloring, I look away.

"And now that you have had your fun," Harken says dryly, "to business." Briefly he lays out the terms of our agreement, turning to me to state my own conditions. I choose my words carefully, ensuring I've covered all that we agreed on the previous night. Gemory's face remains entirely detached throughout, all trace of previous emotion gone. She repeats the terms back to us both, then nods sharply. "Put out your hands."

We do, and she places her own, cool and light, atop them. "Take what you want," she says, in a low, clear voice, "and pay for it."

Somebody once said those words when they bound my siblings and me.

I falter, snatching my hand away. "I don't want to make a Shadow Bargain." I shake my head at Harken. "Our deal didn't include that."

"Keep your threads Woven." Gemory looks amused. "Your bargain isn't with me. I'm merely a witness in this instance."

"But you said the words." I'm deeply uneasy.

"Yes." Gemory's eyes narrow slightly. "*I* said them. Not you. I'm simply witness to the bargain itself."

"And if one of us tries to deny it?" Terribly aware of Harken nearby, I color, but make myself carry on, nonetheless. "What happens then? Do you hold us accountable?"

"Oh, Harken!" Gemory snaps open the fan again, gold eyes dancing above it. "This one trusts you not at all!" The sharp smile flashes again, gleaming and unsettling. "All choices have consequences, child. But in this particular instance, I do not control them, nor have any responsibility for them. I'm here to witness, as I said. And to keep your secrets." She taps me playfully with the fan. "Fun, isn't it?"

The sun has risen while we talked, and the day feels warm on my skin. I glance at Harken to find his face shuttered. To my surprise, I suspect he is quite insulted, if not actually hurt, by my mistrust. I think of what he said yesterday, about being more tightly bound to the Woven Court than I am by my braid.

He can't expect me to take that literally, I tell myself. *And if he truly does feel trapped, then he should understand my concerns. Besides, surely anyone would be wary about anything involving a Shadow?* My thoughts nonetheless feel like justification, just as they did yesterday with the braid end.

"Gemory!" My thoughts are interrupted by Andras appearing behind me. He casts a cynical eye over the newcomer. "I hadn't realized we were to be honored with your presence. And camel mounted, no less." Folding his arms across the rich brocade of his robes, he fingers the pommel of the heavy sword at his side.

"Oh, do, please, try it, Andras." Gemory's smile is utterly lethal. "The knife makers in Basetana are second to none. I'd love to try out my new purchases on such a large, slow target." Her almond-shaped eyes flash with a malicious light. "And camels are the preferred mode of transport in Basetana, not that I would expect an Astrian demon to know such things."

Andras is a demon? I do my best not to react. *Yes,* I think, remembering all I have seen of Andras since we met. *That fits.*

But Andras looks nothing like Magel and Hegal. In fact, now that I think on it, Andras is actually quite attractive—in an extremely dangerous kind of way.

That's it, I realize, studying him surreptitiously. The unsettling edge just beneath the surface that seems poised, at any moment, to leap out.

Catching me looking at him, Andras rolls his eyes and stalks away. "Come find me when you're done with that little sorcerer," he calls to Harken as he leaves.

"Demons." Gemory purses her lips and sniffs. "So tedious, don't you agree?" Looking me over properly for the first time, she makes a slight moue of distaste. "Though given those dreadful clothes, not to mention those most unattractive cuts, I do not imagine you are at all equipped to judge. If one is to appear as a woman," she says, whipping out a mirror from her robes and inspecting her own immaculate appearance with critical satisfaction, "one should at least endeavor to enjoy it, child. You, on the other hand, seem determined to present as a field animal. You may be forced to wear a slave braid, but surely on such a ship one might find a scarf to cover it?"

My lips twitch with a sudden urge to laugh. Gemory reminds me so much of Shimi that my heart twists. How many times has Shimi glared at me with exactly such disapproval, utterly bemused as to why I won't at least try to dress like the other ladies at the Dark and Disorderly? But where Shimi is sharply observant of others, Gemory, it seems to me, is utterly self-involved, even now staring at herself from every angle in the mirror, as if anything at all could be done to improve on such perfection. And what on earth did she mean by *"if one is to appear as a woman"*? It seems the oddest of remarks.

Sensing Harken has more he wishes to say to Gemory, possibly without an audience, I edge away from the two figures. As I go, I hear Harken say dryly, "you might wish to shed your finery, Gemory. It's a little wasted on Andras and me, and we have business to discuss."

"So boring, Harken. And on the way to the Revels, too. Would it kill you to entertain a little? Why have such a magnificent ship—"

"Gemory." Harken's voice is exasperated.

"Oh, fine."

I pause on my way down the deck and look back in time to see Gemory turn on the spot. To my absolute astonishment, when she comes full rotation, she no longer appears to be a woman. In her place is a tall, slender young man, every bit as handsome as his female counterpart was beautiful. In place of the filmy green dress, he wears leather trousers that are, nonetheless, exquisitely tailored, and a linen shirt that reveals finely muscled forearms. "So," he says, bending his head close to Harken's.

But whatever he has to impart is lost to the wind. I give Gemory a last curious glance, then head down into the cabin, leaving them to their secrets.

CHAPTER 25

SAVAGE

I wake when the *Hydra* leaves the sea for the Indigo River.

I can feel it, the slight difference in motion, the thicker quality of the air. Through my open windows come the scents of earth and men, the occasional clang of a bell as we pass some riverside port. I peer through my windows, but I can see nothing. The great ship slides silently through the water, wreathed in a strange mist that blocks even the stars from view.

Oddly restless, I pour myself a cup from the jug on the table. Too late, I realize I've chosen the Darkwine jug instead of water.

It isn't that I don't drink Darkwine at all. Since I've been on the *Hydra*, I've developed quite a taste for Magel's lavenade, which is a lighter, frothier mix with a piquant flavor. But I've spent a lifetime trading Darkwine as a product and seeing it ravage those who turn to it for solace. I doubt I will ever be able to treat it with the casual ease many do. Now, however, in the still darkness of my bedchamber, curled up on a chair by the window watching the night slide past as we go deeper into Astria, the Darkwine feels like a secret thrill.

My thoughts turn to Harken, as they have with increasing

frequency since we made our bargain. When our paths cross, he is always polite but distinctly reserved. Since my questions to Gemory, he has treated me with unfailing courtesy, but with none of the sardonic humor I've unconsciously come to expect and which I secretly rather enjoy. His reserve has had the unfortunate result of increasing my curiosity about his past, the blazing young man in the courtyard who made paradise out of death.

What happened to that youth? I think, my hand stealing up toward the braid at my neck, hovering just below it. *What transformed him from innocence to the Savage King who is on first-name terms with a Shadow and has demons for company?*

The rational part of my mind recognizes that Harken's past, his present transformation, and the reasons behind it are none of my concern. Not so long as he holds up his end of the bargain, and I have no reason to doubt that he will.

But the irrational part of me has relived, over and again and in embarrassing detail, the moments we shared on the deck before Gemory's arrival, craving the easy intimacy that seems absent since we sealed our bargain.

Not for the first time since I boarded the *Hydra*, Garrick's face crosses my mind. *What would he make of this?* I wonder, remembering his grim warnings about Harken. What would he make of my bargain? Of dealing with Shadows and of spying on the Savage King himself?

"He'd hate it." I speak aloud in the darkness, smiling to myself. Garrick, I know, would be filled with dread if he knew even half of it. Not to mention Feivel, who was more disapproving of Harken than I've ever known him to be of anyone. The only two men I've ever looked to for guidance, and both of them told me in no uncertain terms to give Harken a wide berth.

And now here I am. Drinking his Darkwine and contemplating looking into his mind. I know that doing so is a direct betrayal of our agreement. Harken has made it clear enough that he won't tolerate prying.

But curiosity won't let me be. *And besides,* I tell the nagging whispers of my conscience, *I'm not seeking information in order to cause Harken harm. I just want to understand who he is.*

I glance down at my cup. Darkwine, straight from the Woven Court itself, I imagine. Its scent seems to permeate the very wood of the *Hydra*. In the night shadows, the liquid swirls with a dangerous, potent life of its own.

Feeling oddly reckless, I toss off the entire cup in one swallow, then reach up and grasp my braid.

Abruptly, the night beyond the windows spins away, and I am lost in the mists.

I RECOGNIZE *the beautiful Garden of the Fallen almost immediately.*

But the man I'm looking at bears almost no resemblance to the gentle, incandescent figure of my last vision.

This Harken has a face that is twisted into a savage, uncontrolled rage that seems to almost spark from his form. His soft robes have been replaced by hard black leather that shields the tense lines of his body like scales. A black helmet comes down to a peak between his eyes, adding to his fearsome appearance. He strides toward the closed gates and throws them open with an abrupt, contemptuous gesture; they are clearly not locked anymore. Beyond the gates, he turns back to face the garden. He stares at it for a moment, but nothing in his wild expression bears any resemblance to the gentle man who created such beauty. Nor is there any trace at all of the Weaver who built the garden with him. Harken is alone, this much I know.

He drops his arm in a hard gesture of finality, and the gates are replaced by a shimmering, gleaming mist that shields the entire garden from view. He turns away from it and strides across the rubble strewn outside the garden, barely seeming to notice the ruined buildings around him. *Hardly pausing at the high, mist-covered walls that mark the outer edge of his domain, he waves one arm impatiently. They give way for him, and he steps through, into the world beyond. Behind him the mist falls again, the high walls, and the ruins within them, disappearing from view.*

Time shifts as Harken walks into the world, and into scenes of war both terrible and heartbreaking.

Women and children, fleeing in horror from the soldiers ravaging their homes.

Astrids kneeling on the ground, crying as they watch their tapests burn to smoking ruins. Others holding up the cord of their order, touching each of the twelve knots in turn as they plead for their lives. Their despair as the pleas fall on deaf ears, and their final, reverent touch of the golden Astris before they are struck down, their eyes staring lifelessly up at the burning sky.

Priestesses, their robes torn and bodies brutally ravaged, their eyes long gone into madness, half starved and cowering from even the kindest touch.

Through all this horror and carnage Harken walks, a silent, rage-filled witness.

Finally he stands before a battleground, watching armored warriors clash beneath a variety of flags.

With a sudden, chilling shriek of wild fury, Harken cuts a vicious swathe through them all, irrespective of flag or mark, tearing apart any soldier holding a weapon. Indigold and Weaver alike run from his terrible wrath, their faces contorted with fear.

The scene changes again. Harken stands on a cold, silent forest shore, filled with the stench of death and littered with fallen soldiers. Many bear scarlet armor with a symbol of a flaming staff, others blue with an eagle symbol. In the distance, across the water, is the island they have clearly died trying to reach. Bloated corpses, still wearing the indigo robes of priestesses, float on the water, washing up like unwanted garbage. Smoke rises from the island, the sound of women screaming carrying clearly across the water. Harken stands in silent horror as in the distance, another indigo-clad priestess throws herself from the island clifftop into the churning water below.

White-hot rage blazes across Harken's face.

He speeds across the water without any visible effort, landing on the rocky shore like a dark specter of death. He faces a line of Weavers and Indigold, all clad in the aqua or gold of the Waterlands and Dencover, who have come to meet him. Their needles flash in the dull light as they cast their threads in attack. Snarling, Harken sweeps the threads away with contemptuous ease, then sets upon them with an almost gleeful savagery.

The Indigold are smashed against the rocks, killed in an instant. The Weavers Harken unthreads with chilling precision, leaving their mortal bodies as broken corpses and the gleaming, immortal threads of their Woven souls unspooled and torn into dull fragments atop their flesh. Harken's frenzy is wild and untamed, and when he is done, the only souls left alive on the isle are a handful of battered priestesses with vacant eyes, their wits long fled, rocking silently in the ruins.

The scene shifts again to reveal a small group of priestesses stepping from a ship back onto the shore of the isle. They stare, stricken, at the smoking ruins. Harken, standing in front of them, says with lethal finality, "Nobody can harm you now." Raising his arms, he brings the mists down over the isle, cutting it completely from view.

Then he turns and sails away.

The scene shifts again, to show an old Indigold nobleman wearing blue armor with the eagle symbol. He stands before Harken, his face grim and pained. "We are losing this war," he says hoarsely. "Help us defeat them. Help us to end this."

Harken's face twists in disgust, his eyes gleaming under the black helmet. "I will kill any who hurt the innocent. What side they fall on is no matter of mine." He swirls away into the mists, leaving the old lord staring after him with tired, sad eyes.

In the next scene, Harken faces the old lord once more. This time the man has a much younger Andras with him. "At least do something useful, then," the old lord says grimly. "The Kraken Weavers are opening Dark Rips throughout Astria, unleashing all manner of deadly creatures into our world. You say you want to protect the innocent. Then find these creatures. Contain them. My son is a fighter. He will help you."

Harken, his face still dripping blood, faces Andras. "You will find no comforts in my court."

Andras, his red eyes gleaming, wears the scarlet armor with the staff and flame. "Show me the fight—that is all I ask."

Harken's face twists into a hard smile, and he nods curtly. The two men spin into the darkness together . . .

I WAKE IN SHOCK, heart thudding, mind racing with images of darkness and savagery. I'm still in my chair, but night has given way to dawn.

The *Hydra* thuds into something hard and shudders to stillness.

We have arrived at Harken's Water Palace, in the Indigo City.

CHAPTER 26

DEMONS

*T*he mist has gone.

The ever-present scent of Darkwine is lighter here and mingled with summery scents, of flowers and fresh herbs. I come down the gangway to a stone landing over which carved marble pillars form a series of archways. Lanterns of cut glass hang from the center of each. The high morning sunlight gleams off their panes, throwing sparkling patterns across stone steps that divide the building in front of me. Glorious trumpet-shaped flowers of soft pink and cream twine along the wrought iron handrail and stone walls on either side of the stairs. The landing stretches a considerable distance in either direction; the palace must be large indeed. Demons are busy unloading what seems to be an endless store of supplies from the bowels of the ship.

"Not there!" A harried-looking Hegal shouts orders to the bustling army. "Ridiculous," he mutters, shaking his head as he watches the cargo coming ashore. "No warning, no proper plan-ning. All I ask is for one assistant—one! —with a single ounce of sense, but no. How the Woven Lord expects me to ready an entire palace for the Carnival of Revels on less than a few days' notice . . ." He hurries past me, not pausing in his grumbling for a single moment. I struggle not to laugh.

"Allow me." I turn to find a grinning Andras. After last night's braid vision, I look at him more curiously than I did before. In the bright sunlight his skin shines ebony dark, the gold hoops gleaming at each ear. His eyes, though red, have white irises, and the pupils are slightly different than those of the demons I've come to know on the voyage here. His form is unlike theirs too, with no wizened skin, and he certainly isn't small.

"You don't look like a demon," I say as we mount the stairs together.

"Ah. I see Gemory has been telling tales again." Andras's retort is rather sharp.

"I'm sorry." I glance at him. "I don't mean to offend you."

He gives me a cheerful smile. "Oh, you didn't. But I intend to put a knife through that damned sorcerer one of these days." He winks at me. I suspect his threat has no real malice behind it. In fact, over the past couple of days, I've come to the conclusion that Gemory and Andras find some of their greatest pleasure in baiting the other, while also being utterly united by their loyalty to Harken.

"I'm not like the other demons," Andras says. "You're right there."

"You don't need to explain yourself to me," I say hurriedly. "It's none of my business." In the corner of the landing, a beautiful fountain made of the same marble as my bathroom on the *Hydra* grows from the stone wall, entwined in a gloriously lush grapevine dripping fruit and winter jasmine that trails a sweet scent through the air. The fountain runs with clear, sparkling water that smells fresh and clean.

"Beautiful, isn't it," says Andras, seeing my face. "Harken's

Water Palace dates back to the time of the First Woven. You'll find fountains like this all over it. The palace is hidden behind Harken's Woven mists, of course."

I think of the mists in my braid visions, and that which shrouded the *Hydra* on our approach to the Indigo City. "How does that work, exactly? The mist? Does it make places invisible?"

"As smoke on the air," says Andras cheerfully. "And even less noticeable. Places behind the Woven mists simply don't exist, unless Harken himself opens the mists to allow entry. It's a rather special piece of Weaving, don't you think?"

Given what I've seen in my braid visions, I think those mists also come with a deal of loneliness and isolation, but I can hardly say that.

"I've been with Harken most of my life," Andras explains, leading me up the next set of stairs. "My father, Lord Adhair of Goath, had a rather ill-advised affair with a Saber, one of the female warriors who guard the priestesses of the Isle of Nine."

I remember Gemory's snide comment to Harken on arrival: *"I did hear a Breeze that you had been entertaining yourself with a Saber from the Wolf Weald . . ."*

"A Saber." I try not to show too much interest. "They train in the Wolf Weald, don't they?"

"They certainly do, alongside Lady Fearach's Fire Guard. The Weald borders our own lands in Goath, did you know that?" I shake my head, coloring with embarrassment. The list of what I don't know about Astria seems to grow with every moment I spend here. "Don't worry," Andras says cheerfully. "There's a great map painted on the wall in one of the galleries here. I'll show you where it is. Anyway, it turns out that my mother had a little something extra running through her veins, which is not so uncommon for Sabers. My father had a few special elements of his own, so it seems nature took over, and when I was born—well." He shrugs good-naturedly. "I was a bit of a shock to everyone, I gather. Natural-born demons aren't exactly an everyday occurrence in Astria. Luckily for me, my father wasn't the type of man to disown his mistakes, and Lady Fearach is our oldest ally. I was raised by my mother in the Wolf Weald." Andras gives me a sinister smile. "All manner of dark things lurk in those woods. It was good training for demon wrangling, or hunting down other dark creatures, which is how I serve Harken now."

"Goath." I try to recall Feivel's lessons. "That's in the North, isn't it?"

Andras laughs. "Goath *is* the North. Keep going east from the forests of the Weald, and you'll find Goath. My father, Adhair, was lord there for half a century, Guardian of the Northern Peaks."

I remember the worn, grave face of the man in my braid vision. "Was?"

A shadow crosses Andras's face. "He died in the War. My half brother, Kendrick, is Lord of Goath now." He inclines his head. "He's a good man."

"But you don't like him?" I'm trying to make out his expression.

"I wouldn't say that." Andras shrugs. "Kendrick is a stickler for the rules." He winks at me. "I'm not."

Remembering the manner of his and Harken's greeting in my vision, I'm not in the least surprised by that. Harken may no longer wear black scales, nor indulge in widespread murder, but going by his words to me thus far, I'm fairly certain his contempt for the rules governing Astria remains intact. It makes sense that he would surround himself with others who treat them with similar disdain.

We come out of the stairwell into a courtyard so exquisitely beautiful it brings me to a complete stop.

The palace surrounds us on all four sides, rising several stories above. Arched walkways form the edge of each story. An ancient fountain tree stands in the center of the courtyard, though it is nothing like the one in Hiraeth Forest. This is a fig tree rather than yew. It's been shaped so that its roots snake out in every direction, entwining with the marble floor in intricate patterns that create a three-dimensional effect. Despite the floor being smooth and even underfoot, the roots create an optical illusion of contours. The fountain itself is the now familiar starlight-threaded marble, carved on the underside with the same curlicued writing found in my cabin aboard the *Hydra*. The fig tree moves with an invisible breeze, and water runs from the tree into the fountain, and then down into the floor, creating glittering streams that feed out, I imagine, to the rest of the palace. Vines and flowers twine about every surface, and opposite where we stand, an arched breezeway looks out over a series of crisscrossed canals.

"The Indigo City is built on a series of islands in the Waterlands," explains Andras, smiling at my wide-eyed silence. "All travel is on the canals. Few foot alleys exist, and they are easy to become lost in. But you need not fear. You won't leave the palace, unless it is with one of us." Seeming to realize how that comment might not be so welcome, Andras switches subjects hastily. "Anyway, as I was saying, I was raised in the Wolf Weald. I fought in the War, but toward the end of it, new laws came in that outlawed demons, meaning the Kraken's army were shooting creatures like me on sight. Things were looking rather grim until Harken took me in. It was a neat solution for everyone, and so here I've been ever since, guest of, and sworn sword to, the Savage King himself."

Remembering the wild, uncontrolled fury of the man who wandered war-torn Astria in my braid vision, I suspect the old Lord of Goath had saved more than his son by introducing them.

"It must have been nice," I say, smiling at him. "For Harken. To have found a friend like you."

"Ah. Harken has never been one for friends." His red eyes gleam. "Swords, now—those he understands well enough."

"Oh?" Despite Harken's warnings, I seize on the opening offered by Andras's remark. "Was Harken entirely alone in the Woven Court before you came, then?" *After all,* I tell myself, *it's just a conversation.*

Andras's unsettling eyes turn to me with uncomfortable scrutiny. "How much do you know about Harken, Zaria?"

More than I should, and less than I'd like. Guilt and my own ignorance make me feel rather flustered. "I know he was created to guard the Woven Court, but I don't know how or by whom, so I don't really know what that means. I've also heard him called the Savage King." Thinking it best not to elaborate on that, I hastily continue. "I know he hunts down creatures from Dark Rips, but I don't know what he does with them. And he doesn't have a needle, but I know he can Weave, because he healed my wounds." I shake my head, realizing suddenly how ridiculous I sound. "I honestly don't know much at all," I say lamely.

Andras's eyes widen as I speak, and when I finish, he stares at me for long enough that I grow increasingly self-conscious. "I suppose I must seem very uneducated," I say finally.

"Not at all," Andras says politely, which might as well be a confirmation. He regards me thoughtfully. "Some aspects of Harken's existence are a matter of public knowledge, and those, I am happy enough to tell you." He pauses, as if uncertain of how much to say. "Harken's story, however," he says carefully, "is his own. And he guards his privacy closely." He glances sideways at me. "May I offer a small piece of advice, from someone who has known him longer, and perhaps more closely, than many?"

I nod, my face flaming with embarrassment.

"Do not seek to understand Harken's past," Andras says, "nor the darkness that drives him. Those secrets are locked away behind mists even I have never crossed. What I can tell you, from experience, is that Harken's greatest contempt is reserved for those who practice deception of any kind." He holds my eyes. "Harken has brought you into his home," he says quietly. "Whatever his reasons, that alone is a rare trust. If he ever suspects you have betrayed that trust, his retribution will be swift, brutal—and final."

"I didn't mean to pry," I begin, utterly mortified.

"Yes, you did." Andras's tone is even, but uncompromising nonetheless. "And that is perfectly understandable, given your circumstances." His eyes rest on mine. "But even if I could give you answers, I wouldn't. Any questions you might have, no matter how harmless they might seem, I strongly suggest you direct to Harken alone. He may not answer them." He smiles grimly. "But if he suspects you of asking those questions behind his back, he will consider it the greatest of betrayals." He looks away for a moment, as if considering his words, then turns back. "I told you that Harken has never been one for friends." His red eyes are not without compassion as he looks at me. "Might I also suggest that you do not look to him for friendship —of any kind?"

I color; he does not need to spell out his meaning.

"I believe that you and Harken have made yourselves a bargain of sorts." Andras touches my shoulder, a fleeting gesture of comfort. "Bargains, Harken understands. He would sooner put a knife through his own heart than break his word to you. Rely on that and trust him to do exactly what he has promised. But expect nothing more." He waits until I nod in understanding, then steps away.

"Magel will show you to your bedchamber." Andras gestures toward the stairs. "The map room is on the third story, if you're looking for it."

He hesitates, then says, in a careful tone, "Harken often spends time there."

After all he's just said, I can't tell if Andras means to warn me away or encourage me to visit. He leaves before I can ask, and I follow Magel up to my bedchamber.

CHAPTER 27

MAP ROOM

I'm restless, and more than a little unsettled.

My bedchamber is every bit as beautiful as that on the *Hydra*, with a small balcony and a set of external stairs that lead down to a private landing on a small canal. The windows are wide and covered in a wrought lattice that creates geometric shadows on the flamestone floor. Winter jasmine twines with deep indigo honeywort through the windows, casting a soft fragrance through the room.

Magel informs me that a dressmaker will be coming to fit me for the first Revel the following night, but I struggle to focus. I keep thinking of Andras's words and the vision I saw last night, the terrible images of death, destruction and Harken's fury going around my mind.

What happened to change him? I wonder. I know from Harken's conversation with the Lord of Goath that the scenes of destruction he witnessed drove him to avenge the death of innocents. But if the vision is correct, he saw those scenes *after* he left the Woven Court. I feel as if I've missed a step. What pivotal event changed him from the gentle soul who lovingly laid a legion of dead souls to rest into the black-clad, ruthless killer filled with rage who stormed out of the mists and plunged into the world of war? I have no intention of ignoring Andras's warnings. But instinct tells me that the missing step is the key to understanding both what it is that Harken seeks and what has caused him to so deeply mistrust the world around him.

I know I can make the visions happen by touching the braid, but somehow, I doubt I can control what I see. Once I'm drawn into those spinning mists, I'm guided by something quite beyond myself, and, it seems, by Harken's own recollections. *Perhaps*, I think, *whatever is missing from the vision is something Harken himself doesn't wish to recall.*

I find the map room. It's a salon high on the third story, with elegant arched windows that look out over the array of canals, plain tiled floor, and a high, airy domed roof painted to look like a sky. As I look at it, clouds move and shift across the dome, reforming exactly like the sky beyond the windows. I wonder if it darkens with nightfall, stars appearing in place of clouds.

The room is entirely devoted to maps, rolled and neatly placed in a thousand cylindrical openings in the wall. A few large stuffed chairs look out over the canals, with reading stands nearby. On the far wall, amid shelves of books, which appear to contain more maps, is a shelf with decanters of Dark-wine and Weald whiskey.

A rectangular table dominates the room. The base is carved from a single great yew trunk, with the ancient root system forming a multilegged stand. Two vast branches spread out to hold a slab of deep indigo flamestone. A map of the Woven World is etched just beneath the surface. Elegant lines are cut in harmony with the layered colors inside the flamestone, so the rivers and seas are wrought in brilliant shades of aqua and blue that appeared to ripple and move with the light, while the lands are drawn in a variety of opalescent hues. The entirety is finished with a smooth, transparent layer. Currently a map lies open atop it, held at either end by heavy crystal weights. The map looks very old. It shows an island called Sherimah, although I can't see anything with that name etched on the table itself.

On a nearby wall is the map Andras mentioned, a large-scale drawing of Astria with the same inlaid detail as the tabletop, but without all the other countries marked. A golden Astris, the twelve-pointed star of the tapest, gleams above it.

I'm studying the map on the table when I feel a familiar frisson against my neck. I tense, knowing what to expect. A moment later Harken says, "Andras told me I might find you here."

I feel strangely unsure of myself. Not, I realize, because I'm intimidated by what I saw in the vision, but because I'm scared he will take one look at my face and discern my secret. I stay quiet.

"I won't impose upon you," he says with a trace of amusement in his voice. "I sought you out to say that you will have visitors this afternoon. Marissa, Lady Laguia, is a friend. She will come with a dressmaker to help outfit you for the Revels. And you may wish to rest while you can. The Revels often run long after midnight."

"I grew up in a Disorderly House." Indignation sends my previous uncertainty flying. "I've been awake past midnight since I was old enough to pour Darkwine."

"How could I forget?" Now his amusement is obvious.

I touch one of the crystal weights holding the paper map. I have so many questions, and yet I know that if I ask the wrong one, whatever tentative alliance we have will be lost. Everything I've learned thus far makes me certain that Harken will not hesitate to shut his world to me as abruptly as he opened it. That prospect feels far colder and lonelier than I could have imagined only days ago. I cast around for a simple opening to gauge his response.

"Sherimah." I gesture to the map on the table. "It's on this parchment, but not marked in the table itself. I was wondering why that is."

He's standing by the door, linen shirt rolled to the elbows, hands thrust into his pockets. The mercurial lights in his eyes shift like the flamestone, but he's still smiling, or at least, as close to it as he seems to get. "Sherimah was home to the First Woven. The most glorious city ever created, with wonders we can only imagine now." For once, his tone lacks any trace of cynicism.

"What happened to it?"

His smile fades. "What happens to everything, eventually. Ambition. Greed." He lifts a dismissive shoulder. "In this case, Anahita." His fingers move over the paper map, not touching it. "Sherimah was blown apart in the same war that ended Anahita's reign, more than two thousand years ago. All that remains of Sherimah now is the Drop, the hole in the Interweave created by the final great battle." Removing the paper weights, he rolls the map up and returns it to one of the cylindrical holes in the wall.

"Such cheerful conversations, little criminal." He shoots me a wry smile as he makes for the door. "I shall send word when Marissa arrives."

I gather my courage. *Here goes nothing.* "Harken—wait." I move across to the map of Astria on the wall. "I have a question."

"Of course you do." He casts his eyes skyward. "You know," he says meditatively, "I suspect that's the first time you've used my name."

"I should probably stick to 'Master.'" I bite back a smile. "It wouldn't do for a slave to forget her place in public, now, would it?"

Harken's eyes widen in surprise, and he actually laughs. "No," he says, "I suppose it would not. Now." He tilts his chin up, still smiling. "What is your question, my little criminal?"

"I can see various lands marked on this map." I point to the northwest, which shows trees and a symbol of a staff topped by flame, reading the writing under the symbol. "This is the Wolf Weald, bordering the Kept Lands, whatever they are." My finger moves to the east, and an eagle with outstretched wings. "Goath and the Northern Peaks. Together, Goath and the Weald spread south almost halfway down Astria, divided by the river Indigo." I trace the dark blue swathe down the wall and draw a large circle in the middle with my finger. "There are plains and valleys marked here, but nothing else, until close to the Indigo City." I tap the Indigold Cup symbol used by the Paladins. "The Paladins' abbey is marked on the eastern bank, just north of the city. The river goes into the city, which is where we are now, then heads west out to sea. Below that"—I tap another cup symbol, this one without a serpent, amid a mass of rivers and canals—"lie the Waterlands." My finger moves east, to the rocky markings and circular gold symbol of the Serpent Queen. "And south of the city, all the way to the eastern coast . . ." I'm unable to keep the disgust from my voice. "Are the Cave Lands, and the underground city of Dencover."

"I'm not certain why you have questions." Harken inclines his head. "You're clearly an excellent student. Most slaves never even learn their letters."

"Don't be a Fool," I say impatiently. "We had Feivel." His lips twitch. "What I don't see," I say, frowning at the map, "are your lands. Where is the Woven Court located?"

CHAPTER 28

NEEDLE

O dd shadows flicker across Harken's eyes, and his smile is quite gone. "You will not find my court on any map."

When I look at him questioningly, Harken lifts one shoulder. "Isn't that the point of being a savage, my little criminal?" His tone is light, but lightning flashes a warning in the dark eyes. "To remain on the outskirts of the civilized world?"

"But an entire court can't just disappear from the map."

"Ah." He spreads his hands wide. "And yet, behold its absence." Thrusting his hands back into his pockets, he turns for the door.

"Wait." I take a deep breath. "We made a bargain in which we both have roles to play." His brow rises slightly in acknowledgment, but his face is closed. "You said you would tell me all I need to know. But I suspect you overestimate what I *do* know." I smile tentatively, to no response at all. "I just want to understand as much as any normal person in the Indigo City might."

Harken regards me through flat, unreadable eyes. "The Council of Twelve will meet soon," he says tersely, "which means that Feivel will be in the Indigo City. I will instruct him to give you some history lessons."

His dismissal stings. It's also confusing.

"What does the council meeting have to do with Feivel?"

It's Harken's turn to frown. "Surely Feivel told you he has a seat on the council?"

I shake my head, nonplussed.

Harken pauses halfway through the doorway and taps the frame with the fingers of one hand meditatively. Then he slowly pushes himself back into the room. He turns to face the map, his expression shuttered.

"I was created to protect the Woven Court." He nods at the wall. "My protection ensures it cannot be discerned on any map, nor seen, even if someone should ride right by the gates."

That explanation raises more questions than it answers, but I stay quiet, concerned that interruption of any kind will stop him from speaking altogether.

"Feivel sits on the council," he says finally, "because he is the Weaver adviser to the Astar."

"What is the Astar?"

Harken's eyebrows lift in surprise. "The Astar is the senior astrid, head of the Coronastrian Tapest."

"But Feivel doesn't even live in Astria." I'm thoroughly bewildered.

Harken rakes an impatient hand through his hair.

"It's not important," I mutter, turning away in embarrassment. "You're right. I can ask Feivel when he gets here."

Ask him about his role on the council that he's never even mentioned to me. I feel overwhelmed by all I don't know and woefully inadequate to being among Indigold society.

"I've never given a history lesson." When I turn back, Harken's eyes are dark but no longer hard. "I'm not used to— explaining such matters."

I lift my shoulder. "I'm not used to being the Fool in the room."

He gives a huff of surprised laughter. "Well, then, little criminal. We must endeavor to ensure you are not." I feel an odd thrill at the return of our earlier banter. Harken pauses, as if considering how best to start.

"Did you know that for centuries, Weavers were created in the Great Ceremony?" He glances at me questioningly.

"Yes. But I don't understand what that is, or how it works."

"Very few do," Harken says flatly. "Or not in any detail. What all in Astria do know is that before the War, every year, the winner of the Maverick's Race was taken directly from the podium to the Isle of Nine. There they would lie with a priestess, or, if the winner was female, a Paladin, in a closely guarded ceremony. Children conceived of the Great Ceremony were born on the isle, under the protection of the priestesses. If they were born Weavers, they were sent to the Woven Court to be raised."

"You mean not all were born Weavers?"

"No." He glances at me. "Part of the role of the priestesses on the Isle of Nine was to ensure it was never known if a Weaver had been born or not. The Maverick who took part in the Great Ceremony was nonetheless always given a child and expected to raise it as their own, never knowing if the child they took was the one they conceived or an orphan child in need of a home. Most considered it an honor to do so." His eyes are a rich, almost luminous indigo. "They understood that Weavers are children of Astria, each a divine gift born to serve, guide, and nurture all of Astria's people." His lips harden. "Never," he says softly, "to serve a particular family, bloodline, or cause."

He grimaces, as if regretting saying so much. "But none of that matters," he says curtly. Striding over to the shelf, he lifts a decanter of Weald whiskey and raises it briefly in my direction. I shake my head. He pours himself a glass, tossing it off in one swallow. I've never seen him quite so unsettled.

"My point is that for more than two millennia, the conception of Weavers was facilitated by the Astar and his Weaver adviser, in a ceremony so shrouded in secrecy that none were permitted to witness it, not even the Paladin Divine who mixed the Indigold Cup for the ceremony itself. Inevitably, there have always been those who believed those secrets should be shared." He glances at me. "The ceremony is so closely guarded not least because, long ago, Anahita and her followers used Serpent's Gold to try to create Weavers of their own."

"You mean they tried to . . . Weave them into being?"

"Oh, no." Harken's mouth twists in a dark smile. "Weavers are born, not Woven. On that, at least, everyone has always agreed." Something hard gleams in his eyes as he turns to look out one of the open arches. "Weavers are not a race. While they might fall in love, they can't reproduce." His voice is even, though I can hear the tension in it. "But Anahita and her followers believed that, using the right alchemy and the perfect physical specimens, they could change that. They believed in the dream of an immortal Weaver race." He glances sideways at me. "Anahita was a Weaver herself, unable to reproduce. Instead, she sought to create what she called the *perfect vessel*—a physical body into which she could Weave her own immortal threads, that was also able to procreate."

A perfect vessel. I feel slightly sick. It's all beginning to make sense. The Paladin's search for perfection, and their obsession with alchemy. I think of Levin with a flash of alarm. *He is living among them now.* I think of his sweet nature, his love of plants and salving. The thought of those gifts being manipulated in any way makes me angry and sad.

"Is that why Roark went in search of her?" I ask. "Did he want the same thing as Anahita?"

"More or less." Harken nods. "You know that before the War, every ten years the Mavericks raced for the prize of Astria's crown? Of course you do," he murmurs, shooting me an unexpected grin. "Well, little criminal, Roark won his first two Royal Races fair and square, which was a feat in itself, although not entirely unheard of. What was unusual was that he also insisted on competing in the races held in the years between the Royal Races. Traditionally, the monarch presided over those, never entered them."

"He wanted to participate in the Great Ceremony," I say, more pieces falling to place. "Try to make more Weavers."

"Yes." Harken turns back to the window. "And," he says tersely, "to learn as much as he could of how the ceremony worked."

"But wasn't it illegal for him to enter?"

"It was tradition that he didn't race, not law." Harken's mouth twists in a humorless smile. "And traditions only work so long as people of honor respect them. By the time Roark won his third Race, it was clear his ambitions had far outstripped whatever honor he might once have had. Nobody knows when he first began to hear Anahita's whispers. What is widely acknowledged, however, is that somewhere during his third decade of rule, Roark became corrupted by her influence. He in turn corrupted the Race itself. No middle-aged man, Kraken shifter or not, could have beaten the best young Mavericks year after year."

"Why didn't anyone interfere?" I want to ask why the Woven Court didn't intervene, but I'm wary of raising such a sensitive question.

"After more than two decades of rule, Roark's court was full of those who supported his dark ambitions—even some from the Weavers' own ranks." Harken's contempt is palpable. "They helped ensure every Maverick's Race was fixed so he won. Dissenters were cast in his water dungeons, terrible places that drove men mad long before they died." Even in profile, I can see the savage gleam in his eyes. "Roark was from the Waterlands, and the lords of Dencover had long nurtured dreams of returning Anahita to her former glory. Both provinces were Roark's natural allies. By his third decade of rule, they also controlled the Paladins, many of whom were already sympathetic to Roark's views."

The tension in Harken's stance reminds me that he once unthreaded a Paladin Weaver. Sensing we are dangerously close to a precipice, I hastily change the subject.

"What has all this to do with Feivel?"

Harken takes a deep, sharp breath. When he turns back to me, his face is composed, his eyes opaque. "On the day of Roark's sixth Race win," he says, "his followers took possession of the Isle of Nine. They murdered the Coronastrian Astar and stole the golden needle. Feivel barely escaped with his life."

My eyes widen in shock. Harken nods grimly. "The theft of the needle was the beginning of Anahita's reign in Roark's body, as the Golden Kraken. It was also the spark that finally ignited outright war in Astria."

That's what I saw in my vision. I vividly recall Harken standing on the shore, staring grimly out at the isle, surrounded by the corpses of those who had died trying to protect it. But I can hardly mention that now.

"Who fought back?" I ask instead.

"The Northern Alliance," Harken answers promptly. "Which was mainly the Wolf Weald and Goath."

And the Weavers who must have fought with them, I think. I'm beginning to understand the perimeters of Harken's narrative, though, and I know he won't speak of the Weavers, nor his own role.

"Soon after the outbreak of War," he goes on, "the golden needle disappeared again." Harken's face twists in distaste. "Of course, the Golden Kraken and her followers accused the Coronastrian Tapest, and Feivel, of stealing it."

I remember the twisted, charred needle over the tapest in the Seam that Feivel said had been ruined in an act of revenge. "What happened to it, in the end?" I ask tentatively. "The golden needle."

"Nobody knows. Most believe it was lost during the Battle of the Tower, when Anahita was finally trapped."

"Trapped." It seems a strange word to use. "Wasn't the Kraken defeated in that battle?"

"Ah." Harken's expression is cryptic. "That is quite the question, isn't it? Unfortunately, the only person who knows the answer lost his memories the same day he fought in the Battle of the Tower."

My eyes widen in shock. "Feivel!"

"Exactly." Harken smiles wryly. "Three people went into the Tower to battle Anahita. Only Feivel came out. A Weaver's memory is tied to their needle. Every thread they've ever Woven is linked to it. When Feivel lost his in the Tower, with it went anything he might have known about what happened to Anahita or the golden needle. That is supposing the needle was even used in that battle at all." His smile fades. "The worst of Feivel's scars are a result not of the battle itself, but of the torture he endured after it by those who believe he knows more than he will admit."

"You sound like you don't believe the golden needle was ever in the Tower."

Harken shrugs dismissively. "It doesn't matter what I think, nor what the truth is. What matters, for our little lesson, at least"—he almost smiles again—"is that many in Astria, even now, believe that Anahita's immortal threads survive inside the Tower, and that the golden needle is in there with her."

"And those who helped Arkady," I say cautiously, "share those beliefs?"

"It seems a safe assumption, yes." His eyes on mine are unreadable. "But since many on the council, such as our friends from the Waterlands and Dencover, share the same views, our specific enemies can be difficult to unearth. Hence our little charade."

He walks over to stand in front of the map on the wall. "The council force Feivel to sit at their table because the Coronastrian Tapest cannot simply be ignored. It's Woven into the fabric of Astria, in the Indigold Halls of Learning, the Cupbearing ceremonies, salving institutions, and a myriad of things that make life in Astria possible. But to insist that its representatives at council are Feivel, a Weaver without his needle or memories, and Clement, a weak Astar who is little more than a figurehead, is a very public form of humiliation."

I think of Feivel's twisted limbs, the appalling scars that crisscross his flesh when it's exposed. "I had no idea," I say quietly. "Feivel never told us any of this."

"It isn't Feivel's way, to speak of such things." Harken traces the golden Astris, then nods sharply. "And that is more than enough history, little criminal." His tone is light, but his eyes are not.

"Thank you." My mind is racing. I'm very much aware that while Harken has told me a great deal about Astria, he has told me next to nothing about himself. *And the truth,* I can admit to myself, *is that I want to understand Harken far more than I do the history of Astria.*

Harken seems entirely removed from all he just told me and yet in many ways to be the mystery at the heart of it: a Weaver without a needle. *A Woven abomination,* Sereia called him. Even Harken himself speaks of being *created.* And I didn't miss the dark gleam in his eyes when he said that Weavers are born, not Woven. When he pauses at the door, part of me hopes he might offer me some insight into his own story.

Instead, when Harken turns back, all trace of warmth has fled his face. In its place are the remote eyes of a stranger and the hard, sardonic mask of the Savage King. "I don't interfere in Indigold affairs," he says brusquely. "Not their politics, their beliefs, or their petty disputes. Our conversation is the most I will say on these matters. My business, and that of my court, does not concern you."

Something of my hurt must show on my face, because he nods curtly. "It might not be what you hope for," Harken says grimly. "But it's the best I can do."

He tilts his head at the door. "Marissa and the dressmaker have arrived. I can hear them downstairs."

Then he stalks from the room.

CHAPTER 29

DRESSMAKER

I'm in little mood for a dress fitting.

I know I should be content with what Harken told me. I don't need to know the details of his past in order to play my role in our bargain. And after he made such an effort to answer my questions, I certainly have no right to go prying into his memories for more.

And yet the braid at my neck thrills on my skin, beckoning me like a seductive whisper. Everything Harken told me has only served to intrigue me more. The connection offered by the braid feels like carrying around a constant temptation.

I also want time to process all Harken said, to try to marry it with what I've seen in my braid visions. Some things are clearer, put into perspective by seeing the maps and symbols of Astria. I'm certain, for example, that the island I saw in my vision was the Isle of Nine, home to Astria's priestesses and the Great Ceremony. The bodies I saw on the shore, those who had died defending the island, had worn the flame-and-staff armor of the Wolf Weald or the eagle of Goath.

Although it's no surprise to learn that the Waterlands and Dencover had fought together, it strikes me as odd that they have retained so much power, despite, for all intents and purposes, having been defeated. *Foley's father is even the Comitas, I think*, remembering Shimi's excitement. *Head of the Council of Twelve.*

I'm still trying to make sense of it when a knock comes at my door.

I open it to Magel, who, clearly entirely unaccustomed to having Indigold guests, disappears almost immediately. In her place stands a tiny woman with a very pretty face, spun-gold hair, and merry blue eyes that sparkle in greeting.

"Zaria," she says, taking my hands. "But you are a beauty! Now I understand the miracle that made Harken finally open his door." Then she flushes, her eyes troubled as she takes in the still-vivid scars on my face and neck. "Not that I hold with slavery, of course. You mustn't think I agree with it—such a barbaric practice! I can't imagine what Harken was thinking . . ." Her voice trails off awkwardly.

I smile with as much confidence as I can muster. My guest has an easy charm that is impossible not to like. "Lady Laguia, is it?"

"Marissa." She looks relieved.

"You mustn't concern yourself, truly." I ease my hands out of hers. I've never been very comfortable with physical displays of affection. "My master is very kind, I assure you." I turn to the woman standing slightly behind her. "Welcome," I say, smiling, though the irony of a slave welcoming a guest to her master's house doesn't escape me. "Are you the dressmaker?"

"I'm Darcy, my lady."

I struggle not to laugh aloud. *My lady.* The only time I've ever been called anything of the sort was when my sisters were chiding me for ordering them about.

Darcy, I rapidly gather, is one of the most highly sought-after dressmakers in the Indigo City. "It's very late notice," Marissa says rather tartly. "The first Revel is tomorrow night.

Most of the Indigo City have been planning their gowns for months."

Darcy efficiently strips me of clothing during this exchange, wrapping me in a filmy, almost see-through material and measuring me with very little concern for my privacy.

"The Savage—the Woven Lord," Darcy quickly corrects herself, coloring, "has given very strict instructions on the gown he wishes you to wear to the Revel." Her eyes meet mine only briefly in the mirror, clearly doing all she can to avoid looking at my scars. "He has exquisite taste," she says. "If a little . . . risqué." I barely dare imagine what *risqué* might mean in the Indigo City. Her needle flashes around my body, slipping in and out of the air about me, making invisible adjustments to cloth only she can see.

"Darcy is also measuring you for your costume for the Maverick's Race," Marissa explains when the dressmaker pauses and makes notes.

"Already?" I'm rather taken aback, especially given that everyone knows slaves are not permitted to enter.

"Maverick's costumes take a deal of time to create. They must be started as early as possible." Marissa settles herself into a nearby chair, accepting lavenade and cake from a wide-eyed Magel. "Heavenly," Marissa sighs, bestowing a smile upon Magel that turns the demon's face into such a picture of delight that I have trouble restraining my laughter. "It's the only reason I agreed to convince Darcy to fit you," she continues, seeming to have quite lost her earlier qualms. "My three eldest sons have all been in the Race, so I'm something of a veteran. With the wrinkles to prove it. Mavericks!" She casts her eyes skyward. "My third son, Brooks, and his friend Everett might not be competing this year, but they are still the wildest Mavericks you can imagine, and believe me when I say I know of what I speak." She shakes her head with pursed lips. "At least Brooks has his own apartments in the city, which spares his father and me the worst of his Reveling . . . But I digress." She beams at me. "If Harken wants you measured for a costume for the Maverick's Race, then he clearly has plans to unbraid you, at some point." Her eyes meet mine questioningly in the mirror. When I don't answer, she frowns. "If not," she says, fiercely for such a small woman, "I won't indulge whatever this game is that he's playing."

Darcy glances at Marissa, her needle paused in the air, clearly waiting for permission to continue.

I feel caught in a conundrum. I imagine that Harken gave his orders to Darcy without taking into consideration Marissa's clearly formidable powers of intelligence gathering. Our bargain is that I play the part of his slave, but I suspect Marissa will walk out of here without a moment's hesitation if she believes he means to keep me enslaved.

Which makes me rather like her.

I let the filmy material slip, just enough to expose the clear line where my scars abruptly stop. "My previous master was not so kind as my current one." Marissa's eyes narrow. "Were it not for Harken claiming me at the Braid Race, I would still be enduring the beatings that gave me these scars." Marissa's eyes flare slightly at my intentional use of his first name, then narrow further as she works through my words. "It is very important," I go on slowly, "that I appear at the Revels as Harken's slave." I meet her eyes in the mirror. "It would also be . . . unhelpful, for me," I say, with quiet emphasis on the last words, "should anyone believe otherwise."

For an uncomfortably drawn-out moment, Darcy's needle hangs undecided in the air, and Marissa regards me keenly in the mirror. Then, to my distinct relief, she nods sharply at Darcy and settles back in her chair with a satisfied air.

I let out a breath I didn't realize I was holding. "Why are the costumes for the Race made so early?" I'm eager to change the subject.

"Costumes for the Race make themselves." Darcy turns me on the small stool on which I'm standing. "Over the three months between the first Revel and the Race, the costume will develop itself. While it might be stitched by a dressmaker, it is Woven by the competitor's unconscious, in threads of their own soul." She smiles at my surprise. "The Maverick's Race is how the kings of Astria won the throne for over a thousand years. Whatever the Race might have become now, its significance is stitched into the fabric of Astria itself. Every competitor who enters the Race is part of something much larger than themselves."

Darcy turns me to the mirror, her hands resting lightly on my hips, so I can see both her and Marissa in the reflection. "When you present on the starting dock on the day of the Race," Darcy says quietly, "you must be entirely at one with your truest self, racing in a costume that is Woven to not only show your soul to the world, but to enhance your own abilities and give you the greatest chance at success."

My truest self. Anticipation and intimidation lick through my veins. I'm not certain I even know my innermost soul, let alone what it might look like as a costume.

Given Marissa's inquiring mind, I'm reluctant to admit that I know almost nothing about the Maverick's Race, not even how it is conducted. I decide to stay quiet and glean what I can.

"Darcy was apprenticed to one of Astria's greatest Dress Weavers," Marissa says fondly. "Her services are in very high demand."

"It must have been wonderful to be apprenticed to a Weaver," I gently prompt.

"Oh, yes." Marissa's eyes are slightly dreamy with reminiscence. "When I was a girl, every trade was headed by a Weaver, who were themselves trained in the Lotus Palace. They passed on their learning to the Indigold who attended the Coronastrian Halls of Learning."

I only barely hear her after the words *Lotus Palace*. I know instantly that is what I saw in my vision. *That courtyard*, I think, my mind racing, *and the lotus-shaped fountain*. That must have been the Lotus Palace. The center of the Woven Court itself.

"All the Indigold studied for a time beneath a Weaver master," Marissa is saying, "no matter what their trade or profession. But there are so few Weavers left now," she says sadly. She glances at me and stops talking, clearly too diplomatic to mention Harken's role in that particular shortage.

"Does—is your Dress Weaver still in the Indigo City?" I ask Darcy.

"No." Darcy glances at Marissa, who nods. "She died during the War," Darcy goes on. "Fighting for the Northern Alliance, as most of the Weavers did. As I did," she says with quiet pride, "and all my family. Woven in Water we might be, but not everyone in the Waterlands supported the Kraken."

"What happened to Weavers who did support the Kraken?" I watch her out of the corner of my eye, wondering as I do what it is I'm hoping to hear.

"They were unwoven." Darcy's eyes flash with something rather fierce. "Thread by thread—by your new master."

"Darcy!" Marissa shakes her head in a sharp rebuke. "That's enough. And it's not fair, blaming it all on Harken."

"Oh, I don't blame him at all," says Darcy tartly. "They got what they deserved, if you ask me." She subsides under Marissa's reproving eye, though the savage manner in which she wields her needle speaks volumes.

"I wonder sometimes what the Weavers expected to happen." Marissa folds her napkin in sharp folds, pursing her lips. "They created the most powerful being ever to walk the worlds, then left him locked inside a corpse-ridden prison to raise himself." She shakes her head in disapproval. "Any mother could have told them no good would come of it."

Darcy's needle has ceased, but I don't move, silently willing

Marissa to continue. *This is what I need to know. How he came to be, and what went wrong.*

But Marissa, clearly ashamed of having said so much, is already gathering her things. "It must be being back inside this palace that makes me rattle on so!" She stands up as I reach for my clothes. "The dress will be delivered to you tomorrow, Zaria." Her smile is kind as she touches my arm. "And no doubt I will see you at the Revel tomorrow evening."

Thanking Darcy, I accompany them downstairs, where Andras is waiting to take them back through the mists. I let Darcy go ahead and draw Marissa aside.

"You mentioned being back in the palace." I try to make my question sound casual. "Has it been a long time since you were here, then?"

"A long time?" Marissa looks at me curiously. "My dear, I thought you knew."

I look at her blankly.

"Harken visits the Indigo City," Marissa says. "On occasion, he even makes an appearance at a Revel, though that is rare enough. But the Water Palace has been hidden behind the Woven mists, along with the rest of Harken's court, since the War." She gives me a small smile. "Today is the first time I, or any other Indigold for that matter, has seen the inside of the Water Palace since Harken became its lord."

CHAPTER 30

GEMORY

On the morning of the Revel, I dress early, and on Magel's strict instructions leave my hair in a loose knot rather than its customary tight plait.

"I will need to arrange it properly later," she says busily, as she brushes it out, "and I don't want to be ironing out twists." She casts me a beady glance. "What would you like to eat? I can bring up whatever you choose."

"Why don't I just come with you?"

"To the kitchens?" Magel looks horrified, but I doubt I'll ever be truly used to being waited on, and so a short time later, having followed Magel down a series of labyrinthine passages, I'm perched on a counter in the kitchen. I'm oddly comfortable here, watching Magel bake while Hegal, a crisp apron tied over his ruby robes, snaps orders at the small army of demons seemingly required to keep the Water Palace in its immaculate condition. I reach for one of the honey cakes Magel has just pulled out of the oven, and she beams. I take a bite and close my eyes in bliss. A slave I may still be, but I am at least a well-fed one, given the demons seem to take absolute delight in feeding me at every opportunity.

I also have an ulterior motive for being down here.

"Magel," I say, as casually as I can manage, "I wondered if you might be able to tell me what a Saber is?"

"Now, why would you be asking my dear Magel about Sabers?" I spin around on the bench, face flaming, to discover Gemory, dressed today in an exquisite deep purple caftan and matching turban, smirking at me from the door. "I can't imagine what might have provoked such a curious question." A wicked gleam in the golden eyes suggests that Gemory knows precisely what has caused my sudden interest. "Sabers," Gemory goes on amiably, are the female warriors who guard the priestesses on the Isle of Nine. They have quite the, er, *passionate* reputation." Gemory arches an eyebrow suggestively.

Female warriors. Passionate reputation. Everything about that particular combination of phrases succeeds in making me feel both desperately inadequate and deeply uncomfortable. I have an unwelcome image of Harken in the throes of ecstasy with some goddess-like creature, and then immediately wonder why I am thinking of any such thing.

To my infinite relief, Gemory has mercifully shifted their attention to Magel. "Catch," they say, throwing the demon a small package.

Catching the package, Magel casts Gemory a suspicious glance. "I'll not be making any of your bargains," she says warningly.

"Magel." Gemory shoots her a look of wounded innocence. "You insult me."

Muttering beneath her breath about Jezaran sorcerers, Magel undoes the string and parts the paper, revealing seeds of a vivid orange that give off a rich, aromatic scent. "Basetanan pepper!" Magel's red eyes shine as if Gemory brought her the Crown of Astria itself. "Where in the twelve Tells did you get your hands on this? It's been impossible to find for months."

Gemory makes her a gallant bow. "Somebody owed me a

favor." Magel's face closes over like a Seamish storm. "Magel, dear Magel." Gemory shakes their head in mock sorrow. "Owing a favor is quite different than making a bargain. Upon my Jezaran sorcerer's soul, I swear your precious pepper seeds come to you with no Shadow debt attached."

"Well, then." Clearly torn between her innate courtesy and an equally profound mistrust of Gemory, Magel gives them a slightly resentful glance. "Thank you," she says reluctantly.

"Ha!" Clapping their hands, Gemory shoots me a triumphant look. "A Revel Season miracle." Gemory makes Magel a deep curtsy, which the little demon regards with equally deep mistrust, then holds out an arm to me. "Join me, please. There's something I want to show you."

I follow Gemory along a corridor. "Interesting company you choose," says Gemory as we go, casting me a curious glance.

"The servants? Why?" I follow them down a set of stairs. "I'm a slave, in case you'd forgotten."

"They're demons." Gemory turns down another set of stairs. "They have neither soul nor conscience. They may seem harmless enough, but if you saw their genuine form—well." Gemory shrugs. "You may not find them quite so palatable, is all I'm saying."

"Whereas you," I say, halting on the stairs, "are a paragon of perfection, I take it?" I turn back. "I think I'd rather explore alone, thank you."

"Ha!" Gemory touches my arm with a surprised laugh. "Please don't mistake my comment for judgment." The finely sculpted lips curve in an ironic smile not entirely unlike Harken's own. "Some of my best friends are demons, as they say in the Land of Fools." The golden eyes are warm. "I meant to pay a compliment, not insult you." They tilt their head, this time with genuine courtesy, and we carry on together.

After another set of stairs, Gemory pauses at a pair of tall brass doors. "Don't be alarmed."

Their wink does absolutely nothing to reassure me.

Gemory flings open the doors, and I find myself standing at the top of another set of stairs, these ones jutting out from a rough rock wall and leading down into a vast, subterranean water chamber. A high dome overhead is Woven, like the ceiling in the map room, to look like the sky. It's extraordinarily life-like, with moving clouds, birds that seem to actually fly across it, and star-shaped cuts that allow rays of sunlight to filter through. A waterfall tumbles from a rocky slope built out from the wall, and the stairs lead down to a tiled garden interspersed with sea flowers. Beyond that is deep water of the same brilliant aqua as the Stitched Sea. Beneath the surface, bright-colored coral mixes with exotic sea plants. Tropical fish dart between crumbling old arches, while far below, a herd of seahorses gallop across the sea floor, their curled tails kicking spirals of sand into the water above. The chamber is so vast it disappears into mist at the far end.

"It's the ancient city of Tartessos, center of what was once a great civilization." Gemory nods at the crumbling ruins below. "The ruins have the advantage of a thick stone wall at the border of the city. Harken used the wall as a boundary for this chamber, then incorporated it into the palace and built doors into the roof." Gemory nods at the great dome high above, which has a thick seam down the center.

I'm just about to ask why a water chamber would need doors in the roof, when the water before us parts, and a great set of iridescent wings rises directly in front of my face, so close I feel their soft touch. A pair of wide topaz eyes stare directly into mine. Startled out of my wits, I leap backward. A moment later the storm dragon dives down once more, sinking slowly to the sea floor.

"I will say it again." Gemory appears utterly untroubled by such a close encounter with so great a creature. "Interesting friends you make. Storm dragons rarely show themselves so willingly to anyone. And Huxley is a particularly shy girl."

A ray of sunlight catches the storm dragon's wings, turning them vivid aqua, gold, and indigo. One great clawed foot stirs, and Huxley rolls over to follow the sun. Her wings aren't made of scales, I realize, but long iridescent feathers. She looks nothing like what I might have imagined a storm dragon to, if ever I had imagined such a thing. Her face is diamond shaped and quite noble, with a short black nose and a rather elegant mouth, from which protrude two very sharp fangs. Sprawled out in the subterranean rays, Huxley looks like a winged underwater lioness, basking in the sun. As we watch, she yawns widely, displaying rows of lethal-looking teeth and a long pink tongue. One topaz eye cranks open and regards us solemnly, but with little interest, before closing again. A moment later, a gentle snore rumbles through the chamber.

"Why is she kept in captivity?" I feel a stab of sympathy for the storm dragon. She seems far too magnificent to be kept in an enclosure.

"Because," says Gemory quietly, "should she be so much as glimpsed by any in the Woven World, she would be killed immediately. Men would compete for the right to hunt her down and hang her head upon their wall, and none would rest until it was done."

"Why?" I stare at the slumbering dragon in fascination. "Why would anyone want to kill something so magnificent? Is it because she came through a Dark Rip?"

"She was deliberately brought through a Dark Rip." Gemory casts me a sideways glance I can't quite read. "Storm dragons are the most unique of creatures. Renowned for many things, one being their unerring instincts in hunting down treasure, no matter how well hidden."

Treasure. Remembering all Harken told me, I can guess easily enough what Huxley may have been brought to find. *The golden needle.*

"However," Gemory goes on, "that admirable trait rather pales in comparison against the one for which storm dragons are most well-known." Their mouth twitches as if at a private joke. "Hunting for their preferred food: young girls."

"Young girls?" I stare at Gemory suspiciously.

"I assure you it's true," says Gemory airily. "Storm dragons eat young girls. Ask anyone."

"And I suppose you expect me to believe Harken captures young girls to feed it," I say dryly.

"You don't believe me." Gemory sighs. "Disappointing." Their smile spreads. "Hello, Harken."

I spin around just as my braid prickles. *How did Gemory know?* I didn't so much as hear a door open.

"Gemory." Harken's voice is resigned rather than angry. "I should have known." He leans against the rock edge of the waterfall, hands thrust in his breeches. He isn't quite smiling, but at least the grim coldness following yesterday's conversation in the map room has gone.

"Oh, Harken." Gemory taps his arm playfully with their fan. "If I am to put up with that demon Andras, not to mention Feivel's terribly worthy company, you must allow me at least a little fun."

"Your idea of fun is rarely enjoyable for the rest of us," says Harken, rather acidly.

"So tedious." Gemory walks back up the stairs, opening the brass doors. "We were having the most interesting conversation before you arrived." Their eyes brim with mischief from the doorway. "Zaria was just asking me all about Sabers." Shooting me a wicked grin, Gemory closes the doors, leaving me alone with Harken and the storm dragon.

CHAPTER 31

HUXLEY

I cast around desperately for something to say. Anything that has nothing to do with Sabers.

In the end it's Harken who speaks first. "I apologize for any distress you might have been caused by Gemory's tale of Huxley eating young girls."

Desperately relieved to be off the topic of Sabers, I sit down beside the water. "Oh, I knew it wasn't true." I smile tentatively. "Gemory clearly likes their fun."

Harken's shoulders lift with silent laughter. "That much is certainly true." He moves past the waterfall and leans one booted foot up on a large rock a few paces away from me.

"Huxley was brought here by Kraken Weavers, wasn't she?" I glance at him. "To hunt for the golden needle. Gemory said she would be hunted down herself if you set her free."

Harken nods, looking down at the slumbering storm dragon. "Ambitious men rarely consider the repercussions of their ventures. Those who summoned Huxley never gave any thought to what her needs might be. By the time they had given up hope that Huxley would find what they sought, she was starving." He leans down and ripples the water with his fingers.

Huxley raises her great head from the sea floor and shakes it, the iridescent wings rippling in the water. She nudges the surface where Harken's hand is and purrs, a deep rumble that once again vibrates through the entire chamber. "Imagine," he says softly, "how it must have been for her. A baby, as she was then, no more than a few years old."

A brief image flashes across my mind, of the newly created Harken I saw in my first vision, alone in the garden.

"Dragons live for centuries," he goes on. "If Huxley were human, she would have been considered an infant."

Much like a Weaver, I think.

"Her mother, I suspect, died trying to protect her."

Bodies, lying where they had died, defending the Lotus Palace.

"Huxley was pulled into a strange world, utterly alone, with no idea how to forage for food, nor even if there was food here on which she might live."

Harken, burying body after body, with no idea why they died or what could have wrought such destruction.

"Then she was tortured mercilessly, sent out again and again across lonely seas to look for something not even those seeking it truly understood."

Harken, black clad and devastated, walking through the atrocities of war, then hunting the Dark Creatures nobody else understood.

"By the time Huxley fell to land, she was starving, terrified, exhausted, and in pain." The storm dragon watches Harken as he speaks, her wide topaz eyes solemn and unblinking. I have the unsettling feeling she can understand every word he says. When he finishes, she gives a low cry that twists my heart. It's like the caw of a distant bird, lonely and hollow.

"The first person to approach her was a young girl." Harken tilts his head, and the storm dragon's head sways in response. She lifts her two short, powerful front legs up, squealing in pain and memory as she spins away, curling her long tail about her like a dog sleeping in a strange place. "Huxley ate her," Harken says quietly. "Perhaps it was hereditary memory, or perhaps no more than animal instinct. Certainly, it was desperation. Whatever the reason, finally Huxley had found something in this new world that could sustain her. After that, she sought to find the same thing, again and again, until finally I managed to capture her."

"And now?" My voice sounds odd to my own ears, and to my horror, I realize my eyes have filled with tears. I dash them away hastily.

Harken doesn't answer me, but rather makes a gesture with his hands. A small underwater hatch opens, and a torrent of enormous mottled-brown slugs are released into the chamber. Huxley's head comes up, her great mouth opens, and the torrent of slugs disappear. "Sea slugs," says Harken, with a wry smile. "A very particular breed, found only in deep underwater caves. The smaller ones are called trepang and highly regarded in Basetanan cuisine. These ones are a little harder to find, a remnant of a time when our worlds were perhaps not quite so separate as they are now. Huxley can live on them. Perhaps her kind might not have been so feared, had anyone sought to discover an alternative food source."

Huxley eats, then nudges the surface again, crooning softly at Harken before floating across to me. She puts one large paw up on the tiles and looks at me expectantly.

"Hullo." Reaching out a tentative hand, I stroke her head. She curls against my hand, purring loudly. "She's so beautiful," I say, captivated.

"Not to everyone." I look up to find Harken's eyes on me, an odd light in their depths. "Most fear Huxley on sight. And she doesn't trust easily. Storm dragons are loyal," he says quietly. "To their purpose, and to those they love." Moisture drifting through the sunlit rays forms a glistening bridge between his eyes and mine, one of profound peace and stillness. "I respect that."

For an endless moment there is only the soft lapping of water and the still, rich air, given substance by the slow swirl of his words and the meaning they have to me.

Then Huxley nudges my hand and plunges beneath the surface, slapping the water with her tail as she goes. A torrent of water flies into the air, drenching us both to the skin.

I leap up, shrieking with laughter, and collide directly with Harken, who grasps my arms to steady me. His shirt is plastered against his chest, and he's grinning.

Actually grinning.

"Magel's going to kill me." I lean sideways to wring the water out of my hair, which has tumbled straight out of the loose knot. "She made me promise not to touch my hair before tonight."

"I think I like it this way." Harken plucks a long coil from the front of my tunic, slowly trailing it through his fingers. "I didn't know it was so long. It looks mahogany in a plait, but your curls turns to copper when the sun hits them." The coil slips free of his fingers, but he doesn't move. We're so close I can see the mercurial silver shifting in his eyes, smell the heady scent of Darkwine that clings to him.

"Tonight," he says quietly, "we're going into a place far more dangerous than Huxley's chamber." Harken's eyes trace the marks made by Hodda's whip, and my skin prickles in response. "I want to fix those scars. I can't—" His voice breaks off. He takes a sharp breath. "The Indigold nobility are not kind, Zaria. Those scars will make them think they can treat you like a slave."

"I thought that was what you wanted, when you took me." His eyes drop to my mouth as I speak. When they rise again, there's something in them that makes slow heat uncoil through my body.

"I'm not entirely sure anymore," Harken says slowly, "what exactly I wanted, when I took you." The air feels suddenly heavy between us. "I'm used to being alone," he says quietly. "And to knowing my purpose." Strange colors shift in his eyes. "Now I'm opening my home and giving history lessons. My demons, and even my storm dragon, appear enamored of you. And my purpose has never seemed less important." The braid is silken and alive against my skin where his eyes linger on it. "Where I've long been resigned to my fate, even that braid around your neck has never dimmed your belief that you will change yours." His eyes flicker to mine, shadows chasing the light in them. "Your presence makes me forget what I'm bound to, makes me dream of things I have no right to."

I'm so aware of his proximity I can barely breathe. "Maybe you can have those things," I whisper. "Everyone has the right to decide their own fate."

His mouth curves at the edge, silver fire gleaming in his eyes. "So you say. But such dreams are as dangerous for me as they are impossible."

My clothes cling to every curve of my body, and my skin has never felt so alive. Harken's hand trails up my arm, toward the marks on my neck, his eyes not leaving mine. "Let me heal you."

I couldn't argue, even if I wanted to.

The first starlight touches my skin, and my eyes flutter closed.

It's different this time.

There's no dark alley, no shadows where we must hide. There is just Harken and me, and the peaceful sound of tumbling water all around.

The starlight seeps under my skin at my shoulder. I lean my head to one side to expose the scars on my neck and hear Harken's sharp intake of breath. He captures my hair as it sways away from my body with his free hand, the other trailing starlight at my neck, under my jaw, to the tender place just below my ear. I'm exquisitely aware of every tiny movement. The cool thrill takes each scar like a lover, tracking agonizingly slowly down my throat. My head goes back and my lips part, my breath coming short.

My eyes fly open. Harken's face is barely inches from my own, his eyes burning with a hard, fierce light. His hand hovers directly over my heart, while his other one has my hair twined about it in a thick rope. For the briefest moment, I think he is going to pull me forward, hard against him.

For the briefest moment, I think I've never wanted anything more.

Then the starlight is gone, my hair is free, and Harken is standing a full pace away.

"We'll be leaving after sunfall," he says hoarsely, backing away from me. "You should get some rest."

CHAPTER 32

GONDOLA

I lie on my bed, watching the afternoon light dapple across the water and shine on the indigo floor. As sunfall approaches, the last rays find their companions deep in the flamestone, so water and fire dance together. My skin thrills where Harken healed it, but somewhere deep inside, I feel like I'm breaking apart.

I've had only one goal for as long as I can recall. It's been only days since I left the Seam, and I no longer know if I'm closer to the freedom I've dreamed of, or if I'm simply exchanging one form of slavery for another.

I'm bound to my siblings. No matter where they are now, nor who holds their braid end, they're my responsibility. Barely days ago, my bargain with Harken seemed like a practical step forward. Winning the Maverick's Race still feels like a clear goal, one I can understand.

But I feel less in control of achieving my goals than ever. I know nothing about the Race. I'm impatient to begin training, with no idea how that will begin. And instead of learning Race rules and the skills I need to accomplish my goal, I'm playing with captive storm dragons and getting dressed to go to a Revel.

But neither of those things are the real problem.

Harken is.

Love is the worst form of slavery. It's perhaps the first lesson any girl in Disorderly House learns. To love is to be bound more fiercely than any braid ever could. Mallory once told me that the words of the Shadow Bargain have a different meaning for Disorderly girls. *Take what you want, and pay for it,* the words say.

"A girl can take the coin," Mallory told me, *"and pay on her back. Or she can take the man, and pay forever."*

If I cease to remember that the Water Palace is a cage, no matter how gilded, I will no longer strive to find a way through the bars. If for one moment I start to choose Harken over my own goals, I am in danger of taking the man—and paying forever.

Winning the Maverick's Race is the only true way to freedom, the only real escape route, for my siblings as well as me.

I'm still a slave, I remind myself fiercely. Until the braid is off my neck. Until I win the Race and have the coin I need for true independence. *Play your part in his bargain*, I tell myself sternly. *But never forget your own. And never, no matter what, look to him as anything more than the means to get to that goal.*

Don't take the man.

Magel knocks on the door, and I swing my legs over the bed determinedly. I didn't grow up in the Dark and Disorderly without learning at least a few things. And the first of those is how to play a part.

I can do this, I think grimly. Then I catch sight of myself in the mirror, my hair still loose and tangled after being wrapped in his hand, my eyes still glittering with his starlight under my skin, and all I can see are Shimi's copper eyes staring back at me knowingly. "Don't judge me," I say aloud to her imagined reflection. "Don't you dare judge me, Shimi."

I PAUSE for a final look in the mirror. I can hear Harken's murmured conversation below. I've never felt more self-conscious in my life.

The sheer silk dress is the same deep Darkwine color as my eyes, shot through with shimmering gold that seems Woven into the material itself. It has wide-set shoulders that come down to a deep V, clearly exposing the slave braid at my neck, and drops in a straight fall to my ankles. Elegant enough—from the front.

The back is cut to expose my zumi in its entirety and dips low enough to show the faint hollow at the base of my spine. Magel has dressed my hair in a high mass of curls threaded with lotus flowers, leaving every detail of the zumi visible in stark relief.

Taking a deep breath, I open the door and begin the descent to the courtyard.

Harken is talking to one of his demons, his head bent as he listens closely. "No," he says as I round the landing. "Tell Feivel the library remains closed, Foras, until I say differently." He sounds impatient, and the demon, clearly taking the hint, turns to go.

I feel a frisson at my neck, and Harken turns to me.

My braid pulses so strongly that for a moment I think he's touched the braid end. But it's still hanging on the ring at his neck, while Harken's hands are clenched at his sides, his entire body coiled tight as a great cat waiting to leap. Only his dark eyes move, following my descent, the oil lamps on the walls casting flickering patterns in their depths. When I reach the courtyard and still he doesn't speak, I say awkwardly, "Darcy says the gown is made to your specifications. If it isn't right, I can change—"

"No." His voice is low and terse. "The dress is perfect. You are . . . perfect."

Perfect. I can't imagine a word to which I feel less suited, particularly with a slave braid at my neck. It seems the same thought has occurred to Harken; he raises a hand toward it. I shy away.

"We made a bargain." *Remember why you're here.*

Harken's mouth tightens. "Yes," he says grimly. "We did." He almost snatches the cloak from Hagel's hand, though he settles it around my shoulders with infinite gentleness.

The waiting gondola has wide, well-padded bench seats. The gondolier wears the scarlet livery of Harken's senior footmen and has the unmistakable red eyes of a demon, though like Andras, he shows a white iris around the pupil and is powerfully built.

"My name is Zaria," I say as he hands me into the gondola.

"And I am Mantas." He makes me an elegant bow. "You are most welcome to the Indigo City, my lady."

"I'm not a lady. I'm a slave."

"Hm." Mantas's smile doesn't change at all. "One's soul is not described by names or braids." He winks at me as Harken unties the gondola and takes the bench seat opposite. Mantas leans to the side, skillfully steering the gondola around the corner and out of the small side canal, taking us into the wider main thoroughfare.

A hundred gondolas, all richly decorated and hung with lanterns, make the canal a sea of light. The gondolas themselves, however, pale in grandeur beside those sitting in them.

I've never seen gowns so elaborate, a glittering array of color in every shape and size. The cleverly painted faces match the gowns and are often marked with small paste jewels and other ornaments. I see one woman who looks exactly like a mermaid swimming undersea, even as she walks toward her waiting gondola.

"It's a glamour." Harken is watching me. The fierce look in his eyes that sent such a frisson through me has been replaced by his more familiar, hooded expression of faint amusement, which, I tell myself, is a good thing. "The best dressmakers in the Indigo City come from houses that are centuries old. They learn the art of Weaving glamour with cloth in the cradle."

I hear Marissa's voice: *"But there are so few Weavers left now . . ."*

I shake it off. Tonight I have a role to play, and no time for internal pondering.

Some of the outfits are incredibly daring. One woman has both breasts completely bared, though the rest of her body is encased in a kind of jeweled netting that clings to her body. Her nipples are both pierced with silver hoops, from which thin chains snake out to twine with the netting. Her hair has been designed to look like a mass of serpents, moving with a life of its own, and for a brief, heart-stopping moment I think it's Neoma. Then the woman turns, and with a sick lurch, I recognize Sereia, the Paladin Weaver. I look away before she catches sight of me.

"What is it that you expect of me tonight?" I gesture wryly to my backless dress, hidden under the cloak. "I assume there is a particular reason for the cut of my gown."

Harken waves his hand in the air, and I realize he's putting up a shield so Mantas can't hear us. "Every Weaver has a particular style," he says, "that marks a zumi as their creation. Usually one touch is enough for me to discern the story behind any zumi, whether the creator is alive or dead, and whether I knew them or not." He lifts a shoulder. "In your case, however, I cannot. That is curious. I wish to see who, if anyone, recognizes it." He sits back and regards me, his face impassive. "So, yes. There was a reason for that particular design." The manner of his reply and the slight edge to his voice imply he might be regretting his choice, though I'm unsure why.

"Then you wish me to show it off," I say bluntly. "Make certain everyone sees my zumi clearly?"

"Yes." Harken's face looks rather hard. "That is what I had planned."

"Then I will be certain to do so." I sit back in the gondola, watching him. "We made a bargain," I say quietly. "I will ensure I fill my end of it."

Harken frowns. "I don't wish you to feel uncomfortable with anything I ask of you."

My lips twitch; I can't help it. "Other than being your slave, of course."

He gives a sudden burst of surprised laughter. "Well," he says, "apart from that, yes." His eyes are warm on my face, and I feel it again, the odd frisson between us, a tingling in the braid around my neck and something deeper, that I can neither name nor allow myself to think on too long.

Mantas leans on the long oar, guiding the gondola into a long landing. The warmth in Harken's eyes fades, replaced by the hard glitter I know so well. He leaps to the dock and reaches his hand out to me.

"Come," he says. "It's time."

CHAPTER 33

REVEL

I cross the black-and-white checked tiles that in turn give way to a set of shallow steps running across the width of the landing, aware of the curious eyes following us. Harken ignores them entirely, his understated elegance making every other man nearby seem fancifully overdressed.

His scarlet jacket is cut down from the hip, the two sides falling to just above his knee. High points beneath his jaw curl out slightly to show a wide, embroidered black inner collar. In contrast to the elaborate cravats worn by the other men present, Harken's shirt opens at the neck, deliberately exposing the ring-and-braid knot. His jacket is attached by a lone silver engraved button. Black suede breeches disappear into his customary black boots. His costume, particularly with its unadorned black top hat, might be far less elaborate than many of the cloaked layers and soaring hats of the other men present, but every eye turns as we approach the series of arches that mark the palace facade.

Glass lanterns hanging from each arch throw glittering light upon the approaching Revelers. The main entrance is an archway three times the height of the others. The stone center of it is dominated by a symbol etched in what looks like Pathfinder's silver. It's the Indigold Cup, the serpent twining along the stem, its head hissing over the brim. The silver makes the etching move like a river, so the serpent appears to be constantly spiraling up the stem of the Cup, its eye gleaming out at the arriving guests.

"My lord." The footman bows low in greeting. Harken nods curtly and pauses at the entrance, drawing me forward to stand beside him.

It's difficult to see past the wall of bodies in the reception salon, despite each crystal chandelier glittering with a hundred candles. Servants carrying trays of sparkling Darkwine move among the crowd, and many Revelers already carry the telltale amethyst stain on their lips. Heads begin to turn toward us, but Harken, clearly wishing to create a sensation, doesn't move.

Two curved marble staircases rise on either side of the salon to meet in a landing above, from which a gaggle of exquisitely clad Indigold stare down at the crowd, some using eyeglasses held on the end of long sticks to look more closely. They begin to mutter, faces turning in our direction, until Harken and I are the sole focus of the entire room. The crowd on the floor below parts, creating a space before us.

Now that we command every eye, Harken reaches for my cloak.

I step forward, out of his grasp.

I may never have cultivated the art of drama like Shimi, but I've spent my life in Hodda's salon, nonetheless. *If it's a spectacle you wish to create*, I think, not without trepidation, *I know better than any the impact of a slave braid.*

Harken's eyes narrow slightly as I deliberately turn my back to the room.

Slipping slowly free of the cloak, I shrug it from my shoulders, dropping it into a waiting footman's hand.

An audible gasp sweeps the room as my zumi is exposed in

its entirety. I pause, then turn slowly to the front. Gasps turn to shocked murmuring as the watching Revelers take in the braid gleaming at my neck.

A moment later, with little more than a curt nod of his head in my direction, Harken strides past me to the center of the room. I follow dutifully in his wake. Eyes follow me, filled with everything from shock to pity and, in some cases, contempt.

Once, it would easily have been the most humiliating experience of my life.

But this isn't my life. I'm taking what I want, and this is how I pay for it.

Armed with that internal knowledge, I'm not above feeling a secret thrill. *Yes*, I think, catching a particularly disdainful glance from an Indigold woman dressed entirely in Dencover gold. *Look your worst. Despise me for the Weorpan you see, and for the slave braid I bear through no fault of my own.* After a lifetime of serving Indigold men who see me as nothing more than a commodity, I find a certain perverse satisfaction in a charade in which it is I, not they, who has the power—whether they know it or not.

I pause behind Harken, who is staring up at the landing. The watching Indigold there part, men bowing and women curtsying, and a woman steps up to the railing.

It isn't only beauty and her dramatic dress that make her such a striking figure. She moves with a quiet dignity that needs no command to dominate a room and a grace that I recognize, from the many exiled priestesses I met in the Seam, as belonging to the Isle of Nine.

Her mass of black curls is piled high on her head and entwined with deep purple flowers, interspersed with gleaming diamonds that light them from beneath, so the overall effect is like watching an undersea garden float through the air. Her face is exquisitely painted in shades of silver, white, and green, her lips and eyes outlined to dramatic effect in black-edged purple.

Her gown soars up behind her neck in a silver halo that turns first pink, then rose, plunging to a low cleavage, then dipping below her waist into a series of gradually darkening amethyst ripples. The lower skirt ripples out into a long train of dusky midnight silk that moves like smoke.

If her dignified manner hadn't betrayed her training, the dark amethyst shadows behind her eyes are a certain sign. All priestesses use Darkwine to aid their Sight and in their ceremonies. And it isn't just Darkwine I see in those shadows. Even before my braid visions, I'd heard of the cruel experiments suffered by priestesses of the isle under the Kraken's rule. Everything from the woman's quiet smile to the gentle inclination of her head speaks of tragedies endured, lending her beauty a depth and subtlety quite beyond the physical. As she approaches the railing, the chatter in the room dies, every face turned toward her.

"Queen Prudence." Harken sweeps his hat low in a courteous bow that is somewhat undermined by his sardonic smile and the dark, gleaming eyes he raises to the vision on the landing. "As ever, you make a magnificent Queen of Revels."

"My lord Harken." Prudence's voice rings clearly across the ballroom. Despite my first impressions, she is far from a tragic figure. There's an air of amusement in the eyes she turns to Harken, an almost wry hint to her voice as she says, "Your presence in our midst is all the more welcome for being such a rare gift." Inclining her head, she snaps open a gilt fan and waves it leisurely, her eyes resting on me. "And with a slave, no less." She raises a perfectly arched eyebrow. "An interesting addition to our Revels, my lord." Harken's eyes gleam, but he makes no comment. "I expect an introduction before the night is out."

Harken tilts his head in acknowledgment, but the queen has already turned away.

A footman in the corner beats a large brass cymbal, and a set of tall cream-and-gold doors open. The crowd surges through into the ballroom, chattering once more. We are, if not forgotten, at least no longer the center of attention.

"Prudence is Roark's widow," Harken murmurs, "Astria's last queen, and still respected by all. She was once a priestess and suffered at the Kraken's hands as much as any." His eyes, vivid as midnight fire, linger on mine. The braid tingles on my skin. I can sense his tension beneath the hard veneer, and my own pulse quickens.

The game is gathering pace.

"I think," he says, loudly enough to draw attention, "that my slave should precede her master." He opens his arm in a grand gesture toward the ballroom doors.

The game we play lends every exchange an intimate thrill. "As you wish, my lord." I bend my head in a slightly exaggerated attitude of submission.

"Criminal," he murmurs as I pass.

My eyes cut briefly to his. "Savage."

His grin is a dark flash, there and gone.

We enter the ballroom.

CHAPTER 34

QUEEN

The dome soaring high overhead takes my breath away. It also tugs at my heart.

The twelve-pointed golden star, the Astris, gleams on an indigo background, just as it does in the tapest where I learned my childhood letters.

Around the Astris are painted scenes from Caspian the Sailor's legendary voyage, over the Drop and into the Interweave, a story I first heard as a child, from Garrick.

First is Caspian's search for the thief, Tellian, who stole one of the six golden needles. Then, the battle that resulted in the breaking of the needle. The other side of the dome depicts Tellian cutting twelve threads in the Interweave to make his escape. Finally, there is a painting of Caspian the Hero, using his half of the needle to repair the Interweave and tying the twelve Tellian knots that saved Astria.

Staring up at the legend of the first Stitched Man brings Garrick and Doron into the glittering room. My almost playful mood of moments before is replaced by a sickening sense of loss. *They are both out there now,* I think, *lost amid those terrible threads.* Or has the Dark Rip taken Doron further, into a darkness where even the Stitched Men can't go?

What am I doing here? The clawing guilt I've been fighting ever since I woke on the *Hydra* grips me again as I stare around at the opulence no slave in the Seam could ever, in their wildest imaginings, envisage. As if to reinforce my dislocation, the images of Caspian's journey have been dwarfed by a more recent addition: the tentacles of a vast, vividly drawn Golden Kraken. It sprawls in a predatory tangle over the entirety of the dome and beyond, tentacles reaching insidiously across the ceiling. Despite evidence of recent efforts, it's clear the kraken has been powerfully Woven and is not easily undone.

Anahita, I think bitterly. For a brief instant I almost wish I could face that Dark Weaver who has taken so much from Astria—and from my siblings and me.

The kraken's tentacles twine all the way along the ceiling to an Indigold Cup insignia on the inside of the ballroom entrance. In a seeming parody of the traditional serpent rising along the stem, the kraken tentacles seem to choke the Cup itself.

I can't breathe. For a horrible moment I feel as if it's me the tentacles choke, crushing the breath from my body.

Take what you want, and pay for it. It seems the Shadow mantra has become my own, for tonight, at least. In a strange way it gives me the focus I need. I draw a deep breath and gather the threads of my being, relieved when it seems nobody has noticed my temporary mental absence.

Harken is tense beside me, his eyes crystalized into a hard light. I follow them to a small group of Indigold, which includes Sereia's flaming auburn serpent hair. She has her back to us, talking to the ever-smiling Paladin Consul I recognize from the Braid Race: Gareth. I shouldn't be surprised at the other faces, yet still I suppress an instinctive shudder when I see Caspian and Foley beside them. I scour the faces nearby, every nerve in my body alert, but there's no trace of my sisters. There is, however, another familiar face: Arkady's.

Something visceral surges through my veins, a bodily memory of the last time we met, our hands together on the Cup. Harken's hand flies to the ring beneath his shirt, as if he feels my discomfort. There's a momentary warmth as he touches the knot, then he thankfully lets it go.

"Well, well," he murmurs. "If it isn't our Foolish friend."

Standing slightly apart from the other young men, Arkady's dress is elegant but not ostentatious: a navy coat of good cut over white breeches and tall boots. He is entirely unremarkable, but given our turbulent history, for me his presence in the room is jarring, like a wrong note amid a symphony. He doesn't seem to have noticed me. I avert my gaze to avoid his.

Queen Prudence mounts a dais at the rear of the ballroom and quiets crowd and musicians alike with one raised hand.

"Ladies and Gentlemen of Astria. As your Queen of Revels, I welcome you to the Indigo City." Prudence smiles down at the assemblage as if she were still the queen of Astria itself, rather than the widow of a king who died a traitor, and presiding over a carnival that has been stripped of all meaning. It's a measure of her dignity, I think, that she can lend such a sense of occasion to an event so badly plagued by corruption during her husband's long reign.

"Tonight is the first of our Revels." Prudence accepts the ensuing raucous applause with a graceful smile, waiting until it dies naturally to continue. "The Revels will culminate in the legendary Maverick's Race, three moons from now." This time the roar is sustained, particularly from a group of already disheveled-looking young Indigold nobles to one side of the crowd, neckties askew, Darkwine cups held high. By their wild hoots of enthusiasm at every mention of the Race, I take them to be my prospective competition.

"The Maverick's Race," the queen continues, "has been blessed with a particularly rich landholding as prize this year. Helfrach Estate adjoins Hiraeth Forest and is home to the valuable flamestone mines. This year's winning Maverick will be granted title to Caer Helfrach and the entirety of its estate, including the mines. They will also receive this." Four footmen come forward, staggering under the weight of a chest, which they lower to the ground with an effort. The queen's needle flashes, and the chest flics open, revealing an impossibly huge pile of gold coin, to gasps of admiration from the crowd. "For this very generous gift," the queen goes on, "I should like you all to raise your cups to our beloved friend and loyal defender of Astria: Lady Fearach of the Wolf Weald."

She raises her cup to a tall figure, of whom I can see only a top hat through the roaring crowd. Amid the general hilarity, Arkady catches my attention. His eyes are locked on the gold spilling from the chest, and in them I see the same determined gleam I had before the Braid Race.

"Our Foolish friend covets that prize." Harken's undertone is clearly meant for my ears alone. "An interesting development." He nods almost imperceptibly overhead. I don't see Gemory's figure, but I'm certain that's who will be following Arkady.

"You said you think he's a tool," I murmur, "rather than the master."

"I also don't think he is here by accident." Mercurial shadows flit through Harken's eyes. "Helfrach and Hiraeth are the same forest, one on the Seamish side, the other on the Astrian. Both span the most porous part of the Interweave outside of the Drop itself. Helfrach would be the perfect place for anyone inclined to travel to other worlds."

"Then you think he might be acting alone?" I glance surreptitiously at Arkady's slightly detached figure. His expression gives nothing away. Though his sharp features are instantly recognizable to me because of the terrifying manner of our meeting, he has an unobtrusive presence that I suspect helps him disappear into any gathering with ease.

"He may have motives of his own." Harken's tone is thoughtful. "But he cannot have come from the Foolish world without help."

"And that's who you're searching for." I frown, watching the crowd.

Harken inclines his head, but it's me he's watching, and when he speaks his voice is laced with amusement. "Whoever we seek has gone to a deal of trouble to remain hidden. They will hardly announce themselves, little criminal. Tonight is an opening gambit, no more. The game will take time to play out."

Harken draws me through the crowd, still smiling. Despite his easy manner, he eyes every face with a sharp scrutiny that makes me certain he seeks one in particular. Whose face that might be, and why it must be such a secret, I'm equally certain he has no intention of sharing, at least not with me.

The ballroom is round, with several upper levels and circular stages suspended from the roof. French doors open onto small balconies, beyond which lie lush gardens and candlelit canals. On the upper levels are private salons, used for cards, dice, and other amusements, some guarded by footmen with velvet ropes. Dancers and acrobats in exotic costumes perform on the suspended stages, occasionally thrown coins by admiring onlookers. In partially hidden alcoves, couples seeking a reprieve from the crush sit close together on low couches. Through it all, servants carry a seemingly endless supply of Darkwine, some glasses sparkling, some heavy and dark, and still others gleaming with an amber hint of Weald whiskey.

There's no sign of the hearty Drop ale preferred by Garrick and his men, or the dull, heavy aphrodisiac of the Seam.

An orchestra plays a lively beat, surrounded by a glittering tree wrought from gold and wreathed in tiny pearls. The air is thick with the scent of wine, food, and humanity.

Harken is still watching me, the same small smile on his lips. He nods to a room on the second level. "Gemory will keep an eye on our friend. In the meantime—there's somebody I wish you to meet."

CHAPTER 35

CARDS

I precede Harken up the stairs, ignoring the scandalized eyes watching us from behind gilt fans and the hushed whispers that follow in our wake.

A footman and velvet rope guard the entrance to the private salon. The footman frowns at my braid, then, seeing Harken, pulls the rope aside with alacrity. "My lord." He bows low, trying not to stare at me.

"My dear fellow," Harken says agreeably, passing into the salon. The light is lower here, the atmosphere slightly less frenetic. The salon is clearly dedicated to cards. Bottles stand open on small side tables beside the larger ones reserved for gaming. Men have already removed their jackets and rolled up their sleeves in anticipation of the game ahead.

Harken moves toward a table at the center, and I follow.

A very blond man with arctic blue eyes and a spare, rangy figure comes to his feet as we approach. He has burnished skin that speaks of high, snowy places, and his features are vaguely familiar. Harken draws me forward.

"Zaria—may I introduce Kendrick, Lord Halvard of Goath and Guardian of the Northern Peaks?"

Andras's brother, I realize with a shock. It's hard to imagine two men more vastly different. *And the old Lord of Goath's son*, I think, recalling my vision.

"Kendrick—allow me to present Zaria. My slave," he adds, as if it's a careless afterthought. He beckons a footman, who leans forward with a tray.

"Darkwine, my lord?"

Harken's lips quirk as if at a private joke. "I rarely indulge," he murmurs. "Bring a bottle of Weald whiskey and a chair for my slave."

Casting Harken a stern look, Kendrick bows over my hand, for all the world as if I am the equal of any lady at the ball. "Zaria," he says politely. His grave face tightens as Harken gestures for the footman to seat me at a slight distance from the game. "My understanding," Kendrick says in a glacial tone, "is that the privilege exercised by the Woven Court at that cursed Race relates to the freeing of slaves, not taking possession of them for amusement."

"Ah." Harken leans forward to fill the empty whiskey glass of another player as he takes his seat. "Good evening, Lupa," he says politely. It's the tall woman in the top hat who donated the prize earlier: Lady Fearach of the Wolf Weald. "But then, Kendrick," he goes on, turning back to the Lord of Goath, "you and I have always enjoyed rather different notions of what constitutes amusement."

Kendrick shakes his head disapprovingly but doesn't answer.

"Kendrick has the right of it, though, Harken." Lupa allows Harken to fill her glass, but her amber eyes are on me. "I hadn't imagined the Savage Court so starved for amusement—nor you so capricious." She gives Harken a hard glance. Rather than an elaborate gown, Lupa is dressed in dark leather breeches not unlike Harken's own, atop long leather boots with a slight heel. Her hat is set at a decidedly rakish angle, and her rose silk shirt is cut daringly low, exposing a deep, tawny-skinned cleavage that would have earned her a fortune back in the Seam. An enormous ruby gleams on her index finger, and she wears her pitch-black hair in a long, low plait threaded with subtle jewels. The back of her brushed suede topcoat is emblazoned with a staff and flame, picked out in russet and gold, which appears to flicker. *Lupa may look nothing like the fine Indigold ladies in their gowns,* I think, with more than a little admiration, *but she is more unmistakably a woman of authority than any of them.*

"Surely," Harken says in his most arrogant, sardonic drawl, "my reputation for savagery should be enough to preclude such questions? But perhaps," he goes on, his eyes narrowing slightly as a solidly built man with brutish features and thick, salt-and-pepper hair enters the salon and turns to approach our table, "you should be asking a different question."

The man's blunt face and mean eyes are immediately familiar, and even if his gold buttons didn't bear the Serpent Queen insignia, I would still recognize him instantly as Foley's father. I remember Shimi's excitement: *"His father is the Comitas. It's almost like being king..."*

"Why is it, I wonder," Harken murmurs as the man comes closer, "that the same man who takes such pleasure in humiliating you at council seems so eager, suddenly, to seek out your company?"

Lupa's eyes narrow, and a certain sharp interest flashes in Kendrick's as the Comitas reaches us.

"Comitas Ormond." Lupa gestures to the fourth seat. "Won't you join us?"

"Lady Fearach." The Comitas greets her with the barest minimum of courtesy as he takes the proffered chair. "Lord Halvard," he returns Kendrick's polite greeting curtly. Then, his mouth curling with obvious distaste, the Comitas glances briefly in Harken's direction. "Lord Harken," he says stiffly.

"Comitas Ormond." Harken's tone is one of polite disinterest.

The Comitas snaps his fingers irritably for Darkwine, glaring in Harken's direction. "Your Weorpan slave is an insult to every Indigold lady in this ballroom."

"It is fortunate, then, is it not," Harken drawls with an air of supreme boredom, "that we find ourselves in the card salon, rather than the ballroom?"

I fight the urge to smile. Harken has conducted their entire exchange without ever actually looking in the Comitas's direction.

"Lupa." Harken turns to Lady Fearach as Kendrick deals the cards. "That son of yours is somewhere nearby, is he not?"

Lupa tips her chair back, casting Harken a curious glance. "Everett," she says in a low voice. A tall, muscular man appears barely a moment later. Everett has a riot of coal-black curls, strong features and sunset skin like his mother, and warm russet eyes with more than a hint of fire in them. I suspect he would be quick to draw a sword, and handy with it, if he did. Beside him is a young man with a smiling, friendly face.

"And Lord Laguia, too." Harken's eyes gleam. "Excellent."

Lord Laguia! I feel a surge of excitement as I remember Marissa's words during my dress fitting: *"My third son, Brooks, and his friend Everett might not be competing this year, but they are still the wildest Mavericks you can imagine . . ."*

"Dreaver's Tells, Harken!" Taking in my slave braid, Brooks casts Harken a look that is half admiring, half disapproving. "My mother did warn me."

"You do like to knot your threads, Harken, and no mistake." Everett comes up on my other side, shaking his head. "Your slave is quite the scandal of the Revels."

Harken casts me the ghost of a wink. "Zaria—Everett Fearach and Brooks Laguia are veterans of the Maverick's Race." He nods at a low couch against the wall that is directly in the Comitas's line of sight. "No doubt they will be fascinated to hear in person the story of how you raced our young Foolish friend to a draw in the Braid Race."

"Yes, my lord," I murmur obediently. I bite down on a smile as Harken cheerfully ignores the disapproving glares cast in his direction by both of the young men. As I turn to take their courteously proffered arms, I deliberately turn my back to the Comitas, so the light falls directly on my zumi. My ploy must work, because Harken's eyes gleam momentarily as I catch them, his lips twitching with an amusement only I see.

Cards are the very least of his game tonight, I think. And I'd be lying if I said I wasn't taking at least a little enjoyment in playing my part.

I allow Everett and Brooks to seat me on the low couch between them, pretending not to notice the Comitas's surreptitious glances in my direction. "You've both competed in the Maverick's Race, then?" I ask, as Everett pours me a glass of lavenade.

"Neither of us are competing this year, though." Brooks looks positively gloomy.

"Which is a pity," Everett adds, his eyes gleaming with a dangerous light, "since I'd love to take down that Fool Caspian and Foley are putting their money behind. Speaking of whom," he says, looking at me, "I take it the stories are true, then, about you racing him to a draw, back in the Seam?"

"You weren't there?" I look between him and Brooks curiously. They seem precisely the type of raucous young noblemen to frequent the Seam during Race week.

"Us?" Brooks stares at me, and I realize, belatedly, that he is quite insulted by my question. "Dreaver's Tells, no. My mother would have me locked in an underwater dungeon for a year if I so much as mentioned it."

Lupa, having clearly heard the last comment, leans back in her chair. "And Everett would be lucky if I let him ever swing a sword again." Her amber eyes glint with a light very similar to her son's. "That barbaric Race." She shakes her head in clear disgust. "It's a disgrace that it's allowed to continue. No Indigold with any dignity would ever take pleasure from watching such a spectacle." When Comitas Ormond frowns, Lupa raises her eyebrows as if daring him to argue, but he simply purses his lips in clear annoyance and turns back to the cards.

That explains why Caspian and Foley were there, I think. Clearly, neither they nor the Comitas suffer the others' qualms. It's something of a pleasant surprise, to discover that not all the Indigold take pleasure in that desperate spectacle.

"But our distaste doesn't mean we don't want to hear about it," says Brooks, grinning as he takes a drink.

"I don't think," I begin, shaking my head, but Brooks and Everett shout me down, until eventually I'm telling, not the entire tale, but that of the Braid Race itself. By the time I reach the part where I was on the platform, my small audience is hanging on every word.

"Wait." Everett's eyes are gleaming. "You mean you actually had both hands on the Cup at the same time as Arkady?"

"Well, it mustn't have been exactly the same time," I demur. "Arkady was declared the winner."

"Declared the winner by Gareth." Everett's contemptuous tone implies he thinks little of the Paladin Consul. "Which means the outcome was likely agreed on before the race was ever won. Slippery as the alchemy in his damned Cup, that Paladin. No wonder Harken claimed you." Everett casts him a narrow glance. "Never one to miss an opportunity to thwart the will of the Paladins, our Savage King." The slight edge to his tone suggests that despite a certain wary admiration, Everett is not quite so tolerant of Harken's foibles as his mother appears to be.

"Enough about the Braid Race." Thinking it wise to change the subject, I smile at the two of them. "I'm far more interested in hearing about the Maverick's." *That much is certainly true.*

"Well," begins Everett, "the Maverick's Race is much like the Braid Race, only with gondolinos, racing gondolas, instead of carricks—and with a great deal more violence." I settle back into the couch as Everett's and Brooks's faces light with enthusiasm. Their mutual excitement reminds me of a much younger Doron and Levin, and my heart twists a little. Eager as I am to soak up every detail of the Race, I can't help, on occasion, glancing at the card table.

Harken lounges in his chair, playing with lethal precision, by the coin piling up in front of him.

But his eyes are on me, and when our eyes meet, the faintest smile tugs at the corner of his mouth. There's an undeniable thrill in our private game. I lift my eyebrow slightly: *are things going according to plan?*

Harken's eyes flare briefly. *Exactly as planned.*

It's only as I turn away that I catch Lupa's sharp eyes, shifting between Harken and me.

She tilts her whiskey glass to me in an ironic salute, but makes no comment.

CHAPTER 36

COMITAS

"*And so*"—Everett leans across me, using his hands to demonstrate—"on the third circuit of the canals, I steered my gondolino around Brooks, like this, and between us we trapped Caspian under the bridge, which is where he fell into the water. Then Brooks's brother Ford, who'd lost his gondolino earlier in the race, leaped from the bridge into Caspian's and rowed it to the finish line. He nearly won, too."

Brooks and Everett clang their whiskey cups together, whooping at the retelling of the last Maverick's Race. "Caspian hasn't won a race yet." Everett grins darkly.

"Wait." I'm fascinated, absorbing every detail. "You mean that a competitor can still win even if they lose their gondolino?"

"Oh, absolutely!" Everett stretches his arm across the back of the couch, leaning in close as he refills my cup. "The Race is a war, Zaria. The first man to complete three circuits and drink from the Cup wins, no matter how he makes it. Many a winner has lost their gondolino only to row to victory in someone else's. Sometimes they even steal them deliberately." He looks up as his mother throws her cards down on the table, shaking her head.

"I believe the game is yours, my lord." She shoots Harken a wry smile.

Comitas Ormond throws down his hand in disgust and pushes back his chair. "We should perhaps be grateful," he sneers, "that you limit yourself to such frivolous pastimes, Lord Harken. Your savage tactics would not be so well tolerated at the council table. Thankfully"—he casts an unpleasantly suggestive glance in my direction—"you've never shown interest in anything other than your own desires, savage or otherwise."

He's clearly upset, I think. Then, seeing the slight flare of satisfaction in Harken's eyes: *which is exactly what Harken wanted.* I wonder if it is the Comitas himself Harken suspects of opening the Dark Rip.

"That's quite enough, Dirk." Kendrick's icy tone matches his arctic glare.

"Oh, it's more than enough." Comitas Ormond casts a contemptuous glance around the table. "I wonder that you tolerate his society at all, when he does nothing to contribute to ours." Turning pointedly on his heel, Comitas Ormond stalks from the room without another word.

Throwing his cards down impatiently, Kendrick fixes Harken with a grim eye. "Despise the man as I do, Ormond makes a damned good point, Harken. What exactly are you playing at?"

"Why, at cards, of course, my dear Lord Halvard. And rather well, if I do say so myself." Harken lounges back in his chair, legs outstretched, eyeing the Lord of Goath lazily. "It's very gallant of you to defend my honor, Kendrick," he goes on, "but a wasted effort, nonetheless. I've no intention of attending your council meetings, whether as a result of Dirk's baiting or your misplaced displays of loyalty."

Kendrick stares at Harken. "I will never understand you," he says slowly. "After years of absence, finally you appear in society, and for what? To parade an unfortunate slave and taunt

Dirk? He's the most powerful man in the Indigo City, Harken. While you toy with him, your seat on the council remains empty, and Astria is starved of the Weavers it so desperately needs."

A muscle tightens in Harken's jaw, though his bland expression doesn't change. "Perhaps," he drawls in particularly clipped tones, "you might be better served asking more useful questions. Like how a Foolish exile, banished and slave braided by your own father no less, found his way through a Dark Rip and into an Astrian ballroom. I wonder," he adds, in a softer, but no less lethal tone, "how the old Lord of Goath would feel to know you now play politics at a council table with those who most likely facilitated that rather magical change in fortune?"

Kendrick's eyes have turned to flint. "And I would suggest, *my lord*," he says with cutting emphasis, "that if you have something to say that you do so, rather than playing damned cards." Shaking his head, he stands, nodding briefly toward me. "I wish you good fortune, Zaria," he says grimly. "I dare say you are going to need it." He stalks from the room without a backward glance.

Lupa sighs. "Really, Harken," she says, tossing off her glass of whiskey, "there are times when even I find your games tiresome." She eyes Harken resignedly as he beckons one of the footmen and murmurs something in his ear. The startled-looking footman scoops the pile of coin from the table and scurries from the room, casting backward glances as if expecting at any moment to be called to a halt.

"I see in some things you don't change, my lord." Lady Fearach shakes her head in exasperation. "I might just as well have handed my purse to the street urchins on my way in. And you shouldn't aggravate Kendrick." She gives Harken a reproving look. "He's a good man, and your games are quite wasted on him."

"Ah." Harken's eyes gleam. "But never on you, Lupa, which

is why I enjoy your company so very much." Rising, he comes over and extends his hand to me. "If I may borrow Zaria for a moment," he says politely to Everett, seeming amused when Lupa's son gives him a mulish look. "And speaking of charity," he goes on as we return to the table, closely followed by both Everett and Brooks, "you are quite the sensation tonight yourself, Lupa. An entire estate is no mean gift." Harken hands me a glass of lavenade. "Albeit a safe one, given Helfrach will undoubtedly be back in your hands before next year's Revels. How many landlords has it been, now? The last held the castle for less than a month, I believe."

"Ah, Harken." Lupa shakes her head, though she's smiling. "I would give my finest wolves to hear the Breezes you do. I might ask, though, that you keep that particular piece of information to yourself, at least until the Revels are done." She tilts her head at Everett. "Helfrach is the price of my son being named head of the Fire Guard." Her smile fades. "Unfortunately, it seems even appointments on my own estate must be approved by the council these days."

"And the gold?" Harken doesn't react to her comment about the council. "'Tis not like you to be so free with your coin, Lupa."

It's Everett who answers. "I imagine that you heard of the Paladin's ship that was wrecked in an unseasonable storm last month. It was carrying taxes to the Indigo City. A dreadful tragedy, obviously." He drains his glass of whiskey, a dark glint in his eye. "But laws are clear. Any wreckage that washes up on the shores of the Weald is ours to plunder as we see fit."

"Ah." Harken's sardonic smile turns to one of genuine amusement. "Exceptionally well played, young wolf." Everett looks begrudgingly gratified at the compliment.

"That's more than enough foreplay, Harken, even for you." Lupa regards him through narrowed eyes. "Why don't you ask whatever it is you want from me?" The salon has cleared, leaving only our small circle within earshot.

Harken takes a mouthful of whiskey. "My slave," he says slowly, "wishes to enter the Maverick's Race."

Brooks raises his eyebrows. "You do know, Harken, that slaves are not permitted to enter the Maverick's Race?"

"Everybody knows that." Harken smiles silkily. "It is one of the reasons that Caspian, Foley, and Sereia conspired to ensure Arkady won the Braid Race in the Seam."

Lupa's eyes narrow. "You're certain of this?"

Everett snorts and exchanges a derisive glance with Brooks. "You don't need to convince us."

My eyes meet Harken's, and he gives me a slight nod. I turn to Lupa. "Harken and I both heard them planning it."

"But why?" Curiosity flickers in Lupa's eyes as they move between Harken and me. "What do they mean by it?"

"Ah." Harken raises his glass to her. "That, my dear Lupa, is one of many questions. Caspian and Foley's intentions appear straightforward enough; they want this year's rich prize. Sereia's motives, however, are rather more mysterious."

Lupa looks thoughtful. "Then the Paladins have an interest in this Arkady?"

"Perhaps." Harken shrugs. "Or perhaps there are others at play. Either way, when Arkady came through that Rip, he tried to shoot at Zaria. Maybe she was simply in the wrong place at the wrong time." He tilts his head. "And maybe not."

"Dreaver's Tells!" Brooks exclaims, clearly horrified. "That Fool *shot* at you?"

"And then did his damnedest to leave you dead in the Seam," says Everett, his face darkening.

"Ah." Harken's eyes gleam. "I believe you begin to understand why Zaria might wish to exact her revenge on Race Day."

"But meanwhile," says Everett slowly, staring at Harken with a hard expression, "you intend to parade her around the Revels in that slave braid. Like some kind of bait." His mouth twists in distaste.

His reaction is so like my own that I feel an almost irrepressible urge to laugh.

Brooks gives a low whistle. "Dreaver take it, but you play a dark game, Harken." He shakes his head in reluctant admiration.

"It is what I am famous for, is it not?" Harken's tone is deceptively light, but I wonder if it is only me who noticed the rather dangerous flash in his eyes at Everett's words. He turns to Lupa. "Your son Everett has won that Race twice. Brooks here has come close every year. And you once won it yourself."

"Ah, Harken. You could charm the birds from the trees." Lupa's eyes begin to sparkle. "I take it you wish to co-opt my assistance in this little scheme of yours?" I have the impression she is enjoying herself immensely.

Harken shifts infinitesimally, so we are suddenly close enough that when he inclines his head, I can sense his heat on my skin. A thrill of excitement races down my spine, whether from the prospect of the Race or Harken's nearness, I'm not certain. Despite there being no impropriety at all in the way we're standing, every breath of his touches the bare skin of my shoulder, and I'm almost painfully aware of his lean, hard body so close to my own.

"Zaria could have no better coaches," he says evenly, though I note he doesn't look at Everett as he speaks.

Lupa's eyes rest on my braid. "I take it she will be freed in time to race?" Everett's lips purse in disapproval as Harken gives a curt nod. Lupa's eyes move between the two with some amusement, then shift back to look me up and down in frank assessment. "You mean to enter the Maverick's Race, then, girl?"

"I don't mean to enter it." I meet her eyes squarely. "I mean to win it."

"Ha!" Lupa hits her hands together as if I've told a great jape, her eyes gleaming. Brooks whoops aloud, then looks about furtively when Harken shoots him a quelling glance. Lupa nods at me. "Have Harken bring you to the Fire Hall. Best if we train you away from prying eyes, I think."

"As you might imagine," Harken says, "this particular Breeze is one I wish kept very close." He fixes Brooks and Everett with a stern eye. "Am I understood?" The two of them nod, Brooks fervently and Everett with a more resentful acquiescence. "Excellent." Harken puts out his arm to me. "Now come, slave," he murmurs, in a voice that sends a thrill down my spine. Lupa looks between us sharply, her eyes narrowing.

"It's time for you to meet a queen."

CHAPTER 37

ZUMI

I descend the stairs increasingly uncertain of exactly what the game has become. Harken touches the base of my spine fleetingly as he turns me toward the dais. I feel the almost delicious thrill of his nearness, but I am also disconcerted. I initially thought our game an intensely private one. Now the perimeters are beginning to feel uncertain and Harken himself increasingly unpredictable. Harken has repeatedly said that he doesn't involve himself in Indigold affairs. And yet his behavior tonight implies, if not actual involvement, certainly more interest than what he might claim. I'm beginning to suspect that despite his protestations, Harken may be more interested in the world he purports to disdain than he cares to admit.

The queen's throne seems at first glance to be made of pale driftwood. As we near the dais, I realize it's ivory, Woven long ago into an intricate cross pattern. High on the back, towering even over the queen's elaborate coiffure, is a great pearl shell, into which has been carved the Indigold Cup. The serpent ripples on the shell, creating a spiraling optical illusion that's hard to look away from.

"My Lord Harken." The queen gives him a rather reproachful smile. "You've caused quite the savage scandal at my Revel." She casts her eyes sideways, to where a glowering Comitas Ormond, his son Foley, Caspian, and Arkady eye us with palpable hostility.

If Harken's goal is to set a cat among the pigeons, I think, my skin crawling under their scrutiny, *he has certainly achieved it.*

"Prudence." Harken steps forward and kisses the queen's hand, holding it a little longer than necessary. "Forgive me. I did not mean for my games to cause you distress."

He means it, I realize. His manner implies a level of intimacy between him and Prudence that I hadn't imagined. The queen's deep amethyst eyes soften.

"It has been too long since you graced our city, Harken."

"I doubt many here would agree," Harken says dryly.

"If you never allow society a chance to know you," Prudence reprimands him gently, "you can hardly complain when they choose to believe the worst. And I think we can both agree that this evening's display has been particularly provocative." Her gaze rests pointedly on the slave braid at my neck. Arching her eyebrows at Harken, she turns kind eyes to me. "My dear." She smiles. "Rest assured we are not all so terrible as Harken undoubtedly paints us to be."

I note her unspoken assumption that Harken himself is not terrible, one that so far seems to be shared by many of those he has introduced me to—Marissa, Lupa, and now Prudence.

"Your Majesty." I make my best curtsy, though I suspect the gesture entirely lacks the grace Shimi or Neoma might have given it.

"Prudence, please." She waves me to my feet. "I'm an honorary queen at best, these days. Kept simply to be rolled out on ceremonial occasions." She turns to Harken. "Perhaps it's time you told me your purpose in coming here tonight."

"Zaria." Harken touches my shoulder lightly. "There's a

juggler at the rear of the ballroom." He turns me gently under the guise of pointing it out, though I know his purpose. I feign fascination as Harken murmurs, "You were once a priestess of the isle, Prudence. You also knew all the Weavers who served your husband. Do you recognize the hand that made this zumi?"

His fingertips skim the lotus and serpent dagger on my back, his touch as intoxicating as Darkwine.

"It is the finest work." I turn back to find Prudence slowly shaking her head. "With all the subtlety and skill of the isle. But there were so many priestesses used and discarded at the Kraken court, and I myself was imprisoned for so much of that time, that all I can say for certain is that it is likely priestess Woven." She smiles at me sadly. "I wish I could tell you more, child. Tragically, too many of my sisters were lost in the Kraken's attempts to produce perfection." She presses my hand. "I will say that whoever wrought this on your back must have cared for you a great deal. Every thread of that beautiful zumi was Woven in love. Whatever Shadow Bargain was made to get you out of Astria, I imagine it was done to keep you safe."

Having never hoped for either answers nor explanations of my origins, I'm surprised by a sudden rush of emotion at Prudence's words. The way she speaks of the lost priestesses brings home to me the heartbreak our unknown mothers must have known, the danger they undoubtedly faced in seeing my siblings and me safe. I smile, not trusting myself to speak, and withdraw my hands before she can see my emotion.

"My dear Prudence!"

Feivel? I freeze at the familiar voice. *It can't be.* I'm almost scared to turn around. Though I knew Feivel was coming to Astria to attend the council, meeting him here feels like an improbable convergence of two separate realities: the struggle to survive in the dark alleys and poverty of the Seam, and the strange game Harken and I are playing in the glittering world of the Indigold.

Despite his habitually harried air, Feivel beams as he kisses the queen's hand. "Time cannot dim your beauty, Prudence."

"Oh, Feivel." Prudence taps his arm fondly with her fan. "Your company is always a highlight of the Revels."

"You flatter me. And I see you've met my favorite pupil." Feivel grasps my hands, and I cling to them, his kind face swimming in front of my eyes. His gentle hands instantly recall the precious, stolen hours spent in the rear of the tapest, sheltered from the harsh world beyond by his unfailing goodwill.

Prudence looks between us in surprise. "You know one another?"

"Feivel taught my siblings and me our letters when we were children." I manage to get the words out, though my voice is slightly hoarse. "He taught all the orphans in the Seam. Fed us, too, more often than not."

"Ah." Feivel dismisses me with a wave. "Zaria was a terrible student." He winks at Prudence. "Far more interested in racing carricks and using her sword than in Astrian politics."

Harken, leaning by a nearby pillar, makes a disparaging noise. "I would consider that a sign of rather exceptional intelligence." His dark eyes shift between Feivel and me with disquieting scrutiny.

Feivel glares at him. "I imagine," he says tartly, "it is too much to hope that Kendrick might have convinced you to grace the council with your presence during your stay?" He nods to where Kendrick is talking to Gareth, the weak-faced Paladin Consul, and another, taller man with austere features who I can only see in profile. Beside them Sereia is staring at us, her vivid emerald eyes dark with spite.

"Hope is a dangerous thing, Feivel." Harken's eyes rest on Sereia. All trace of his former intimacy with Prudence has fled, his glittering mask and contemptuous smile firmly back in place. "I doubt any of you should enjoy it very much," he says, his sardonic drawl particularly pronounced as Kendrick breaks away from the group and approaches us, "should I ever choose to make my presence felt on that council."

"Until you do," Kendrick says coldly, "very little is likely to alter in Astria." He glances pointedly at Sereia, then back to Harken. "Though many things may well grow a great deal worse."

"That," says Harken lightly, "sounds very much like a problem for you, Kendrick." Turning away pointedly, he begins a murmured conversation with Prudence that clearly excludes the rest of us.

Kendrick, looking resigned rather than annoyed, turns to me. "And are you enjoying the capital?" he asks politely, once again conversing for all the world as if I were just another lady in the ballroom, rather than a slave in the company of the Savage King.

I answer his questions, but over his shoulder, I'm watching Harken. His eyes roam the crowd as they have all evening, but this time they settle on a particular face: the tall man whose profile I saw earlier. He has a rangy, powerful build and auburn hair clipped meticulously short. He turns toward us as if pulled by some invisible force, and when his eyes meet Harken's, the current between them is filled with such potent emotion it momentarily takes my breath away. I have the impression of deep-set eyes that might be green and an aquiline nose that gives him a rather hawkish look, but so fleeting is their glance that I might have imagined it. The other man turns abruptly away before I can gain any real insight, striding from the ballroom almost as Harken himself might. By the time Harken turns to answer a question from Prudence, his own face is inscrutable once more.

"Who is that man?" I ask Kendrick abruptly, nodding at the tall figure disappearing through the doors.

"A Weaver named Torsten," says Kendrick as he follows my eyes. "He's the Indigold Weaver on the council. Comitas

Ormond's personal adviser." He lowers his voice. "I shouldn't mention his name in present company, if I were you." Kendrick frowns at the doors through which Torsten just left. "I'm rather surprised he dared show his face, knowing Harken would be here."

I'm absolutely certain it is Torsten's face for which Harken has been searching all night. *He suspects him of being behind Arkady's presence here*, I think, though why, I don't know. I'm trying to think of a way to ask Kendrick when I overhear a snatch of conversation that makes me turn slightly, straining to make out Prudence's low voice.

"I don't know why he came, Harken. He never attends the Revels." She puts a hand on Harken's arm in an almost comforting gesture. "But I hate to see you dwell on old enmities. I had hoped that your attendance tonight might mark a new beginning."

She's talking about Torsten. I'm quite certain of it.

"You have always been too kindhearted, Prudence." Smiling grimly, Harken gently twists free of her grasp. "But don't waste your hopes on me. I'm quite beyond them, I assure you."

I turn back before he notices me watching, to discover that Kendrick, too, appears to have been listening. "I sometimes think," he says, almost to himself, "that Astria might have been better served if Harken had simply dispatched that damned Weaver during his rampage after the War."

I'm desperate to ask what he means, but Harken's approach prevents my question. Kendrick steps back and says in a more public tone, "It has been a pleasure, Zaria. I hope you enjoy the Season of Revels, for as long as you remain in our city." He eyes Harken rather dourly. "However long your master decrees that might be, of course." There's no mistaking his disapproval.

Harken, however, merely smiles coldly in acknowledgment. "My compliments, Prudence, on a spectacular evening." He glances briefly at me as he makes a gallant bow, and I take the hint.

"Thank you," I say to Prudence, meaning it. "It was lovely to meet you." She presses my hand kindly as Lupa, Brooks, and Everett join us, Feivel at their side.

Feivel hugs me, touching my cheek briefly. "I hope to see you soon." He meets my eyes. "I haven't seen your siblings yet," he says quietly, "but if I do, I will tell you. I promise."

I nod, swallowing the lump in my throat, then turn to bid farewell to each of the small group in turn. Everett leans gallantly over my hand. "I really will look forward to training you," he murmurs, holding it longer than he should and casting me a wicked look. I roll my eyes and he grins, winking conspiratorially. I bite my lip to stop myself laughing.

"My dear Harken." Opening her fan, Prudence eyes Everett and me over the top of it, her eyes brimming with mischief. "I suspect you may have competition."

Lupa coughs into her glass of whiskey, and even Kendrick looks mildly amused. Brooks is openly laughing.

Harken casts his eyes skyward. "I think," he murmurs in my ear, "that we've created more than enough scandal for one night, little criminal."

CHAPTER 38

URCHINS

I sleep uneasily and wake tangled in the sheets, my body hot and my mind restless.

When I venture downstairs, I'm informed by a typically harried Hegal that Harken has already left for the day. I strongly suspect Harken's absence is connected to the encounter, no matter how fleeting, with Torsten. I hoped he might confide in me during the intimacy of our gondola ride home last night. Instead Harken made only lighthearted conversation before bidding me a courteous good evening as soon as we reached the palace landing, leaving me intrigued and frustrated in equal parts.

Given the almost vicious emotion I witnessed between Harken and Torsten, not to mention Kendrick's comments, the two clearly share a turbulent history. But given the stark warnings I've been given about prying into Harken's past, it seems reckless to start doing exactly that. I spent a sleepless night consciously avoiding the temptation of seeking answers in the braid connection.

I'm relieved when Gemory informs me we are going upriver to Fire Hall, Lupa's city residence. I'm grateful to be turning my thoughts toward the Race and away from the mystery of Harken's past.

"You look peaked." Gemory eyes me from beneath an elaborately embroidered parasol as Mantas poles the gondola through the canals to the Fire Hall. "Restless night?"

I turn away from the suggestive golden eyes. "I drank too much lavenade," I mutter.

"Harken must have drunk from the same barrel." Gemory twirls the parasol with an annoyingly smug smile. "His endless pacing of corridors quite kept me from my rest."

I toy briefly with the idea of questioning Gemory, but instinct warns me not to take the risk, and I'm relieved when they drop the subject of Harken. The gondola travels further north, until the canal narrows and buildings give way to sloping green banks and lush fields. Finally, a copse of dark trees appears, several chimneys poking up in its midst. Mantas draws the gondola up to a small wooden dock, where Everett and Brooks are waiting. The Fire Hall is on an isolated bend of the river, tucked into a hollow far distant from any other estate.

"I have matters to discuss with Lupa." Gemory waves the parasol at the two Mavericks in a vaguely threatening manner. "I'll be watching you two. Treat Zaria with respect, or I'll have Harken's storm dragon eat you both."

"Does he really have a storm dragon?" Brooks looks distinctly impressed. "I thought that was a rumor."

"When speaking of Harken," Gemory says with an amused smile, "I've always found it wise to assume every rumor true." Leaving us with the disturbing images they no doubt meant to provoke, Gemory strolls up the bank.

"Well, that's terrifying." Everett casts me a wry glance. "Harken does approve of you being here, doesn't he?" I do a good impersonation of laughter, rather than actually answering the question, which seems to work. Talking over one another in their eagerness to boast about previous Races, Brooks and

Everett lead me toward a branch of the river that wends behind the vast manor house. A table has been set up in anticipation of our visit, with water flasks, cakes, and other easy to eat foods.

Training is clearly a way of life at Fire Hall.

"First," Everett says, gesturing to an array of sleek vessels beneath an ancient towering oak, "the racing gondolino." He pulls one out to show me. "They're narrower and deeper than a normal gondola. They come in all shapes, some bent up at the ends like a banana, others low at either end, like this one. There's endless debate over what size is faster. Competitors spend months preparing them, fitting them with all manner of weapons—spiked balls, spears."

"Everett even tried a flamethrower, one year." Brooks grins as Everett throws a cake at his head. "Needless to say, it fizzled."

"Not before it singed Caspian's hair, which was largely the point." Everett glares at him. "Anyway. The gondoliers are called Mavericks, a leftover from the bad old days, when those who competed were either peasants or Indigold nobles who'd severed ties with the house they served in order to compete for a title of their own—or, in a Royal year, for the crown. They were known as Mavericks, since they had no fixed allegiance." He nods at the gondolino. "Climb in," he says amiably. "The rules come later. Let's see what you can do."

An hour later, I'm thoroughly wet, and all trace of formality between the three of us has utterly disappeared.

"No, not like that!" Hooting with laughter, Everett pulls me out of the water and back into the narrow gondolino, where I land in an inelegant sprawl. "Don't ever seek to topple another Maverick at the expense of your own safety. The gondolino is all you have. The moment you fall from it, your race is over."

Panting, dripping wet, I prop my knee against the cavalo, the raised arch used to brace against while rowing. "Give me that oar."

Everett, lounging against the stern, throws it, then trips me so I land for the umpteenth time that day on my back, cracking my head against the cavalo as I do.

"Your first lesson," Brooks says, grinning from the gondolino beside me. "Be aware of everything in your gondolino, all the time."

Everett nods. "I've seen more than one Maverick undone by a carefully thrown stick or piece of rope."

"She needs to learn balance," Brooks said.

"Rubbish." Everett frowns. "She needs to learn to fight."

"Right now," I say, rowing toward the bank, "she needs water." Seizing the water flask from the bank, I pull the cork with my teeth and drink greedily, rubbing my head. "So, back to the Race. How, exactly, does it work?"

"Ah." Everett leans forward in the stern and clasps his hands. "Every Maverick must row their own gondolino with a single oar, just as you see the gondoliers do. The course is Woven to alter every year and revealed only when competitors gather at the start, so it's impossible to practice the turns beforehand. Spectators are advised of the course as soon as the field have gathered, and the race for positions is almost as fierce as the race itself."

Brooks grins. "The street urchins in the city make a fortune from securing the best vantage points and selling them off to the highest bidder. Servants in Indigold houses might sleep in warm beds every night, but none of them know the alleys, bridges, and canals of the city as the street children do. One of those children once earned enough selling places to buy themself a gondolino and compete. He won that year and now lives in a lovely villa in the River Lands." He nods to the north.

"How wonderful." I can imagine that triumph better than they might imagine.

"Don't be seduced by the pretty picture he paints." Everett gives me a warning look. "The Maverick's Race takes a lot of skill and is utterly ruthless. Competitors must make three circuits. On each circuit, the course will pass beneath two bridges, and each time competitors pass the bridges, they must pluck one of the ribbons from it and tie it to their oar. The bridges are where it gets violent. Spectators hang over them and try to beat the competitors off, prevent them from getting a ribbon. Meanwhile the competitors are busy fighting one another. It's made more difficult by the fact that there are never enough ribbons, which means anyone too slow to grasp one is eliminated."

"The organizers always ensure that the first turn is brutal," chimes in Brooks, his eyes gleaming with recollection. "Nerves and haste on that corner clears the field. Then the last lap is particularly violent. Anything goes. Mavericks have been known to leap from their own gondolino into another's, if they think it is faster, and if they think they can beat the other person in a fight. The fights aren't lighthearted, by the way. People die every year."

"Die!" I look at them in astonishment. For some reason, I always imagined that kind of barbarity reserved for slaves like me, in the Seam.

"Oh, people die, all right." Brooks's face sobers. "The Indigo City might look rich, from the palaces and manor houses of the Revels. But there are plenty of hungry people in it who would happily put a knife in their neighbor if they thought it might win them lands and title. And the prize is always rich. The Indigold nobles who donate the prizes like to show one another how much wealth they can afford to lose."

"I see." I've grown up on tales of the Braid Race. I know every possible way to cheat death, or bring it, on that old, deadly circus track. But I'm a stranger here, and everything about this Race is new, from the gondolinos to the obstacles. "What can give you the advantage?" I ask. "What are the downfalls?"

"There are plenty, of both." Everett plucks a stick from the boughs overhead and stabs the cavalo with it as he talks. "First, you need to learn how to fight—but in your case, with a blade, not an oar. Some of Astria's most hardened warriors enter. You can't hope to match them in strength, so it's skill you will need." He grins. "Last year the Race was won by a Stitched Man who had glamoured a great sea whale to help tow him. At least four corpses were floating by the time he was done."

"You can do that?" I ask, taken aback. "Use animals?"

"Shifting into an animal yourself is strictly forbidden, of course. Beyond that competitors may glamour any creature they choose." Everett shrugs. "But the Race is held on water, and sea creatures are notoriously fickle. After Roark's years, most are wary of using anything from the depths." His mouth curls. "The fear of the Kraken remains," he says quietly.

A leaf drifts down, followed by another. I didn't grow up in Hiraeth for nothing; I glance up into the boughs above, just in time to catch a glimpse of the urchins shimmying out along the branches. "Hey!" I call, and a shower of leaves fall as they scurry away.

"I'm so sorry." Frowning, Everett comes out of the gondolino. "I'll have some of our Guard track them down."

"No, please."

Brooks and Everett turn to me in surprise. The threads of my old life twist uneasily with the new. "You mentioned earlier that street urchins secure the best vantage points." I force myself to speak in a calmer tone, reminding myself to have patience. It's not Brooks and Everett's fault they didn't grow up in alleys, scrapping for coin. *They've never known what it is*, I remind myself, *to need hope.*

"They're no threat," I say. "They're only here because they want to know as much as they can about the competitors."

"And nobody is supposed to know you're a competitor." Brooks steps out of his gondolino, frowning. "I'll have them whipped—"

"No, you will not," I say fiercely, leaping out of my own gondolino and facing him on the bank. "Don't you dare."

Taken aback, Brooks stares at me. "They might tell Arkady," he says. "Ruin Harken's plans."

"I don't care if they do." My anger takes me by surprise. It makes me tremble, and it makes me reckless. I could never afford to feel anger during my life in the Seam. Anger is a privilege, one not permitted to either slaves or street urchins. Now it rips through me with a fury that is almost frightening. "You won't hunt them down," I say tightly, "and you most certainly won't whip them. They've followed us all the way from the city out of curiosity, and because they might make a coin, or gain an advantage, if they learn something others don't know. They've probably run the entire way here. If we don't want them to betray us," I say, raising my voice enough to be heard throughout the surrounding trees, "all we have to do is ask." I gesture to the table. "We won't eat all of that, will we?"

Everett shakes his head, watching me curiously. "No," he says slowly, "I suppose we won't."

"Well, they will." I glance around at the old oaks, grinning as I see the telltale movement where the boughs bend. "Let's go up to the house," I say loudly. "But leave the food here. I might want to train later."

I glance back at the river when we near the back door.

All the food from the table is gone.

Smiling to myself, I go inside to speak with Lupa.

CHAPTER 39

DAWN

*I*t's dawn, and I'm training with my new sword.

The early mornings are mine. A time when the city sleeps, and mist drifts over the canals beyond the Water Palace. The small stone landing below my bedchamber has become my favorite place to train. I keep a racing gondolino tied there in which I practice on the days I can't get to Fire Hall, and in the early mornings, like now.

I've developed something of a routine since I began training.

Given that Everett and Brooks are, as Marissa put it, the most dreadful Mavericks, they rarely emerge from Brooks's city apartments before noon, and usually even then still pale and fragile from the previous night's antics. We meet most days in the early afternoon, out at Fire Hall.

Mornings I spend in the map room, with whoever is free to answer my questions, usually Gemory or Andras. Occasionally, when he has time, Feivel.

The evenings belong to Harken.

After sunfall, I swap my tunic and trousers for one of the gowns Darcy sends. I meet Harken in the central courtyard, and Mantas takes us by gondola to whatever event we are attending.

But despite the seemingly endless round of glittering balls, banquets, and everything in between, the easy intimacy of our first days has disappeared entirely. Harken is unfailingly courteous and always polite—at least to me. To the nobility of the Indigo City, he is alternately contemptuous, provocative, and at times, downright rude. It takes several events for me to realize that the easy manners he displayed at the first Revel were a singular effort. A calculated means to gain Lupa's trust, discover what Prudence knew of my zumi, and ensure the Indigo City knew me as Harken's slave. Since that night, he has brought to every event a cold, almost clinical detachment. Our appearances are inevitably brief, just long enough for Harken to scan the crowd, presumably for Torsten's face. He hasn't offered any further information about what he has discovered, or what he might suspect Torsten's game to be. Other than polite inquiries about my training, Harken rarely discusses anything with me.

And he shouldn't have to. Balancing on the cavalo, I cut the air with my blade, spinning under an imaginary attack. *You're training for the Race. Harken is doing . . . whatever it is Harken does.*

I slice the air almost viciously.

He didn't promise to give you updates as part of the bargain, I tell myself sternly. *Especially when his concerns are clearly connected to some old conflict.* The narrow gondolino rocks precariously. I breathe, steady it, and jump for the imaginary ribbon. The gondolino nearly upturns entirely when I land, but I consider any landing a triumph. I've fallen into the water so many times my hair seems permanently wet.

Take what you want, and pay for it. I say the mantra over and over as I move through my training routine.

Take what you want—thrust—*and pay for it*—slice.

I pause, panting, leaning on the high stern of the gondolino. My fingers inch toward the braid, and I clench them firmly away.

It's taken all my willpower, but I've refused to allow myself the guilty pleasure of using the braid to spy on Harken. He is not only fulfilling his part of our bargain; he has surpassed any hopes I might have had. Everett, Brooks, and on occasion, when she has time, Lupa, are the best Maverick experts I could have. I want for nothing in the Water Palace, except my siblings, whom Harken can hardly be expected to provide. Given that I have no reason to believe Harken won't free me, using the braid connection simply to satisfy my own curiosity crosses an unmistakable ethical line. The Dreaver on my shoulder might whisper that I have a right to know of anything that might place me in danger or affect the outcome of our bargain. But my life isn't one that has allowed for self-deception. I know that I'm not curious about Harken's past because of fears for my own safety or that he might renege on our bargain.

I crave insight into Harken with the same hunger I do his starlight touch on my skin. That desire has as little to do with reason as my longing for his touch has to do with healing. *"Your presence makes me forget what I'm bound to,"* he said in Huxley's water chamber, *"and dream of things I have no right to."* His words torment me, not least because they echo a whisper in my own soul. The truth is that I hadn't realized the solace I took in our intimacy until after the ball, when I noticed the hole left by its absence. Although I still don't entirely understand his circumstances, the aching loneliness I sense behind his words is the same that I feel knowing that I can never be truly free so long as my siblings are not. It is the bittersweet resignation of freedom for the binds of responsibility and loyalty.

I've never known true intimacy of the soul. Even with Doron, I necessarily kept my innermost thoughts to myself. With Harken, however, I feel an uncanny understanding, as if he sees the loneliest, most hidden part of my soul and knows it even better than I do myself. That feeling of connection is headier than any dose of Darkwine, an addiction that keeps me awake at night and sends me here, to train at dawn, until my body is tired enough that I don't see Harken's indigo eyes every time I close my own.

I spin savagely in the gondolino, thrusting at an invisible foe. *Take what you want, and pay for it.* For perhaps the first time in my life, I understand why I might take the man, even if it means paying forever. *Perhaps*, I think, *I was wrong all this time. Perhaps it isn't love itself that is the greatest form of slavery, but rather the longing for it.* The thought grips my heart with a ferocity so startling I freeze in the gondolino, my sword midair, just as a shadow passes overhead.

I look up in time to see the first dawn rays flash from the brilliant underside of Huxley's wings. She's soaring high above, on her way back to her chamber, no doubt. I watch as she cups the breeze, angling to one side as she arcs lower. There's something unusual in her shape.

It's only when she flies closer that I realize Harken is on her back.

Huxley caws as she passes overhead, a low, sweet sound that I find unbearably poignant, no matter how many times I hear it. I sense in Huxley some of the displacement I feel myself, in this strange glittering world where nobody is what they seem and secrets lurk in every shadow.

I watch until Huxley disappears, then turn back to my training in an effort to quiet my unruly heart.

A few moments later, as the light begins to change, I feel the familiar frisson at my neck. I spin around in the gondolino to find Harken on the landing, watching me with a frown.

"Surely those wolves aren't teaching you the sword," he says abruptly in greeting. "A blade won't win you that Race."

"Oh?" I lean on the high, carved stern, facing him. "I thought you didn't concern yourself with Indigold matters, like the Race."

His eyes narrow. For a moment I half expect him to turn and stalk off, ignoring my questions as he does any of the Indigold matters he seems so determined to avoid. Instead he leaps into the gondolino, his booted feet finding purchase without any discernible difficulty. I gave up wearing shoes during training, not least because I spend so much time in the water. I'm mildly annoyed that he should balance so easily.

"Show me." He produces a blade from thin air. When I raise my eyebrows in surprise, he tilts his head with a faint smile. "Being me has its advantages."

I bite my lip.

"Careful." Shifting colors dance in his eyes, sending a thrill through me. "You almost smiled, then."

We spar, Harken spinning around me with mercurial ease. "Not like that," he says, easily dodging my thrust. "You might as well announce it with a banner. Or that." He grins, parrying another stroke. "And you won't have time for fencing, anyway." He leaps easily over my sweeping cut. "That move is at least more likely to be of use." He holds up a hand in an ameliorating gesture. "But you leave yourself exposed. I could grasp the blade, like this." Suddenly I am caught, my back against his chest, my sword in his hand, both of his arms locked about me. Heat races through me like a Hiraeth fire, lightning fast and breathtaking. "Once I have you like this," he murmurs in my ear, "there is no escape. Your race is over. Your life is mine, should I choose to take it."

He tosses the blades with one hand. They clatter onto the stone landing, but his arms don't move. One covers my upper chest, the gloved hand holding my shoulder. The other is firmly about my waist. I've never been so close to him, not even when he's healed me. I can barely breathe.

"Huxley found something on our flight this morning." The hand on my shoulder opens to reveal a deep purple, almost black flower. "It's a desert rose." His lips move to my other ear, so close I almost feel their caress. "It has petals like velvet." He trails the flower up my throat, its rich, cinnamon scent filling my senses. "Its scent reminds me of you."

My blood has slowed to a thick, heady pulse. The dawn mists gleam and swirl in the coming sun, glittering like a thousand diamonds.

Only they aren't dawn mists. They're Woven mists, behind which everything is imprisoned. Even Harken.

Especially Harken.

I bend at the knees and twist free in a sudden movement. I face Harken from the other end of the gondolino. I'm trembling, every sense afire. His glittering eyes are like the mists themselves, sunlight and sunfall in them at once.

"My life already is yours," I say quietly. My hands clench so tightly I can feel them cut into my skin. "Body and soul. Remember?"

Harken's eyes drop to the braid at my neck. His mouth stretches hard, and he makes a noise almost like a snarl.

"It's time that braid was gone." He raises his hand, and I feel the visceral, savage pull of freedom.

Then I think of the emotion in Harken's face when he looked at Torsten. Of the answers I don't have, and perhaps never will, once the braid comes off.

At least, that's what my rational mind thinks of. My heart clings to the intimacy of the braid connection as if it is light woven in darkness. My innermost soul has found in that connection a lifeline out of loneliness, whether real or imagined, and is reluctant to relinquish it.

Take what you want, and pay for it. I take a deep breath.

"Does that mean," I force myself to say, "that you know who helped Arkady and why?" Harken halts with his hand midair, searching my face. "Are you freeing me because you already have answers," I say, "or because whoever it is you seek has not taken the bait you offered?"

Harken's eyes narrow. "Does it matter?"

"It does," I say quietly, "if the answers affect me. Do they?" Reaching out, I cover his raised hand with my own and slowly draw it down. "What is it that you won't tell me, Harken?"

The mists swirl in his eyes, full of the secrets he won't share. "I thought freedom was all you wanted," he says roughly.

The braid on my neck writhes like the mists themselves, its frisson poignantly familiar. "I thought so, too," I whisper.

Harken's hand beneath mine clenches with a sudden ferocity, and the light flares in his eyes.

Then he leaps from the gondolino and is gone.

CHAPTER 40

HUNTED

*T*wo days later, I still haven't seen Harken.

It's late afternoon and I'm in my bedchamber. I trained earlier today at Fire Hall with Lupa and my new sword.

I should be happy.

My hands hover over the braid. *Don't*, I tell myself fiercely. Whatever it is I'm hoping to find, I've no right to use the braid connection to go looking. Far worse, I suspect I'm reaching for the visions because what I really want to do is reach for Harken himself.

And that scares me to the Dreaver's Tells and back again.

Take the man, and pay forever.

I play the scene in the gondolino over in my mind, as I have every hour since I saw him. *I just want to know the truth*, I tell myself. But what truth is it, exactly, that I'm hoping to find?

Whether it's Torsten or someone else who is behind Arkady's appearance in the Seam matters little to me, or to the bargain Harken and I made. Our encounter in the gondolino has only served to make me even more uncomfortably aware that my curiosity has much less to do with logical answers and much more to do with who Harken is.

But, I argue with myself, *something happened in that ballroom when he met Torsten*. That much I do know. In the brief moment of their encounter, the twisted smile and reluctant humor of the man I thought I was coming to know fled, replaced by a dark stranger I've seen only in my visions. He's been distant ever since.

Harken has left me no choice, I tell myself. *He's made it clear he won't talk about his past. If I want answers, I will have to go in search of them myself.*

I reach for the braid with the same relief an addict does Darkwine and fall willingly into the mists.

HARKEN IS SITTING *on tumbled rocks, staring over the sea into a distant storm.*

He still wears the black armor, the helmet that removes any humanity from his face. His eyes are dark, the storm swirling in their depths.

"Aren't you bored yet?"

The voice is as startling to me, in the vision, as it is to Harken, who leaps to his feet, face twisted in a ready snarl, eyes gleaming with violence.

"Oh, please." *Gemory is sitting barely paces from him, their face entirely unconcerned.* "You couldn't catch me even if you wanted to kill me, which I happen to know you have no desire to do."

Harken's eyes narrow. "You're a Shadow."

"How very observant." *Gemory's tone is dry.* "But then, I shouldn't imagine you have many opportunities to hone your conversational skills, locked away with all those demons behind your walls. Though I will say you've organized that court of yours with quite ruthless efficiency."

Harken stares at them. "What do you know of my court?" *He moves menacingly toward Gemory. "I would not advise you to test the shadowscyes behind the Woven mists."*

"As if you could possibly know when I do." Gemory looks amused rather than intimidated. "Your mists matter not at all to the House of Thread and Shadows, Lord Harken. But we keep our secrets close, never fear."

"Then what do you want?" Harken's tone is cold and utterly disinterested. "Out with it. I have business to attend to."

"Yet more demons?" Gemory raises an eyebrow. "You have the delightfully ruthless Andras and a small army of wranglers to do your bidding in such matters. I come to offer you a more interesting challenge."

Harken's eyes narrow, but he doesn't answer.

"I'm sure you are familiar with a certain Paladin Divine." Gemory glances sideways, taking in Harken's gleaming, furious eyes. "Yes," Gemory says calmly. "Quite. Well, it seems that Divine has developed a fondness for Serpent's Gold. He's also become rather adept in opening Dark Rips and has been searching them for a particular creature. One with very interesting gifts. It seems, however, that after finally discovering the creature, and cutting a Dark Rip to bring it through, our Paladin friend now finds himself unable to control it." Gemory meets Harken's eyes. "There is a storm dragon loose in Astria. And it needs your help."

The vision shifts, taking the rocks and Gemory away.

Now Harken is lying on a high cliff, clearly waiting for something. A moment later, a black silhouette appears high in the clouds, descending at a terrifying pace toward a village below. This is not the gentle, wide-eyed Huxley I've met in the water chamber. This storm dragon is a fierce killer, topaz eyes gleaming with fear and rage. She soars down like a deathly arrow from the sky, intent on a group of small children playing in a field. The children scatter, shrieking in fear, all but one small girl whose legs are too short to keep up. She stumbles and falls in the grass, her little face turned in terror toward the black-winged death coming toward her.

Huxley swoops in and rips the girl from the ground in one terrible stroke of her taloned paw. As the villagers watch in horror, she rises into the air again, eating the child in two great, ravenous bites as she goes. A piece of the girl's dress, all that is left of the child, flutters to the earth as Huxley flies away.

The vision shifts. Huxley lands atop a tapest in a distant city. Tearing the golden Astris from the roof as people cower in fear, she flies away with the gold between her paws, Harken following at a distance. The storm dragon takes the Astris to a scarred mountain cloaked in the acrid, sulfuric stench that marks a Dark Rip of terrible size. I know instinctively that this is the place she was brought into this world. Harken watches as Huxley lays the golden Astris lovingly on the black, scorched stone, a great tear rolling down her leonine features.

Time passes in the vision. Harken follows Huxley as Indigold and Weaver alike hunt her, trying to bring her down with their needles, swords, and spears.

He takes the Hydra *when she flies far out to sea to escape the hunters. He watches from behind his mists as she curls the air into terrible storms that throw the sea into chaos, killing the men in ships who have come in search of her. He follows again as she flies back to land, screaming her pain in a terrible yowling that sends terror through all who hear it.*

For months Harken studies her, watching as Huxley grows thinner and more desperate, retreating out to a small island at sea that she makes her own, filling it with all the gold and precious stones she can find. I can sense her terrible loneliness, her desire to recreate something of the home she no longer knows.

Harken watches as Huxley tries miserably to eat everything, from sea creatures to cattle to crops in the fields. He sees her grow sick and weak after these experiments, with a terrible, gnawing hunger that grows and grows until finally, mad with starvation, she sets out for another village, another helpless young girl. Harken sees her aware-ness, her knowledge of the pain in her actions, and her utter inability to do anything about it. Over time, the attacks on her become more sustained, her injuries more terrible, her life force slipping away, and still Harken watches.

The vision shifts again. Armored men approach the island by stealth, attacking the storm dragon with spear and sword. Huxley, terrified and bleeding, limps into the air, but her wing is broken, her body so weak she can barely summon the wind, let alone build a storm. The men advance on her with needles, casting thread after thread, and Huxley falls slowly to the earth, cawing in heartbroken defeat.

Then suddenly, Harken is there, black clad and infinitely more terrifying than the broken Huxley. Facing down the approaching men with ice-cold fury, he sweeps their needles away contemptuously.

The men, eyeing him in terror, fall to their knees, clearly antici-pating death. Harken stares down at them, and the savagery in his eyes fades, replaced by something less visceral, though no less lethal. "There's been enough killing," he says curtly. "The storm dragon belongs to my Savage Court. When I'm done with her, I'll come back to deal with your War."

He disappears, Huxley's broken body swirling away with him into the Woven mists.

CHAPTER 41

MOONBEAMS

*W*hen I wake, my heart is thudding slowly, tears still drying on my cheeks. The vision may not have answered my mind's questions, but it has, temporarily at least, sated the dark loneliness of my heart. The waxing moon is high, casting soft light over my room, but I know I won't sleep. I need to see Huxley.

I slip out of my bedchamber and follow the stairway down the tall brass doors.

Huxley's water chamber is a soft kaleidoscope lit by the moonbeams falling through the cuts in the high dome above. The strange, shifting colors come from coral gleaming beneath the water itself. No lanterns burn down here. It's a world of flickering shadows, the interplay of moonlight and water. Huxley must have sensed me coming. Her wide topaz eyes meet mine as I come down the stairs, and she caws softly in greeting.

I sit on the edge, my feet in the water, and Huxley croons as she rubs against me. She dips and dives playfully through the water, her wings flashing in the silvery light, darting away then coming back to me again.

"You're safe here, aren't you?" I smooth her sleek head,

feeling her wild heat under my hand. She makes a sweet noise, and for a moment I almost swear she's smiling.

"Yes, she is safe here." I spin around, heart thudding, to find Harken sitting atop the rocks beside the waterfall. "But she's also a captive."

"I didn't see you." I scramble to my feet. "I'll go."

"No." Harken leaps easily down and comes to stand nearby, but not too close. He's barefoot, his shirt unbuttoned over his breeches, hands deep in his pockets. The light casts deceptive shadows across his face. "I'm glad you're here."

"You are?" I tense, ready to flee at the slightest moment.

His half smile flashes in the darkness. "Yes. I am." He hesitates. "The Water Palace is your home. Or it is for now, at least. I wish you to feel as safe here as Huxley might, but I do not wish to keep you captive as she is." He stares past me, into the shadows. "Our recent encounter reminded me that so long as you wear that braid, this palace is no more than a prison—and I the master of it." He meets my eyes, though his are quite impossible to read. "I offered to unbraid you because even as a ruse, I find the role of slavemaster abhorrent." His face hardens. "Not for any other reason."

There is a certain stiffness to that last remark. *What other reason does he imagine?* I wonder.

"We made a bargain." I search his face, seeking a clarity that is hidden in the shadows. "If you haven't found the answers you seek, then—"

"You need not fear. I will honor my part." I'm about to deny I have any such concerns, but he cuts me off again. "I will continue to provide all you need for the Race."

"I'm sure you will, but—"

"I am unaccustomed to being much in public, just as I am to guests in my home." Harken continues brusquely, as if I haven't spoken. "Sometimes I lack the manners expected in such company. I fear that has regrettably been the case during the recent Revels, and then again, when I interrupted your training. I hope you will accept my apologies."

I nod uncertainly, unsure what exactly to say.

"I give you my word," Harken says quietly, "that I won't ever make you feel uncomfortable again."

I wonder why it is that his assurances should leave me feeling bereft, rather than comforted.

He nods at my braid. "Let me take that thing off."

Perhaps, had his words come before our encounter this morning, I might have seized the freedom he offers. But now it feels as if freeing me is Harken's way of placing more distance between us, not less. I have a cold suspicion that removing my braid is simply one step closer to removing me from his home. And once I am beyond the Woven mists, I fear I may never find my way behind them again.

That thought terrifies me in a way that even slavery never has.

"Wait." I'm clutching at threads I barely understand myself. "You said that Huxley was brought through a Dark Rip to search for the golden needle. Who was it who opened that Rip?"

"A Paladin Divine." Harken's tension is palpable. "Aided by a very old, very powerful Weaver."

Torsten? He didn't strike me as old, but then I know Weavers age differently.

"How did they open it?" I know I'm treading on fragile ground.

Harken's eyes narrow. "They used a very rare, very powerful knife. One forged with Serpent's Gold."

"That knife." I watch him closely. "Was it ever found, after the War?"

Despite the gloom, Harken's frown is unmistakable. There is a long silence, during which I sense he is debating how much to say. "Many such tools were recovered, after the War." Harken measures his words carefully.

"But not that one." I feel a growing sense of excitement. "That's why you stayed in the Seam, after Arkady came through. You were trying to find that knife—or whoever was wielding it." I try to think through all that has happened since. "If Arkady was brought here the same way Huxley was, then it's likely for a similar purpose." My mind is whirling, a great many threads trying to knit together. "But why would they think Arkady can get to the golden needle, when even you can't enter that Tower?"

"Why indeed." Harken's voice is studiedly neutral. "But none of this has anything to do with you, or with that braid on your neck."

"Yes, it does." He looks at me in surprise. "You say you want me to feel safe." My heart is thudding. If I previously stepped over an ethical line in my pursuit of the braid connection, I'm now firmly moving into the shadowy world of moral ambiguity, in which that line has been left far behind. "You have ensured that whoever holds that knife now sees me as a piece in their game. One so valuable that you claimed me as your slave rather than leave me in play." I feel a flash of satisfaction at his visible consternation. "Isn't that why you took me in the first place? To send a signal that I have value only you understand?"

"None of that matters now," Harken says roughly. "I can unbraid you—"

"And then what?" I take a step closer to him. "Like it or not, you have put a target on my back. Whoever holds that knife will likely come for me, even if it is just to satisfy their curiosity. So long as I'm your slave, I can't be taken. The braid is a bond, unbreakable so long as the words remain between us. While I wear it, you need only touch that knot at your neck to discover my whereabouts. So long as I wear this braid," I say softly, "I am safe, Harken." I desperately want to touch him, but his stance is rigid, every muscle tense, the lightning flashes in his eyes harder than I've ever seen them. "Don't you think whoever you are seeking knows that? If your suspicions are right," I say, "then the moment you unbraid me is when they will come."

He stares at me, his face gaunt. "You are safer out of this palace."

"Why?" I search his face. "Why would I be any safer unbraided and beyond the Woven mists? Better that I should play the role for which you took me in the first place, at least until we can discover who it is that holds that knife and what they want."

I know I'm playing a dangerous game. *But then this game has been dangerous from the start.*

"The last two people who held that knife are dead." Harken's voice is harsh, wrenched from somewhere deep inside him. "I hung the Paladin Divine on the gates of the abbey."

I'm suddenly back in the tapest, listening to Feivel tell me about the Savage King.

"The Paladin Weaver, I unthreaded." Despite Harken's almost menacing expression, I don't look away, and I don't flinch. "I wrapped his body in his own immortal threads. Then I hung him beside the Divine, so the Weaver could look upon his friend for so long as his eyes might see." His voice is flat, cold, and utterly devastating. "I made very certain," he says, eyes gleaming in the darkness, "that the Weaver was still watching when the birds picked the last flesh from the Divine's rotting corpse. That is the man you are trusting to hold your slave braid," he says hoarsely, his eyes no more than fathomless, dark pits. "And to keep you safe."

Harken's face is barely a breath from my own. *He wants me to run,* I think. *He's trying to scare me, just as Feivel did. As Garrick did.*

"I trust you." I meet his eyes squarely. "And I already knew that story."

"This is a bad idea." Harken inhales sharply and turns away from me. He strides to the stairs, taking them in a series of leaps, then pauses at the heavy brass doors. "You once accused me of being a savage." His head is bent, his voice low and rough. "I told you then that much is true. I also told you never to forget it." He glances back, his eyes hooded. "I suggest, little criminal, that you do not."

The doors close behind him, and I am alone in the darkness.

CHAPTER 42

LIBRARY

I'm disappointed but not surprised when I don't see Harken for the next few days. I train hard, avoid even looking at the temptation of my braid, and try not to worry that I might have encroached so far into Harken's forbidden world that he has simply disappeared into the depths of the Savage Court forever.

Fortunately for me, Feivel has had some time to visit the Water Palace. I've taken advantage of his presence to learn all I can, on a range of topics.

"Pleased as I am that you are taking such an interest in your lessons," he says now, glancing at me across the map table, "forgive me if I wonder why I am teaching you needle lore when you still wear that." He nods at the braid in distaste. He's not the first one to make pert comments. Despite it being my idea to keep the braid on, it's becoming increasingly difficult to maintain the facade of being a slave. I particularly dislike lying to Feivel.

"I hope Harken knows what he's about, with this game of his." He shakes his head disapprovingly. "Given the Dark Rips that opened in the Seam before you left, I should have thought he had more important things to worry about than causing a scandal at the Revels." He seems unusually agitated, constantly glancing at his pocket watch.

"Is something wrong?" I think it best not to comment on the Dark Rips.

Feivel shoots me an apologetic smile. "It isn't your fault, child. But if I am honest, I very much need to see Foras at the library. Would it be possible for us to continue our lesson as we walk?"

I'm rather taken aback. I've only left the Water Palace in Harken's company or to train at Fire Hall. I'm not sure how Harken will feel about me passing through the mists without his permission. But he isn't here to ask, and I don't wish to delay Feivel, so I keep my concerns to myself.

Shortly afterward, Mantas is poling us through the canals to a different part of the city. There is more parkland here, and the buildings are large and very old, nearly all with the golden Astris on their roofs. Many are shuttered, and others are in a state of disrepair. "The Coronastrian Halls of Learning," Feivel says as we slip past them. "Not as busy as they once were, of course, now that the Paladins have begun building halls of their own." His mouth purses, and I can see the frustration and pain he clearly doesn't want to openly express. "Each is designed according to its subject." He points at a building shaped like scales. "The Law Halls," he says. "And those, of course, are the Salving Halls." He points to a rich green building in the shape of a twelve-pointed lotus. Feivel's eyes linger on it lovingly.

"You like the Salving Halls," I say, watching him as we pass.

"Yes." Feivel glances at me, his ravaged face oddly beautiful with remembrance. "Many of my personal memories may be gone, but I can still recall exactly how the Salving Halls smelled. I think I might have liked to have been a salver, had I not ended up serving the Coronastrian Tapest. I've always thought the art of salving to be the highest of callings. Ah." He nods at a tall building in gleaming white stone, designed to resemble a tied scroll standing on one end. "Here we are." We follow a spiraling pathway into the scroll, which is made of various wings, none of which are open. What I now recognize as shimmering Woven mist hovers over all the doorways, effectively rendering them locked. At the center of the spiral, we come to what is clearly the public reception area. There is a long line, dealt with by a small team of very harried-looking demons overseen by Foras, whom I've previously seen in the Water Palace talking to Harken. Foras has a forehead set in a perpetual frown and four quills hovering in the air around him, marking four separate parchment checklists.

"Dreaver's Tells," he greets Feivel irritably. "Does Harken have any idea how busy it is here, with Indigold from every corner of Astria here for the Revels? The Paladins might have their own halls, but they don't have a library. Now it isn't just the Coronastrian masters who come here for materials, but the Paladins too. Hello, dear," he greets me absently, not waiting for my answer before continuing. "Without access to the Great Library in the Lotus Court, and Weavers to run it, we're doing everything by hand—and I'm only one demon, Feivel! With a handful of creatures I've trained straight out of Dark Rips! Can't you talk to him?"

Feivel makes sympathetic noises, but having already heard both of them plead this exact matter with Harken on a number of occasions, I know his words are empty comfort. "Now," I hear Feivel say, when Foras pauses in his exasperated complaints, "I came looking for a particular book. I can do the search myself," he goes on hastily.

I stop listening and look about instead. It's a rare treat to be out in the city during the day. I wave to a handful of street urchins who are wending through the waiting masters, selling everything from cups of water to sliced fruit. They wave back, giggling. One of them mimics falling off a gondola, and I laugh aloud. I've become accustomed to their curious eyes and hushed laughter as I train, and Everett has become resigned to laying out a rich table of food that mysteriously vanishes at the end of every session.

"Zaria!"

I'm startled to hear my name, especially when I realize who it is—and who is with him.

"Leo." The Paladin Divine from the Seam looks as nervous as ever, his face pale over the enormous pile of books he's carrying. Whether his nerves are caused by meeting me or due to the tall, austere-featured man standing slightly behind him, I don't know. "I didn't know you were in Astria." *And what are you doing here with Torsten?*

"It's partly because of your brother." My heart leaps, Torsten momentarily forgotten.

"Levin?" I try not to betray my eagerness. "You have word of Levin?"

"I helped him gain entry to the Candidate year," Leo says, blushing. He's wearing glasses now; they do nothing to help his sickly appearance. "My Uncle Saxan was so pleased with me for helping him find such a strong recruit that he let me come here, to Astria. I'm going to be a Cupbearer in this year's Maverick's Race," he says proudly.

I nod politely, trying not to let my impatience show.

"Leo." Torsten nods stiffly at me. "We should be going."

"Wait." I grasp Leo's arm. "Is there anything you can tell me about my brother?"

"There's not much heard from the Candidates, of course." Torsten's face tightens with visible impatience, and Leo shoots him a nervous glance. The telltale dark stains on his fingers are almost black, his hands tremble, and the eyes behind his glasses bear the violet shadows of Darkwine. "But from what I've heard," he goes on hastily, "Levin is among the best of his class.

As far as I know, the Candidates are currently in the Basetanan desert."

The thought of my smiling youngest brother out there, in the fierce wastes where only camels and nomads survive, makes me shudder.

He's taken his chance, then. And made the most of it, by this account. I'm passionately relieved to know Levin's alive and thrilled for him that he has achieved such success. But my time in Astria has left me feeling more than a little ambiguous about the order my brother has joined. It's hard not to feel worried, particularly given Leo's present company.

"Leo!" Feivel is coming toward us, waving a large, very heavy-looking tome. "Torsten," he adds, nodding with cold courtesy. Torsten, I notice, doesn't return the greeting. His eyes on Feivel are utterly devoid of warmth.

"Dear boy." Feivel takes Leo's hand, smiling kindly. Unfortunately, his gesture results in Leo dropping all he is carrying. Books and his leather roll of alchemy tools spill open onto the ground. We all start gathering his belongings, Leo's hands shaking so much he's barely able to help us. Feivel's smile fades. "Such good work you did, Leo, back in the Seam." He casts Torsten a look of severe reproach. "Helping abandoned slaves find their families. You made a difference to so many lives."

"Oh, not really." Leo drops his eyes and colors as Torsten silently hands him the small herb knife Feivel gifted Leo back in the Seam. As Leo tucks the knife away and carefully binds the leather roll, Torsten folds his arms and watches in disapproving silence. He's clearly unimpressed by Leo's friendship with Feivel. His intimidating scrutiny causes Leo to fumble the knot. I feel a surge of resentment at whatever hold the Weaver has over him. Leo might have been a hopeless Divine, but he's always been kind to us.

"I do hope you still tend an herb garden." Feivel's eyes on

Leo's bent head are full of visible concern. "You took such pleasure in it."

Torsten lifts a derisive eyebrow. Leo's smile fades. "There's no time for that now." He grips the tool roll nervously. "Divines concentrate on alchemy."

I feel a flash of anger. *Clearly Leo has little choice in the matter.*

Feivel glares at Torsten. "A good teacher encourages students to concentrate on their strengths." He pats Leo kindly on the shoulder. "And yours, dear boy, do not lie in alchemy. Call on me anytime," he adds, "if you wish to seek an alternate path."

Looking mildly horrified at this exchange, Leo barely nods at us before hurrying away, Torsten a dark shadow beside him.

"Those damned Paladins are clearly forcing the Divines into ever more dangerous alchemy in their bid to replace the lost Weavers." Feivel's eyes flash.

"Is Torsten a Paladin, then?" I ask cautiously. "He doesn't wear their uniform."

"No, he's not. And loathe Torsten as I might," Feivel goes on grimly, "I don't believe he supports their ambitions, no matter what Harken thinks of him."

I frown. "Then what is he doing with Leo?"

"Torsten teaches herb lore to the Paladin Divines." Feivel shakes his head. "He studied under me, long ago. He was a good student, according to the journals I kept at the time; I thought he would be a better teacher." He grimaces in frustration. "Good or bad, Torsten shouldn't be forced to teach for the Paladins. The abbeys are the only place left to teach, since Harken won't so much as lift the mists on the Indigo library, let alone help rebuild the Coronastrian Halls of Learning."

I think of Kendrick's words, at the first Revel: *"Astria might have been better served if Harken had simply dispatched that damned Weaver . . ."*

"But Torsten was a Kraken Weaver, wasn't he?" I'm rather

surprised that Feivel is so philosophical, especially after seeing the hostility between the two Weavers. "Isn't that why Harken won't work with him?"

Feivel purses his lips. "Yes," he says reluctantly. "But the War is over, and Weavers are few enough. Those of us who are left need to work together—even Harken. *Especially* Harken," he says, as we settle into the gondola. "It's infuriating that he won't take part in the council; but it's also a tragedy. While Harken keeps our world locked away behind his mists, ignorance grows. Children are born who will never know the kindness and love of a Weaver teacher. Great buildings fall into decay, and with every passing year, our world becomes a little less sophisticated. All because Harken is too proud to involve himself in what he calls Indigold affairs." His mouth tightens. "Whatever his past crimes, Torsten is at least trying to rebuild what was lost. Meanwhile, Harken stands by watching, seemingly without care, as Astria crumbles to darkness."

Feivel casts me an apologetic glance, covering my hand with his own. "Forgive me, child. None of this is your fault, of course."

"I thought," I say, as casually as I am able, "you said that Harken murdered most of the Kraken Weavers, after the War. Why is Torsten still alive?"

Feivel passes a weary hand over his face. "That," he says resignedly, "is a question only Harken can answer." His eyes drop briefly to my braid, and he gives me a sympathetic smile. "I gave up, long ago, trying to make sense of his choices."

The gondola moves slowly away from the shore, leaving my unanswered questions hanging in the air.

CHAPTER 43

SABER

*T*he moon is full again, and Harken and I are in the gondola, on our way to Fire Hall for the second major Revel of the season.

"You're oddly quiet." Harken sprawls on the padded bench seat, arm thrown over the back, long legs stretched out before him. Despite his seemingly casual attitude, I can read his tension in the carefully splayed fingers, the odd stillness of his long limbs. Harken isn't relaxed at all.

Neither am I.

"I'm accustomed to rather more questions on our journeys, little criminal."

You won't answer the only real ones I have. But that way lies a dangerous conversation, so I keep my eyes firmly fixed on the bank. "I've traveled these canals for weeks on my way to training. They hold few surprises."

"Of course." Harken's voice has a slight edge. "I forget how much time you've been spending with the wolves." A moment later he breaks a slightly tense silence by saying, in a more amiable tone, "Tonight will, however, hold entertainments even your jaded eye might find interesting."

"Oh?" My eyes flicker briefly to him, then away again.

"At midnight," Harken says, "The Fire Guard will all shift to wolf. It's always quite the spectacle. The entire council will likely attend."

"Good." I turn to meet his eyes squarely. "Perhaps you can speak with them about the library." Harken's eyes narrow. "Feivel took me there," I go on. "It was chaos. Poor Foras can't cope at all."

"Poor Foras," says Harken tersely, "is well aware of why the library is closed. And Feivel shouldn't have taken you there. It's not safe beyond the mists."

"Hiding behind them doesn't help us discover what we need to know. And besides, there's a whole world out there." I give Harken a rather challenging look as I gesture toward the distant city lights, fading as we move north upriver. "One that won't rebuild itself."

Harken's eyes flash dangerously. "I see Feivel has been free with his opinions."

"Feivel is frustrated." I meet his eyes squarely. "And understandably so. Keeping the Woven Court closed doesn't help good men like Feivel or Foras to do their jobs."

"Clearly, if they've resorted to using you as their mouthpiece." Biting off his words, Harken looks out over the darkened fields, every line in his body hard with tension. When he faces me again, his icy mask is back in place, with no trace of his momentary lack of control. "If you wish to visit anything in the city," he says in a clipped, curt tone, "all you need do is ask. I will have Gemory or Andras accompany you. Feivel no longer has his Weaver's needle, and he is physically weak. He can't protect you if anything goes wrong."

We travel the rest of the way in silence. Harken hasn't moved an inch since we left the palace. Though he might be sprawled over the seat with every attitude of nonchalance, there is a lethal tension in his body that, combined with the restless light gleaming deep in his eyes, and the unusually grim tilt to his customary sardonic smile, does not bode well. I find myself less concerned by that than I might normally be.

I've spent quite a lot of time thinking through our encounter in the water chamber, and my conversation with Feivel. It's increasingly clear to me that Harken's world, behind the Woven mists, is as much a prison of sorts as my own slave braid. What I don't understand is whether it's a prison in which he is forced to remain or one he chooses. I'm beginning to suspect that it is, at least in part, the latter. For someone who has spent a lifetime seeking freedom, the idea of choosing captivity, in any form, is anathema. Particularly when Harken's isolation appears to be coming at such a high cost to Astria itself. I can't help but feel he is holding Astria hostage to some personal vendetta of his own, one which none understands but him.

And so long as he won't trust me enough to explain himself, I think, fighting the urge to grasp the braid, *I'll likely never know the truth.*

I'm not unhappy when my thoughts are interrupted by our arrival. Unfortunately, from the moment we step onto the landing, it's clear that Fire Hall is about to live up to its name, in more ways than one.

"Zaria!" Brooks and Everett are among a group milling about the landing, greeting new arrivals. Everett is wearing his new uniform as head of the Fire Guards, carmine edged in gold. "Don't you look handsome," I greet him, smiling as he helps me out of the gondola. Beside him is a tall, slender girl with deep-set forest eyes and a supple athleticism. She's dressed in a tight-fitting indigo pant suit that is clearly some kind of uniform, going by the number of similarly clad women close by. I instantly feel infinitely overdressed in my silver silk dress that, as usual, exposes my zumi.

"Harken," the girl greets him in a low, sultry voice. "I thought you'd never arrive."

"Tanwen." Harken's customary sardonic tone softens as he returns her greeting. "At least I shan't die of tedium."

Tanwen kisses Harken's cheek in a remarkably familiar gesture. As she turns side on, I see a saber symbol on her sleeve. Instantly I hear Gemory's voice: *I did hear a Breeze that you had been entertaining yourself with a Saber from the Wolf Weald . . .*

And what does he mean, die from tedium? I think indignantly. *It's hardly as if I ask to be brought to these occasions.* Turning my back on them both, I accept Everett's outstretched arm on one side and Brooks's on the other, leaving Harken, with Tanwen on his arm, to follow.

"Fire Hall looks amazing." I smile at Everett, determined not to show my disquiet. It certainly does, with blazing urns of fire, in place of lanterns, turning the front gardens to a brilliant gold and two enormous staffs either side of the door burning with white flame. The engraved wolf over the hall entrance breathes a flame that changes color according to the dress of each person entering beneath it.

"Mama has outdone herself, of course." Everett winks at me. "She always enjoys a chance to remind the council that Dencover isn't the only province in Astria with money—nor the Paladin Blades Astria's only military force."

We are walking as part of a broad group. Brooks and Everett, on either side of me, talk over each other in their habitual way as they point out the attractions. Harken and Tanwen are off to one side, slightly removed from a small group that includes Kendrick of Goath, who has arrived with Feivel. It must be our recent conversation, I think, that causes Harken to greet them both so coldly. He practically ignores the other nobles, head bent instead toward Tanwen. When I do glimpse his eyes, they glitter dangerously, and there is a hard, muscular tic in his jaw.

"Harken. Thank the Great Weaver." Lupa casts her eyes skyward as we meet her in the formal greeting line. "At last, some much needed entertainment amid this tangled knot of a Revel."

"I do always aim to entertain." Harken's tone is light as he bows over Lupa's hand, but she must see the same warning signs I do, for her eyes narrow briefly. There's little time to do more than greet, however, and a moment later we're in the ancient stone and wood ballroom. It's lit in all corners by fire: in sconces on the walls, in a central chandelier of three burning gold-and-indigo rings, and even in the opalescent colors gleaming deep within the flamestone floor.

"No lavenade for you tonight." A grinning Everett hands me a deep amber concoction with flame licking the top. "Ember wine," he says, winking. "Go lightly, though." I sip cautiously, chatting easily with Brooks and Everett as I greet several other Mavericks and nobles. Some I've met during my days at Fire Hall, others at the many events I've attended over the past weeks. I'm more at ease here, however, in such familiar surroundings, than I've been at other events where Harken has often been my only anchor.

"Are the Breezes true, then, Kendrick?" Formalities over, Lupa rejoins us, her remark drawing our circle closer, including Harken and Tanwen. "About there being a genuine plot afoot, among Anahita's old followers, to breach the Tower?"

Kendrick frowns. "I don't think now is the time, Lupa—"

"Oh, but I do." Lupa, utterly resplendent in the same vivid carmine and gold as her son, takes a cup of Weald whiskey from a passing footman. "I rather like discussing the Kraken army while in my own hall." Her lips curl in a particularly lethal smile. "It reminds me how many of them I killed during the War."

"Lupa." Kendrick shakes his head reprovingly, though he's smiling. "There have been interesting Breezes, it's true." His low tone draws us all slightly closer. "Some say the Paladins have begun to hear her whispering from the Tower. If true, it gives credence to all those who still believe she was never truly destroyed."

"And the Paladins would be listening, of course." Lupa's mouth twists in contempt. "Who knows what Tellian tangle those Darkwine fanatics are cooking up?" Her eyes cut to Harken, who leans against a nearby wall, regarding us all with an expression of utter boredom. "Care to enlighten us with your thoughts on the matter?" she says, not without irony.

Everett snorts. "That would be a first." His tone has a biting edge that is almost a challenge. His mother shoots him a warning glance.

Harken's mouth curls contemptuously, though he doesn't answer. His eyes are on the entrance, where Comitas Ormond and the Paladin Consul Gareth have just arrived at the head of a small group. I know Torsten is among them by the sudden, fierce frisson at my neck, even before I catch sight of his tall figure. Harken's tension is almost painful. Before he lowers his head slightly, I see the same sudden, dark savagery I did at the first Revel, a deeply disturbing flash, there and gone in a moment. Once again it appears to have gone unnoticed by the others. Torsten doesn't so much as glance in our direction, almost as if he can sense Harken's cold anger.

"I'd far prefer," Feivel is saying pointedly, "to be enlightened at the council table."

"My dear Feivel." Harken's sardonic drawl is more pronounced than ever. "If you want me at that table, then start by cutting away the dead wood." He nods at where Torsten stands behind the Comitas. "I would suggest you start with the malignant roots."

"Might *I* suggest," Lupa says dryly, "that you might have better served Astria by including at least one of those malignant roots in the rather savage pruning you did after the War, given that you intended to deprive us of your vote?" The lethal gleam in Lupa's own eyes as she eyes Sereia and Torsten across her hall makes me suspect that she would need little persuasion to burn away those roots herself.

"I wouldn't bother, Lupa," says Kendrick dismissively. "Our Woven Lord hasn't explained himself in almost two decades. I hardly think he's going to start now, no matter the quality of your Weald whiskey."

"Finally, Kendrick." Harken holds out his glass for the footman to fill. "Something on which we can agree. I would suggest the rest of you listen to the worthy Lord of Goath."

Raising his glass in an ironic salute, Harken steps away from the wall. His eyes flicker briefly to me, still standing in between Everett and Brooks, both of whom are eyeing Harken with the same disapproval as the rest of the small group. Holding his arm out to a nearby Tanwen, he says, "I believe the river is particularly beautiful under the moon. Shall we?"

Nodding curtly to the group, he turns away.

"Zaria." Everett touches my arm, frowning. "I'm sorry you had to witness that."

But I'm no longer listening. I'm staring at the door, and suddenly nothing matters, not Harken or his Saber, or the pitying expressions of all those looking at me in the wake of his abrupt departure.

Following the Comitas is Caspian, Foley, and Arkady.

And with them are my sisters.

CHAPTER 44

SISTERS

*E*verything in the blazing hall seems to disappear. I move through it oblivious to the greetings of those I pass, or of Everett and Brooks asking where I'm going.

All I can see are my sisters. They stand slightly apart from their masters, clasping glasses and looking around warily.

Shimi's aqua gown is so sheer her nipples are clearly visible through it and tight enough to make it abundantly clear she isn't wearing underwear. Her braid has been Woven to look like a gold choker. I find the illusion even more offensive than the braid itself.

Neoma, beside her, is clad head to toe in shimmering gold. It's even threaded through her hair. Her braid has likewise been glamoured to resemble a choker, though I sincerely doubt any are fooled by the illusion.

"Shimi." I push past the last person, blurting my sisters' names out as I come closer. "Neoma."

Shimi's eyes widen immediately, then flare in warning as they shift to where Caspian stands nearby. Neoma, standing slightly back, is staring somewhere past me, her eyes not only vacant, but almost dead. I halt in my tracks, trembling with the abrupt juxtaposition of past and present. Neoma's eyes terrify me. The expression in Shimi's brings home with a jarring shock how much my life has altered in these past weeks.

No matter what complexities exist in Harken's world, I realize with an odd flash of awareness, somewhere in the past month I have ceased to feel a slave's fear, the ever-present threat of a master's hand on the ring.

My sisters, however, seem to have learned fear in ways I'd spent a lifetime trying to spare them, and that hurts far more than it ever could if it were me in their place.

"Zaria," Shimi hisses through her practiced smile, "are you insane? Don't make a scene, or they'll know we're slaves like you." Her eyes drop pointedly to my braid. "I guess your plans didn't quite work out as you'd hoped." Her voice is brittle and hard, as it always is when she's defensive.

I glance around, relieved to see Caspian and Foley engaged in a conversation, not looking our way. "I'll be freed before the Maverick's Race," I say in a low undertone meant only for the two of them. "I've been training for it. I mean to win, Shimi." I'm speaking in a whispered rush, unsure how long I can go unnoticed. "And when I do, we'll have a home, at last, and enough coin to pay whoever we need to for your freedom." I keep glancing at Neoma, but her eyes are fixed on something I can't see. She makes no indication of having recognized me.

"Are you still so stupid," Shimi mutters angrily, "as to believe in miracles? Look at us. Doron is most likely dead. Levin is gone. You're the most notorious slave in the city, from what I hear. And as for Neoma and me . . ." She breaks off, shaking her head abruptly. "My point is," she goes on, "surely you know what they're like by now? He won't ever free you, Zaria." She shoots a wary glance at Caspian. "None of them will free us. Not ever."

My stomach churns uneasily. Up close, I can see the dull exhaustion in the bronze eyes and, worse, the faint imprint of bruises on her skin. "Shimi." I catch her hand. "Where are you staying?" My eyes shift to Neoma. "And what is wrong with Neoma?"

Shimi stares at me, her hand slack in mine. "We're in an apartment close to the palace. Caspian and Foley keep us there with . . . some other girls." She looks away, and I don't need her to elaborate to know she means an Astrian version of a Disorderly House. "I keep Neoma dosed with Darkwine," she says quietly. "It's easier that way. Otherwise, she gets . . . upset." Her eyes shy away from mine.

Once, when Neoma was an adolescent, a man caught her on his lap and refused to let her go, laughing that she had to tell him a good fortune before she could be freed. Neoma's eyes went suddenly dead, then a moment later she went quite insanely wild, screaming and thrashing so badly we had to restrain her. Thinking of what might happen if she has a turn like that in the company of men like Foley or Caspian makes me shudder with horror. I can understand why Shimi has dosed her, though it pains me even to imagine it.

I look down at the dark marks on Shimi's own arm. "You're hurt," I say quietly.

Shimi meets my eyes squarely. "I chose this, Zaria." There's a hard set to her jaw, a fierce light in her eyes that I know is pride. I want to kill whoever made those bruises. I want to throw my arms around her in a shield.

And I know she'd never forgive me if I even thought of doing either.

"Levin is alive," I say instead. Shimi's eyes flare momentarily. "He's in the Paladins, one of the best Candidates, by all accounts. And Garrick has gone to the Drop to search for Doron." I press her lifeless hand. "I know you're not safe," I say quietly. "But at least we're here, together. Sisters."

"They're your sisters?" Having made his way to my side, Everett stares between us in surprise. His eyes narrow as he takes in the gold chokers. Taking out his needle, he waves it briefly, removing the illusion and revealing the braid. The agony of humiliation on Shimi's face is heartbreaking.

"Everett." I touch his arm. "Please don't do that."

But Everett shakes me off. "How dare they bring slaves into my mother's hall," he says furiously. Realizing what he's said, he glances at me. "It's different with you—Harken, you know—but this." I've never seen Everett truly angry before. "Well, at the very least, I can buy your sisters and ensure they're freed."

I know what a terrible idea this is before the words are out of his mouth. Even if I didn't, one look at Shimi's face would be enough to signal it. "Everett," I begin, but I'm too late. Everett's anger has caught Caspian and Foley's attention. The two move instantly to Shimi and Neoma, pulling them close in a clear declaration of ownership.

"You want a slave, wolf, then go buy your own." Caspian pulls Shimi hard against his side, so her thighs almost straddle his and her breasts are pressed against his arm, clearly outlined beneath the sheer material. "And I'd like to see your mother throw out the same council members who only recently voted to confirm you as head of her precious Fire Guard." Caspian smiles unpleasantly. "A vote which can, I assure you, easily be revoked."

"Besides," Foley adds, his pudgy fingers kneading Neoma's arm, "this one tells fortunes. I'd ask her to read yours—but if you keep going as you are, you won't have one."

The encounter is beginning to draw the attention of the crowd. Eyes widen, shocked whispers coming from behind fans. I close my eyes briefly, wishing I could unsee the mortification on Shimi's face.

Neoma's eyes sharpen momentarily. "He's coming," she says a little dreamily, her eyes slightly unfocused. "He's coming for you, Zaria." As soon as my name is out of her mouth, her eyes widen with a sudden clarity. She stares at me, color draining from her already pale face. "Zaria," she whispers.

But whatever Neoma might have been about to say is cut short by Harken's sudden arrival in our midst. "Zaria," he says sharply, thrusting me behind him.

"That's right," Foley sneers. "I'd keep a tighter hold on your slave if I were you. Unless you fancy taking her while she still smells like wolf."

The braid on my neck seizes with such savagery that I gasp, fear racing through me. Foley's smile fades abruptly, and even Everett stands back. Harken has his back to me, but if his face resembles anything of the ruthless fury I feel about my neck, I suspect that Lupa's hall will soon be covered in blood.

"Foley." I feel an icy shock as I realize the speaker is Torsten. "You and Caspian will take your games elsewhere." His voice is low, refined, and silken as a tiger's purr. Foley, I note, falls back immediately, despite casting Torsten a resentful look. Torsten's needle flickers in the air, and suddenly Caspian and Foley are across the other side of the hall, my sisters with them, and the crowd is dispersed, chattering as if nothing has happened. I push past Harken, but his hand on my wrist stops me in my tracks.

"Don't follow them." His voice is flat and hard. "You'll make it worse."

"How could it get any worse?" Everett rounds on him furiously. "I'd say being a slave is as bad as it gets, Harken. Enough of this damned game of yours. It's long past time you unwove that damned braid."

Harken's face is as terrifyingly cold as I've ever seen it. "Unless you intend to end this night as ash, watch your claws, wolf."

A nearby clock chimes midnight, and from the distance comes a bloodcurdling howl. Everett's eyes gleam.

"Run along, now." Harken's lip curls. "Your mother is call-ing." He looks down at me. "Enough of this."

He waves an impatient arm, and the room disappears in the familiar, glittering mist.

CHAPTER 45

FIRE

*E*ven behind the mist, I can smell smoke and fire.
Harken carries me to the internal courtyard of the
Water Palace, but even here, the air feels acrid and hard on my
skin. It takes a moment for me to realize the feeling is inside my
body, not outside.

Harken releases me and I slump to the floor, my silver dress
pooled about me, my face in my hands. I'm not sobbing. My
grief is a dry, racking pain that twists inside me so I can barely
breathe.

"Zaria." Harken's voice seems to come from far away. "Zaria,
look at me." He touches my arm, and despite collapsing a
moment earlier, I leap to my feet, stumbling away from him
until I feel the edge of the fountain tree behind me.

"Don't touch me." My voice is quivering with anger. "Don't
you dare touch me."

"Very well." Harken folds his arms, his eyes glittering once
more. "Out with it, then."

"You could have bought them. Both of my sisters." My fists
are clenched so hard my nails dig into my palms. "If not back in
the Seam, then certainly here. And don't deny it. I know you're

powerful enough to make Foley and Caspian do anything you wish them to."

Harken sniffs dismissively. "Showing any interest in your sisters would have given the council a bargaining chip they would not have hesitated to use. That is how these people think. I don't deal with them, and I advise you not to, either." I stare at him incredulously. "As tonight proved beyond doubt, it would only have made your sisters' lives worse." He grimaces. "We just succeeded in making this a game for Caspian and Foley, and I assure you, such men love nothing more. Left alone, they might have tired of your sisters soon enough. But after seeing your reaction tonight, now they never will."

"You could have bought them long ago, back in the Seam—"

"But I didn't." Harken cuts me off curtly. *Too curtly*, I think, seeing the fleeting shadow in his eyes.

"It's too late for regrets now." I'm trembling, heat and cold racing alternately through my body. I shake my head when he remains silent, his face impassive. "I can see that you regret not buying them, back then. But you're too stubborn to admit it, just like you're too stubborn to help Feivel and the others make changes on the council."

He makes a harsh sound. "I told you once before that I find the buying and selling of slaves abhorrent." His voice is rough, without any trace of either the humor of a moment ago or his earlier anger. "I've killed men for it. Many times." We stare at each other across the courtyard. "That's why I didn't offer to buy you, or your siblings, when first we met in the Seam. Purchasing you, no matter my reasons, would make me no better than those I'd punished for doing the same. I had never so much as considered something so wholly vile as owning another human, until—"

His voice breaks off abruptly. He thrusts his hands into his pockets, frowning, his mouth clamped shut.

"Until what?" Despite myself, I need to know. And despite

everything inside me telling me to leave the room right now, and to the Tells with Harken's regrets, something else has me rooted to the floor, every fiber of my being aware of his glittering tension.

"Until I saw what that bastard Hodda had done to you." Harken bites out the words. "Until I realized you were going to race anyway. Risk another beating, or more likely death, for your freedom. For your siblings' freedom." He stares at me hollowly. "Yet still I hesitated, when what I should have done was walk into that Disorderly House then and there, purchase you all, and set you free." His jaw clenches hard. "It was a mistake, Zaria."

I'm so taken aback I'm lost for words.

"I don't expect forgiveness," he says shortly. "But I will get your sisters out of the clutches of those men. That much I promise you."

"I've known men like Foley and Caspian my entire life." I eye him across the courtyard, still angry, despite his disclosure. "Do you think that I don't understand how it feels to deal with them? To pour their wine, when I despise them, or take their coin, when I want to throw it in their face? I understand better than anyone why you don't wish to speak with them, let alone deal with them." Old injustices surge through me in a hot torrent. "But that isn't why you didn't free my sisters."

His eyes narrow, boring into mine.

"It's because of that man who came tonight." When he doesn't immediately answer, hurt stokes the fire inside me. *Even now*, I think, *he won't trust me.*

"Torsten." The name lands in the room between us like a caged animal clawing for release. "The Weaver who is adviser to the Comitas. I saw your face," I go on when he doesn't speak. "At the first Revel, and then again tonight."

"You *saw my face*," Harken repeats sarcastically, his eyes glittering. "Evidence, indeed."

"It's Torsten you've been hoping will take the bait all along." I'm too angry for caution. "Everything else—my sisters, even our bargain—are just pieces in whatever stupid game the two of you are playing."

"Stupid game!" Harken paces furiously across the floor to the stairs and turns around, glaring at me. "Do you have any idea of the pure evil we are discussing? The Kraken Weavers betrayed everything—*everything*—the Woven Court stood for."

"And yet you spared two of them: Torsten and Sereia." Seeing my sisters has made me impatient with Astria's intrigues, and even more so with Harken's part in them. "Torsten and Sereia are the malignant roots you mentioned, the reason you won't sit on the council, but you choose to let them both live, for reasons not even Kendrick or Feivel understand. You use me to try to bait them into the open, but you won't tell me why, or even what exactly it is that you think they're trying to do."

"I offered to free you!" Harken is staring at me, his face white with anger. "You were the one who wanted to keep that damned braid!"

I shake my head in exasperation. "Even now, you're avoiding my questions. You know the braid isn't the issue here."

"And you know that my business is none of yours," he fires back.

"It seems to me that your business is everyone's problem." Anger and frustration make me reckless. "I've fought my entire life for freedom. For the right to have the kind of voice that seat at the council table gives you. But instead of taking that seat, and using your voice, you stay locked behind these mists in self-imposed exile, fighting some old vendetta of your own while Astria crumbles. My sisters are enslaved to evil men, all because your games are more important to you than taking even the smallest interest in the world beyond your own court." I clench my fists in frustration. "I'm starting to wonder if you ever even cared about discovering the truth behind Arkady, or the Dark

Rips. Do you have any evidence that Torsten is the person behind this? Or has hatred clouded your judgment so badly that he is the only villain you can see?"

"You know nothing." Harken spits the words with a cold fury that momentarily halts me. "Of the evil I have seen, nor of the role he played in it."

"Then tell me!" I throw my arms up in exasperation.

"Explaining myself wasn't part of our bargain," he says icily. "It still isn't."

A sound escapes me that is half laugh, half sob. "It seems to me that our bargain is whatever you wish to make it, in any given moment."

Harken's eyes flash with anger. "Have I not held up my end?" He thrusts his arm out in an almost vicious gesture. "You train every waking minute with that damned wolf—"

"Everett would never have left my sisters to rot in the Seam," I fling back at him. "Offering to buy them was the first thing he did tonight."

"Oh, I'm certain Everett would love nothing better than to play the part of a hero." His voice is hard and pointed. "And from what I saw tonight, it looks like you'd be more than happy for him to play that part—"

"How dare you!" Incandescent with rage, I face him across the courtyard. "Everett might be a Maverick," I throw at him, "but he's an honest one. And he's honorable too, you know he is, or you'd never have agreed to let him train me. And besides." Hot rage surges through me, making me reckless. "You can talk, carrying on with that Saber, Tanwen, who you clearly have more than a passing friendship with!"

Harken's icy control finally snaps. "Tanwen doesn't try to tell me how to run my court!"

"Of course she doesn't!" My own control is entirely gone. "I have no doubt that conversation is the last thing on either of your minds."

We stare at each other across the courtyard. I'm panting and furious, tears so close to the surface I can barely breathe. Harken's face is set and pale, his eyes sparking like one of Lupa's fire urns. I never do this, lose my temper so completely, and suddenly I loathe myself and Harken in equal measure.

Running across the courtyard, I go right past him without looking, up the stairs and straight to my bedchamber, closing the door hard behind me.

CHAPTER 46

DARKNESS

I'm far too angry to sleep.

I stalk around my bedchamber, anger and indignation churning within in equal measure. Gradually the latter gives way to a creeping sense of shame, and I sit down on my bed, knees drawn up. I've always loathed conflict. Losing my temper is a weakness I've rarely succumbed to. I'm honest enough to recognize that a good part of my anger is a result of my shock and grief at having seen my sisters. And I can't so much as think of Foley and Caspian without wanting to either throw up or throw something, hard.

None of that, though, helps my anger that Harken won't intervene on my sisters' behalf. And as for his accusations about Everett—I cut off that thought with an involuntary hiss that serves to remind me I am still dangerously angry.

I stalk around the room again. I can't settle. Even a bath doesn't help, nor brushing out my hair, which has always soothed me. Finally, opening my bedchamber cautiously, I peer out into the darkened corridors. I don't dare go to the kitchens. Even at this time, there will undoubtedly be a demon hard at work. Instead I head for the map room and the decanters on the shelf there.

I push the door open cautiously, but the room is silent, night clouds drifting over the dome above. They're oddly comforting. I go to the shelf, pour myself a glass of Weald whiskey, and drink it down in one long gulp. The taste reminds me of the Weald, which in turn reminds me of Everett.

Foley's loathsome face and insinuating comments pass through my mind: *I'd keep a tighter hold on your slave if I were you. Unless you fancy taking her while she still smells like wolf.*

Fury and shame grip me hard. I spin around, throwing the glass with all my might through the open window, listening to the satisfying smash as it hits the stone below, the night breeze whipping my hair about my face.

"Stealing again, little criminal?" Horrified, I realize Harken is sitting in one of the open archways barely a few paces away, long legs crossed before him, his body hidden in the shadows. A decanter of Darkwine is beside him, and his eyes glitter in the darkness.

Folding my arms over my chemise, I pick up the nearly empty decanter and sniff it, putting it down hastily. "You can't drink it undiluted," I say, more sharply than I intend. "That's strong enough to kill even you."

He raises his cup. "I'm very difficult to kill." He pours a large amount of Darkwine down his throat, as if in proof.

"What a pity." I turn away, too upset for games.

Harken leaps easily to his feet from the archway to stand before me. He is barefoot, his shirt hanging loose, the sleeves roughly pushed up.

"Torsten and Sereia are brother and sister." The words seem wrenched from the darkness itself. They shock me into stillness. Harken nods grimly at my surprise, his jaw taut and set. "Torsten was born of Roark's first Great Ceremony, Sereia from his fourth." Harken's mouth curls. "Nobody should know that, of course. Weavers are children of Astria, entrusted to the Lotus Palaces. But such traditions meant little to Roark."

Reaching for the decanter, he pours another cup of Dark-wine, then turns away, facing out through the open archway. I barely dare breathe lest I break the spell of his confidence.

"In the fifth decade of Roark's reign, he claimed them both as his children, an unheard-of sacrilege." The tension behind his voice is like lightning licking a distant horizon. "Sereia," he says roughly, "was a mere decade old when Roark put her into the hands of one of the most evil, corrupt men ever to walk this earth: an ancient Paladin Weaver named Mortimer. You already know," he says quietly, staring out into the night, "what became of him."

That particular story has long ceased to shock me. I remain silent, focused on the angular figure silhouetted in the light of the distant city. Harken seems carved from the same stone as the buildings themselves, his only movement the slow turn of the wine cup in his hand.

"Torsten was placed in the household of Roark's greatest ally: the old Lord of Dencover." Harken takes a very measured sip of his wine, then turns slowly back to me. "The old lord did not survive the War." The gleam in his eyes matches that in his cup. It leaves me in no doubt as to who brought death to the Lord of Dencover.

"I let Torsten and Sereia live because I was taught that children, even Weavers, should not suffer for the sins of their fathers." Harken's eyes bore into mine. "No matter how vile those sins might be."

His waiting for my reaction places me on the edge of a precipice. I sense that one wrong word will send Harken flying into the void, leaving me standing on the broken ground of his trust.

"You call them children," I say tentatively. "But Torsten must have been fifty when war broke out."

Harken nods curtly. "Young, still, by Weaver standards." His mouth hardens. "Though old enough," he says softly, "to have attained the knot of harmony, and his zumi, in the Woven Court. He was forty when he left for Dencover, his first posting in the outside world."

Old enough, I think, *to know better.* I sense that is the point at the core of Harken's cold anger. Remembering how intimidated Leo seemed by Torsten, I don't blame Harken at all. On the brief occasions I've met him, Torsten has displayed none of Feivel's kindness, nor the benevolence usually ascribed to Weaver teachers.

"And now," I say slowly, "you believe Roark's children are working for their father's ambitions once more? For Anahita?"

"I believe it is more than possible." Harken places the cup down on the stone ledge. "But if my suspicions are right, then two of Astria's last Weavers must die." His voice is heavy. "And it will be my responsibility to see they do."

When he turns back to me, his hands are thrust deep in his pockets, his face in shadow. "There is a reason I keep my affairs private." His voice rasps like old stone. "My sole purpose in this world is to guard the Woven Court. What may seem selfish to you is the one reason for my existence, and the only thing to which I must remain loyal."

I want to step toward him, to reach past the fathomless darkness in his eyes, but I'm afraid that if I so much as move, this moment will be gone, and Harken with it.

"I was Woven, Zaria. Not born." There is a bluntness to his disclosure that seems devoid of emotion, yet it is there, a potent shadow behind his studied detachment. "I am not a man, but a being drawn from the very threads of the Woven Court itself. I am bound to my court, just as it is to me, our existence Woven together for eternity. My bondage is not one from which there is freedom, Zaria. Not now." The carved lines of his face seem deeper in this light, his eyes no longer either hard or cold, but filled with an ancient sadness. "Not ever."

I know he means to give me a warning. He cannot know that his words forge a link between the man I have sensed in my visions and the one I have met. Most of all, he cannot know that in binding vision to reality, he has unwittingly upended my oldest and most deeply held conviction—and with that, undone the last of my reason.

Until now, I have always believed love to be the worst form of slavery. It is only in seeing Harken deprive himself of it that I know the truth for the first time: that love is perhaps the only true freedom there is.

Even a slave can love.

It is a revelation as blinding as it is utterly right, and it leaves me breathless. I step forward involuntarily, but Harken rears back, inhaling suddenly, a sharp breath that hitches in his throat.

"I do not say this for pity." His voice is harsh. "You need to understand who, or rather what, I am." His voice grows harder with every word. "I'm not just a dark creature, a *Savage King*." He says the name with bitter irony. "I *am* the darkness, Zaria. That is why I can walk through a Dark Rip or sail the *Hydra* through the Nexus. I am created from the very stuff others fear. The nightmares Fools see in their sleep makes up the fabric of what soul I was given."

"Do you think that frightens me?" This time when he would move away I take his hand, tugging him back. I turn it over in my own, seeing the beautiful, newly woven being of my visions, as well as the wounded savage he was forced to become. "I know why you hate them," I whisper. "I understand. And I don't blame you, no matter what I said tonight."

The hand in mine tenses. I stand utterly still, unsure if he will flee.

Then, slowly, his other hand comes up, brushing my hair

away from my face. Harken tilts my face up toward his. In the starlit room, his eyes are infinite as the night sky beyond.

"Do you have any idea," he says hoarsely, "how you've turned my life upside down, Zaria? My home, my court. Your scent is like a desert rose on a winter morning, lingering in every room, filling my senses until I'm mad with it."

I can't move. His hand curls against my own, and my heart curls with it in my chest, thudding so fast it hurts. Harken steps closer to me still, the Darkwine heat of his body touching every cell of my own.

"I can't sleep," he murmurs, "for seeing your face." His hand is at my neck, his thumb stroking my cheek with breathtaking tenderness. "And every time you leave to go to that wolf, all I can think about is him seeing you like you are now, with your hair down and wild, and so damned beautiful I can barely breathe for wanting you."

I glance up at him from beneath lowered lids. "What of the Saber?" I whisper fiercely. "Tanwen?" It isn't until I say it aloud that I can admit to myself how much it hurt, seeing Harken with her.

He gives a rasp of a laugh. His hand slips from mine to my waist, pulling me against him. His lips are so close I can almost taste them. "I've known Tanwen since she was five years old." He half smiles. "And believe me when I say her tastes do not extend to males, of any species."

I almost laugh, a choked sound of relief, and then his lips find mine, stealing my words, along with my senses.

Everything that I've felt this night, all the passion and jealousy, the fear and rage, finds an answer in Harken, as if the fires we saw earlier have been burning all this time, just waiting to burst into a roaring blaze. I can feel his loneliness and pain, just as I can his utterly lethal power. His mouth owns mine with a skilled certainty that leaves no place for thought and turns my body to liquid heat, flames licking along every vein.

The kiss goes on for a long time, and by the time it stops, I want only for it to continue.

It's Harken who steps away from me, his eyes burning, raking a hand through his hair. "I won't do this," he says hoarsely. "You're still enslaved, Zaria. It's wrong—"

"It's my choice." I sway toward him. "Do you think I don't want you too, Harken? I don't care about the braid. Not anymore."

"I won't be the man who takes his slave." He steps out of reach, eyes darkening. "I can't be. And I won't unweave you for that. Not now, not like this." He stares at my mouth, his body taut, his eyes burning. "Go to bed, Zaria." His hands clench reflexively. "Go," he says roughly.

For a moment, I think about arguing. But then I realize that I'm standing in the middle of the map room in nothing more than a chemise, practically begging Harken to rip it from my body.

That's when I flee.

CHAPTER 47

NEEDLEMAKER

I'm not entirely surprised when I don't see Harken the next day. A part of me is even relieved.

But one day turns to two, then several more. Relief turns to anxiety, then to gnawing fear.

I deal with my anxiety by training, every waking moment, on the gondolino below my bedchamber. I cut the air with my sword and swing low, trying to block out the seemingly endless round of thoughts in my mind.

The list of what I imagine could go wrong is long, and ever changing. Perhaps top of that list is Harken disappearing behind the Woven mists to his Savage Court and simply never emerging. After all this time, he's never trusted me enough to take me there. Perhaps he never will.

I thrust, almost topple the gondolino, and slump to the boards, my head in my hands.

"Oh, enough." I look up to find Gemory balanced on my balcony railing, watching me with a rather bored expression. "Watching you is like observing a montage from a badly written tragedy, and I've always found the theater tedious. Come. I'm taking you out." They eye me disapprovingly. "I've already chosen your outfit."

After changing into Gemory-approved wear, and a short gondola ride, we are walking through dingy alleys in a part of the city I've never been to before. I wrinkle my nose. "There's quite the stench here." I glance at Gemory. "And I grew up in the Seam."

"We're in Glosbe," they say cheerfully. "It's the tannery quarter." They point to the gutter, where multiple bright colors swirl in the running water. "Dyes mix with the runoff from washing the leathers. Yes, it stinks."

"Is there a reason we're in the tannery quarter?"

"We're here to meet a needlemaker." Before I can ask why we would seek a needlemaker in the tannery quarter, Gemory stops in front of a small, dark, shuttered shopfront. "Ah. This is it."

The shop is even less attractive inside. What few goods line the dusty shelves are basic leatherwork, and not particularly fine examples at that. The windows are dirty, and much of the dust seems to have lain undisturbed for some time.

Gemory rings the bell on the counter. A thin man emerges from the rear of the shop, wiping his hands on a cloth apron.

"Gemory!" The man's face lights up. "Had I known you were coming, I'd have made sure there was almond cake."

"No need, old friend." Gemory throws the man a packet. "Serzan, this is Zaria, a friend of mine. She will likely require a needle, soon. Oh, don't look so surprised," they say impatiently to me. "If you win that damned Race, you'll be chasing a needle in moments, and you know it." They nod at the man behind the counter. "Serzan is the most talented needlemaker in all Astria."

Trying not to show my excitement, I take Serzan's hand and return his greeting, then follow him to the rear of the shop, where he sets about making mint tea in a silver teapot. Serzan walks with a limp and has a face so scarred it's even worse than Feivel's. But Serzan's scars do not glitter, nor do his eyes flash with Darkwine and gold, as Feivel's do. These scars are ugly gashes that were never treated, his limbs broken and never repaired. One eye is a sunken socket. The other is the dark, empty pool of a broken soul. I should know; I grew up stepping over many such blank stares in the gutters of the Seam.

"I've always been curious as to how needles are made." I smile at Serzan, thinking it better not to mention the War.

"Needles are alchemy." Serzan seizes the topic eagerly, his deathly face suddenly reanimated. "Made by Weaving threads of Pathfinder's silver with the threads of the bearer's own soul, then binding the entirety with Indigo, the most mysterious substance of all. Of course," he says, tilting his head, "we are speaking of Indigold needles. A Weaver's needle is a physical part of their own body, born with them as infants. The process of extraction is known only by the priestesses on the Isle of Nine. But the alchemy of Indigold needlemaking is an art, one I learned from my own Weaver master." A shadow crosses the lone eye, and some of his animation fades.

"How do you find the Indigo?" I ask hastily, seeking to divert him.

"The Cupbearing ceremony," Serzan answers promptly. "The sediment left in the Cup after an infant's Cupbearing is placed into a pendant or amulet of some kind that they wear on their person, until they are nineteen. The sediment changes over time, learning from the bearer, absorbing their soul. When it is placed into the Cup that they drink at their needlemaking ceremony, the sediment becomes the Indigo thread that holds the key to the person's soul." Serzan smiles, rather sadly. "That Indigo thread is an individual signature that can never be recreated or imitated. It is the product of past and present, of who we were and what we are destined to become. Even a needlemaker is never entirely certain how the Indigo thread will alter the needle, until the Work is done."

"What if the person never had a Cupbearing ceremony as a child?"

Serzan's eyes drop to my braid, then meet mine. "Needles have a way of finding a home," he says quietly. "Not all needles are made. Some are found. Some others are stolen. Yet more are gifted. When it is time for you to hold a needle, your hand will be filled, and your own thread will join with it." His face falls. "Needles can also be taken away," he says softly.

His face doesn't invite questions, but I'm curious, and Gemory's silence is unusual enough that I interpret it as an invitation, so I ask my questions anyway.

"Did you have your needle taken?"

Serzan folds his arms. "I did." He meets my eyes squarely. "I fought in the War. Unfortunately, it was on the wrong side."

I don't dishonor him by looking away. "In the Seam, we say there is no right or wrong side, only those who live and those who die." I smile at him. "You're alive. That means you're on the right side."

"Ha." Serzan glances at Gemory. "I like her."

"Oh, give her time." Gemory casts their eyes skyward. "She can be quite as tedious as any other, I assure you." Serzan laughs, though it's more of a strangled cough.

"Would you tell me more?" I say, encouraged by his good humor. "You don't have to," I add hastily.

"No, no." Serzan gestures wryly at the empty shop. "I'm hardly busy." He pours me another glass of tea, which is minty, strong and sweet, served in a small filigree glass. "I was needlemaker to the old Lord of Dencover." He glances at me, clearly gauging my reaction. I strive to maintain a neutral expression. "When he went to war for Roark," Serzan continues, "I accompanied his army. You must remember," he says, slightly defensively, "by the time of the sixth Race, when war broke out, Roark had been in power for five decades. He was Dencover's ally, the only king I'd ever known—and, we were taught, a great man." Serzan drops his eyes. "Nobody realized he'd become the Golden Kraken. Even if we had, I'm not sure it would have mattered." He lifts a helpless shoulder. "We'd been raised to be loyal to the king, and to Dencover. Both told us that the Woven Court had been corrupted by ambitious men who wanted to seize power for themselves."

Serzan doesn't attempt to hide his cynicism.

"Roark had long claimed that was why he had taken his own children, to save them from persecution. Now, he said, those ambitious men had imprisoned innocent Weavers—including the Paladin Weaver Mortimer and Roark's own daughter, Sereia. And we believed it," he says bitterly. "Of course we did. We were loyal.

"We didn't know that the imprisoned Weavers had attacked the Isle of Nine and stolen the golden needle. Let alone Woven the Serpent Queen into the Kraken." He shakes his head. "When the Lord of Dencover ordered his son, Mason, to march on the Woven Court, we thought we were going to free innocent Weavers and liberate the Lotus Palaces for Roark, and for Astria. We couldn't wait to fight."

He breaks off. I don't want to push him for answers. I've seen the horrific destruction of the Lotus Palaces in my visions. I know what Serzan doesn't want to say.

"The gates were Woven closed, of course, but they opened to admit one of their own: our Weaver, Torsten." He shudders slightly. "They thought he was there to negotiate."

"He attacked his own?" I stare at Serzan in horror. "It was Torsten who freed his sister and the Kraken Weavers?"

Serzan nods miserably. "The Kraken Weavers opened the gates to our army, then turned their needles onto the Weavers themselves. Amid the confusion, it took time for Mason to realize that those he had liberated were bent on destroying what he thought he had come to protect. Mason was a good man," Serzan adds with a faint edge of defiance, "no matter what his father was. He tried to turn his army against the Kraken Weavers, but it was like trying to turn back an ocean tide. In the end, the Weavers did manage to close the gates, but it was too late. The damage was done. The Kraken Weavers had escaped, the Lotus Palaces were all but destroyed, and the bulk of Astria's Weavers lay in threads on the ground."

The dead are so many they cover the ground almost entirely. I need only close my eyes to see the terrible destruction of that first braid vision. *A blue lotus floating in a pond.* I swallow my pain. *A garden of lilies that is perfectly intact.*

"Mason died." Serzan's voice is hoarse with his own pain and regret. "Most of our army didn't survive. Those of us who did were thrown into dungeons for the duration of the War, no matter who caught us. Most went mad, with guilt and grief."

He stares into the past, his face sad and old. "All of us had trained under a Weaver at some time. We all knew the beauty of the Lotus Palaces. No man should ever have had to see what we did that day, or be asked to destroy the very soul of the Woven World. That day should have been the end of the War. Sadly, it was only the start."

My tea has gone cold in my hand. All I can see is Harken, standing amid that terrible destruction, lost and alone.

"Serzan has his needle back now." Gemory interrupts the silence, their quiet voice entirely devoid of its customary sarcasm. "He wants to make needles again. To take an apprentice and pass on what he knows."

Serzan's face brightens a little, then darkens again. He holds my eyes, the desolation in his daring me to turn away. "My master died that day," he says quietly, "defending the Lotus Palaces. A Weaver who never lifted his needle for any purpose other than to bring beauty to the world, forced to stand against an army bent on his destruction." His eyes fall away from mine in shame. "I watched him die."

His words hang in the air between us, as stark as they are heartbreaking.

Serzan glances at me briefly, then turns away again, coloring. "Passing on his skill is the only way I know," he mutters, "to honor his memory."

I reach out and cover his hand with my own. "I hope you can," I say, meaning it.

His face lifts in surprise, and for the briefest moment, he almost smiles. Then it fades.

"There are no more apprentices in Astria," Serzan says quietly. "And unless that council changes, there likely never will be."

"*W*hy did you take me there?"

Gemory and I are in the gondola, nearing the Water Palace. *Is it because you wanted me to know what Torsten did? If so, then why?*

Does Gemory know what Harken has told me? Or is there another game afoot?

I feel driven half mad, both by Serzan's story and by my own emotional turmoil. I'm tired of trying to make sense of Astria's intrigues, and I feel heartsick at what Torsten did. I understand more than ever why Kendrick and Feivel question Harken's sparing him. I'm also quietly furious that a man such as Torsten should be the barrier to Harken taking his place on the council, preventing good men like Serzan from rebuilding what they helped destroy.

"Well?" I prompt Gemory, who is looking at the passing gondolas rather than me. "You wanted me to hear Serzan's story. You must have had a reason. You always do."

"Obviously." Gemory casts me a slightly bored glance.

"Why?"

"Because some stories are important to hear." Gemory waves

their needle lazily, clearing a way through the mists. "You needed to hear that one before today's council meeting."

"Today's council meeting? Why?" I look around, suddenly suspicious. "Is it being held here for some reason?"

Gemory makes an impatient noise. "Do you know what a shadowscye is?"

I'm taken aback by the rapid change of subject. "I assume it is similar to a silverscye," I begin.

"Never assume." They leap to the landing and tie the gondola, extending a hand to help me out. "Your answer is that you don't know, so I will tell you."

It can be incredibly frustrating having a conversation with Gemory.

"All scyes are openings," they say as they lead me upstairs. "A Weaver can open a scye from any location and step through to their destination of choice. A Pathfinder must use a silverscye, which is a fixed opening made specifically to move silver from one designated place to another. Silverscyes are carefully monitored, as are the Pathfinders who pass through them in silver form. Pathfinders are forbidden from shifting to silver unless they are using a silverscye." Gemory winks. "Never trust a Pathfinder."

"And Shadows?" I ask.

"Ah." Gemory smiles cryptically. "Shadows don't need scyes of any type to move from one place to another. We do, however, like to listen to things." They wink. "Shadowscyes are one of the ways we do that."

We've come into a room I haven't entered before. In fact, although I've walked down this corridor many times, I'm certain I've never seen this door, let alone the room behind it.

"No, you haven't been here before," says Gemory, with their uncomfortable habit of knowing exactly what I'm thinking almost as rapidly as I do myself. "And nor will you find it again, should you come searching." The golden eyes cast me a stern look. "Even if you were able to find it, you couldn't use it. The House of Thread and Shadows keeps its secrets, and shadows-cyes are one of them."

The room is windowless, bare but for two comfortable armchairs, with a small round table between them. Gemory waves their needle, and a tray of Magel's cakes appear, along with some lavenade. "I like to be comfortable," they say, shrugging. "Council meetings are notoriously tedious."

"We're going to listen to the council meeting?" I'm more than a little shocked. "You have a shadowscye in the Indigo Palace?"

"The House of Thread and Shadows has shadowscyes in every room in Astria." Gemory tilts their head. "Well, every room that matters, and many that others don't think do. But regardless, yes, today we're listening to the Indigo Palace." They hold up a warning finger. "Without comment, mind. Once I open the shadowscye, they can hear us, just as we can hear them. That means sip your lavenade silently, don't clink your glass, and if you need to pass wind, do it silently or leave the room. Am I clear?"

Before I can express my indignation at any or all these suggestions, Gemory waves their needle, and a shadow appears on the wall before us. It's the size of a large window, and as the grainy light begins to clear, it reveals a large, circular flamestone table. The base looks like a golden tree trunk, with boughs that split out from the center, dividing the table into twelve separate places like the golden Astris itself. The entirety gleams with a strange light, almost as if it's alive.

As the room comes slowly into focus, so do the faces. Though I can see mouths moving, the sound is still muffled, like listening through a window. I can't make out the words.

Comitas Ormond's chair is marked by the symbol of a lone golden needle. To his right, Torsten's chair has the same symbol with the twelve-pointed lotus beneath it. Kendrick's, next to him, is marked with the eagle of Goath. On the Comitas's left, Foley's chair is marked with the Serpent Queen of Dencover. Caspian's bears the plain Cup of the Waterlands. Gareth's is next, with Sereia beside him. Both their chairs bear the serpent-twined Indigold Cup, but Sereia's also has the twelve-pointed lotus beneath it. Next to Sereia are two empty chairs.

One bears the pomegranate symbol of the Isle of Nine. The other, directly opposite the Comitas, bears the twelve-pointed lotus.

The Comitas and the Lord of the Woven Court. They're clearly meant to sit opposite one another. *The priestesses don't attend, either*, I think sadly. After all they have suffered, it makes sense. It also seems a tragedy.

The following chair is occupied by a very thin man with a pale face and downcast eyes. Given the golden Astris on the chairback, I assume he is Clement, the Astar, head of the Coronastrian Tapest. Feivel sits beside him, with the same symbol and the lotus beneath it. Lupa, with the staff and flame of the Wolf Weald, sits in the final place between Feivel and Kendrick.

The last of the grainy shadow disappears, and the conversation suddenly bursts into the room where Gemory and I are sitting. I'm so startled I almost leap from my chair. Gemory purses their lips, rolls their eyes, and gives me a warning frown. Too terrified to move again, barely daring to breathe, I sit still and listen.

"Paladin's Water is a sacred gift from the Great Weaver," Feivel is saying. "The fountain in the abbey is the only one of its kind and was given to the Paladins by the Lotus Palaces centuries ago, for use in the Divine Cups. It was never meant to be used in dangerous alchemical experiments."

"What are you suggesting, old man?" Sereia leans over the table, a hard glint in her eye.

Feivel's own eyes flash. "Are you denying that your alchemists are mixing the Water with Serpent's Gold again, when your Divines are clearly going mad with their experiments?"

He's talking about Leo, I realize, recalling how our old friend's hands shook when we saw him at the library.

"And what of your precious Savage King," Sereia spits venomously, "and the storm dragon he sends out daily? It's obvious he's using it to hunt for Serpent's Gold. After the atrocities he's committed, the contempt he's shown for this chamber, do you expect us to believe he doesn't mean to get into the Tower and take the golden needle himself? And what of that slave he's taken in? She plays a part in his schemes too, mark my words."

Too stunned to even turn to Gemory, I am hanging on every word.

"We've been over this." Lupa hits the table with an exasperated hand. "Zaria is no more than a slave from the Seam, exiled after the War like so many others."

"A slave with a zumi from the Isle of Nine and a very suspicious backstory," snaps back Sereia. "Who just happens to be training for the Maverick's Race. We're not Fools, Lupa."

Comitas Ormond and Torsten remain silent throughout this exchange. Caspian and Foley are watching as avidly as if it were theater; I almost expect them to call for wine. Kendrick is quiet and watchful, while the Astar keeps his head bowed. Gareth, the smooth-faced Paladin Consul, clears his throat and beams his false smile around the table.

"The matter at hand is the Shadow Braid she wears." Gareth spreads his hands and tilts his head in affected concern. "You speak of unnatural experiments, Feivel, but the truth is that the darkest of those were the children born to priestesses of the isle during the Kraken's reign. They are the products of unions with all manner of creatures, from Pathfinders to Shadows, not to mention the alchemical cocktails consumed to aid their conception." He frowns regretfully. "We all know Shadow Braids were used by the priestesses and their allies to smuggle out infants who might otherwise have been killed at birth, and to disguise their origins. How can we know this slave isn't corrupted in some way? She might well be full of silver—or even Serpent's Gold. What if Harken's plan is to use her in the Great Ceremony, or for some other dark game of his own? After all"—he looks around the table with a pious air of concern—"the Woven Lord is an unnatural being himself. We should not forget the savagery which made his name."

My heartbeat has slowed to a dull, heavy thud, and I'm gripping the arms of the chair so tightly my knuckles are white. It's all I can do not to run at the shadowscye. I want to beat the politician's smile from Gareth's brutish face. I want to teach him the meaning of the word savagery in a way he'll never forget.

I'm clearly not the only one.

"You dare speak of unnatural in my presence, Paladin?" Lupa's tone is coldly contemptuous, but I can see the wolf lurking in the back of her eyes. I'd say Gareth surviving this chamber is very much an option rather than a certainty. "While you order your alchemists to play Great Weaver again? That way lies the madness that turned a great king into a hideous mutation possessed by Anahita herself." Lupa's eyes narrow. "I had thought," she says in a lethal tone, "that you would have learned the errors of following such a path by now."

"Using Pathfinder's silver in alchemy is no different than the silver in your blood that makes you wolf." Sereia's voice is shrill and furious. *She is dangerous*, I think, watching her. *Unpredictable.*

"It may be the same substance, but you know the difference as well as I." Lupa's lip curls. "Silver has been running in Indigold blood for millennia. Shifting form is what Indigold do. It's part of our heritage. Woven in Air, Water, Fire or the dark Earth of Dencover, we can all shift form, if we only bother to master the skill." Lupa's face twists in disgust, her amber eyes gleaming with a savage light to match Harken's own. "But your father tore Pathfinders apart, just so he could use their silver in his experiments."

Her tone is lethally quiet, her words deliberate enough to make Gareth wince.

"Roark melted them down," Lupa continues relentlessly, "and mixed them with Serpent's Gold. Dark, profane Work the Lotus Palaces would never sanction." She eyes Sereia coldly. "Your father brought Anahita back. Almost gave her a body, and yet you dare to speak of unnatural to me, Sereia? You," she spits contemptuously, "who draws breath only because, for some unfathomable whim of his own that I will never understand, Harken didn't murder you and your brother along with the rest of your damned House when this city fell."

An ominous silence falls over the table. Even from the remove of the shadowscye, I can sense the danger in the air. One false move, and whatever uneasy peace exists at that table could be lost forever.

It's Comitas Ormond who breaks the tension.

"The matter at hand," he says with his heavy-handed bluntness, "is whether or not to outlaw the unweaving of Shadow Braids." The Comitas looks around the table. "Until now, the removal of such braids has been automatically sanctioned by this council at the request of any lord who petitions on the slave's behalf. But I believe we might need to consider imposing a complete ban—one that would outlaw the removal of Shadow Braids completely."

CHAPTER 49

COUNCIL

J breathe deeply, trying to still the desperate fear churning inside me. Gemory eyes me warningly. My nails dig into my palms with the effort of remaining silent.

Breath in. Breathe out.

The Comitas's blunt delivery left no room for misinterpretation.

They're trying to ban the removal of Shadow Braids.

I close my eyes briefly, then open them when Comitas Ormond speaks again.

"The Maverick's Race," he says pompously, "has a noble history. It was once how we chose our kings."

"Until Roark made a mockery of it," Lupa fires back immediately. "He rigged at least three, and possibly four, of the Races that gave him the Crown of Astria. And in doing so, he proved to us all how fragile our world really is." She gestures contemptuously at Gareth. "Roark took the Paladins from their original purpose of serving the Tapest and made of them a militarized force that even now believes itself above the role it was created to fulfill."

She turns back to the Comitas. "Weavers had always been

raised by the Lotus Court, no matter who conceived them. Roark took these two"—she flings a hand at Sereia and Torsten — "and made them servants of his crown. Don't ever speak to me of noble histories, Dirk. That Kraken bastard your own father helped put on the throne stole every shred of nobility from the Race, and from Astria itself."

Sereia looks ready to leap over the table, and Lupa more than ready to meet her. Torsten's face remains impassive.

Kendrick puts a calming hand over Lupa's. "I suggest," he says coldly, eyeing the Comitas with arctic penetration, "that you make your point and get on with it, Ormond."

It's Caspian, however, rather than the Comitas, who answers. Up until this point he has lounged in his chair, watching proceedings with a slight smile.

"If this girl should be freed," he says now, "and by some miracle wins the Maverick's Race, we cannot be certain that Harken will not take her behind the Woven mists to the Isle of Nine and create some Dark Ceremony of his own."

Feivel tenses, and Lupa grips the table. Kendrick shoots them both a quelling glance. Foley smirks beside Caspian.

"Leaving Harken's games aside," Caspian drawls, "if the slave wins, she will be custodian of one of our oldest and richest estates. The equal to any in this room, or close enough." He gestures carelessly around the table, his disgust at the idea palpable. "A girl who has been raised in the Seam and never learned so much as how to wield a needle. Clement." He turns to the pale-faced Coronastrian Astar. "Surely even the Tapest can see the danger posed by such a proposal?"

Clement makes a half-hearted gesture with his hand, looking around the table nervously. I remember Harken's contemptuous description of Clement: *A weak Astar who is little more than a figurehead.*

Kendrick's lips tighten. "What I see, Lord Carliss," he says to Caspian, "is that the opinion of the Tapest matters very little, so long as Dencover, the Waterlands, and the Paladins hold the balance of power at this table. If you want to impose such a ban, you will. You know full well the Woven Lord will not attend this chamber so long as two of Roark's children sit at the table. And while he does not, nor will the priestess Islene." He turns back to Dirk. "This council is yours, Comitas, as you are well aware. You may make what decisions you wish, no matter my opinion, nor that of any other at this table."

His stark words leave an uncomfortable silence in the room. Foley still hasn't spoken at all. I imagine his only purpose is to vote as his father commands. Torsten also has remained silent, but in his case, I can't make out his thoughts or motivations at all. His face is austere, detached, and utterly inscrutable, as it has been on the other occasions I've seen him.

"The danger, my lords and ladies," says Sereia sharply, "is that Harken brought that girl here because he has plans to use her—whether in a ceremony, or to breach the Tower and retrieve the golden needle." She sits back in her chair with a small, spiteful smile. "What manner of madness will be unleashed if the golden needle should fall into his hands?"

Feivel throws his hands into the air in exasperation. "None of us know if that needle is even in the Tower." When Sereia, Caspian, and Foley exchange skeptical glances, he shakes his head wearily. "We don't," he says, with the resigned tone of a man who has been tortured for that very information. "And Harken, for all his faults, has never given the slightest indication of being interested in wielding power for his own ends."

Torsten taps a long finger slowly on the table in front of him. "Perhaps not for his own ends." His low, refined voice is measured and precise. "But if his efforts were on behalf of someone else, then I think we must consider the possibility."

This time the silence is even more uncomfortable, though I don't understand Torsten's meaning.

Is it Anahita they're talking about? I wonder. *But why would Harken want to help her, after all he saw her do?*

I don't have time to ponder the thought, however.

I feel a familiar frisson at my neck, then the shadowscye abruptly closes.

"What do you think you're doing?" Harken's back is to me, but his low, furious tone makes it all too easy to imagine his expression.

"It's my fault," says Gemory quietly.

"Of course it is. That doesn't answer my question."

"She has a right to know what they plan, Harken." Gemory's eyes briefly meet mine. "To know what's at stake for her."

Part of me wants to speak. But whether it's shock from all I've just heard, or simply an unwillingness to cause more tension between Harken and myself, I can't find the words. Instead, I sit there, letting it play out.

"And what then, Gemory?" Harken's tone is hard with tension. "Do you think a slave from the Seam, without so much as a needle in her hand, is going to face down the entire council? Force them to finally deal with the rot in their midst?"

Gemory comes to their feet, their eyes glowing deep gold, like a cave of untapped treasure. "It would be more effective than chasing Dark Rips and taking Huxley out to search for Serpent's Gold."

Serpent's Gold? Why is Harken hunting for that? I'd thought Sereia's accusations nothing more than lies.

"You step on dangerous ground, Shadow." Harken's voice is utterly cold.

"We've been teetering on that precipice for some time now, Lord Harken." Gemory places a heavily sardonic emphasis on the word *lord*. "Perhaps it's time to leap into the abyss. Or would you prefer to return to the Savage Court and cower with Huxley in her gilded cave?"

For what seems an endless moment, Harken stands perfectly

still and silent. Gemory stares back at him without any discernible trace of fear.

Gemory, I think, *is the only one I've ever seen face Harken that way.*

Then he tears the door open with such ferocity it almost falls from its hinges and stalks from the room without another word.

"Well," says Gemory mildly. "That went well, don't you think?"

"You did that on purpose." Despite being grateful for what they've done on my behalf, I'm still annoyed with them. "Surely there was a better way," I say. "One that wouldn't antagonize Harken so badly."

"Ah." Gemory's golden eyes are catlike. "But then, you assume I didn't wish to antagonize him, when the truth is that I had every intention of doing so."

"But why?" When all I get in response is Gemory's enigmatic smile, I shake my head impatiently and go to the door.

Harken, however, is long gone, and I'm left to ponder all I've learned.

CHAPTER 50

TRAINING

When Harken is absent the following morning, I
decide to train alone.

I need time away from the Water Palace, and more importantly, away from anyone else. I feel like I haven't been truly
alone ever since I came to Astria.

I beg Andras to take me through the mists, but when we get
to Fire Hall, I simply wait until he's gone from sight, then take
one of the racing gondolinos and pole slowly downriver.

It's a peaceable way to think. The sun on my back is
comforting, and the steady motion is relaxing. I take a turn
close to the Paladins' abbey, then another into a network of
smaller canals nearby. I've been this way before with Everett
and Brooks. It's a good course on which to practice speed and
turns. I set about training hard, spinning the gondola this way
and that, losing myself in the pleasure of physical exertion.

I try to think through all that I heard in the shadowscye, but
in the end, there's only one thing that matters.

They want to ban Shadow Braided slaves from being freed.

That means not just me. It means my sisters. Levin. Even
Doron, if he's still out there somewhere.

It's just like back in the Seam.

I stab my oar viciously into the water, turning the gondolino sharply.

We're Weorpan here, too, even if the Indigold are too nice to say it to our faces. They mistrust us just as the Seamish did.

I've never obsessed over my parentage, never blamed my unknown mother, but right now, I bitterly wish she'd found another way of saving me from whatever fate she'd thought worse than the one I face now.

I know I need to see Harken, as soon as I get back. Whatever my reasons for holding on to the braid at my neck, the time for such luxuries is gone. The braid needs to come off, as soon as possible.

Otherwise, it may never come off.

The sky overhead darkens, a restless wind stirring the flowers on the bank. In the Seam the wind was often restless. In Astria the breezes are polite, with none of Hiraeth's savage unpredictability.

Perhaps the winds tired of savagery after Astria's War. Or perhaps they save their energy for special occasions, like the Race.

I will find out soon enough.

I spin in the gondolino, bringing my sword down in a sharp cut.

If I'm freed to Race.

I push that thought away. Harken has already offered to unweave the braid, and I've no reason to doubt his word. I know the simple answer to my problem is Harken; the simple answer is always Harken.

He can vote on the council. He can free my sisters.

But there's nothing simple about Harken. Especially when his sole method of dealing with conflict seems to lie in avoiding it altogether, whether it's with me or with the council.

The wind is picking up. I glance uneasily at the sky. I've never seen storm clouds in Astria, despite it being winter here.

Occasionally it has rained during the night, and I've woken to a sparkling world. But hard winds and low, sullen clouds are something new. *Particularly clouds such an ugly orange*, I think, squinting upward. And that smell!

I feel a horrible premonition of danger at exactly the point that I remember what that smell signifies.

"A Dark Rip," I gasp aloud. There's no time to wonder why a Dark Rip would be opening in Astria, and right in front of me. All I know is that I must get out of here—fast.

I thrust the oar through the water, powering the gondolino upriver, toward Fire Hall. But I'm deep in the network of canals and must spin around corner after corner. The wind is picking up, the terrible sulfuric smell growing harder and more acrid.

The wind is so hard now I can barely lean forward, the sky overhead glowing sickly orange against black. I know it's too late. I know the Rip is here.

And then it opens.

Directly in front of me, with the same stunning, terrible darkness that took Doron. This time it isn't across a clearing, but so close I can touch it, the terrible elliptical eye sucking me into the rippling, fathomless darkness. I'm frozen, unable to move, surrounded by a terrible void that claws at my body even as the gondolino is whipped away from beneath me. In a moment, I know with a terrible certainty, Astria will be lost to me forever—and I to it.

Then Huxley is there.

The topaz eyes appear directly in front of me, but there is nothing in them of the placid creature I have seen in the water garden. This is the storm dragon Huxley might have been in her old world, a fierce creature with shimmering eyes and a lethal mouth opened in a roar, her great paw outstretched as she snatches me from the void just as I am falling away from the world.

Her enormous claws close around me, her heated breath scorching my face as she roars.

The braid on my neck seizes, so viciously that my sight fades.

I am spinning away, into the mists of vision.

HARKEN IS STRIDING down a long tunnel. Narrow slits in the walls show deep sea rather than sky. Water drips down the walls and splashes beneath his boots. The air is dank and cold, a terrible silence cut only by the incessant dripping and, far more horribly, by people screaming.

He goes down more stairs, to a deeper level. Here the screams are louder. Round doors cut into the walls of the tunnels have grates over them, through which the odd eye can be discerned, pressed hard against the tiny openings.

"Please," those trapped inside cry to Harken. "Help us."

But Harken does not heed them. He strides directly past them all, until he reaches the furthest, deepest dungeon. Pausing outside the door, he takes a deep breath, as if steeling himself. Then he thrusts his arm into the air and the door is blown open.

A man hangs from the ceiling, suspended by his joined wrists. His head is down, his body slumped, and he is clearly unconscious. His back is a vicious mess of raw flesh, old whip marks overlaid by fresher ones. Every inch of his flesh is scarred and bruised, his limbs twisted and broken.

"Darien." Harken's voice breaks on the name. Moving forward, he cuts the chains with a sharp flick of his fingers and catches the tall, lean body carefully in his arms. The man opens one purple eyelid, and despite his battered face, his lips move in a slight hint of a smile.

"Child," he says quietly. "Thank you."

Harken makes an inarticulate noise of such pain it hurts to hear it. He strides through the dungeons, flinging each door open as he passes, stalking grimly by the broken bodies inside, pausing only long enough to strike them free of their chains. A final door, and he is standing on a stone landing, facing a woman who wears a shawl over her face.

"You must come with us, Prudence," he says. "It's not safe for you here."

"They will need care," the queen says quietly. "And I have help."

Harken's face twists with fury. "Don't trust any of them," he says bitterly. Pressing Prudence's hand briefly, he spins into the air, bearing the broken body before him.

They come to rest in a cool, shaded room I don't recognize. It must be in the Woven Court, for it looks out over fields of Darkberry. Harken lays the man in a vast bed. He does not call for demons, nor anyone else, but bathes every inch of Darien's body with the same care he once did the wounded Weaver he'd rescued from battle. I wonder if Darien is that same man; they share the same lean, spare form, though I never saw the other Weaver's face.

Darien recovers far more quickly than the other Weaver did, however. His skin heals before my eyes, his body rapidly regaining strength, though he seems to need only Darkwine to recover. Darien stares at Harken's face as he is tended, his eyes lingering on the hard planes, the taut expression.

"Harken." He halts Harken's hand. "What has happened to you?" he says quietly. "What have they done?"

"To me?" Harken laughs, a hard, ugly sound. "You know there is nothing they might do to me. But what they have done to each other . . ." Shadows cross his face. "Horrors beyond imagining," he says quietly. "Horrors you could not have envisaged, Darien."

"I have lived a long time." Darien sits up weakly. "I can imagine more than you might know. What of the Lotus Palaces?" He studies Harken's face. "I was captured soon after you were Woven and know little of what took place after. Let me see what they did."

"You don't want to see the Lotus Palaces." Harken shakes his head, his face dark. "I don't go to that place."

"I must." Darien swings his legs over the bed. "Take me," he says,

and there is a hint of command in his voice that even Harken seems to obey.

They travel through the rainbow mist and into the Garden of the Fallen.

Harken stands under one of the old archways, his face a hard mask. Darien leaves him and walks into the sea of flowers, the heavenly symphony of melodic notes and sweet scents. Kneeling down, he places his hands on the earth and closes his eyes.

He is reading the story of the garden itself; I know it by the way his head slowly lowers in sadness. He remains like that for a long time, listening, feeling, his head down so I cannot read his face. He shifts faster than my eyes can follow and is suddenly by the tall Songtree, touching the indigo leaves and their carmine veins in wonder.

"I'm sorry." Watching from beneath the archway, Harken draws a weary hand over his face. "I know you Wove me to save this place. But I failed, Darien. I was too late. It was already gone—"

"Failed!" Darien turns from the tree, his face twisted with sorrow, tears falling freely down his cheeks. "How can you ever think you have failed? You took mindless destruction and made from it a paradise. You took our greatest work and made it a sacred masterpiece." Striding across the garden, he takes Harken's face in his hands. "No," he says fiercely, when Harken tries to push him away. "Look at me." He forces Harken to meet his eyes. "I left you," Darien says gently. "We made you, our greatest creation, and then we shut you inside the scene of a massacre. And yet all this, you did. Alone, in the darkness, still you found a way to show love to another, and to create exquisite beauty." Darien shakes his head slowly. "Fail me?" he says softly. "I have never been more in awe of another being, not in all the many years of my existence."

But Harken shakes his head, tears glittering in the mercurial eyes. "You don't know what I have been," he says harshly. "What I have done."

"Oh, my Woven child." Darien's face softens into a smile, so ancient and wise it seems otherworldly. "If you think me a stranger to

315

savagery, you are more mistaken than you can imagine. But I am here now. And we do not have the luxury of time." Stepping back from Harken, he holds out his hand. "Will you come with me?" he asks quietly. "I would walk with you through time. Teach you all I might, before our hours together must come to an end." His expression becomes wry. "We may have limited time in this world," he says, with a half smile reminiscent of Harken's own, "but in the worlds I walk, time moves differently. Come with me, Harken. I can never make up for the years you have spent alone. But at least allow me to show you how to face the years that lie ahead."

Darien waves a hand, and the two spin into nothingness, a place where I cannot follow.

CHAPTER 51

WOVEN

I wake with tears drying on my own face, the scent of Darkberry rich all around, and Harken leaning over me.

The air is different, and yet familiar. I know its touch, just as I know the vast bed on which I'm lying and the sound of water trickling in the distance.

"The Woven Court." Harken's fists are clenched against the bedcovers on either side of me, his arms rigid with tension. I touch his face. "You brought me home."

"I thought you were gone." Harken's face is pale and set, a distant storm crackling in his eyes. "I felt the Rip open, and you near it, and I thought I'd lost you forever." His hand hovers over the braid knot at his neck. "I felt your fear—" He breaks off, turning his head abruptly, the breath hitching in his throat. He passes a hand over his face. When he turns back to me, the light in his eyes is more violent than ever, a shifting torrent of color. "I can't lose you." His voice rasps like rusted metal. "I can't, Zaria."

"Then don't." The words escape me like a sigh. "Please, Harken." I touch his rigid jaw, and a muscle there flickers. His eyes narrow, then darken with the same fear that has lived within me for so long. I feel it, the moment he steels himself to pull away. My hand tenses on his face. "Please don't shut me out."

Harken stares down at me, still holding himself away from my body. "I wanted you from the moment I saw you in Hiraeth," he says roughly. "But I have loved you since I healed you, the night before the Race."

His lips twist into the half smile I have grown to crave. *"I'm not little,* you said to me then, *and I'm certainly not yours."* His thumb steals out from the clenched fist to stroke a curl on the pillow beside me, lightning burning deep in his eyes. "I knew even then there was nothing small about who you are, or what you meant to me. And beyond all reason, I knew that I had never wanted anything more, in my entire existence, than to make you mine."

"Body and soul." I could never have imagined those words might sound sweet.

He nods slowly. "Wanting you terrified me then." His eyes search mine. "It still does."

We stare at each other, the space between us rich with tension and longing. I don't dare reach for him.

"I never should have claimed you as my slave." The muscles in his arms on either side of me are corded and hard. "Nor made that ridiculous bargain with you. But so long as you wore a braid, I told myself, I couldn't touch you. I wouldn't. I didn't leave that braid on your neck to draw others to you," he says hoarsely. "I left it there to keep myself away. And then, when I was finally past caring, you insisted on keeping the damned thing."

A sigh of laughter chokes in my throat, stoppered by the guilty shadow of my deception. But the shadows flee under his hands, one twined in my hair, the other so close I crave its touch, his eyes searching my face. "I have run as far as Huxley can fly," he says. "Drunk the Water Palace dry of Darkwine. Even hunted demons with Andras, just to take my mind off wanting you." His sharp inhale brings his head up, then back to face me. "Staying away from you has been the hardest thing I have ever done in my life. And I can't do it anymore, Zaria. No matter the danger." His thumb brushes the skin of my neck, just below the braid. "This has to come off." Lightning flashes in his eyes. "Before I go mad with wanting you."

"No." My answer comes from a place behind the shadows and surprises even me. "Not now." My hand covers his own. "Not yet." I'm not ready to let go of the intimacy, the connection that has been comfort and solace since the moment I felt the heat of his body radiate through my own. *In the morning. He can take it then.*

But not now. Not while loneliness and pain are still a shadow inside me, and Harken's writ in every ravaged line of his face.

I want to take the man, I think suddenly. *The man he was in those visions, the man he is now. I want to be bound to him and pay forever, if I must.*

"I want you," I whisper, reaching up to the braid knot at his neck. He shudders as I touch it, his eyes closing briefly, and I feel his heat race through me. "I want to be bound to you, like this, so I can feel you. I need to be, Harken." His eyes fly open, the last vestiges of control fleeing the wild lights in his eyes, and the braid writhes into my body like a sensual river. "I need you, Harken. All of you. I want to be yours—body and soul."

Then his hand is in my hair, the other beneath my body as he gathers me to him. He turns my head, and I arch against him as he tears the shirt from my body and traces my skin with his mouth. He has my clothes off in moments and my legs wide, his mouth on me until I'm groaning aloud. When finally he rears over me again, his burnt-sienna body is hard and hot on my own, indigo eyes blazing with silver and gold. The starlight stream with which he once healed me sets every place he touches on fire, seeming to find a liquid current inside me that craves even the slightest touch.

"I need you," he says roughly.

My hands go around his body, drawing him close. "Then take me."

He does, with barely restrained savagery. I twine about him, his heat and darkness setting me alight. He holds me beneath him, lifting me as he thrusts far inside, to the place where no separation exists. We move together until the starlight explodes within me, and from some distant place, I hear him cry my name.

Later, we bathe together under the waterfall in the bathroom, my back to Harken and his hands on my body as the gloaming grows over the Darkberry fields. I turn to him as the first stars gleam above, kissing him hungrily, and he lifts me to the open ledge and takes me there, slowly this time, his mouth on mine.

CHAPTER 52

DARIEN

*I*t is night, and the waxing moon high, when we wake again. I'm lying across Harken, his heartbeat thick and heavy under my face.

"This palace is completely private." His hand twines in my hair. "Nobody comes here. Not Gemory, not Andras—no one. You're safe here, I promise."

I nod. I know I'm safe here. "I didn't mean to call Huxley," I say. "I know it's dangerous for her to be seen."

Harken's hand stills. "Not as dangerous as a Dark Rip." I can hear the echo of fear lingering in his voice. "Don't hesitate to call her. Not ever. She can always bring you back here."

"Wait." I prop myself up on his chest. "Where is here, exactly?"

Harken's lips curve. "The Woven Court is located upriver of the Paladins' abbey. If you were to look on the map, it would cover the entirety of the eastern river plains, from the abbey in the south to the estates that border Goath in the north. That's why that part of the map lies empty now."

"Then it still exists." I study his face, luxuriating in every detail.

He laughs softly. "Oh, yes. But like the Water Palace, none can find it, let alone enter it. Not unless I allow it to be so."

For a time I lie there, content listening to the nightbirds sing and smelling the Darkwine on the air. There's something I want to ask, but I debate myself, unwilling to betray what I've seen in visions. I settle on a compromise.

"Who is Darien?"

The heartbeat races under my cheek, then gradually slows again.

"I should have known someone would have mentioned that name by now." He doesn't ask who, for which I'm grateful. "Darien was the greatest Weaver Astria has ever known. It was he who first defeated Anahita, long ago, in Sherimah. He was also one of the three people who went into the Tower to fight Anahita this time—and one of the two, along with a priestess named Danae, who never came out."

Beyond the windows, a flock of night birds cross the valley in a muted rush. They shadow the indigo sky as they pass into the mountains beyond, leaving silence in their wake.

"Darien was the one who Wove me, at the start of the War." He inhales sharply, drawing his hand down his face like a mime. He moves slightly, the War an inch between us now in the bed, and he a profile against the valley's darkness as I lie on my side watching him. "He used the golden needle of the Coronastrian Tapest to do it."

Breath fills my chest. "Darien stole the needle?"

"He stole it back. From the Kraken Weavers, and from Anahita." There is only the faintest edge of rebuke, but I feel it, nonetheless—the hole made of his memories that I can never be part of. "Darien knew that without the needle, Anahita's power was limited, her threads trapped in the clumsy Kraken form. He also knew she'd stop at nothing to find it—and that if she did, Astria would be lost."

The braid at my neck is quiet. This is history, not Harken's memory. This is a place I can't follow.

"As the Kraken armies marched on the Woven Court, Darien called the greatest of Astria's Weavers here and closed the gates. Not all came, of course." His voice hardens momentarily. "Some had already chosen a different path. Others had been imprisoned for their part in Roark's ambitions."

Sereia, I think, remembering the needlemaker's story.

"Darien asked for the Weavers' permission, and their combined skill, to Weave from the threads of their Woven Court a guardian for it. A truly immortal being Woven from the best of them, strong enough to be a shield against Anahita and with an allegiance to the court that was impossible to break. One made of the court and bound to it."

"Body and soul." The words escape me like a sigh.

His outward breath is a reluctant huff of acknowledgment. From my sideways position, his lips are like a marble sculpture, timeless and eternal.

"Darien's request went against every law of the Woven Court. To Weave the threads of life itself was the very vanity that had destroyed Sherimah. But Darien had already faced Anahita once, and he knew what she was capable of. It had taken a thousand years and more to rebuild even half of what was destroyed when Sherimah was blown into the Interweave. Creating me was the only way Darien knew to ensure our world was not lost again."

His head twists to me, his eyes pinpricks in the darkness. "The Weavers agreed, or at least those still loyal to the court agreed. Even though it violated the law they were sworn to uphold. Even though they knew it could mean their death."

There is a stark clarity to his words that precludes sympathy.

"The Weavers held the Woven Court safe for the full day and night it took to create me. They contributed threads of their own, but ultimately, it was Darien, with the golden needle, who truly Wove me into being." Harken has turned away as he speaks. Now he stares up into the night, his eyes far from me. A loose thread from the drapes overhead gleams in the starlight. He turns it slowly between thumb and forefinger.

"By the time they were done, the Kraken armies had come to the gates. Still, we might have been safe. The Woven gates were not easily opened, even before they were behind the mists.

"But the Weavers were not naturally suspicious, especially of their own." He rolls the thread with studied precision. "When a Weaver called to them asking for entry, they opened the gates in good faith."

"Torsten." The needlemaker's story impacts even harder, now that I understand what had happened on the other side of those gates before Torsten's arrival.

Harken gives the barest nod. He releases the thread, and it turns slowly in the still air. "The Weavers had never trained to be fighters," he says finally. "And they were exhausted after their efforts. Most died where they stood. Darien ensured the golden needle was safe, then, in a final act, closed the Woven Court and sent it into the mists, beyond sight of this world. He was utterly spent. The Kraken Weavers took him then, when he was at his weakest, and threw him into the water dungeons beneath the Indigo Palace."

Harken swings out of bed in an abrupt movement, striding naked to the terrace. He leans his elbows on it, his hands clasped behind his neck, head down. After a moment, I follow him, the night air wrapping about me like a sweet song. When I come alongside, Harken raises his head with a harsh exhalation and grips the terrace, staring out into the valley.

"Darien never told anyone, not even me, where he put the golden needle, though Anahita's Krakens tortured him for five years without mercy. Most, even many Weavers, assumed I had it." He shakes his head curtly. "I didn't," he says, shortly. He glances at me, as if to ensure I heard him. "I don't."

"Did you ever meet him again?" I ask tentatively. "Darien?"

Harken nods slowly. "We met the night before he went into the Tower." Starlight shows his half smile. "I know it makes little sense, but time is a changeable tapestry, as Darien used to say. It exists in countless threads, all of which are present at any given time. They simply weave together in different patterns, at different times.

"Darien took me walking into that tapestry. We had only one night and day of Astrian time. But Darien and I walked together for centuries."

His fingers drum restlessly against the terrace. "He tried to show me all he could. We stepped into ages past, myths and legends now lost into the mists of time." He glances at me with a short, twisted smile. "We even appear in some of them, which is always amusing when I spend time in the Foolish world." His smile fades as he turns away again. "Darien taught me how to follow the threads and navigate the Interweave. He tried to teach me everything I might need to keep the Woven Court, and the many worlds connected to it, safe. Safe from the ambitions of the Indigold, other Weavers, and even Fools.

"You asked me who Darien was," he says quietly. He twists his head to me, still gripping the terrace. "To me, Darien was everything."

"And then you lost him." I ache to touch him.

"Then Astria lost him." Harken passes a hand briefly over his face. "And our world has been darker for it ever since." He turns to me, drawing me close. "But now you are here." He kisses me, and we don't speak for a long time.

It's the early hours of the morning when I wake to find Harken standing on the terrace once more. Something in his stance instantly alerts me.

"What is it?"

Harken turns, his face as stark and hard as I've ever seen it. "A Breeze came from Goath." He holds out his hand, and a single snowflake drifts through the moonlight, bringing with it a chill wind and Kendrick's voice.

"Council has voted to outlaw the removal of Shadow Braids." The words echo bleakly around the chamber. *"I thought you would want to know."*

CHAPTER 53

FREEDOM

*T*he moon is full. It's the night of the third Revel, the final one before the Race. It is to be held at Caspian's estate, Caeruleis, in the Waterlands.

Harken and I are not attending, of course.

"We need to decide what to do." I'm standing in our bedchamber as the moon rises over the Darkberry orchards, lighting the silvery threads that twine in the deep-colored berries. In the days since I've been here, we've barely left the Summer Palace, as Harken calls it. He's standing by the window now, shirtless, hands thrust in his breeches, staring across the valley toward the mists that shield the Garden of the Fallen. I call them the *rainbow mists,* in my mind, since when I've seen them in my visions they've shimmered with colors the Woven mists do not. But I can't talk about that.

We talk about the council decision a lot. But there are other things we don't speak of. Those things are beginning to weigh on me, like air heavy with the coming winter. I fear that weight will drag us down if we do not address what has been left unsaid.

"It was my fault, Harken." I bring winter into the Summer

Palace. "You wanted to take the braid off. It was me who told you not to."

Because I didn't want to lose the intimacy it offers. Because I'm afraid that without it, your world will close to me. That perhaps I will wake up one day and find myself on the other side of the Woven mists, unable ever to find my way behind them again.

"I can unbraid you anyway." He turns back from the window, the moon lighting his unsmiling face. "The council can't stop me. They never could."

"But they can stop me from racing." I move closer to him. "Without their vote, I'm still enslaved, whether you have unwoven my braid or not. In their eyes, I would still be an outlaw."

I'm wearing one of his linen shirts and little else, and my hair is down. His mouth curves in the half smile that makes my heart turn over. He moves, and suddenly I am held before him, my back to his chest, his lips on my neck as we look out across the orchards. It is sublimely beautiful behind the mists, like a different world. Even the air tastes different here, sweeter, as if two thousand years of peace are distilled in every breath.

"I want to show you something."

"I think you've done that. Several times." That's how we have dealt with the weight of the council's decision, by losing ourselves in one another. Here it is easy to stay lost. The Woven Court holds the weight of winter at bay.

Harken's laughter rumbles against my back, his arms tightening about me.

"And I plan to do it again. Soon." He turns me in his arms. "But for now, come with me." I look down at my lack of clothing and raise an eyebrow. Harken shakes his head. "It doesn't matter, not where we're going."

I nod, and he spins me into darkness.

We alight on a beach head. Rocky cliffs surround us, the sea glittering under the moon. The *Hydra* lies at anchor off the shore. Harken points to a small island, not far from shore. "Can you see Huxley?" I frown, staring into the moonlight, until a great tail shifts, the colors caught by the light.

"It's her home," Harken says quietly. "The coast of the Woven Court is behind the mists, quite a way out to sea. Huxley is safe here. She can fly and hunt for her own food, without fear of those who would harm her." He faces me, his eyes grave. "Huxley still hunts for Serpent's Gold," he says quietly. "I know you heard that, through the shadowscye. I want you to understand the truth." He brushes my hair back over my shoulders. "She doesn't fly into the Interweave. I don't send her to find the missing fragments that are lost there; that is a mission for Fools and madmen. But I do send her out to find Serpent's Gold in this world. Not because I wish to use it, for anything." A shadow of distaste passes his face. "Because I know how powerful it is," he says quietly, "and what might become of Astria, should too many Rips be made in her fabric. And because I have seen, in my time walking with Darien, how such gold can be put to work by the ambitious in their efforts to become immortal and all-powerful. I will do all I can to protect our world from that."

He nods out to sea, where Huxley slumbers peacefully. "She brings it back here, to her cave on that island. It makes her feel safe—and there could be no safer place for the gold to lie. Huxley would defend it with her life."

We stand there for a time, the foamy sea running over our bare feet, watching dolphins leap through moonbeams. A soft Darkwine breeze dances on the air, and Harken's arms about me are the home I've never had.

But the braid about my neck is still there. And the home is Harken's, not mine.

"Gemory called it a gilded cave." I turn in Harken's arms so I can meet his eyes. "They didn't only mean Huxley's cave. Gemory was talking about this, all of it." I nod behind us, where the vast acres and glorious old buildings of the Woven Court stretch as far as the eye can see. Though I've seen little more than the Summer Palace and the restored palaces Harken uses as his Savage Court, I can nonetheless grasp the scope and magnificence of his domain. "It was never meant for one man and dark creatures, Harken. And so long as I stay here, behind the mists, I am as much a captive as I ever was." My arms twine about his neck, though he is very still. "As much as you are," I say quietly.

Harken makes an impatient noise and moves out of my embrace. "I know my role in this world," he says shortly. "I learned it—" He stops abruptly.

"From Darien." I finish the sentence for him, though he flinches at the name. "You learned all you know from Darien." An image of the teacher I saw in my visions crosses my mind, there and gone. Harken has not mentioned him again, and I have not asked. I can't; to do so would be to reveal knowledge that now, since he began to speak to me of his life, feels like more of a betrayal than ever before. "Do you truly believe that Darien would have wanted you to remain locked up in here?" I move closer to him, touching his bare arm. "To cut yourself off from the world beyond the mists?"

"Go behind the mists, Zaria." Neoma's whispered Sight, her unfocused eyes the day I said farewell to my sisters in the Seam, come in a flash of unbidden, sudden memory. It's eerie to hear her voice, and those words, here, behind the Woven mists.

I don't have time to think on it, however.

"The world beyond the mists isn't safe. Not for you, not for anyone." Harken's eyes are hard. "I told you I can unbraid you. I can unbraid your siblings, too, and bring them all here. The council's approval matters for nothing inside my court." He looks down at me, and his face softens, the moonlight dancing in his eyes. "You can make this your home," he says. "Here you're beyond the reach of the council. Of any of the Indigold and their petty games. You will want for nothing, I promise."

I touch his face, and he kisses me. I can feel the ache between us, the divide, between what he wants for me and what I know is right for myself.

When finally we draw apart, I measure my words carefully. "If you unweave our braids, the council will consider us outlaws. Unable to own property. Unable to wield a needle."

Harken frowns. "Why would you want a needle? I can Work enough for us both, and there is an army of demons able to serve your every need—"

"You've never had a needle." I cut him off. "Never needed one. You and your threads are one and the same, your ability to Weave an extension of yourself. But for slaves in the Seam, a needle is a symbol of power and freedom. It represents the right to create a life of one's own choosing. Of course I want a needle, Harken." I search his face, willing him to understand. "I want to win that Race, just as I promised myself I would. To win an estate of my own, and coin enough—"

"That nobody can ever buy you again. Yes, I remember," Harken says impatiently. "You told me this when we made that damned bargain. But there's no need for that now." He shakes his head, frowning. "I can buy you any estate you want. Build you a palace to rival anything in the Woven Court. There is nothing stopping you from attending all the Revels you wish if that is what you choose."

"The Revels can go to the Tells." I'm more upset than I realized. Harken's face begins to close over, and I take a deep breath, trying to find the right words. "Once, long ago, I made choices for my siblings. Plans that I believed were right, and my right to make for them. That arrogance might not be the only reason they are all where they are now, but I have wondered ever since if it might all have been avoided, had I simply trusted them more, listened in a better way. You are offering me everything." I step toward him. "And I trust you implicitly. But I can't make those choices for my siblings again, no matter how much I want to save them. The only thing I can give them now is their freedom, and their right to make a life of their choosing. If you unbraid them, I'm simply making the same mistakes again. I can't do that, Harken. I won't."

Harken's eyes narrow as I speak, and by the time I'm finished, his hands are thrust in his pockets once more, his eyes glittering like the cold stars above. "You're asking me to sit at that table," he says slowly.

"I'm saying that it won't end here." I want to take his hand, but he is cold and remote, and I know it would be a gesture too far.

"No matter how much Serpent's Gold Huxley finds, there will always be someone searching for more, or another way to gain power, just as they are doing by banning the unweaving of Shadow Braids. What will it be next time that they decide is unnatural? Lupa's wolves? Pathfinders? And all the while, they tolerate Arkady in their midst."

It's this hypocrisy that has stung the most, ever since Kendrick's Breeze came through the window.

"Arkady came through a Dark Rip." I hold Harken's eyes, not flinching from the hard anger in them. "That is what began all this. We still don't know why he's here, nor who is helping him —and meanwhile, those same people who want to ban me from racing because I am some kind of unknown creature are quite willing to drink Darkwine beside Arkady and sponsor him to race. Why would they do that? What if they really are trying to find a way into that Tower, as Kendrick said?"

"I said I will get to the bottom of it, and I will." Harken's voice is terse.

"And then what?" I shake my head. "You kill or imprison those you find responsible? That won't stop them, Harken." I know I've pushed too far, can see it in the rigid line of his jaw, the hard gleam in his eye. But I can't simply stand by and say nothing, live in this wonderland to be waited on by demons, while the world beyond crumbles into darkness.

"What is it that you want of me?" He bites the words out.

"Meet with Lupa and Kendrick. Invite them here. Into the Savage Court, if not to the Summer Palace. Talk with them, at least. Hear what they have to say."

He stares at me. "I can't sit at that table," he says roughly.

"I'm asking you to listen." I step closer to him, touch his cheek. "That's all, Harken. Just listen."

CHAPTER 54

FAMILIAR

*W*e are sitting on the terrace of what Harken rather darkly calls the heart of his Savage Court. The interior is a vast expanse of carved ocher walls, filigree archways, and trickling fountains. It is where Harken conducts his business and during the day is often quite busy with his wranglers and demons coming and going.

The outer terrace, however, is a tranquil place facing out over the river and the plains beyond that lead to the mist-covered gates. It is a long garden with winding mosaic paths and a fountain that runs the length of it, water shooting glistening arcs into a lotus-filled pool. Flowers climb across the walls, and in the circular end of the terrace where we sit now, wisteria hangs overhead. We are at a large mahogany table inlaid with mother-of-pearl, an exquisite array of dishes before us, but the conversation couldn't be more at odds with the idyllic surroundings.

"You're a stubborn bastard, Harken." Kendrick's voice is clipped and hard, his eyes arctic shards. "Breezes don't lie, and Goath has been Keeper of Breezes for as long as the Woven Court has stood. Someone is using Serpent's Gold to open Rips, for what purpose we don't know. The Paladins are mixing ever darker brews, and their military arm is greater than it's ever been. Dirk and his Paladin helpers seem bent on crushing the last life from the Coronastrian Tapest and gaining ever more control over the rest of us." He puts his cup down on the table with more force than necessary. "We need you at that table. We need your vote. We need to find a way to keep these bastards in check."

Harken sprawls long legged in his chair with every appearance of boredom. His public mask is firmly in place, the glittering, hard eyes, slightly cruel smile, and pronounced sardonic drawl. He lifts an indolent brow as Feivel adds his voice. "The ban on Shadow Braids is likely just the beginning." Feivel sounds tired and stressed. "It's how it began last time," he says. "I may have lost my memories, but I can read histories as well as anyone else. And there's something else." He passes a hand over his face. "I returned to the Seam a few days ago, to collect some things. My rooms there had been thoroughly upturned."

"Your rooms?" Lupa frowns. "What was taken?"

Feivel shakes his head. "Nothing, that I could discern. But I think we can all imagine what they were looking for."

"A pointless search," Harken says dismissively. "They tortured you for years to find your Familiar. If they didn't find it then, they're hardly likely to find it now." But his eyes have narrowed slightly, and I can sense interest behind them.

"That's all you have to say?" Kendrick laughs derisively, sitting back in his chair and eyeing Harken with palpable frustration.

"What's a Familiar?" I look between them. "I haven't heard that term before."

"It's something Weavers make." Feivel gives me a strained smile. "I'm not the first Weaver to have faced the loss of their needle. In a long, immortal life, it is a real risk. A Familiar is an object in which the Weaver places a thread from his needle.

Insurance, if you like. Should the needle be stolen, lost, or otherwise destroyed, the Familiar acts as a lodestone that can instantly locate it. In the worst case, a new needle can be fashioned from the Familiar itself."

"What kind of object?" I ask.

"Many fashion them into jewelry. A ring, a pendant. But a Familiar can be anything." Feivel shrugs. "One Weaver I read of made his into a birdcage. Of course, there are those who like to use the thread to imbue one of their everyday objects with particular power. A metalworker might place it in their hammer, for example, or a salver in the cauldron used to mix potions. Usually, Weavers like to keep their Familiar close. It is a part of them, and infinitely precious."

"But Feivel lost his memory with his needle." Harken waves dismissively. "So he can't recall what his Familiar was or where he put it."

"What Feivel is too polite to say," Kendrick says, giving Harken a reproving look, "is that his Familiar is the chief reason he was held in the dungeons for so long and tortured with such determination. Dirk and his supporters knew that if they could locate the Familiar, it would link Feivel to his needle."

"And that, in turn, would take Feivel back into the Tower." I nod, understanding.

"But they didn't find it." Harken's tone is blunt. "And since Feivel here can neither recall what form his Familiar took, nor where it might be, it seems to me that a search is rather futile." Despite his dismissive manner, long fingers drum against his leg under the table, and his eyes have a distant look in them.

It seems I'm not the only one who notices.

"Harken." Lupa leans forward, hands clasped on the table. "If someone is searching for that Familiar, there's only one reason why. I've been saying this for months: they're trying to get back into that Tower, either to get the golden needle or to awaken Anahita, if that is even possible. Either way, we can't afford that

Tower being breached. We might never be able to Weave its like again—" She stops abruptly, coloring faintly. I know she means because they no longer have Darien, and by the sudden, fierce gleam in Harken's eye, he does too.

"The Woven Tower is behind my gates." Harken's voice is clipped and hard. "To even approach it, they would have to come through me, and you know as well as I that is impossible."

"People thought resurrecting Anahita was impossible, until Roark managed it." Kendrick's voice is cold and dispassionate as Harken's own. "You are assuming that any attempt on the Tower will be made directly at your gates. But we're dealing with Paladins and alchemy, Harken." When he doesn't immediately respond, Kendrick pushes his point. "Nobody can pass your mists. All of Astria knows that. But what is the first lesson a Weaver teaches the Indigold holding a needle?"

"Having never held a needle myself, Kendrick, you might need to enlighten me." Harken's tone is scathing, but again, I sense something behind his eyes, a gleam that tells me he is perfectly aware of the answer and is simply using this as a distraction to take a moment of thought for himself.

It's Feivel, in his patient way, who answers. "In all Weaving," he says quietly, "for every warp there is a weft."

"In other words," Lupa interrupts impatiently, seeing my confusion, "all Weaving begins with something that is solid, or in place. The needle Weaves, or Works, around what already exists."

I try to think this through. "Does that mean that instead of trying to Weave their way through Harken's mists, somebody might be trying to work with things that are already in the Tower? To—Weave a thread around something inside it, to gain entry?"

Kendrick gives me an approving glance. "I begin to see why Harken likes you so much."

Lupa chuckles. "Wait until you see her with a gondolino."

I color. Harken, however, seems entirely oblivious. *I know that expression*, I think, watching him. *He has a suspicion, but he won't share it.*

Feivel, too, ignores the side conversation. "They would still have to find a way through the mists, not to mention past Harken." He shakes his head, frowning. "I can't see how anyone could do that."

"Neither do I," Lupa says, "but Kendrick and I wonder if whatever is planned might have something to do with the Maverick's Race."

"The Race?" Harken's head jerks up, suddenly attentive.

"The ban on Shadow Braids seems rather . . . timely." Kendrick meets Harken's eyes. "And begs the question of whether someone might have a very good reason to keep Zaria out of that Race. The Braid Race in the Seam was used to free Arkady. Is it possible something may be planned for this one too, something that relies on Arkady winning it?"

"This was exactly how Roark won his six Races." Lupa takes up where Kendrick stops. "By simply disposing of any in the field who might pose a challenge. Everyone knows once the Race is in play, cheating is impossible; the Work binding the Race itself is too arcane and strong to have it go undetected. But killing the competitors before they ever get to the starting line —well, that is something else again. And whatever else you deny," Lupa says quietly, staring at Harken, "you told me yourself that someone has tried very hard, more than once, to kill Zaria."

Harken doesn't answer. One finger toys with a glass on the table, turning it slowly in place, but his face is utterly inscrutable.

A short, rather tense silence is broken by Kendrick. "Dreaver's Tells, Harken." He rakes a hand impatiently through his hair. "You love the girl," he says bluntly. "It's plain to us all, has been from the day you walked her into that damned Revel."

Lupa gives an unladylike snort of laughter. Even Feivel looks slightly amused. My face is afire.

"If you won't sit at that table for the rest of us," Kendrick says, "then do it for her. You claimed Zaria before the ban; you have every right to challenge it. Lodge an appeal to the council to have that damnable braid removed. Otherwise," he says, "you're tacitly agreeing with them that Zaria is Weorpan. Unwanted, and unfit to sit at any table at all." He holds Harken's eye grimly. "You might be savage, Harken. But I've never thought you cruel."

Harken is lethally still. For a terrible moment I think he will lean across the table and tear Kendrick's head from his shoulders. Then his eyes shift to me and soften slightly.

He spins his wine cup on its stem in a decisive gesture. "Almost twenty years," he drawls, "I've kept these gates closed and enjoyed peace. I open them for one night. One," he says, glaring around at them all, "and any trace of peace is gone." Picking up the cup, he drains it and places it back on the table with infinite care.

"Very well," he says finally. "I'll lodge the appeal."

CHAPTER 55

WEFT

*H*arken leaves the next morning.

"I may be gone for a few days." We're in the Summer Palace, in the bedchamber that has, despite my urging Harken to leave it, become my favorite place in all the world. Harken, tawny in the early morning sun, is in the chair, pulling on boots over his breeches. "Kendrick says he might have found something in Goath's records about Arkady. I want to take a look." He pulls me down to his knee, kissing me so thoroughly I begin to lose track of time. "Andras will be in the Savage Court," he murmurs. "And if you need me, all you need do is touch the braid. I will feel you."

I pull back, frowning. "You feel it? If I touch the braid?"

"I feel—something." Odd shadows shift over Harken's face. "Emotions, I guess. And I know where you are. Physically, I mean." His lips touch my neck. "Mentally," he murmurs against my skin, "you might be miles away. I can't tell what you're thinking. It drives me mad sometimes."

I'm glad he can't see my eyes.

"I want you to know." He pulls back so I can see his eyes. "I will lodge the appeal. But I don't know if I can sit at the council table." His mouth tightens. "I need you to know that."

I nod slowly. "I know you will do what you can," I say quietly.

He kisses me again, long and sweet. "I'll be back as soon as possible."

I spend the next days either riding Huxley or training.

The first time she takes me flying it's at night. I wake to find her staring at me through the window, her topaz eyes brimming with mischief. A moment later I am atop her warm, leonine back, clinging to the iridescent feathers as we silently wing through the night sky.

After that first, exhilarating moonlit flight, we fly every day, and gradually I gain a real sense of Harken's domain.

The Summer Palace is located on the side of a mountain, the tallest point of the Woven Court. Below it, the hillside stretches to the vast Darkberry orchards. Beyond the orchards is a deep valley. On the other side of it, the old Lotus Court is hidden behind a shimmering rainbow mist. I know, from my visions, the Garden of the Fallen lies behind that same mist. I fly Huxley close to it, but never cross the line.

Following the valley downhill leads to the restored palaces now known as the Savage Court. Though Harken treats them dismissively, to me even the Savage Court is a place of wonders.

A tributary of the Indigo River runs through the center of it, wending about from the other side of the mountain to the Summer Palace. An ancient stone lane runs beside the river, with smaller mosaic plazas coming off it that lead to different palaces. Each building is dedicated to a different function of the Savage Court, with an entire circus devoted to the larger animals Harken's demons capture and a great aquatic chamber for those that come from the sea. Many of the buildings have clearly been repurposed; most seem to have existed in some way before. Ancient fig, yew, and pomegranate trees grow amid the mosaic plazas, with winter jasmine and citron adding freshness to the Darkwine air.

The Savage Court is a busy place, though run with ruthless efficiency by Andras and his team of demon wranglers. They come in all shapes and sizes, some demons themselves, others creatures I've never seen but who seem to have found a home in service to Harken.

Largely, though, I spend my time training in the canals and flying on Huxley.

Harken has been gone for three days when I touch the braid.

I'm not certain I mean to, exactly. One moment I'm standing in the bedchamber, staring out toward the Lotus Court and thinking of all Harken told me about Darien. The next moment, my hand is on the braid, and I'm there.

I'M STANDING *by the Songtree in the Garden of the Fallen. The night sky above is studded with stars. Harken and Darien face one another, close by.*

"You have to let me go." Darien's face is extraordinary, angular and smooth, like old slate that has been sculpted into gleaming perfection. He has a remote quality that makes his presence slightly surreal, neither Indigold nor Weaver, but something else entirely. "We have no choice. It is for this moment that you were created, and for which I have been preparing for longer than I can recall."

"I can't do this without you." Harken's voice is filled with pain and loneliness so deep it hurts my soul to hear it. "At least let me fight her at your side."

"I wish it could be different." Darien grips Harken's shoulder. "But the Woven Court can't be risked. Even broken as it is, still the power of Astria itself is contained in every inch of its soil. It isn't only the books in the library or the learning in the walls. The very threads of our world are held here, in the Woven Court." He speaks with sad finality.

"It cannot fall into the wrong hands. We almost lost it once, and if Anahita escapes, we easily could again. Too much is at stake."

"What of Anahita herself?" Harken's eyes are hollow caverns. "What if you, Feivel, and Danae cannot defeat her?"

"We can't defeat her." Darien's calm acceptance is heartbreaking. "I know that, Harken. I've shown you what happened the last time we fought." He stares past Harken, into the past. "Sherimah was blown into the Interweave," he says quietly, "and Anahita with it—but she didn't die. And nor will she, so long as she can gather enough Serpent's Gold to find her form again. That's what you must do now." He turns back to Harken. "Seek out that gold, no matter how long you search. Send the Stitched Men into the Interweave, if you must. Collect it all, and find a way to give it back to Astria. I thought I'd done it, all those years ago." Shadows chase over his eyes. "But the six golden needles are gone, some stolen, others lost. And Anahita doesn't need all of them, Harken. She only needs one—or enough fragments to make one."

Harken's hands clench in fists of frustration. "What does any of it matter, if you can't defeat her? Why even go into that Tower in the first place? And why are you so certain you can get her in there?"

"Because I know Anahita." Darien's voice is as curt as I've heard it. "I know her weaknesses. I can offer her something she can't resist: a body, and my help to bind her into it. Danae is head priestess of the Isle of Nine, experienced with Darkwine trance, trained in embodiment. She eluded Anahita last time; now she offers herself willingly in exchange for a cessation of war, or so Anahita will believe.

"Anahita has been smoke for two thousand years, Harken. Finally, she succeeded in threading herself into a living form—only to find herself trapped in the body of a Kraken for five years. The Kraken was Roark's shifter form, never meant to hold something as powerful as her. Now that Kraken body is dying—and Anahita is desperate."

He touches the Songtree with one hand, his face softening. "Once Anahita is in the Tower, Danae and I can bind her. Feivel believes he can hold her until it is done. And I would trust Feivel with my life." Pain darkens his face. "Though it hurts me to use him that way. It will *be nothing short of a miracle if he survives. I will do all I can to ensure he makes it out alive, but you must be there, Harken, to pick him up when he is thrown from that Tower. If he falls into the hands of the Kraken Weavers, he might as well be dead."*

"And I am supposed to simply stand by and watch." Harken's tone is bitter.

"You are supposed to survive. And with you, the Woven Court." Darien's tone is quiet but resolute. "The Tower was made with the help of the House of Thread and Shadows, Woven specifically to hold Anahita. If we succeed in binding her inside it, Feivel will leave the Tower, and immediately Shadow mists will cloak it so that none may enter—not even you." Harken flinches as if he has been struck. "Eternity," says Darien quietly, "is something I understand better than most. I do not wish yours to be tormented by curiosity. The House of Thread and Shadows is the only power in Astria capable of both creating a completely impenetrable barrier and holding it—even against you, if necessary. It is an added layer of protection.

"But for the duration of the battle with Anahita, the Woven Tower must be left outside the Woven mists. If she should defeat us, Harken, and escape that Tower, the Woven Court must be protected. Nor can the Tower be left vulnerable, for the Kraken armies will descend the instant they realize their queen is trapped. Mine won't be the only battle fought when dawn comes. Many will fall in the time it takes for Danae and I to bind Anahita." Stark lines cut Darien's face, new, raw cracks in a statue worn smooth with time. "Seal the Woven Court behind the mists, then Weave your own threads around the Tower. You must hold the Tower, hold it safe, while that battle rages."

He grips Harken's shoulders. "No matter what you see," he says roughly, "what you witness, your place is here, holding the threads of this earth together. So long as the Woven Court is behind the mists and bound to you, it cannot fall. And you must hold those threads." Tears glisten in Darien's eyes. "It is why you were made," he says again. "Neither you nor I are truly of this world, Harken. And that means we must be its most faithful servants."

For a long time they stare at each other, pain and love one and the same between them.

When Harken finally speaks, his voice is like old stone. "Tell me what to do."

Darien closes his eyes briefly. Releasing Harken's shoulders, he steps away. "Hold the threads until Feivel falls from the Tower," he says quietly. "If he does not, then Anahita will have won, and your sole responsibility will be to hold the Woven Court. If Feivel falls from the Tower, then we have succeeded. Anahita will be bound and the Shadow mists will rise, locking the Tower behind them. Then you must take the Shadow Bound Tower back into the Woven mists with you. Don't lift them again, not until you know the Woven Court is safe."

"When will that be?" Harken says fiercely. "And how will you ever leave that Tower?"

"It is better that I should never come out of that Tower." Darien meets his eyes. "I wish I did not have to leave you with this burden— but I do know you can bear it." His smile is beautiful. "You are Woven from the best of us. Everything that is good in this world was given to Weave you. No other can be trusted to safeguard our world and our knowledge. I wish I could remain with you, but I cannot. I am the only one who can bind Anahita. And once it is done, you must never search for me, not in this world or any other. The Shadow Bound Tower must be kept separate even from the Woven Court, Harken. Weave it with threads of your own devising, and Weave them strong. Keep that Tower safe. For every warp, there is a weft." Darien frowns. "There is always a pathway, no matter how well Woven the Work. And there are those who will never cease trying to find a way through this one. Do you understand?"

Harken bends his head. "Will there ever be an end to it?" he whispers.

"For you, there is no end." Darien braces his hands on Harken's shoulders. "You were not born, and you cannot die. You are the only Woven Lord, Harken, created from every thread of this world and spun into being by greatest of our kind. I have taught you all I can,

taken you through worlds and times, tried to walk a thousand lifetimes with you in the short time we have had together. You are the keeper of our world now. I wish it did not have to be so lonely a task. But I also know there is none better made to bear that burden."

Harken meets his eyes and his shoulders stiffen, as if to take the weight that has just been dropped to them. "I want you to know that I will never forgive them." Harken's voice trembles with emotion. "If it takes a thousand lifetimes, I will find those who did this to us and see they pay for what they have done."

"No." Darien shakes his head. "Such hatred will only make eternity more painful. Take it from someone who has lived more lifetimes than most men can dream of. Let it go." Darien steps away, drawing his cloak about him. In his smile I see a shadow of Harken's own, a strangely familiar twist to his mouth. "Now bid me farewell, and let an old vampire go and taste his last meal."

Vampire!

If I could gasp, I would. I'm not certain I ever believed such a creature truly existed, outside of Feivel's books and the tales told by Fools. Vampires belong to Dark Rips and Foolish legend, not to Astria.

Something in my reaction, though, must somehow have penetrated the braid vision, for Harken stiffens.

"What was that?" He swings around, his eyes roaming the garden.

Darien looks exactly at me, and for a moment I would swear he can see me. His smile becomes enigmatic. "Now that," he murmurs, "is what I would call hope."

CHAPTER 56

SONGTREE

*H*arken returns, bringing the outside world with him.
"A dinner," he says, casting his eyes skyward.
"They're all coming. Kendrick, Lupa—even Prudence." He
smiles wryly. "My demons are in ecstasies." I hide my face in his
chest, along with my guilt. I need to tell him about the braid. I
can't hide the truth anymore; I don't want to.

The conversation I witnessed has haunted me since I woke
from it. It is at once unbearably poignant and a sick, guilty
shadow on my soul.

I should have told him long ago.

It was selfish, my craven holding to the braid. A way of
prying into a man who has offered me nothing but truth. I can
no longer fool myself that my deception is anything other than
a lie—one that is now forcing Harken to take steps toward those
he despises and a world he rightly mistrusts.

But in the bustle leading up to the dinner there never seems
to be a right moment. A dozen times the words hover on my
tongue, weighty as marbles in my mouth, but smooth and slippery, easily swallowed again.

Too easily, I think in frustration. It is evening, and we are dressing for the dinner Harken has organized. I am fixing my hair with my back to him. His torso is bare, his corded back to me as he pulls on his breeches.

"I told you about the blank entry in the records of Goath."

"Yes. You thought it might have something to do with Arkady?" I'm only half listening, still wondering if I shouldn't speak now, even though we are about to face the others. *There will be no right time.*

"Goath keeps careful records of every judgment made by its lord. Although it's forbidden to ever disclose Shadow Bargains, Goath of course has found a way around that—by leaving a blank entry." Harken's tone holds a grudging note of respect. "Goath also has authority over Pathfinders in Astria. It is Goath that monitors the silverscyes, and keeps meticulous records of every Pathfinder born and their movements. Even their black-market dealings with little criminals in the Seam." He shoots me a sly grin in the mirror, then turns back to his dressing. "Kendrick found an entry dated at the start of the War, a report of a Pathfinder who was caught spying, a woman who had one child—a son called Arkady."

My hands still.

When Harken turns to me again, his face is grave. "It's a grave crime to exile a Pathfinder, even slave braided as this one was. Astria keeps Pathfinders close; we all know they can't be trusted. It must have killed the old Lord of Goath to do it, but a Shadow Bargain isn't something you can refuse to repay."

Take what you want, and pay for it. Some long-ago Lord of Goath made an unknown bargain of his own. Generations later, a Shadow had come calling, requiring his heir to exile a Pathfinder and her son, and leave no record of it.

"Then Arkady is part Pathfinder?" My head reels with what that might mean.

"It explains how he came so easily through that Dark Rip." Harken smiles grimly. "He couldn't use a silverscye, not while he wore a slave braid, but he could certainly navigate a Dark Rip. Pathfinders are able to travel the threads of the Interweave itself, one of the reasons they are so carefully monitored and restricted to silverscyes. Amusing, is it not, that the council is so concerned about your origins, while nurturing a treacherous piece of silver in their midst?"

"Are you going to tell them?"

"No." Harken pulls on his boots and stands up. "Kendrick and I thought it might be interesting to see what game our slippery friend is playing—or rather who might be using him for one of theirs." There is an unaccustomed warmth in his voice when he speaks of Kendrick.

Almost, I think hopefully, *as if they could be friends.*

"We thought it prudent to keep the matter between ourselves, for now." He gives me the ghost of a wink. "Feivel has rather the honorable turn of mind. He may not approve of us allowing a Pathfinder to taint the nobility of Astria's sacred Race."

"OH, HARKEN." Prudence stops at the entrance to the salon Harken's demons have prepared for dinner and claps her hands to her mouth. "I had forgotten how exquisite it is here."

Tears spring into her eyes, and she reaches for my hand. "My dear," she says softly. "How can we ever thank you? I had feared I may never lay eyes on the Woven Court again."

I'm relieved when I glance back to see Harken already talking to Kendrick and having missed that last comment.

I have never felt less worthy of thanks in my life. It's my own foolishness over the braid that has led to Harken being forced to open his court to the others. I find it difficult to celebrate my own perfidy. Prudence, though, isn't the only one clearly thrilled to be admitted to the palaces beyond the terrace of the Savage Court, where we last met.

"I have to agree with Prudence." Lupa eyes the soft teardrop lanterns suspended from a roof made entirely from the ancient boughs of a great yew, and the floor made from a carpet of flowers, amid which small paths lead to our table. Made of the same white marble shot with gold as the fountains, the table grows from the tree itself. A fountain on one side flows with Darkwine of varying strengths, another with water, while crystal decanters rest on a curved shelf between them. The table is set with silver, and tiny candles hidden among the leaves light the whole with a soft forest glow. Even Lupa seems misty-eyed.

"It has been so long," she says quietly, "since any of us have had the privilege of being among the wonders of your court, Harken."

"Thank my demons." Harken deflects the compliments with his customary cynicism. "They've never been happier." He casts his eyes skyward, and everyone laughs.

It's a small party. Only Prudence and Clement are the additions to the previous group of Feivel, Lupa, and Kendrick.

"So." We've barely begun the first course when Kendrick speaks. "As Comitas, Dirk can't vote."

"Might a woman eat her soup first, Kendrick?" Lupa says dryly.

"No." Kendrick almost smiles, but his eyes are grave. "I want to make certain we all understand what will happen. As I said, Dirk can't vote. That leaves Torsten, Sereia, Caspian, Foley, and Gareth—the same five votes that have defeated Lupa, Feivel, Clement, and me until now. With Harken, we can equal the vote. Which is where you come in, dear Prudence." He covers her hand with his own.

"I'm not lifting the mists on the isle." Harken says it with clear finality. "I won't ask Islene and her priestesses to sit at a table with those who took so much from them, nor expose the isle to danger. But as Lord of the Woven Court, I can nominate a proxy in their stead, so long as the nominee is priestess trained."

Prudence nods. "I will be happy to represent the pomegranate vote." She smiles softly. "And Harken took me to visit Islene personally. I have her mark of authority." Reaching into her robes, she brings out a deep lapis heart-shaped leaf, shot through with carmine.

There is a moment's silence at the table, broken finally by a misty-eyed Feivel. "The Songtree," he says softly. "A miracle, even in the Woven World. It seems forever since I have seen one."

I don't dare look at Harken. He is very still, his face shadowed by the great trunk of the yew tree. I suspect he chose that seat on purpose.

"Of course." Lupa smiles at Feivel. "You, who worked most closely with the priestesses, are the only one of us, other than Prudence, to ever see the Songtree." Her face is oddly soft. "I should give a great deal," she murmurs, "to see such a marvel."

"At least the one we have is safe." Kendrick cuts through the sentimentality, casting an uneasy glance at Harken. He looks relieved to see Harken making polite, if quite clearly bored, conversation with Clement. I hide a smile.

Kendrick, I think, is entirely focused on the job at hand, and not at all willing to risk losing his chance. "Prudence," he says, "keep the leaf hidden, unless there is any challenge to your vote." His mouth takes on a grim look. "I wouldn't put it past any of them to take it and try to grow a Songtree of their own."

"I doubt any could rival the beauty of that on the isle." Prudence smiles sadly, turning the leaf over in her hand. "I miss the Songtree, very much."

"I can only imagine how beautiful it is." I cross my fingers under the table against my own lie, as Magel changes out my soup plate for a delicious dish with roasted walnuts and pomegranate. "I've only ever seen pictures of Songtrees in Feivel's books about the Lotus Palaces."

The words are barely out of my mouth before I wish I could take them back. If I didn't already regret mentioning the Lotus Palaces, the awkward silence that falls on our side of the table makes it clear enough that I've said something wrong. I'm passionately grateful to discover that Clement is still talking to Harken.

"You must have been confused," says Feivel, smiling at me. "There is only one Songtree in Astria—on the Isle of Nine." He gives me a curious look. "Which book of mine was that? I don't recall any that show the Songtree."

"Oh." My face is aflame. "I can't remember now."

"It's an easy enough mistake to make." Prudence smiles kindly and pats my hand. "The yew tree isn't dissimilar." I realize, with a flood of relief, that their silence is more pity at what they take as my ignorance, rather than suspicion at my words.

Why would they be suspicious? I think miserably. *I'm the only one at this table, except Harken, who knows what grows in the courtyard of the Lotus Palaces.* I know what I saw in my vision wasn't a yew tree. But clearly it once was, and that makes my slipup potentially catastrophic.

When finally I do glance at Harken, he's deep in conversation with Kendrick and seems not at all perturbed. I bend my head to my meal and barely speak for the rest of it.

EVEN AS OUR GUESTS LEAVE, I feel miserable, all my earlier excitement gone.

Now is the time. My mistake at dinner has taken me over the edge. I'm suddenly impatient to tell Harken the truth, no matter the outcome.

Really? whispers my heart. *Even if that means losing him altogether?*

Sick fear rises slick and cold in my throat. Harken has opened his home to me. His heart. What might such a betrayal do to a man who has already experienced so much of it?

More than once I've considered not telling him at all. Simply never touching the braid again, and never speaking of what I have learned from it. It could be my secret to carry, a burden I hold myself instead of yet another weight on Harken's already overburdened shoulders.

But the dinner has left me shaken. *What if Harken heard my comment? What if I slip up again?* And above all of that is a far more basic truth: I am no longer Harken's slave. I am his lover, the only person to truly be allowed into his world.

The braid visions are a betrayal, one that has abruptly become sickeningly unbearable.

I wait until the last figure disappears through the mists, then turn to Harken. "Can we talk?"

"Always." Harken smiles, touching my cheek. "But I've promised to check something for Kendrick before the council vote, and I should like to take care of it right away. Can our conversation wait until my return?"

I swallow hard. I don't want to wait. I want to speak now and be done with the lie that suddenly seems to weigh more than the braid itself ever has.

I force a smile. "Of course."

Huxley has flown to our terrace, as she sometimes does. Her eyes glow as she watches us. Harken puts a hand on her head and stands there for a moment, almost as if he is having a conversation with her. Huxley closes her eyes, and I smile. Sometimes, the storm dragon seems more like a kitten in his hands.

When he turns back, his face is already distant, as it often is when he leaves the Woven Court. "I will be back tomorrow night," he says. He looks oddly sad, and I wonder what it is that Kendrick has asked of him. He touches my face briefly, then his hand falls away.

"Take care," he says softly.

CHAPTER 57

MISTS

I can't sleep.

The night grows high, and still I toss restlessly. The things I have seen in the braid visions mix uneasily with the reality of my presence here, so close to the place I've only ever seen in those dreams.

My braid itself seems restless, prickling against my skin. I've never been so aware of it. I want to fling it away, and I want to take hold of it. In my inability to do either, finally I mentally summon Huxley. A moment later she is on the terrace, purring softly. I've discovered it rarely takes more than my thought for her to come.

We soar high over the orchards and valleys, flying in wide circles above the Savage Court. The rainbow mists draw me in a way they never have before. I feel almost a compulsion to fly through them. I'm about to confess my lies to Harken. *Perhaps I just want to know that what I saw is real before I do.*

I curse myself for trying to justify my actions and almost turn back. Then I hear Neoma's voice in my mind: *You have to see past the mists, Zaria. See the truth.*

Huxley senses my decision before the thought is finished. Turning, she soars on an invisible wind, directly toward the rainbow mists. *Of course she can pass them*, I think, as we are momentarily enveloped. *Huxley has flown through here a hundred times alone.* The Woven Court, all of it, is her home, as Harken once said.

I sense the difference in atmosphere the instant we are through.

If I thought the valley and outer palaces of the Woven Court an enchanted land, the Lotus Palaces feel sacred.

The air here is substantial, rich with an invisible force that is palpable, as if the threads of life are somehow more densely Woven. It feels expectant, like a living thing.

I fly over buildings that were crumbled in my visions, but which now stand fully restored to their former glory. Exquisite tiling gleams amid curlicued carvings in the walls, visible even in the deceptive night shadows. There is something heart-breaking in the empty archways, as if the rooms lying behind the sensual curves and ocher walls are crying out for souls to fill them. I fly over towers and turrets, arranged, I realize, in a twelve-petaled lotus cluster, of which the Garden of the Fallen is the very center.

I see the Songtree first, the carmine-and-lapis leaves gleaming in the darkness. As I fly closer, I hear its sweet song whisper on the night, held in the water and trickling through the earth itself.

I want desperately to land, to touch the earth Harken once nurtured back to life. But I know I cannot, know that even this flight is a betrayal of his trust. Instead I soar up on Huxley again and, with a last glance at the lonely splendor of the Lotus Court, fly out of the mists and back to the Summer Palace.

Huxley lands on the terrace. I tumble from her back, my heart twisted with emotion and confusion.

"Find what you were looking for?"

My heart stops. Lounging in the shadows, long legs stretched out before him and a glass of Weald whiskey in his hand, is Harken.

Not the Harken I have shared my heart and body with these past weeks. Nor even the sardonic, masked Harken who goes into public. This Harken is hard and detached, the vicious Savage King who killed legions without a backward thought. All that is missing from his icy rage is the peaked black helmet.

"Darien's name should have been my first clue. If I hadn't been so desperate for your body, perhaps I would have paid more attention."

There's something almost crude in his phrasing that summarily dismisses whatever emotional connection might have existed between us.

"Nobody, not even Gemory or Andras, speaks Darien's name in my presence. It is not a name used lightly by anyone, even the Indigold." He turns the glass slowly in his hand, his eyes never leaving mine. "And then, of course, there was the odd connection I felt in the braid. I respected your wishes never to touch it, do you know that? Never once. Not even when it burned my skin or twisted against me like a live thing. Not when it kept me awake at night, or when I could feel your anger or loneliness. Still I didn't touch it—because you asked me not to."

His mouth curls. "What a Fool," he says softly, "I have been.

"But it was the Songtree that gave you away." He takes a meditative sip. "As far as anyone knows, the Songtree on the Isle of Nine is the only one in the entire Woven World. Rich men have spent their last coin searching for another, to no avail. And nobody, not even a slave from the Seam, could mistake a yew tree for a Songtree."

I want to speak, but I know I have no right. I stay silent.

"Something you may wish to know about storm dragons."

His tone is flat and remote. "They hold a flesh memory of every flight they ever take. One can read their journeys like a book, if one knows how. I touched Huxley earlier tonight. She'd flown through the mists many times, alone. But never with you aboard.

"That was something, at least, I thought. Perhaps your visions had been only brief things, flashes of insight. I can understand why you might not share those, though still I must wonder why you wouldn't tell me of them. But then tonight, barely hours after I left, you flew straight through those mists. Do I need to touch Huxley, Zaria, to confirm what I already know?"

I shake my head mutely.

Reaching behind him, Harken takes the leather cord from around his neck and tears the braid end from the ring. I feel every touch, my braid twisting painfully against my skin.

"There." Harken throws the braid end at me. It hits my body and flutters down to lie uselessly on the terrace, the featherlight touch of its rejection more painful than Hodda's whip ever was. "You won't ever have to worry about me touching that braid end again," he says scornfully.

Turning to the side, he twists his hand in an almost brutal movement. A scye opens between us, a gaping hole in the Woven mists through which I can see Fire Hall, flame torches burning at the entrance.

"You will be safe at Lupa's," he says coldly. "And no doubt you will flourish among the Indigold, who thrive on lies and deceit." He nods at the scye. "Go. Your possessions will follow."

"Harken." It hurts to speak, and I know I have no right to. "Please, not like this."

His eyes narrow slightly. "How, exactly, would you like it to be, Zaria? Because the only other way this scene ends is with me tearing that body of yours apart and hanging it in pieces over my own gates. And I fear that even I am not capable of doing that."

His hand makes a savage twist, and I am thrust into the scye, powerless to stay in a world that no longer wants me.

The braid end lies where it fell, discarded and forgotten on the ground.

CHAPTER 58

ABYSS

I don't tell Lupa what happened between Harken and me. Wisely, she doesn't ask.

At first I don't leave my room. Lupa informs me, the morning after my midnight arrival, that the council hearing has been postponed for a fortnight, which means a decision won't be made until barely days before the Race itself. I don't ask her who postponed it or why. It doesn't matter anymore.

None of it matters.

I close the door and go back to bed.

I lie in the darkness, the braid on my neck dead and cold. I hadn't realized how accustomed I'd become to Harken's warmth enlivening it, the slight friction against my skin a constant presence on my body, in my life.

Now there is nothing, only the braid itself, bound as it has ever been, though to what, now, I wonder. Harken no longer holds the braid end. Yet I remain enslaved; I know it deep inside. I am a slave with no master. I have come all this way, and it has all been for nothing.

Worse, it is entirely my own fault.

I know there is no way back from this. I haven't just lost

Harken, and the life I was beginning, tentatively, to call my own. I've lost the Race before it's even begun. Whatever the reason for the postponement, I know Harken will never attend that council now. Why would he? Everything in my deception only serves to confirm everything he's ever believed about the perfidious games people play. Why would the man who has carried the unbearable burden of the Woven Court, alone and unassisted, for years now, go to the defense of a girl who couldn't even dignify him with honesty?

I roll over, but I don't sleep, and I can't eat.

All I want is to forget.

"GET UP." Lupa throws open the door and strides into the room, wrenching open the curtains and glaring at me when I cower under the covers. "The Race is barely weeks away, and you haven't swung a sword in days. You will get up, and you will train."

I don't have the strength to argue with her. I rise silently and go with her to the canals, where I obediently move through the training exercises I've practiced every day for weeks now.

The first day Lupa says nothing, simply trains with me. The following day she sends Brooks and Everett to fetch me. I go through the same motions with them, though their banter goes over my head. Soon they stop telling me their stories, and we train in silence.

My nights are haunted by horrific dreams. In place of the braid visions, Dark Rips open before me, taking each person I have loved, one after the other. I watch each of my siblings tumble backward into the abyss, each calling to me as they go.

Shimi, her face twisted with the fear she never allows anybody to see, screaming that it's because of me that Caspian was so determined to buy her. Blaming me for the council ruling that means she will never be freed.

Screaming that it's my fault Harken didn't unbraid her and Neoma.

Neoma, her beautiful eyes dead and empty, lost in her own world—and now lost to mine, forever.

Levin, his eyes gleaming with the fanatical light of the Paladins, turning away from me deliberately.

And of course, Doron. Over and over, Doron. I live every moment of his loss again and again, knowing each time that the fault for it is mine alone.

But the worst dream by far is the one I have of Harken, grim faced in his black helmet and staring into an endless mist, utterly alone and dead inside. That vision is the one that jolts me awake, screaming into my pillow, my body drenched in sweat and racked with loss.

After several more days, the boys stop fetching me for training. I close the drapes and return to bed, grateful to be left alone.

But it isn't meant to be. Lupa wakes me again, drags me down to the canals. Again, I go through the motions, turning obediently, jumping for the makeshift ribbons on the bough.

"Enough!" Exasperated, Lupa throws aside her sword, wiping the sweat from her face. "Fight like this," she says, glaring at me, "and the costume Darcy delivers will be that of a water rat. Every day in training, you create the person who will win that Race. Every time you swing that sword or jump for a ribbon, you build the winner who will hold that Cup. Forget that, and you forget who you are and what you came for. And once that person is forgotten, Zaria, believe me when I say that finding her again will not be easy."

I lay the sword down. Stepping out of the gondolino, I wade through the water to the shore.

"What are you doing?" Lupa calls to me angrily.

I turn to face her. "That person is already lost," I say bleakly. "Harken will never go to that council. My braid will never come off. I will never race. It's a lost dream, Lupa." I meet her eyes. "And I have nobody to blame for it but myself."

She throws her arms into the air in exasperation, amber eyes flashing. "What can possibly be so bad you would throw away everything you've worked for?"

"I lied," I say bluntly. "I lied to Harken, and I betrayed him."

Hesitantly at first, then in a rush, I tell her about the visions, leaving out the details of Harken's life, but telling her of how I searched for them, from the very first day I came aboard the *Hydra*. "I could have ended it, then," I say bitterly. "Harken offered to give me the braid end during our first conversation. I could have taken it. Given up my view into his mind and memories, or at least told him of the connection. I knew it was wrong. And still I chose it."

Lupa casts a stone into the river without looking at me. "Do you know why you made that choice?"

"I thought I did." My elbows rest on my knees, hands clasped behind my neck. She waits without speaking. "Maybe at first it was because I wanted to have control over whatever I might face."

"Understandable." Lupa throws another stone.

"No, it isn't." Shame curdles inside me. "And that's far from the worst of it. I lied to him long after I knew Harken was trustworthy." I pluck a branch from overhead and tear the leaves from it, one by one. "He saved me from certain death," I say, "and gave me hope. Opened the gates of his home to a world that has shown him nothing but pain, on my behalf. He gave me what he could." I cast the branch into the water. "But it wasn't enough, not for me." I'm filled with self-loathing. "I knew what I was doing. And I did it anyway."

"Because you love him." Lupa's tone is matter-of-fact. "And

because you were afraid that if he unwove the braid, it might all disappear."

I stare at the water drifting slowly by, a current spiraling in the center.

Afraid, I think dully. *Just as I was afraid of Doron leaving.* For someone who has always been fearless regarding my own life, there is a certain humiliating justice to the realization.

"I wasn't afraid of losing the life he gave me," I say, staring into the river, "the Water Palace or the Woven Court." I glance at Lupa, my face aflame. "I was afraid of losing Harken." *The way I feel when I am with him.*

Lupa twists her head in acknowledgment. "And now," she says quietly, "you've done just that."

I put my head in my hands. "Andras warned me, right at the start. He said that if Harken ever suspected I had betrayed his trust, his retribution would be swift—and final."

And now retribution has been delivered, my worst fears realized. I am shut outside the Woven mists, probably forever.

"Andras is a demon, and Harken's servant." Lupa rests her elbows on her knees, her face thoughtful. "He may be Harken's friend, but a friend is not a lover. I would not give up on Harken so easily."

She turns to me, her eyes glowing in the afternoon sun. "Fear caused this," she says simply. "Yours and Harken's. You both fight it by seeking control over your own destiny—and over each other's." She smiles wryly. "But love can't be harnessed, Zaria. You can't capture it and hoard it like gold in a cave. You can only feel it, allow its light to enter you, and let the memory of it strengthen your soul when the darkness falls."

She stands up, brushing the leaves from her breeches. "I know you're in love with him. But I'd lay half my gold that he loves you just as much."

I glance up at her, startled.

"Any Fool could see it, the first night he brought you to the

Revels. But Harken has been alone a long time, with nothing but demons, Shadows, and memories for comfort." She picks up her sword, turning it in the sunlight as she wipes dirt from the blade. "It's going to be as hard for him to comprehend your fears as it is for you to understand that despite what he might have been created to do, and what hardships he may have suffered, he is still a man in need of love. He'll come around." She nods decisively as she sheathes the sword.

I shake my head. "I doubt it."

Lupa shrugs, dismissively this time. She is impatient now. "Fear has already cost you a great deal, Zaria. Don't let it steal what future may still lie ahead."

That night, for the first time since I arrived, nobody comes to make me attend the dinner table. I think dully that it's likely Lupa will ask me to leave. She is not the kind of woman to indulge either sentimentality or failure.

I stand before the mirror and stare at the dead, cold braid about my neck.

I no longer think of touching it, even if Harken was still on the other end of it. Even the thought of doing so makes me feel sick. I will never touch the braid again.

I don't deserve to.

CHAPTER 59

VOTE

*I*t's Gemory who takes me to the city for the council
vote.

We travel the canals in relative silence. Gemory, at least,
doesn't admonish me to cheer up.

We disembark on the wide checkered landing in front of the
palace. I can't help but recall the last time I was here, in
Harken's company, for the Revel. Today the landing is deserted,
the tiles pale in the early morning light. The entrance to the
council chamber is down a few alleys. Our footsteps echo
hollowly off the stone. I cannot remember ever feeling more
alone.

"Look." Gemory tilts their head to the walls. I follow their
gaze to a row of tiny figures, high on the roofs above. It's the
street urchins who have watched me train for the Race. "Look at
their necks," Gemory whispers.

Each of the urchins is wearing an imitation braid.

Some are no more than a twist of rag, others parchment. I
force a smile, raising my hand as we pass, and the urchins shout
back, waving their braids eagerly.

"I've let them down." Shame curdles inside me. "I wanted to give them hope."

Gemory casts me a sideways glance. "You are here," they say quietly. "That is hope enough. And you see them. That is all they ever needed. To be seen, and to be given even the glimpse of a dream they might live for."

We enter the reception area, an imposing marble room in which every sound echoes. "This is where I leave you." Gemory winks at me. "Though I shall be listening, of course." I smile faintly in return. I doubt there will be anything worth listening to.

An unsmiling footman escorts me to a small antechamber, where I wait alone to be summoned. I try not to think of the empty chairs at the council table. I remind myself that Harken will not come, that there is no hope left.

Even so, when the doors to the chamber finally open, my eyes fly past the familiar faces, going immediately to the chair with the lotus symbol on the back.

It's empty.

As I knew it would be.

But knowing it and seeing it are two different things. That empty chair is the death of whatever small hope still lived within me. I stand in the place the footman guides me to and wait for my fate to be delivered.

"You know why you are here, slave." Comitas Ormond's tone is cold. "Your Shadow Braid may conceal powers, qualities, or a nature that pose a threat to Astria's security. Today we will decide whether it is safe to unbraid you or whether you will remain a slave. Members of our council will ask questions, and you will answer. Our decision will be handed down at the end of the session."

I nod obediently, but I wonder dully why they are going through the motions when the outcome is already certain.

"What do you know of your parentage?" Sereia's question is

sharp and fast. "What do you recall of your life before the braid was Woven?"

"Nothing," I say. "My first recollection is of being in Hiraeth Forest, with the braid on my neck and my siblings at my side."

"You say siblings." Gareth smiles patronizingly. "But they aren't relations at all, are they? Merely other War orphans with whom you found yourself."

"We were part of the same Shadow Bargain." I stare at the table, seeing not the flamestone, but the small trolley, the five bags of coin. "We were each bound to a bag of coin, Woven to refill."

"Who told you the bags would refill?" The question comes from Torsten, in his resonant, precise tone and without obvious emotion of any kind.

"Nobody." I lift a shoulder. "I just knew that was what I had to say."

"You just knew." Sereia repeats the words in a smug tone, as if they are some kind of dark evidence. "And now," she says, "those bags have stopped filling. At the same time as Dark Rips began opening, near you. What do you know about that?"

The questions go on, one after another. *Did you open the Dark Rips? Do you know who did? Why do Dark Rips open near you?*

"She's a slave," says Feivel, in some exasperation after one such question. "She could hardly open a Dark Rip undetected."

"That remains to be seen." Caspian leans forward, his eyes gleaming malevolently. "And what of your alliance with the Savage King, Harken? Are we supposed to believe that association to be entirely by chance?" When I don't answer, Foley cuts in.

"Do you deny you conspired with the Savage King before the Braid Race? Why else would he have freed you?"

"He healed me," I say dully. *A starlight stream, wending life into the broken places within me.* "After the first Rip opened, when I was wounded."

"Wounded by a Foolish pistol," Kendrick interjects pointedly. "Wielded by Arkady, when he came through the Dark Rip you accuse Zaria of opening." His eyes meet mine briefly, but he doesn't expose what he knows of Arkady.

Lies and deceit, I think, recalling Harken's contempt. I am back among the games he despises, and they sicken me.

"Harken healed you." Sereia ignores the mention of Arkady. Her lip curls. "You expect us to believe that Harken healed an unknown slave simply out of the goodness of his heart, and for no personal gain?"

"Twice," I say quietly. "First when I was wounded, then again after my master beat me." I meet her eyes. "He was kind to me."

There is a moment's silence during which the entire council stares at me. The Northern Alliance with pity and regret, the others with open derision.

"Kind." Sereia spits the word. "Kind!" She looks around, and Caspian and Foley laugh obediently. "All here know Harken's savagery." Her eyes flash dangerously. "Many of us have witnessed it firsthand. Regardless, it appears he has tired of whatever little game he was playing with you." The suggestive way she runs her eyes over my body makes it entirely clear what manner of game she means.

My legs around his waist. His hands in my hair and the smell of Darkwine all around us.

I close my eyes and breathe deeply. No cheap words can take those moments away from me. For as long as I live, I will have them, a flame of love and light in the darkness that is my life from now on.

Comitas Ormond spreads his hands wide. "We all know the reputation of the House of Thread and Shadows," he addresses the entire table. "For the entirety of Astria's history, Shadow Bargains have masked dark deeds. More sins have been hidden by their murky dealings than can be counted. We all know that

Shadows keep their secrets—and that they are only called upon when secrecy is required."

He sits back in his chair and eyes me with a show of regret. "We may never know what secret is hidden behind your braid or Woven into the zumi on your back. But the very fact that someone felt compelled to not only buy a Shadow Bargain to conceal it, but also bribe a master to take you, must be taken as an indication of a potentially fatal flaw. I have not heard any evidence here today to dispute that."

The Northern Alliance sit, stony faced and silent. They know as well as I that nothing they say will have any bearing on this case.

Sereia smiles silkily around the table. "Shall we vote, then?"

The door behind me flies open, and I see the sudden shock on every face.

"I believe we shall."

The flat drawl is so impossibly dear to me that I wonder if I am imagining it. I don't dare turn. I feel no frisson at my neck, *but then*, I remember tiredly, *I won't, ever again.*

Stalking past me to the table, Harken pulls out the pomegranate chair and ushers another figure into it. "Prudence." He waits until she takes her seat before taking his own and looking around the table with hard contempt. "You wish to vote," he says coldly. "Let's vote."

"You can't just . . ." Comitas Ormond stammers, glancing between Harken and Prudence.

"I can." Harken's rebuttal is cold and concise.

Sereia leaps to her feet, eyes flashing, pointing at Prudence. "She isn't a priestess."

"Harken is within his right to nominate a proxy." Kendrick's tone is grimly satisfied. Lupa is openly smirking, Feivel smiling quietly, and even Clement seems stirred from his customary timidity, looking around the proceedings with actual interest.

"Dirk!" Sereia turns to the Comitas. "There is no evidence Prudence represents the isle—"

"Sit down, Sereia." Torsten's precise words cut through the bluster. Sereia looks for a moment as if she might protest, but the eyes he turns to her are so glacial she subsides, sullenly taking her seat. "No such proof will be necessary." Torsten nods curtly in response to Dirk's indignant face. "There is precedent, Comitas. The Woven Lord is within his rights."

Harken ignores this exchange entirely. The Comitas glances around, as if seeking a last-minute reprieve, but nothing materializes.

"All opposed to unweaving Zaria's Shadow Braid," he says slowly. Sereia, Gareth, Caspian, Foley, and finally Torsten, all raise their hands.

Five opposed.

"Those in favor of unweaving Zaria's Shadow Braid." Comitas Ormond's reluctance is palpable. The hands of the Northern Alliance rise, Harken's no more than the briefest gesture.

Six in favor.

The Comitas scowls. "The motion is passed."

I am frozen, numb, unable to truly comprehend the enormity of what has just taken place.

Comitas Ormond raises his needle and twists it contemptuously in my direction. "Unwoven," he says.

I feel the strangest sensation at my neck, a slow, insidious unspooling that spirals through me, releasing a tension in every cell of my body I never knew existed until it was gone. The relief is at once so total and unexpected that it momentarily stuns me.

Dimly I'm aware of Harken pushing back his chair, gesturing with cold civility for Prudence to go before him. As the threads within me gradually disperse, Harken turns on his heel and strides from the chamber as abruptly as he entered it, looking neither right nor left, and without acknowledging my presence in any way.

"My dear girl," Feivel says mistily, somewhere nearby. "You are free . . ."

I see the faces swimming before me, Lupa's triumphant, Kendrick's glittering with satisfaction, but they come from a great distance.

There is a roaring in my ears, and the chamber fades as if through a scye, or into the dark maw of a Rip.

"Excuse me," I say faintly.

I make it to the small antechamber before the darkness reaches for me. I sink into it willingly, and am gone, beyond the mists.

CHAPTER 60

TORSTEN

I am in the Garden of the Fallen, in the early days of Harken's Woven life.

The garden is not yet finished. Harken is still clad in simple robes, his face shining and innocent, his beauty almost incandescent. He holds his hands over the earth in which he has just buried a corpse, tears rolling down his face as he gently coaxes flowers from the soil.

The teacher he nursed back to health comes to stand beside him. His face is hidden by a wide-brimmed hat, his tunic still torn and faded from battle. In the sunlight, I can make out the faint outline of the symbol that had once been emblazoned there: the Serpent Queen of Dencover.

The teacher puts a hand on Harken's shoulder. "To cry is to know our own pain," he says, "and that is important; but when our tears water a new creation, the pain is transmuted to love, and like this, we honor those we have lost."

The young Harken wipes his eyes, nodding slowly.

The teacher takes his hand, and together, the two Weave the flowers into being.

The vision shifts. The garden is long finished, and many of the surrounding buildings have been lovingly Woven back to completion.

Harken turns to his teacher. "I can't stay in here forever. There is work to do, I know it."

His teacher shakes his head, stiff with tension. "There is nothing beyond these walls but heartache, savagery, and treachery."

The conversation continues over days, then weeks, as the sharp, destructive cries of war cut through the mists and into their peace. Each cry halts Harken in his Weaving, makes him gaze toward the gates, both with sadness and curiosity. Finally, Harken faces his teacher. "I must go out there. I need to help them."

"No." His teacher grips his shoulder. "That world is too brutal for one so beautiful as you. Stay here. Wait for it to be over. Leave men to their wars."

Harken's eyes fill with sadness. As he turns away, his face becomes resolute.

The vision shifts to night. Harken dons a dark cloak and low hat like his teacher's. He pauses at the outer gates and glances back, as if in deliberation. Then a cry comes from beyond the gates. Harken's mouth sets determinedly. He draws the Woven mists aside with a slow, tentative gesture and steps through.

Harken slips through the streets of a nearby town, both enthralled and horrified by what he sees, by the cacophony of humanity milling in the streets, loving and living, fighting and dying. He sees a group of men wearing tunics bearing the same symbol that marks his teacher's faded cloth. They're standing about a barrel, drinking ale. Harken edges closer, listening to their conversation.

"What about Dencover's Weaver?" one of them says. "The Golden Kraken insists he's still alive, says she can feel him, somewhere hereabouts."

"No." One of the others shakes his head. "I saw him fall. He called for the Weavers to open the gates, and they did. He led Dencover's army through to the Lotus Court, and then he fell."

"I'm telling you," says another, "I saw him move. And I swear as those mists fell I saw something leaning over him."

The others laugh, though without humor. "You're imagining it," *says one. "We were all drunk on Darkwine that day. And who could blame us? The Woven Court is gone because of what we did. Killing Weavers." The man's face darkens, and he downs his cup, calling for more, shaking his head. "That I should live to do such a thing," he says bleakly. "See such beauty destroyed . . ." The men drink silently, none looking at the other.*

Harken edges away from the group, his face beneath the hat pale with horror.

The vision shifts again.

Harken stands before his teacher, confusion and hurt carving the first lines into his face. "They were talking about you. I know they were." His teacher's head is bowed, his face still hidden. "Won't you even try to deny it?" Harken stares at him, almost pleadingly. "Tell me this wasn't you." His voice breaks to a whisper. "Tell me you weren't the one who opened the gates. Who did this . . ." He gestures to the Garden of the Fallen. I know it isn't the flowers he is seeing, but the corpses from which they grow.

The teacher faces him, his back stiffly upright. "I can't deny it." His stern, precise voice resonates around the old stone. "It was I who asked for the Woven gates to be opened. I led the army to the Lotus Court."

Harken's eyes are black, stark with shock. "You did this," he whispers. "All those bodies. All that death." He stares past the man, ashen faced. "You helped me bury them." His whisper rasps painfully from deep inside him. "All that death was by your hands, and yet you let me heal you with mine. All your talk of healing, of tears . . . it was lies." He meets the man's eyes. "It was all lies."

The teacher has not moved, remains rigidly upright, meeting Harken's eyes without flinching. "Yes," he says simply. Nothing else, just that cold, hard affirmative.

Harken's black eyes narrow. No light shifts in them now. The smooth lines of his face are deepening, hardening into flat planes and precise angles as stark as they are merciless. His mouth curls at the edges, the soft lips that have always smiled in wonder now twisted with cold fury. "I should kill you."

The Weaver faces him, making no effort to protect himself.

"Tell me why I shouldn't kill you!" Unshed tears freeze, diamond hard, in Harken's eyes.

"Because to do so would destroy your soul." The teacher's voice is sad and quiet. "And that would be the greatest tragedy of all."

"No more of your lessons!" Harken roars, his face a broken landscape of rage and pain. "You disgust me. Go." He sweeps a contemptuous arm toward the gates, flinging them open. "Go with your life. May it be long, and your suffering with it. May you know every day the destruction you have wrought and feel it in your own soul tenfold. Be gone, and pray to all the twelve knots of your broken faith that you never see my face again."

The teacher takes the full force of Harken's words, standing stolidly as they blast into his body. The garden begins to shimmer, the light gleaming oddly. It's only as the teacher turns to the gates that I finally see the austere, elegant face, etched with such deep grief it seems carved in granite.

Torsten's face.

CHAPTER 61

ASTRIS

*I*t's dusk, and I'm standing in Fire Hall's small private tapest, seeking solace amid the wood, stone, and centuries of fragrant prayer.

It is the day after the council ruling and two days before the Race. Lupa carried me to Fire Hall last night. After what I'd seen in the vision, I was too stunned to speak or eat. I slept, and for that I'm grateful.

But this morning I woke early. I've spent the day rowing the canals aimlessly. I don't know if I'm trying to find something or to escape the knowledge of what my pride has wrought.

Harken honored his promise despite my betrayal of his trust. Despite having to sit at a table with Torsten, possibly the only person to have betrayed him even more badly than me.

I'm not certain how I am supposed to reconcile my sins. Perhaps that is why I find myself here, in a tapest.

Any desire I may have had to Race has fled. When I think of what my ambitions have cost Harken, not to mention my siblings, even the thought of racing turns my stomach.

I will make a life for myself, I think, kneeling before the Astris. *A humble life, one without pretensions like winning Races.*

I think of the needlemaker, Serzan, and his resolve to simply pass on his knowledge. I think of the street urchins. *I know how to read and write*, I think. *Perhaps I can teach, or care for them.*

Either way, I promise myself silently, *this is the last night I will spend dependent on Lupa's charity.* After all the suffering I have brought Harken, the damage I have done, I want only to crawl quietly away and make a new start alone. One that doesn't involve grandiose ambition.

One that doesn't cause pain to anyone else.

I pray in the darkness, trying to find a glimmer of light on the lonely road ahead.

I'M PACKING a bag the following day when Lupa appears in the door.

"I've tried." Lupa gestures at me, but it's Kendrick, I realize with surprise, that she's addressing. "She says she won't race tomorrow. Nor will she stay in my house or accept help." She ushers Kendrick in with an exaggerated gesture. "Good luck," she says dryly, closing the door behind him.

Kendrick walks over to the tall French doors and looks out over the rolling lawn, toward the canals where I've been practicing for months. Bracing myself for another lecture about wasted training, I'm rather surprised when he says instead, "Harken did us all a favor, you know. At the end of the War."

He glances back at me, his stern face unusually meditative, then turns back to the window. "In essence, Harken administered rough justice. It might have been brutal, but it was final. It needed no adjunct. There were no trials, no endless handwringing or debate. Harken cauterized the wounds left by the Golden Kraken's atrocities. The Kraken Weavers were unthreaded. The Indigold who had aided them were publicly and brutally executed. Harken simply removed the guilty and left the rest of us to get on with governing."

"The Paladin Divine I hung beside him, so the Weaver could look upon his friend for so long as his eyes might see . . ."

I move forward to stand near Kendrick at the window. "Did Harken ever tell you," he says, not looking at me, "that it was the Paladins who were behind the coup that overthrew the Lotus Court and stole the golden needle?" He nods at my surprise, his mouth twisting in a wry smile. "I didn't think so. Harken rarely sees a need to explain the reasons behind his decisions."

"I know about the punishment he inflicted on them," I say quietly.

Kendrick's smile fades. "A savage story, indeed," he says quietly. "One that few people truly understand. It might be helpful to hear the whole, if you would permit me."

I can't imagine how his story could possibly help, but I shrug my assent anyway.

"Paladins weren't always the military force they are now," Kendrick says. "Once, *Paladin* was simply the name given to those who trained under Weavers to learn the sacred mystery of the Divine Cup. The water they use, even today, comes from a specific fountain, of which there is only one, in all Astria. Only the Paladins, and the Weavers who taught them, had access to it. It was the idea of one of those Weavers, Mortimer, to make of the Paladins a militant arm solely dedicated to protecting the sacred well."

Mortimer. I recall the way Harken described him: *"One of the most evil, corrupt men ever to walk this earth."*

"The Tapest agreed," Kendrick continues, "and even the Woven Court saw the value in the idea. The abbey was built on the site of the well, and the Paladins were made official custodians of the water, which is how it got its name. Paladin's Water has remarkable healing properties that can cure almost any ill." Kendrick glances sideways to me. "Mixed with pure Darkberry in the right quantities," he says quietly, "it is even rumored to grant eternal life. A dangerous promise, one that has cost the lives of countless Paladins over the centuries. Especially since the alchemists must use lethal doses of Darkwine, as they are never granted access to the pure berry itself."

I nod; I've heard the stories of Paladins mad with Darkwine and alchemy, their minds gone and bodies left as no more than husks.

"Just as Darkberry had always been grown far away from the sacred well, and mixed only under careful supervision, so had those who mixed the Cup been kept apart from the ceremonies in which it was used. The Paladins were custodians of the Indigold Cup, while the Tapest held the golden needle that was the key to the mystery of the Great Ceremony. It was one of many separations of power that helped Astria function. Some things, the old Weavers knew, were too dangerous to exist too closely to one another.

"The Paladins were ostensibly neutral, loyal only to Astria and their sacred duty." Kendrick's face tightens. "Mortimer, however, had other ambitions, and the time to dedicate to fulfilling them. By the time Roark won his first race, Mortimer had been Paladin Weaver for a thousand years and had, almost single-handedly, built the Paladins into a real force—one loyal to him.

"Mortimer had also been diving into the Interweave for centuries, gathering Serpent's Gold and likely experimenting with it." Kendrick shakes his head sadly. "He had Divines he'd indoctrinated with his own beliefs, a military arm, and now a weak and ambitious king. By the time the Indigold realized the threat posed by their unholy alliance, Roark and Mortimer had been conducting their sick experiments for years, their Divines coaxed into attempting ever more dangerous alchemical experiments. Some, me included, believe it was Mortimer to whom Anahita first whispered. However evil Roark might have been, ultimately, he was Mortimer's tool. It was undoubtedly Mortimer who betrayed Sereia and Torsten's existence to Roark, convincing him to pull Sereia out of the Lotus Court before she was even inducted as a Weaver. Torsten was strategically placed in Dencover."

Kendrick meets my eyes and smiles faintly. "Now," he says, "to my point. Mortimer always knew Roark could not get away with winning a sixth Race; all of Astria knew his corruption by then. But Mortimer didn't need him to win. He just needed the Indigold distracted long enough to achieve his objective: the golden needle.

"Mortimer knew the golden needle would already be on the Isle of Nine, in preparation for the Great Ceremony. The isle was carefully guarded during the Race, and before the ceremony. Only one person was permitted through the guard."

"The Paladin Divine," I breathe. "The man who had mixed the Cup."

Kendrick nods. "While most of Astria was in the Indigo City for the Revels, the Kraken armies rode out in secret. The Divine went with them. The rest is brutal history."

Bodies on the shore, dead where they had stood, to the last man defending the isle.

"That is the story of how the golden needle was first stolen." Kendrick turns away from the window and takes a seat, hitching his robes in a businesslike fashion as he folds one leg over the other. "The isle fell before the Race was run. None in the capital even knew there had been a coup. The Weavers did, of course, and closed the Woven Court; but they had no forces to defend it against the Kraken army. The Paladin Blades surrounded the Indigo City itself, supposedly to defend it, but in reality to prevent any from going to the aid of the Woven Court."

Kendrick passes a hand over his face. "Those were the darkest days," he says soberly. "Mortimer used the golden needle to thread Anahita into Roark's body. It was, I think, meant to be only a temporary measure, though we will never know. A week of endless nights followed. The streets of the Indigo City ran with blood. As the fighting went unchecked, Mortimer and his chief Divine used the golden needle in dark parodies of the Great Ceremony. Neither knew exactly how it worked, of course, though they killed hundreds of priestesses in their efforts to learn. It is said they emulated the ceremony, using every combination of Pathfinders, Paladins, and priestesses, forcing them to lie together in their efforts to create the perfect vessel for Anahita to inhabit. Somewhere amid the chaos, the golden needle was stolen, and Anahita was left stuck in Kraken form."

By Darien, I think, but don't say.

"It took almost five years," Kendrick says, turning back to me, "and untold horrors, before the Northern Alliance finally retook the Indigo City and bound Anahita in the Tower. Astria was still in chaos when Harken found Mortimer and the Paladin Divine who had stolen the needle. He dealt with them before there could be any discussion of right or wrong." His eyes shift meditatively. "Had he not, what lies might they have told? Mortimer had many supporters, Weaver and Indigold alike, who believed he was on a sacred mission. It's an uncomfortable truth nobody wants to confront to this day, that there were many who believed in some version of Anahita's promises, and still do.

"Harken's retribution might have been swift and terrible, but it was also decisive. In some ways, his clinical act of revenge turned a situation away from potential civil war to a world where justice had been dispensed. Certainly, none dared challenge him. And there was also a certain balance to his actions.

"Sereia and Torsten were spared, despite having broken the laws of the Woven Court by fighting for their natural father.

Most felt it was the best of Weaver justice, not to hold the children accountable for their father's crimes."

I flinch despite myself at the recollection of Harken's voice. *"I let Torsten and Sereia live because I was taught that children, even Weavers, should not suffer for the sins of their fathers . . ."*

"I've always believed Harken had different motives, however." I glance at Kendrick in surprise. "In the old days," he says, "Sereia and Torsten would have been brought before the Lotus Court, subjected to discipline by their own order. By leaving them instead to the judgment of the Indigold, Harken made outcasts of them. He passed judgment but took no responsibility for the outcome.

"With that decision, Harken effectively ended the Weavers' authority over their own, and when he did, he removed any accountability Weavers might once have faced for their actions. This has proven incredibly dangerous—as you saw, when you met Sereia."

Kendrick turns to me. "I don't think that Harken ever foresaw the consequences of his choices. In sparing Torsten and Sereia, and closing the Woven Court, he likely thought he was leaving the way open for Astrians to find their own way back to the twelve values of the Lotus Court and the Tapest. I think that Harken, deep down, has always believed that right would eventually prevail. And with every passing year that he has watched Astria choose self-interest over good, I believe his grief has grown.

"Many in Astria believe that Harken abandoned them." Kendrick shakes his head. "I think Harken believes Astria abandoned him."

Betrayed, I think dully. *Over and over, he has been betrayed.*

"I say all this," he says gently, "because I believe that Harken saw something in you that helped him believe good still exists. Whatever has happened between you, abandoning him now will not help. It will only confirm what Astria has already taught him, over and again."

Kendrick takes my hands. "If there is one thing that a lifetime of listening to Breezes has taught me," he says, "it is that not all things are lost; and not all lost things are lost forever.

"Harken backed you to win that Race, Zaria. Don't abandon him now."

CHAPTER 62

MAVERICKS

I'm still at Fire Hall when I wake on the morning of the Race.

Lupa, never one for either crowding or coddling, left me be after Kendrick's visit. I went to sleep uncertain of what the future holds, but equally unable to dismiss his words. I know I must race. Kendrick may or may not be right in what he said about Harken, but he is, at the very least, an intelligent and objective observer, and I no longer have faith in my own judgment.

The morning doesn't allow time for further doubts. I'm barely up and dressed when Everett and Brooks knock on my door.

"Maverick's Breakfast." Everett shoots me a mischievous, if rather wary, smile. I've barely seen him or Brooks lately. He thrusts a flaming cup through the door. "Weald whiskey," he says, grinning.

"It's tradition," adds Brooks.

I drink it down despite my skepticism. It spreads a reassuring flame through my stomach, and even a tremor of excitement. Whether that is likely to last the distance of the Race is questionable, but it's infinitely preferable to the gray dullness I felt before it.

"We can't stay," Everett says. "We're Cupbearers."

"Go on." Brooks grins. "Ask us what that is, I beg you. Do you have any idea how many intolerable lectures on the history of the Indigold Cup Everett and I have had to endure this season, when we could have been drinking instead?"

Feeling that I've had rather too many lectures on Astrian history lately, I give him a sideways look. "Lessons aren't my strong point. Give me the Maverick's version."

"Created after the fall of Sherimah," calls Everett.

"By seven of Astria's greatest Weavers," says Brooks.

"Has seven rings, each a coil of the serpent."

"And four flamestone pillars. The Cup itself is—" Brooks frowns. "Everett?"

"Don't ask me. Crystal or something." Everett shrugs. "The serpent twines about it from base to mouth and comes alive when it is filled with Darkwine and Paladin's Water, at the start of the Race."

"Long ago, the Cup filled the first time by itself," Brooks says, waving his hands in the air as if he is Weaving, "with an unknown substance known to us all now as . . ." He does a dramatic imaginary drumroll and says, "Everett?"

". . . The Water of Eternal Life," Everett intones, making a dramatic bow. "A mysterious elixir thought to contain Serpent's Gold, Pathfinder's silver, Paladin's Water, and pure Darkberry." He counts each ingredient off on his fingers, ending with a triumphant flourish. "Though none really know for sure," he adds, shrugging.

"The Indigold lords were gathered together," Brooks says with theatrical grandeur, "and all dropped their blood into it. Then they all drank from the Cup."

"And since that day," says Everett with mock gravity, "all Indigold have been stronger and more beautiful than other mortals. Endowed with gifts according to their element, and with the ability to Work and shift."

They both step forward and take a grandiose bow. I applaud them, laughing despite myself.

"And what do you two reprobates do, then," I ask, "as Cupbearers?"

"Ah. I'm so glad you asked, Zaria." Everett gives me a scholarly nod. "Brooks?"

"Thank you, Everett." Brooks puts on an imaginary pair of spectacles. "To honor our history, seven noble Cupbearers"—he and Everett point to one another—"will, later this very day, carry the Cup from the palace through a series of underground tunnels to the Cup Chamber, where it is placed on a specially designed plinth."

"In years past," says Everett with an air of tragedy, "the Cup would have been blessed by the Astar and his golden needle. However!" He casts his eyes skyward. "Since, as we all know too well, said needle is missing, the Astar will just say a blessing." His voice returns to a mundane tone. "Then we all take a sip of Darkwine, including the Paladin Divine, who then pours the remainder into the Cup, adds the rest of the stuff, and does the Work that wakes the serpent." He says the last in a tone of complete disinterest, this part clearly being out of his remit. "Then," he says, brightening, "the Cup rises to the surface of the canals on the plinth. The consul announces the Race, the Darkwine wakes the serpent, and once it breathes fire, the Race starts."

"Wait." I've largely followed all this, but remembering Leo telling me he might be a Cupbearer, I have a moment of sheer dread. "Please don't tell me," I say, looking between them, "that the Divine is a Paladin called Leo?"

"The acolyte?" Everett gives a hoot of laughter. "Dreavers Tells, no. They'd never let that shaking creature near something so important."

"Besides," Brooks adds, "the council has been Cup-shy ever since Roark's Divine poisoned the Cup one year. Although," he says dryly, "the Paladins have conveniently short memories. That Divine's brother, Saxan, heads up the Blades now."

"I'd say Saxan learned his lesson." Everett's tone is rather grim. "Given he had to walk to work beneath his brother's body every day during his training."

"Wait." I stare at them in surprise. "Saxan's *brother* was the Paladin Divine hung over the abbey gates by Harken?"

"I wish I'd seen that." Brooks's face wears an almost wistful expression. "My mother flatly refused to take me to the abbey to have a look." Everett snorts with laughter.

I'm still shaking my head at them, not to mention at the startling revelation that the Paladin Divine of whom I've heard so much was another of Leo's relatives, when there's another knock on the door. This time it's Gemory, with Darcy, the dressmaker.

"That's our cue." Everett and Brooks both buss me roundly on each cheek. "We'll see you at the start landing."

I watch them go with a bittersweet feeling. I wonder if, after today, I will ever see them again. If I win, I suppose I will be an Indigold noble, though I can't imagine myself attending Revels. If I lose, however, I will be little more than one of the street urchins who have come to watch me train.

And winning, I think, *seems very unlikely.*

"Enough brooding." Gemory closes the door briskly behind the dressmaker. "Darcy—unveil the masterpiece."

Gemory's golden eyes are gleaming, making me thoroughly nervous. Then Darcy takes my costume out of its wrappings, and all coherent thought flees my mind.

The glittering mesh gondolier's armor is the same Darkwine color as my eyes. The iridescent storm dragon emblazoned upon it writhes like a living creature. The helmet is a fearsome thing of intimidating design, made to look exactly like Huxley's strange juxtaposition of lion and dragon. It fits around my head like an extension of me, and when I draw it on, something inside me trembles and shifts, as if the helmet itself contains part of Huxley's nature.

"The armor may seem light," Darcy says quietly, when I don't speak, "but it is imbued with the essence and power of the creature that inspired it." She stands behind me as I stare into the mirror, unable to recognize the fierce creature staring back at me.

I think of Huxley's lonely past and her noble nature. Huxley is Harken's companion, not mine. "I'm not worthy of this," I say, almost to myself.

Darcy's lips purse disapprovingly. "The costume is Woven in threads from your own soul," she says, rather tartly, "and guided by the hand of the Great Weaver themself. It is not for you to approve, or disapprove; the costume simply is. With the aid of my needle, of course." She touches one of the gleaming feathers that adorns the back.

"Say thank you," mouths Gemory in my ear.

"Thank you!" I say, horrified to have forgotten. "It's magnificent," I add, smiling at Darcy as I remove the helmet.

"Careful," she says sharply. "And don't play with it. The next time you put it on, it is for the Race. Do you understand?" I nod obediently. Darcy gives me a satisfied once-over, then leaves.

"Right." Gemory eyes me in the mirror. "Make your preparations, then Lupa will meet you downstairs."

"You're not traveling with us?" I ask.

Gemory shakes their head. "I will scye. But this is no time for you to slink from one place to another like a Shadow. Today, you are a Maverick." They wink at me. "And Mavericks arrive in style." They're almost through the door when an unsettling thought crosses my mind.

"Gemory." They pause, looking back inquiringly. "The

Paladin Divine that Harken hung over the gates of the abbey," I say. "Do you know if he had any children?"

They give me a quizzical look. "Divines don't marry, nor father children. And like all Mortimer's acolytes, his Divine was obsessed with Darkwine and even darker experiments, and little else." The sound of impatient voices rises from downstairs.

"Hurry, now," Gemory says. "Lupa isn't one I'd keep waiting."

CHAPTER 63

SERPENT

I'm oddly shaken by the news that Saxan's brother was the Paladin Divine Harken punished. *Perhaps*, I think, *that is why Leo was in the Seam in the first place, as a kind of punishment for his family's indiscretions.* That seems unlikely, however, given how high his uncle has risen.

I shake off my thoughts. Gemory is right: this is hardly the time to think on it.

I reach for the discarded threads of my slave braid as I leave my room, tying them about my neck. I know it seems a strange talisman, but they are the only link I have to Harken, no matter how tenuous. I'm oddly grateful that Lupa rescued them from the council chamber.

In some strange way, this Race is full circle from where I began, back in the Seam, and the braid, no matter how I once hated it, has been a part of that journey. I wear it today to remind me of the girl who trained in Hiraeth with Garrick and dreamed of freedom.

Garrick. My heart clenches fiercely. *What I would give to hear his gruff voice today.* To feel his rough hand on my shoulder.

But Garrick is not here, and it's time to go downstairs.

Style, in this case, is Lupa's flying carpet.

"I'm Woven in Fire," she says rather smugly, when I halt in front of the exotically Woven carpet, clearly impressed. "Our carpets are part of our naturally given Work."

Climbing tentatively aboard, I wonder if Astria's marvels will ever cease to amaze me.

Lupa casts her threads and murmurs a command, and the carpet rises into the air. I can't imagine a more fitting arrival for a dragon than atop a carpet of smoke, surrounded by blue-and-orange flame. *Unless it was on Huxley herself*, I think, but then, I realize with a pang, it's unlikely that I shall ever sit atop the storm dragon again.

As we fly into the city, Lupa points out the banners of other competitors, hung at various vantage points above clusters of supporters. "That's the eagle of Goath," she points out. "Pallas, Kendrick's sister, is racing with it today. That's Tanwen's," she says, not without pride, pointing to a Saber banner. "I trained her for her first Race. Dencover," she says disapprovingly, passing the Serpent Queen. "Foley is racing himself, Dreaver take him. The Waterlands banner next to it"—she points to a Cup on aqua—"is for Arkady. Caspian has offered him his own banner."

Of course he has.

There is a good sprinkling of Paladin Blades among the banners. "Saxan won the Race," Lupa says, "before he became First Blade a few years ago. Proof that not all apples from the same barrel go bad." Again, I'm shaken by the reference to Saxan's brother, but before I comment, I have the dislocating experience of seeing my own banner, amethyst with an iridescent dragon, hanging high up on a roof.

And not just on one roof.

Far above the crowds of Indigold nobles and their ornate pavilions, the street urchins are gathered in the gutters and atop the roofs of the city buildings. They hold up my banner as we fly past, cheering until their faces blur before me.

Finally, we soar over the roof of the Indigo Palace, and Lupa brings the carpet down gently onto the checkered white-and-black tiles, where the competitors are milling about. I'm assigned a number eleven by a harried-looking official.

Feivel bustles over, smiling. "Dear girl." He kisses my cheek. "They allow me to join the salvers on Race Day," he says, winking. "It's my favorite hobby, and of course there are plenty of injuries. It's also the only time I'm ever allowed to touch Paladin's Water, so I never miss it!"

Paladin's Water. A loose thread tugs at the corner of my mind, an odd flicker that feels dangerous, but I don't know why. *Probably just nerves.* I shiver, and Feivel gives me a reassuring smile.

"I know that if Garrick were here," he murmurs, "he'd tell you to show the bastards what you can do."

He presses my hand, and I swallow hard, unable to speak to thank him as he bustles away.

"Remember your training," Lupa says as she walks me over to my amethyst gondolino, emblazoned with the iridescent dragon. "Above all," she says, lifting the helmet onto my head, "don't hold back. You may not be born wolf, but you've as much fire in your soul as any from the Weald." Her eyes find mine behind the helmet. "This Race is like life. There's a time to play in the shadows, and another to let that fire blaze. Your costume Wove as the storm dragon." She grips my shoulder. "Find the storm within, Zaria, and let your dragon find you."

Her words are like fire in my veins, and I turn to my gondolino as Gareth, the Paladin Consul, mounts a raised platform off to one side of the tiled landing. I see Saxan standing nearby, his white hair gleaming. It's hard to imagine someone so dignified being related to the corrupt Divine who committed such dark deeds.

"Lupa," I say on impulse, as she is turning to leave. "The

Paladin Divine that Harken hung over the gates. What was his name?"

Lupa's eyes narrow. "That seems a rather odd question for such a time." When I don't speak, she casts her eyes around warily, then lowers her voice. "Jaxan," she says. "His name was Jaxan."

In an instant, I am transported back to the abbey in the Seam, Leo's alchemy tool roll on the table beside him as he studied. I can still remember the name stenciled on the leather there: *Jaxan.*

"You have to find Feivel." I grip Lupa's arm and she turns to me, startled. "Tell him to look inside Leo's tool roll," I say in an urgent undertone. "I think I know who has been opening those Dark Rips."

Lupa frowns. "Who's Leo?"

But I don't have time to answer her, for Gareth is calling the crowd to attention.

"Mavericks!" Gareth holds out his hands in a benevolent gesture. Lupa backs away with the others, though she is still frowning, which I hope means she's taken my warning seriously. *If Leo is doing anything untoward*, I think, *Lupa will discover it soon enough.* There's nothing more I can do about Leo now. I put him out of my mind and focus on what is ahead.

Prudence, as the Queen of Revels, sits on a Woven throne in the tiered stands behind Gareth, Dirk beside her. Other spectators pack every viewing point on either side of the landing. "When I call your number," Gareth calls, "you will enter your gondolino and row to the start line. Number one!"

Every competitor receives a cheer as they step into the gondolino. Some I recognize, like Tanwen in her Saber's costume, and Pallas, in sky-blue armor emblazoned with the eagle symbol of Goath. There's more than a dozen Paladin Blades, all dauntingly huge and clad in variations of indigo and silver. There are a few competitors in colors I don't recognize, some men, others women. I try not to turn around as Foley, unmistakable in gold, steps into an equally garish gondolino.

"Number eleven," calls Gareth. I'm barely aware of the cheers as I step into the gondolino. I'm so nervous I'm barely aware of anything other than the oar, and the water in front of me.

It's only when number fifteen is called that I recognize Arkady, clad in the aqua and gold of the Waterlands. He receives rather muted applause, and not a few murmurs. It's hardly surprising; his helmet is a white-gold kraken, its tentacles wrapping about his face, both sinister and intimidating. His eyes meet mine as he steps into his gondolino, and I see the same grim determination in them that I recognize from the Braid Race.

He means to win.

The realization completely focuses my attention. Sweeping away the confusion of the past weeks, the emotion that has dulled my soul like old smoke, on a savage internal breeze.

Whatever Arkady came here for, this Race is part of it, just as the Braid Race was. Every enemy I have in Astria wants him to win.

Which means that I need to see he doesn't.

This is what I came for, I think fiercely. I may no longer be racing for my own foolish ambitions, or even for my siblings. But I can race to stop Arkady. To defeat those who stole all that is beautiful from Astria. Who were responsible for so much cruelty in their sick desire for perfection and power.

And I can race for Harken. He kept his side of our bargain. He faced his greatest enemy to ensure I have this chance. I will not dishonor that sacrifice by abandoning him now.

I'm going to Race. My mind narrows down to a razor-sharp focus. *And I'm going to win.*

The start line is the middle of a long, straight canal, which ends seemingly in a blank wall. Everett warned me that the course is Woven in illusion, of which that turn is clearly the first. I have no idea if it goes to the right or the left.

"Welcome!" Gareth throws his arms out dramatically, his voice carrying across the canals, immediately silencing even the chattering street urchins. "Today we bow to the bravery of Astria's Mavericks and wish them well in this greatest of competitions. The Maverick's Race has always represented an opportunity for the lowest born in Astria to take their place at the highest table. On the canals, every man is equal, with the only advantage that which they earn at the end of the oar."

This sally receives a sustained cheer, especially from those on the rooftops and clinging to lampposts, and good-natured boos from the wealthy Indigold, many of whom sit in velvet-covered chairs with servants behind them holding jugs of wine. "Yes, yes." Gareth holds up his hands to quiet them, smiling broadly. "The Maverick's Race is open to all who dare—and the prize, presented by our very own lovely Queen of Revels, is rich indeed." He bows to Prudence, who smiles and raises her Cup. The other council members, I notice, sit at a notable distance from her. Clearly, they have not forgiven her presence at my hearing.

"And now," Gareth says, with great dramatic effect, "The Cup will rise on the winner's plinth, where it will fill with Darkwine. As soon as the Cup is filled to the line, the serpent will call, and the race will begin.

"The plinth will reemerge during the final circuit. After completing all three circuits, and collecting their six ribbons, the first competitor to raise the Cup with both hands and drink its contents will be declared the winner."

He raises his needle. The water bubbles directly in front of us, and the Cup breaks the surface.

It must be Woven to repel water, for it appears perfectly dry, the flamestone and crystal glowing with an otherworldly light. Gareth twists his needle, and Darkwine rises behind the crystal.

As it reaches each of the seven lines, another coil of the serpent writhes into life, gleaming with an odd combination of indigo, gold, and silver that makes it seem remarkably real. The Darkwine scent wreathes through the air, rich and intoxicating, reaching for me like the orchards from the Summer Palace, seducing me with heady promise. For a moment I see Harken's eyes, starlit in the night: *I am the darkness . . .*

The Darkwine reaches the final coil, and the serpent's head rears above the great flamestone cup. Its mouth opens, and indigo fire roars into the air.

Flamestone petals rise from the base of the Cup and furl around the open mouth, enclosing the Cup and its contents just as the plinth descends suddenly into the chamber below, taking the Cup with it.

The Race has begun.

CHAPTER 64

RACE

*I*n the churning water and clamor of the crowd, my first stroke is so panicked that I nearly upturn the gondolino. I'm not the only one. Amid the chaos of nearly thirty gondoliers taking their first stroke, several competitors are toppled into the water, their races over before they've so much as left the landing. Choking fear makes my movements jerky and uncontrolled, which only worsens as most of the field shoot out ahead of me, racing toward the first turn. The gondolino is so light and narrow it feels like a blade on ice rather than a vessel in water, so delicate I'm afraid the slightest movement will upturn it. Then I feel the comforting arch of the cavalo beneath my knee, and my hands find their place on the oar. I thrust down, rock forward, and the vessel shoots forward like an arrow from the bow.

I'm just finding my pace when I hear a hoarse cry and the clatter of wood on stone. Up ahead, where the wall looms, a gondolino is on its side, its gondolier floundering in the water.

I hear Brooks's voice in my head: *"The organizers always ensure that the first turn is brutal."*

Nerves and haste, I remind myself, remembering Brooks and

Everett's advice. *That is what clears the field.* I can't see anything beyond the approaching wall. The buildings on both sides of the canal are tall and jut out, hiding the way forward, but after three gondolinos turn to the left, I trust my instincts and steer mine to the outside of the field on the right, slow my stroke, and allow plenty of room to round the corner.

It's the right choice.

The corner is absolutely brutal, a tight hook turn that upturns a sea of vessels. Some competitors hastily pull themselves back in. Others try to right their gondolinos. But several are clearly beyond saving, and one competitor is being hauled out of the canal by spectators, blood running from beneath his helmet. Others have taken advantage of the chaos to maim either those in the water or their gondolinos. It takes all my concentration just to steer a path through the wreckage. The canal ahead gradually narrows then takes another sharp turn, again to the left. I stroke toward the turn, trying to remain out of reach of the other gondolinos. I'm starting to settle into my pace. Ahead I can see one of the Paladins locking oars with Tanwen. Pallas is just ahead, and in front of her are the bulk of the Paladins. Foley and Arkady are pulling swiftly ahead of us all.

For every one of my strokes, the men ahead move half as far again as I push myself. Tanwen seems almost as strong as the men as she grapples with the Paladin. Pallas, like me, is trailing the Paladins and the two men in the lead. And one look at the rigorous battle between the Paladins and other competitors midstroke is enough to send ice through my veins. Brooks and Everett had not been exaggerating in their advice regarding oar-to-oar combat. Even one of the blows I see exchanged would be enough to throw me straight into the water.

I keep rowing, fighting despair as I watch the field pull ahead, trying to stay focused on the turn. The bridge after it is narrow and tall, and lined with screaming spectators. It's only as

I draw close that one of the voices rises above the others, sending a shock of recognition through me.

"Zaria!"

Shimi and Neoma stand in the center of the bridge, staring down at the approaching competitors. Neoma's face is oddly animated as she calls my name again, her Sight clearly able to recognize me beneath the helmet. Shimi, face set and hard, glances around warily and grasps Neoma's arm to prevent her calling again.

Shimi's reaction is a hard reminder of the fears that have governed us all for too long, and that have cost so much. My oar slices down with ruthless efficiency, and my gondolino leaps forward, just as the bridge is upon me.

There are several gondolinos still to pass it, but only two ribbons left. The endless hours of training in which I have sought escape are now honed by fury to a single point of focus. Bracing, I jam the oar in the lock and leap into the air, my hand closing around one of the ribbons. For the briefest moment I stare straight up, directly into Shimi's fierce bronze eyes; then I'm falling, landing catlike back in the gondolino. My hands close around the oar and I lunge forward, passing under the bridge and out into the open, just in time to take the next corner.

My momentary despair is completely gone. Every sense is focused on my oar, the shift of the water beneath me. I can sense the eddies and currents, know just where to place the oar, how to move for the greatest speed. The corner is a hard dogleg. I go right, into a narrow, deep canal where the walls are sheer on either side and there's barely room for two gondolinos side by side. Wreckage floats all around, evidence of the treacherous nature of the narrow pass.

A competitor in front of me thrusts a spear from his vessel intended to ram a hole in mine. I keep well back, knowing it would be fatal to leave my position in the bow to go forward and deflect it. Another Paladin comes up on my right. The gondolier raises his oar and thrusts it at me. Too late, I realize it is spiked at the end. I gasp as the spike sinks into my hip, right at the place where the mesh armor is thinnest. To my passionate relief, the mesh doesn't so much as flex under the spike, but the pressure alone is enough to skew the gondolino, throwing me off-balance. Thrusting his oar back in the water, my attacker shoots past me and turns the corner, going left into the second part of the dogleg.

Steely determination makes my movements sharp and focused. Instead of the wide turns I took on the other two corners, I lean into this one, almost putting the gondolino on its side. I take the corner in a spray of water, rounding it on the inside of the competitor who just passed me. He shouts in surprise that turns to annoyance when I whip around and shove his stern with my oar as I pass, causing him to veer off and hit the wall on his right.

The canal widens again, the second bridge ahead. I stroke toward it, steadying myself. This bridge is also lined with spectators. They all seem to be yelling something at me, but I'm focused on the ribbon and ignore them. This bridge is wider and flatter, the few ribbons left easily spaced. I stroke hard then leap, snatching the ribbon a split second before another competitor reaches for it. I drop back to the gondolino, mentally thanking myself for the thousand times I've practiced that landing, and the competitor, in unrecognized colors, drifts away. Their race is over.

But just as I think I'm safe, I realize why the spectators were yelling. Two of the Paladins must have been slowed by the dogleg, for they're barely ahead of me. After the others missed out on gaining a ribbon, it's just Pallas and me. The two Paladins are rowing in a pincer movement, forcing Pallas and me to drop back. It's the same strategy Arkady used in the Braid Race. *The Paladins are acting together*, I realize, probably under orders. Arkady, or whoever controls him, wants me out of this Race—and they're prepared to sacrifice bodies to achieve that end.

Pallas pulls a long, lethal-looking sword, and thrusts deftly at one of the Paladins, forcing him to give way. The other, though, looks to be cutting me off completely, and by the studs on his oar, any attempt to argue will result in a fatal blow.

Making a split decision, I pull my oar against the current, stop, and pivot, almost hitting the bow of the Paladin's gondolino as I come around his other side. Pulling my oar up, I push against him to move my own gondolino out of his reach. By the time he reaches around with his oar to take a swipe, I'm already moving ahead, into the more open water. We round the corner, Pallas on the inside, and come down the straight, past the landing from which we began. A silver line has been Woven across the water's surface, at the point where the plinth and Cup stood. I pass it.

I've survived the first circuit.

Now that I'm on the straight, I can see Tanwen up ahead, crouched in the bow of her gondolino and rowing with long, powerful strokes, every slight movement of her body controlling the vessel with masterful precision. She's on a level with Foley, who has fallen behind Arkady. The Paladins are spread behind them.

Protecting them, I think scornfully. The Paladins have effectively made a defensive wall, which is taking down any gondolino that looks to gain ground on Arkady.

Tanwen moves to head off Foley as they hurtle toward the wall at the first turn. Foley, clearly determined to force her into crashing, is rowing hard into the treacherous turn. But at the last moment, as Foley would have turned to the left, Tanwen gains just enough to thrust her oar into the water and pivot her bow around, so it smashes into Foley's gondolino with a thud that echoes off the stone and sends Foley crashing painfully into the wall.

I feel a savage stab of exultation. Tanwen no doubt has her own hatred of Dencover. But mine is personal.

That, I think fiercely, *is for Neoma, you bastard.*

As I approach the bridge on which Shimi and Neoma stand, Shimi's tense stance, and the rigid control of her face, sends a clear message that something is wrong.

"Zaria." I see her mouth my name as I leap for the ribbon and grasp it. I understand Shimi's warning when I land and find two Paladins with spears out, waiting for me. I have no time to protect myself. Their spears thrust through rings at the sides of their vessels, straight for my unprotected legs.

Steel slides through my right calf like cold fire, instantly crippling. I scream, high and fierce, as the spear slides out again and fall forward as my right leg collapses underneath me. The other spear strikes me in the knee but delivers only a glancing blow. Instead of withdrawing it, however, the Paladin slashes the tip upward, piercing the opening in the armor just behind my armpit and driving it into my bicep. I cry out again, clutching at my arm, struggling to hold my oar. The Paladin waits long enough to ensure his spear has driven home. As I try to twist free, my eyes meet his.

Caspian.

The triumph in his eyes tells me he entered in a Paladin's disguise for just this purpose, to be the one who ends my race.

He is still leaning forward, thrusting his spear in deep with the full weight of his body.

I'm abruptly transported to a dawn morning on the landing outside my room, and Harken's seductive teasing: *"But you leave yourself exposed. I could grasp the blade, like this."*

It isn't a sword, and this is no game, but the principle is the same. Gritting my teeth against the pain, I grasp the spear and thrust my body backward, hard enough to almost topple myself from my gondolino.

Caspian's eyes flare in rage and shock, then a wrenching pain tears through my shoulder as he falls forward. The spear rips through my muscle, but my ploy works. Caspian has plunged headfirst into the water, his gondolino rendered useless when Pallas thrusts her own spear through it as she passes. The current carries my gondolino out of Caspian's reach, and dimly I see him swimming toward the bridge.

Pallas raises her arm in salute, but I still have Caspian's spear embedded in my own, and I'm trembling with shock and pain. I can't move so long as the spear is stuck in my arm. *It's already half out*, I tell myself grimly. *It will have to be pulled free, sooner or later.* Gripping it with my right hand, I close my eyes and pull.

The pain is both terrifying and liberating. Terrifying, because for a horrible moment I think I will faint. Liberating, because it's so all-encompassing that it blocks out any other sensation.

I have absolutely no strength in my left arm. I use my right as I turn to grasp my oar and see my sisters on the bridge behind me. They're gripping the stone wall, their faces white with fear.

Blood is running down my leg. I can barely stand, let alone hold the oar. Pallas has passed me, and the field is getting farther and farther away. In the distance, I see Tanwen take a glancing blow to the head from Arkady's studded oar. I think she will go down, but she struggles determinedly to her feet. She shakes her head and slowly puts her oar back in the water, doggedly taking another stroke, even as two of the Paladins close in on her.

Her resilience inspires me. *It isn't over*, I remind myself. *This isn't over until that Cup is drunk, or I am dead.*

I heave my own oar up, wincing with the pain, switching my

stance so I can stroke using my right arm. It's awkward, but I can still move forward.

We're coming into the dogleg. I brace myself, half expecting to come into an ambush, but I've fallen too far behind. There is only Tanwen, and as I near her, I see a jagged hole in the side of her gondolino through which water is pouring. Blood is seeping through her armor.

"Go!" she screams, maneuvering her ruined gondolino out of my path. "I'm finished, but you're not, Zaria. Go!"

The Paladins are closing in on Pallas. Just as I think they will take her down, she leans forward on her oar and sends a sharp, clear call onto the wind. Two vast albatrosses, both with wingspans upward of twelve feet, swoop into the narrow pass. Picking up Pallas's ropes in their beaks, they beat their wings and move forward. Pallas's gondolino surges beyond the Paladins' reach, so fast it leaves a churning wake.

Animals.

I've been so focused on trying to survive, I've forgotten we are permitted to use them. This isn't the Braid Race, fought between slaves with no power to shift or summon. This is Astria, where anything is possible.

But I have no needle. Nobody has ever taught me to shift, and the only creature I know how to summon would be killed on sight.

The second bridge is approaching. I'm barely moving, drifting with the current, blood streaming from both my wounds. I brace myself in the bow, squinting to focus on the ribbon. *It isn't over.* I say it again, like a mantra. *The only way this is over is if you give up.*

I'm going so slowly I can see the faces of the spectators on the bridge. They aren't cheering me so much anymore as they are showing pity to a sure loser. I'm passionately grateful that I'm right-handed, or I'd have no chance at all of even trying for the ribbon. As it is, even the thought of trying to propel myself off my wounded leg is daunting.

I take a deep breath and leap anyway.

At first, I think I've missed the ribbon entirely, but then my fingers close over the end, and it comes away. My leg gives way beneath me when I land, and I grunt with pain. The crowd groans in sympathy. Just as I gain my footing, a shadow leaps from the bridge, and suddenly there are two of us in the gondolino.

I have the barest glimpse of a Paladin's uniform and narrow, angry eyes, then a fist smashes into my helmet, slamming the metal against my nose with enough weight to momentarily stun me. "Slave scum," Caspian hisses. Behind us, the crowd on the bridge is cheering wildly at this twist to the Race. Vaguely I recall Everett telling me that competitors can steal another's gondolino to complete their race.

"Get out!" I push ineffectually at him with the arm that isn't wounded. Caspian bats me away easily. His fist comes up again. This time it smashes into the shoulder his spear pierced. Red-hot pain flashes through me, and I cry out, crumpling beneath his fist.

"Didn't anyone warn you," Caspian sneers. He kicks me where I lay, his boot knocking the breath from my belly. "People die in the Maverick's Race. Nobody asks questions. Particularly not when that corpse was recently a slave."

Surreptitiously, I grope for my knife, trying to judge distances. "You can't use my ribbons to win."

"Do you think I care about winning?" I hear the rasp as Caspian pulls his sword. "There's far more at stake than a Cup, Weorpan." He raises the sword. There's a shout of warning from the bank, a flash of rope, and suddenly the blade is gone, wrenched from Caspian's hand. It flies through the air, tumbling into the water. Confusion and anger war in Caspian's face as he looks around for the culprit. I roll over swiftly and lunge upward with my good arm, thrusting the knife with all my strength. I feel the blade slide into flesh, high on the inside of Caspian's thigh. He screams in pain, groping at his groin, where blood is seeping through his armor. Lunging upward, I ram my good shoulder into him, and Caspian topples into the water, to the screaming approbation of the crowd on the sidelines.

I come shakily to my feet and reach for the oar. From the corner of my eye, I see a cluster of urchins scatter along the bank, throwing the rope they used into the water, shrieking with triumph as they disappear into the alleyways. One of them turns at the corner and raises her hand to her mouth: *food.*

It is forbidden, I know, for any outsider to help a competitor. The urchins knew that and took the risk anyway. I doubt they care whether I win or not. They did it to save me from a predator, just as I did when Everett threatened to whip them. They knew my life was at risk and acted without thought for their own safety.

Just as Huxley once did.

I see Lupa's face: *"Find the storm within, Zaria, and let your dragon find you."*

I see Harken's: *"Don't hesitate to call her. Not ever."*

"Come on!" calls one of the street urchins from a distant rooftop. "Show us your fire, dragon!"

There's a time to play in the shadows, and another to let that fire blaze.

I close my eyes.

Huxley, I think.

CHAPTER 65

DRAGON

*T*he gondolino drifts around the corner, guided by the barest touch of my oar, toward the straight and the silver line that marks the second pass. The other gondolinos are hardly even visible in the distance, already rounding the hook turn at the end. I'm so far behind them I can't hope to catch up.

Huxley.

I feel her mind with my own, her tremor of fear as she sees the scene through my eyes, the lines of screaming humans, whom she has only ever known as either prey or predator. I feel her shrink into her gilded cave, unwilling to leave her sanctuary for a world that has shown her only danger since she fell through that Dark Rip.

I understand.

I slump back against the high stern, my eyes closed. *It was wrong*, I think dully, *to ask such a thing of her.* No matter what Harken said, summoning Huxley amid the mass of humanity will mean her death. I've no right to ask that of a creature who has known only loneliness and suffering her entire life.

Zaria. Neoma's voice is a memory rather than reality. *You are strong. He made you stronger than you were . . .*

I close my fingers around the oar.

Take what you want, and pay for it.

The mantra that has ruled my life floods through me, firing my veins with the strength that was born the night I found myself standing in Hiraeth with four infants and no memory. The strength that learned to defy pain on the floor of Hodda's office, at the end of his whip. The strength drawn from the belief that no matter what darkness I might endure, I would, one day, win freedom for us all.

I chose this, I tell myself grimly. *I've taken what I wanted, from the very first.* In my mind I see the faces of my siblings, feel the unbreakable bond that has joined us from the first day, and will, until my last. I see Doron's terrified face as he fell into the Rip and feel the familiar, aching pain of loss and shame.

And now it is time for me to pay.

No matter what world Doron is in now, we are bound, the five of us. We always will be. And I won't give up on any chance, no matter how remote, to find a way to give back what I have taken from them.

What has been taken from us all.

I open my eyes.

The landing is to my right. The crowd is mostly staring after the gondolinos rounding the corner, but a few desultory cheers come my way, half-hearted shouts of encouragement. High on the rooftops, the urchins wave their slave braids at me.

Gripping the oar, I stroke forward.

The gondolino surges a little, earning a few more cries. Pain sears through my arm, but I no longer feel it. I know pain. Pain and I are old friends.

I stroke again. And again.

Suddenly the gondolino is picking up pace, skimming down the canal as if the current itself is carrying me. The cries of the crowd grow, the street urchins chanting from the rooftops as I fly toward the wall at the end. "Dragon!" they cry, beating the walls with their feet. "Dragon!"

I lean into the turn, arcing the gondolino with my body so it pivots sharply, then surging forward. The other gondolinos, I realize, aren't so far ahead after all—and they're virtually neck and neck as the canal narrows, forcing them to slow down, with Arkady's sleek aqua vessel in the lead. He's stroking strongly, maintaining his pace, though he's down to only a few Paladin defenders, one of whom is fighting Pallas on the approach. Shimi and Neoma are leaping up and down, clutching each other as they see me coming, clearly beyond caring about the scathing looks of the Indigold nobility nearby or what Caspian or Foley make of them. I see the fear in their eyes as I come closer and they see the blood flowing from my wounds.

"Don't worry," I try to say, but the words won't come out of my mouth. I stare at the approaching ribbon. It seems so far out of my reach as to be untouchable. The thought of pushing off from my toes is excruciating.

Don't think about it. I suck in my breath and leap.

The ribbon is in my hand.

I land in a mass of agony that casts a red film over my eyes. But I have the ribbon. I have it. And this isn't over yet.

I thrust into the dogleg—and straight into Sereia.

She's standing on the wreckage of Foley's golden gondolino, wedged across the pass, and I know full well none can see into the dogleg. There is nothing here but high, sheer walls and deep black water.

Sereia twists her needle in the air, and the water beneath my gondolino begins to churn uneasily. "You should never have made it out of the Seam," she sneers. "You should certainly never have survived a Dark Rip." The first tip of something dark and sinuous emerges from the water, and her sneer twists to something darker. "But there's no Savage King to save you now, and from what I saw, his storm dragon won't be coming for you either." Tentacles rise from the water, thick and covered in horrible growths. Suddenly I realize the significance of Arkady's helmet. *The Kraken Weavers have owned him, all this time.*

Sereia casts the tentacles a triumphant look, then twists her needle to open a scye and disappears.

I thrust my oar at the golden wreckage, clearing a path forward so I can escape whatever Sereia has summoned, but my gondolino is no longer moving. The tentacles have curled around the sides, holding it fast. I hack at them with my sword, but they are too many. The tentacles snake over the gondolino, coming up toward me. I'm about to be pulled underwater.

I feel a flash of absolute fury that it should be Sereia, whom Harken spared, despite her terrible deeds, who will be my end.

"No!" I throw myself at the tentacles, hacking at them with my knife, ignoring the searing pain in my leg and arm. I stab repeatedly, wheeling around and thrusting my knife at everything I can reach. The tentacles writhe and buck under my assault, but they keep on coming, rising until they surround me. I slash my knife overhead, trying to hit what I might, but I know it's futile. Nothing can combat such strength. The tentacles begin to close over me, and the water beneath gives way, as if some invisible gate has opened.

Just as I am slipping into that dreadful abyss, a huge, winged figure rises out of the water beside me, mouth open and roaring in fury. Great clawed feet reach down and rip the tentacles from around the gondolino, long fangs tearing into others.

Huxley.

I close my eyes in tremulous, shaking relief.

From beneath the water comes a subterranean shriek of rage that shakes the surface. Huxley answers it with a primal roar of her own. Above, storm clouds begin to gather. Slashing and gnawing at the tentacles, Huxley savages them one by one, until finally, bleeding and raw, the tentacles slip back into the water, the kraken Sereia raised crying in anguish and fury.

The fight has taken us out of the dogleg and into open water. "Go," I shout to Huxley. "You must go! They can't find you here!"

But instead of leaving, Huxley turns, her large topaz eyes fixing upon my own. In the fleeting moment of connection, I see what she read in my mind, the image and emotion that summoned her, even beyond my own conscious wish: Doron's face, as he fell into the Dark Rip, and the wrenching horror I knew in that moment. In the same instant, I see through Huxley's eyes the moment when her own mother, a hunter's bolt through her heart, dropped from our world into a Dark Rip. I feel Huxley's own terror, pain, and loss.

She knows why I race, I realize. *Our pain is the same.*

Huxley does not wait for my permission. She lifts the coils of rope from the deck that are tied to the rings, twining them through her claws. Then, with a mighty beat of her wings, she flies.

The gondolino streaks through the water at such speed it sends a huge wake arcing into the air.

The slightest shift of my body could easily topple it, so I brace as best I can and hold on. We're gaining fast on the other opponents, but so far, they seem oblivious to what is behind them. The spectators on the surrounding banks, however, are screaming their excitement, and ahead on the bridge, they wave their arms and call out as Huxley's great wings draw us onward. Pallas, a Paladin hard at her stern, is about to draw level with Arkady, but as they approach the bridge, Arkady leans across and stabs his spear viciously through the breast of one of the albatrosses. It shrieks in pain and fury. Pallas turns to meet Arkady's attack with her own sword, but her momentum is lost. Arkady shoots forward, and with one dead bird and the other floundering, Pallas has no choice but to lean forward and cut them both loose. Immediately, her gondolino begins to sink, and I realize there are great holes in either side. Pallas's race is over.

Arkady is in the lead coming into the bridge, his last Paladin hard behind him. Huxley draws my gondolino alongside the Paladin, and as he thrusts his oar at me, I crouch beneath it, gasping at the pain, then spin up, my sword cutting across his neck in the move I've practiced a thousand times. The sword catches him in the narrow band between armor and helmet, and the Paladin falls like a stone.

The urchins are on the bridge now, pushing their way to the front, screaming in delight, waving their braids and dragon banners in the air. Huxley dives low as we approach the bridge, slowing her pace so she might pass beneath it. She's still going too fast for me to jump and land. I see the gleam in Arkady's eyes as we pass him and know he has made the same calculations. I feel a moment of sheer panic that I should be so close to my goal, only to see it pulled away. At a loss to know what to do, I close my eyes, showing Huxley the ribbon in my mind, trying to communicate what I need. We're right on the bridge. I watched the ribbon approach and brace myself; I have no choice but to try.

I leap, and my hand closes around the ribbon. I fall.

And hit the water.

Even though I knew the landing was impossible, still the water is a shock. Weighed down by my armor, I sink like a stone. Trying to thrash my way to the surface uses all the muscles that have been savaged by the spears, sending blinding agony through every part of my body. I kick through it, reaching for the light above. It's dangerous for me in the water, I know. This is the domain of sea creatures. Of the kraken.

The memory is enough to cut through the pain, and I reach for the surface in desperation. *I must get out of the water, or I will die here.*

I feel the first insidious touch at my leg just as I break the surface, thrashing furiously and lunging for my gondolino, but I'm still under the bridge, and although Huxley has stopped, the gondolino is still out of reach. A rough tentacle snakes about my leg, and I scream. Arkady's gondolino noses past me. I look up in time to see him viciously thrust down with his studded oar. I can't turn in time to avoid it, and the oar strikes my helmet a stunning blow. The tentacle is weaker than the last time the kraken attacked, but still, it is closing hard, drawing me below the surface. Arkady doesn't pause. He thrusts his oar into the water, pushing forward.

I began to slip underwater.

There's an explosion of bubbles all around, and Huxley is beside me, topaz eyes gleaming through the water, her claws ripping at the tentacle on my leg. She's bleeding from a vicious wound at her shoulder. *Arkady must have used his spears on her as well.* The thought fills me with a rage that burns away my own pain. Her mouth is open, fangs bared in a savage snarl, and for a terrible moment I think she has lost all sense with the pain and will kill me without thought. But then her teeth close gently on the amethyst mail, and she is lifting me out of the water.

I can breathe once more.

A moment later, I'm dropped into the gondolino, and Huxley has the ropes between her claws, surging forward at a hard pace. I drag myself to my feet and realize the severed tentacle is still wrapped around my leg, a writhing, horrible thing that, despite being cut from its owner, is still alive, still trying to bind me. I draw my knife and hack furiously at it as we round the corner into the home straight, coming level with Arkady. This time there is no gleam in the other's eyes. He stares straight ahead, thrusting his oar with grim determination. I can feel his fear as Huxley beats her wings and, with a final thrust, pulls me into the lead.

The urchins high on the roofs are screaming the word *dragon*, over and over, chanting it as they beat the stone in excitement. The crowd is on their feet, roaring. The water bubbles and surges as the plinth, lit from beneath, rises through the water, until the flamestone petals break the surface and unfurl to reveal the Cup, Darkwine swirling behind the crystal.

Huxley slows, tilting her wings so she arcs around the plinth, bringing the gondolino close enough for me to reach for it.

My hands close over the two handles as I lift the Cup to my mouth. The dark, potent brew tastes like no Darkwine I've ever known, but rather lethal, like the serpent writhing on the Cup itself.

From the corner of my eye, I see Arkady's hands fall away from the plinth, fear and resignation in his eyes. His features are weirdly distorted, as if they are losing their shape. On the landing behind him, Leo is on his feet, his meek features twisted in a snarl of rage, a knife raised in his hand. Torsten leaps toward him, needle out, his eyes blazing and mouth open as he roars a warning.

Then Leo's knife comes down, tearing a Dark Rip open.

I swallow the serpent's Cup, and the world disappears.

CHAPTER 66

TOWER

I'm inside a round room I've never seen before. And accustomed as I am to visions, this, I am certain, is no memory. I am here—or at least a part of me is.

Did I fall into the Dark Rip?

I don't think so. I'm dimly aware of my physical body, lying inert on the landing back at the Race. The part of me that is here feels more conscious than the shadow I was when I visited Harken's memories. I'm aware of everything around me, and I try to absorb what I can of my surroundings.

At the center of the room is a fountain tree, but one unlike any I've ever seen.

It's a pomegranate tree that seems to grow from the stone floor itself. In place of roots, it has black tentacles of gleaming marble that twist in and out of the tree, like a cancer frozen in the act of spreading. A sinister seam of gold runs upward like a slow, deadly snake writhing through the marble tentacles, all the way to the kraken's head, which is split open to form the fountain bowl. A lone pomegranate hangs over the basin. It is gashed open by a single streak of gold, which is surrounded and held by rich, moist seeds of vivid crimson.

I'm inside the Woven Tower. I know it, just as I know that gold is Anahita, or whatever is left of her.

Of course it is I. Anahita's voice is all around me, a sibilant hiss that permeates my consciousness. The gold stream runs agitatedly through the marble. *Who else could have survived such a prison?* Her voice is almost scornful.

The pomegranate quivers on the branch, crimson seeds gleaming in response.

Danae, I think, my heart twisting. *This is what is left of the priestess who gave her life to bind Anahita.* I've no sooner had the thought than the voice comes again.

You are not the one I was expecting.

Searing pain rips through my invisible soul, more excruciating than any of the bodily injuries I have sustained through the Race. This is different, like a Dark Rip itself opening within me.

All my plans, Anahita's voice hisses furiously. *All the preparation . . .*

Her fury tears my soul again, and if I could cry out, I would. But whatever part of me has somehow found its way into the Tower lies inert and silent on the floor, crippled in pain.

The stone walls are covered by a thicket of Darkberry vine. Berries hang from it, rich and potent, the same lightning that lives in Harken's eyes twisting in their indigo depths. Like the pomegranate seeds, the berries quiver with life and power. They have been Woven, I sense, as some kind of barrier.

There's only one gap in the thicket: a narrow silver line made, I assume, by the silver needle on the floor in front of me.

Feivel's needle. I know it, instinctively, just as I know that the silver line is the gap through which Feivel was once thrown—and through which I have just come.

For every warp there is a weft, I think, recalling Kendrick's words. Feivel's needle must somehow have made a crack in the Darkberry barrier. One Anahita is clearly aware of.

Not his needle, Anahita gloats. *His Familiar. The only thing able to reach through the defenses Woven by his needle. It needed only the barest fraction, melted into the Cup, to create a crack. Then the right mix of Darkwine, gold, and silver in the Cup. Just enough to activate the Pathfinder's own silver and bring him to me.*

Arkady, I realize. *It's Arkady she meant to bring here. That's why he was brought through a Dark Rip; that's why they were so determined he win the Race. Anahita knew a Pathfinder could come through that crack—and that she could wind her threads into his body.*

I wonder if Arkady knew he was coming here to die. If anyone told him his purpose.

And then, like a slow, sickening tide, a horrible suspicion rises in me. *Am I dead?*

This can still work. Anahita ignores my thought. There is a note of surprise in her tone. *I can still make your body mine.*

Her presence within me changes, becomes more insidious. The pain leaves, and instead I feel a magnetic pull toward the fountain. The golden stream moves faster, swirling up the tentacles, reaching for me, drawing me forward.

What are you? she whispers, her voice coiling through me as if she is searching my being—for what, I don't know. *You cannot be Indigold, or the Darkwine in that Cup would have killed you by now.*

Desperately fighting her golden pull, I barely hear her. There is a presence in the very air of the room that holds me like a counterforce to the golden stream, binding me to the floor where first I landed. It swirls within the moist crimson pomegranate seeds and inside the gleaming indigo Darkberries. I recognize it; the air here is rich with the potent, densely Woven threads of the Lotus Palaces.

Drink, Anahita commands, her voice shrill with tension. *If you drink, we will become one. If you do not, you will die here. Hurry.*

But I can't drink. As I think the words, the golden seam surges upward, reaching for me. *I have no body*, I mentally protest. *How can I drink with only my mind?*

Fool! The golden stream gleams with Anahita's hard, savage presence. *Only your mind has power. And your mind owns your body. Drink, and you will summon your body. It is the servant, you the master. Rise, as if you would stand.*

The gold reaches for me, pulling and pushing at whatever invisible essence of myself is in the room. It's a strange, disembodied feeling, her pull too strong for even the Woven threads in the air to fight. I think to stand, and then I am upright, or whatever it is of me that is in this room is upright.

You must come to the fountain. Her voice is tense with excitement. *Now.*

Her command draws me forward until I am looking down into the wide bowl of the kraken's head. The water is the crystal clear purity of a mountain stream, with a faintly silver sheen. As I watch, gold flows upward and into the bowl, where it is immediately dispersed by the water into thin, insubstantial fragments that writhe furiously for a time before being sucked back down into the black marble tentacles. There is something insidious about the way the fragments move, as if they seek to rejoin. It almost reminds me of the Pathfinder's silver, separate parts of a whole. The resemblance ends there, however. Pathfinder's silver has a certain inevitability as it merges, whereas the gold in the fountain is fractured and broken as soon as it enters the crystalline water. The frayed golden threads wave beneath the surface, forever doomed to reach in vain for each other.

The water itself is profoundly still, undisturbed by the restless movement of the gold threads. In it I sense Darien's ancient, still presence. *He is here, holding Anahita, for all eternity, if he must.*

I cannot drink. I know it with the hard certainty I knew I must survive that Race. *If I drink, those pieces will take hold inside me.*

If you do not drink, comes Anahita's voice immediately, *you will die here. None can enter my tower, not even the Woven One. Your mind will remain here while your body dies. It will remain here forever, or until you go mad enough to drink. And you will go mad here in this nothingness.*

I stare down at the broken, writhing gold, dimly aware that somewhere beyond this Tower, my body is dying.

CHAPTER 67

GOLD

The thought of ingesting the sickening golden threads makes every instinct in me recoil.

What did the Woven One do to you? Anahita's thoughts probe my being. *How did you pass through a crack through which only silver should come?* Then, as if to herself: *It doesn't matter. You don't know how long I have waited for this.* There's an edge of manic excitement in her voice. I can feel the agitation behind it, the urgency. *There may never be another chance.*

Despite my own internal resistance, I can feel my being reaching toward the water. I don't need to physically drink it, some part of me knows. Just dive into the fountain itself. The gold will become me and I it, the threads finding their way into my body, so it will be my soul bound here forever, while Anahita—

You intend to wake as me. Everything that I am in this ephemeral, disembodied form freezes in shock. *You will wake on that landing, and all will think it is me who wakes, but it will be you.*

Perhaps it is still possible. Her thoughts are like restless winds inside me, rapid and disturbing. *I had thought to wake as a Pathfinder, able to walk where others cannot, a form I can twist to any*

I choose. None would have suspected the Fool. The restless winds twist inside me. *But now this, you . . . Yes, perhaps this is even better . . .*

Then the restless winds of her thoughts go suddenly quiet. *Enough!* Her command is deep and sonorous. *Drink now, or it is all for nothing.*

Her strength grips every particle of my being. All that is Anahita is focused now upon bending me to her will, forcing me to drink.

I'm no match for her strength.

My ephemeral form floats down toward the bowl. Even fragmented gold as she is, Anahita is powerful in ways I can't begin to fathom. It's like trying to fight a hurricane inside a Dark Rip. I can feel her strength in the magnetic pull drawing me, smell her dark power on the air—

No, I realize, deep inside myself. *That isn't her power I can smell.*

That scent, rich and intoxicating, comes from the Darkberries lining the wall. Suddenly I hear Feivel's voice, as immediately as if he was standing before me, just as he did long ago, in his tapest back in the Seam: *"Darkberries are a strange, powerful fruit . . . incredibly dangerous. But they also have a consciousness, containing within them the Indigo threads of life itself. Like fear, a lone Darkberry can kill, and usually does. If it doesn't kill, it can wipe all sentient thought from a mind, leaving it an empty vessel, the body it inhabits no more than meat. But Darkberry is also the most powerful medicine there is. Taken at the right time, in the right circumstances, there is no poison or illness in a body that Darkberry cannot cure . . ."*

I think of my braid vision, the conversation between Darien and Harken: *"Once Anahita is in the Tower, Danae and I can bind her. Feivel believes he can hold her until it is done."*

I think of Feivel's memories, left behind in here with his needle.

What if his words to me about Darkberry were an unconscious memory, one linked to the part of him that is still inside here? What if he bound the Tower with the one thing guaranteed to kill anyone whom she might try to inhabit?

Feivel has always loved the mundane: his herb garden, salving. It would be just like him to bind the Tower in something as simple, and lethal, as Darkberry. *If my body is dead,* I think coldly, *she can't use it.*

Anahita tightens her grip on me, cutting into my being painfully. But it also gives me hope. *She doesn't like that thought,* I realize.

The water is right below me. Anahita is forcing me down, focused on driving me into it. Despite the resistance in the very air about me, the potent blend of the three great Weavers who have given all they have to bind Anahita, I'm slipping into the fountain's bowl. The morass of toxic, writhing golden threads that are the remnants of Anahita's soul are pulling me down. But while she is focused on pulling me into the bowl, she does not have the strength to prevent my own thoughts from reaching out.

I can sense that, sense that she can control only a part of me, not all of me.

With the part of my consciousness that is not enslaved to her, I reach out toward the Darkberry on the wall.

Toward Feivel. Toward Harken. Toward the Woven Court from which the Darkberries come.

I reach for home.

Anahita's scream inside my head is one of pure fury that cracks me wide open, tearing the fabric of my soul itself. As the very threads of my being begin to separate, I feel all that I truly am going with them. I know that if I do not find a way to reach the Darkberry, all that is now *Zaria* will be gone forever, as impossibly rent and adrift as the lost gold threads in the bowl.

I feel a strange, familiar prickling, and suddenly, in a

different reality, Harken's face is floating above mine, the lightning in his eyes flashing with uncontrolled fury. The scent of Darkberry surrounds me, and I reach for it as a lifeline, inhaling it, the torn threads of my soul seeking to find the source from which it comes. Then he is gone.

I seem to fracture, so a part of me is facing the wall, the Darkberry right before me and Feivel's needle below. The rest of me is still being drawn inexorably into the bowl. My awareness is split, and it is the most terrifying feeling I have ever known.

Part of me feels the insidious touch of the gold threads as they swim into my being, choking my own ephemeral form with their presence, like a toxic alien intruder.

The other part of me reaches desperately for the berries on the wall. That part, though, is weak, fighting against Anahita's terrible pull.

The water begins to stir, and I feel Darien's deep, ancient strength rising to help me, fighting the broken fragments of Anahita's soul as she tries to draw me under.

For what seems an eternity, I can do nothing but hang useless in the air. The water in the fountain shivers as Anahita floods it with gold, sucking her sickening torrent up from the tentacles into the bowl, where it hits Darien's crystalline barrier like fireworks hitting the indigo night. Part of my soul is slipping into the basin, helpless against Anahita's lethal pull.

In another, increasingly distant reality, I am dimly aware of my physical body jerking and convulsing, a hubbub of confusion around me.

But the finest sliver of my soul remains here, suspended in the air, facing the Darkberry vine. The berries are close enough to touch—yet I am powerless to reach for them.

I am going to be lost here, I think in terror, *lost while staring at the one thing that could save me.*

Despair and agony rip through me with every parting thread

of my soul coming slowly undone in the fountain bowl. The Tower begins to fade down a long tunnel. My distant body ceases moving, and I feel the last breath leave it. The gold is reaching for me, trying to take me, and I know there is very little of myself left.

Then, like looking down a telescope, I see Harken leaning over my body. His hand comes up, clasping the ring at his neck where the braid knot once hung. He closes his eyes and I feel him, as if the lightning in his eyes reaches through the braid itself. A bolt of energy licks through me, and the last fragment of *Zaria*, the same thread that once faced Hodda's whip and that more recently forced me to reach for my oar when all logic told me my race was done, surges forward, to the Darkberry.

I do not so much consume the Darkberry as find myself inside it. One moment I'm staring at the strange color shifting inside the berry, and the next, I'm surrounded by it, the light within like the starlight stream Harken once used to heal me. It runs into and through me, stitching the torn pieces of my soul back together again as Harken once mended the wounds on my skin. Light shoots through my being with an almost unbearable intensity, searing me clean and filling me with a richness that feels embodied, like my physical body in liquid form. It roars toward the gold threads of Anahita's soul and thrusts them from my being in a great indigo wave.

She screams aloud, but though the pain is obscene, her cry can no longer rend my soul.

The silver line on the wall tugs at me, and I'm rushing away from her, carried on a Darkberry tide. Just as I reach the gap in the wall, Feivel's needle gleams in front of me. I throw out a thread of consciousness, reaching for it, and then I am sucked back through the wall, toward the place where my physical body lies.

As the bare tower room spirals away from me, I see the

crystal water surge up and reach for the golden threads, sucking them back down into the fountain.

Then the Tower is gone.

"DRINK!" For a moment I think I am dead, and it is still Anahita's voice calling me, but then the voice comes again, this time more urgently. "It's Paladin's Water. You must drink it, Zaria." I feel something silvery and cool at my lips, and realize I am somehow, miraculously, not dead. I crack open my eyes.

I'm lying on the tiled landing, Feivel and Harken both staring down at me. Feivel is holding a cup to my mouth. "Drink," he says again, and I do.

I feel something warm and sharp in my hand. "Feivel," I say weakly. "I found your needle."

And then I pass out.

CHAPTER 68

DEAD

I wake on our bed in the Summer Palace, as sunfall turns the orchards deep indigo. Nothing has ever seemed so beautiful to me.

Harken is standing by the open arch, his back to me. His hands are thrust deep in his breeches, his shoulders straight and hard beneath the linen shirt. In the fading light, he's as still as cast bronze, his hair stirring in a light breeze the only moving part.

My heart twists with bittersweet longing before I am truly conscious of any other part of my body. I want to drink this moment in, absorb him while I still can before he disappears and is lost to me, forever.

I move tentatively beneath the sheets, bracing for pain, but to my surprise there is none. My body feels utterly different, as if it belongs to someone else. *Harken must have healed me.* Then I remember the cup Feivel gave me to drink. *It was Paladin's Water that healed me*, I think sadly, *not Harken.* Harken won't ever heal me again. I wonder why he's brought me here at all.

"I know you went into the Woven Tower." Harken begins

speaking without turning around, his voice detached. "What I need to know is how you came back."

Dread grips me at the hard edge in his voice. I push myself up against the pillows, marveling that I am not in an agony of pain. He turns toward me and begins speaking again.

"A lot of people are going to ask you questions." He is unusually pale, his eyes on mine sharp with scrutiny. "Before they do, I need you to tell me what happened in there."

Had anyone else asked me to relate what had happened, I don't think I could have told them. But it is Harken who brought me back, Harken's hand on that braid that stopped me from dying.

It is his story, too.

In halting sentences, sometimes struggling to find the words, I tell him everything that happened from the moment I drank from the Cup. When I reach the part about the gold threads entering my body, Harken's eyes flare. Stepping forward, he tilts my chin up abruptly, scrutinizing my eyes.

"You stopped breathing," he says curtly. "I felt your pulse stop with my own hand. How did you come back?" he asks again, his eyes narrowing, boring into mine. "Did any of those threads survive inside you? Is that what now exists, in the place where Zaria once was?" His hand tightens reflexively on my chin. I know what he is asking, and suddenly, I know why he brought me here. First and foremost, Harken is bound to protect the Woven Court. I can feel the lethal power behind his grasp. I know that part of him is wondering if he should simply break my neck, here and now, and eliminate whatever threat might live inside me.

"I could feel myself dying, it is true." I meet his eyes, trying to let him see inside me. "But part of me was still alive. Able to remember things—like what Feivel once told me about Darkberry." I almost smile. "He told me that taken in the right circumstances, Darkberry can cure any kind of illness, work as an antidote to any poison. There were Darkberries all over the walls of the Tower. I think—I suspect," I correct myself, unable to explain exactly how I knew it was true, "that Feivel Wove them there to hold Anahita during the battle, and to bind her after it was done. I could feel him, in there." Tears spring to my eyes. "I could feel all of them," I whisper. "Darien, Danae, Feivel —it was like all of them were Woven into the air itself, protecting me from Anahita."

Harken's hand drops away, and he pulls back, his eyes unreadable. *Darien*, I think dully. *I came out, but Darien didn't.*

"I knew I couldn't let her inside me." I force myself to continue. "I knew I had to eat one of the Darkberries and kill the body she wanted." I swallow convulsively. "But I was insubstantial. I don't know what part of me was in that Tower, but it wasn't a part that could eat. I was staring at the Darkberry, knowing it was my salvation but unable to grasp it."

I break off. Of all the moments in that Tower when I was afraid, that one, I know, is the one from which nightmares are made. The sheer terror of knowing salvation to be so close, yet being incapable of reaching for it . . . I shudder, pushing the recollection away.

"Salvation?" Harken's face has paled. He looks almost sick, but at least the hard light of suspicion has faded from his eyes. "You were trying to reach for Darkberry as salvation? You know as well as I do that people die if they eat Darkberry. Indigold, Weorpan, or Fool—Darkberry kills them all, Zaria."

"If Anahita had succeeded, I would have been dead anyway. She wanted to . . . thread the pieces of her soul back together inside my own. Make my body hers, as she once did the Kraken." I shake my head, wanting to rid myself of even the memory.

Harken blanches. Standing abruptly, he strides away from the bed, raking a hand through his hair. He takes a deep breath, then turns back again, his eyes oblique. "But she didn't succeed?"

I shake my head slowly. "I thought she was going to. I felt the last breath leaving my body, but she was still forcing her way into my being, and somehow, I knew there was enough life still in it for her to find purchase." I pause, the nightmare reaching for me again, trying to find the right words to describe the next part. "Then I—felt you." I meet his eyes. I'm reluctant to mention the braid end, after all it has cost us both. "It was you who pulled me back." I glance at the ring about his neck, but the braid end isn't on there.

Maybe, I think unsteadily, *it never was. Maybe I imagined it all.* I want to touch Harken, but he is beyond my reach, remote and detached.

"It seemed as if your strength ran through me. Helped me reach for the Darkberry." I can't meet his eyes, can barely speak. I look down at my hands on the coverlet. They seem different.

Everything seems different.

"You gave me the strength to go . . . *inside* the Darkberry. And when I did, Anahita was powerless. Every part of her was thrust from my body. I was suddenly whole again."

I'm still staring at my hands. My skin is the same deep ocher it has always been, but now it seems to glow with an umber sheen, almost like Harken's own. "Except I'm more than whole," I say slowly. "And I don't think it's just from the Paladin's Water. I feel—changed."

When I look up, Harken is nodding slowly, a few paces away from the bed. His eyes are distant, and I can sense the rapid thoughts racing through him just as I can the strange new invigoration in my own body. *It's like the starlight stream from his hand is everywhere inside me now.* Within the very fiber of my being. Not an invader but . . . the essence of who I am.

"Do you think she's dead?" I ask tentatively. "Anahita?"

"No." Harken's voice is certain. "I think she is more dangerous than she has ever been—and that it's only a matter of time until she escapes that Tower.

"There is a reason," Harken says slowly, his eyes turning to mine, "that the Paladins, and the priestesses on the Isle of Nine, take a concentrated form of Darkwine for their ceremonies. Of course, it can be lethal. But as Feivel told you, it can also, in certain circumstances, heal almost anything. It is the origin of life and the cause of death. In this, it is eternal."

He pauses, then comes over to the bed. Sitting down on the mattress, he takes my hands in his own, turning them over as he looks down at them. "Eating a Darkberry," Harken says, "will kill whatever lives inside you." He raises his eyes to mine, allowing his words to make their full impact. "No matter what stories Indigold wish to tell themselves, they are, at their essence, mortal. Their forms are modified, it is true. It is the reason they live longer than a Foolish life and are more powerful, with Indigo gifts. But their forms are mortal, nonetheless. They do age, and they do die." He holds my eyes. "Concentrated Darkwine is dangerous enough. But to eat an actual Darkberry means certain death, for even the strongest Indigold." Harken turns my hand over again, looking down at the glowing ocher skin. "I think you can feel the difference in yourself. See it—as I can."

The dense, rich particles of the Woven Court swirl in the silence that follows his words, gleaming with a light I had only sensed before now. I know what he is saying, but my mind is still trying to process it.

"What do you mean, then?" I grope for the words. "Do you mean that I'm . . . dead?"

Harken's eyes find mine amid the golden sunfall between us. "I mean that the mortal part of you was already dead before you entered the Darkberry," he says quietly. "I felt the last breath leave your body on the landing, and I think you did too."

I nod slowly. I know he's right, but I still don't know what it means.

"I think that because your own mortality was gone, the

Darkberry's destructive forces attacked the only living thing inside you: the broken threads of Anahita's being. After those were destroyed, the regenerative forces of the Darkberry took root in your being. Nobody in living memory has ever seen that happen, because nobody has ever survived eating a Darkberry. But you didn't eat it. You, or rather an ephemeral part of you, *entered* the Darkberry. I think the Darkberry recognized something inside you that it could join with. It brought you back to life—or at least, it brought your intact soul back into your physical body.

"The Cup you drank from didn't hold only Darkwine. If I am right, and I believe I am, it held a precise blend of concentrated Darkwine, Serpent's Gold, and Pathfinder's silver that killed your body, as it has many before you. Then, when only Darkberry in its most pure form sustained you, Feivel gave you Paladin's Water. You consumed the mystery elixir, Zaria. The very Water of Eternal Life the Paladins have spent centuries seeking to create.

"I do not think the combination brought you back to a mortal form, nor even that of a powerful Indigold." Harken holds my eyes. "I think it brought you back as pure Indigo. Not Woven, as I am, but grown, as the Darkberry itself is. I think," he says slowly, "that when you sacrificed yourself by entering that Darkberry, you inadvertently became the very thing Anahita has always desired the most: what the Paladins might call a *perfect vessel*. And that," he says grimly, staring at me, "makes you the most valuable—and dangerous—being that Astria has ever known."

CHAPTER 69

KNIFE

The perfect vessel.

I close my eyes, listening to the slow beat of my heart. *It's still there*, I think. *I'm still me.* And I am. But I'm different, too.

I can't begin to think about what those changes might mean, should others learn of them, nor what new dangers I might now face. All I really care about, in this moment, is what Harken himself thinks.

He said I am dangerous. My heart jolts painfully. *I'm a threat now. To him. To the Woven Court he's sworn to protect.* His hand is still on mine, but it feels cool, impersonal.

"I have only one question." I open my eyes to find Harken looking at me closely, his own eyes more inscrutable than ever. "You didn't see the golden needle in that Tower," he says. It isn't a question so much as it is a confirmation.

"No." I shake my head slowly. "The only needle I saw was silver, a Weaver's needle. Feivel's, I'm sure of it." I frown. "What of Danae's needle?"

"She never took it in." Harken withdraws his hand smoothly, with no flicker of emotion. "Danae was always intended to be the anchor, and she didn't require a needle to become that. Hers was destroyed before she ever entered the Tower. And Darien hadn't used a needle since his was lost in his first battle with Anahita.

"I need to see Feivel," Harken says abruptly, standing. "I want you to know," he says in an oddly stilted tone, "that your siblings are safe. They will be with you by tomorrow, at the latest."

A part of me wants to ask how, but there is too much in my mind for now.

"Will you wait here," Harken says, "until I return?" It seems such an odd question under the circumstances, and my mind is turning so fast, that I simply nod.

He goes, and I'm alone.

Night has fallen while we spoke. I slip from the bed and pull the remainder of my broken costume from my body, standing under the waterfall for a long time. My body no longer hurts. Not at all. And despite all that has happened, I don't feel tired. I dry off and walk naked to the mirror.

I am altered.

It isn't my imagination, nor some lingering illusion granted by the Darkwine. I turn slowly in the soft light cast by the oil lamps on the wall, examining every inch of my skin. My skin is richer, more lustrous, pliant rather than soft. My limbs feel both finer and more resilient, like tempered steel in contrast to heavy bone. On the surface I have both filled out and become smoother, the lines of my body supple and curved with a symmetry my previous form lacked. Even my hair has altered, from tangled curls to gleaming mahogany ripples that shimmer with a life of their own. But the greatest change is in my face.

My eyes are no longer light amethyst but the deep, almost shocking shade of Darkberry itself. Threads of dark indigo edged in silver shift in their depths. Not quite the lightning flashes of Harken's, they are more like moonbeams far beneath the surface of water, flickering and ever changing. They, more than any other change, seem to me a physical manifestation of the starlight stream held in my own body.

And my body itself feels strong. It is liberating, freedom of a kind I've never felt before.

This form, I sense, is intrinsically powerful, in ways not even the Indigold nobles could comprehend. That power, and the profound sense of freedom it affords me, makes me feel beautiful in a way that has nothing to do with my physical appearance, dramatic as I know that is. It lives inside me, in the place where my strength has always been, only now the last barrier has fallen between me and the once seemingly impossible dream of freedom. *I didn't just win my right to freedom in that race,* I think, *or the material riches of its prize.*

I defeated death itself.

And now I will be with my siblings again.

Every part of me is glad, and grateful. But of all the many questions that remain, my greatest one is for Harken—and he doesn't seem at all inclined to answer it.

He saved you, I tell myself. *Whether he meant to or not, he did. And he brought you here. Maybe just start with that.*

But it's not enough. Not nearly enough. Worse, going by his remote demeanor since my miraculous return, I'm beginning to suspect that detached civility may be the best I have to hope for.

Be grateful he offers that much, I tell myself sternly, pulling on a tunic and trousers that are thankfully still in the room. I wonder idly if tonight's Revel is still being held. I don't particularly care.

I don't care about much at all, I realize. It's an odd feeling. More liberating, in some ways, than either being unbraided or discovering I'm immortal. That thought strikes me as so unexpectedly funny that I find myself laughing, so hard it almost hurts.

I'm still laughing when I realize Harken is back in the room, watching me.

He isn't laughing at all. In fact, I've never seen his face so grim.

He walks to the terrace and leans on the stone wall there, his hands clasped before him. The full moon is high, lighting the Darkberry orchards below.

"I knew you were in danger." He speaks without turning around. "I knew it before that Race ever began. But I was so damned angry—" He twists his head sharply, dropping his chin. When he continues, his voice is low and harsh. "It was only when Huxley flew from here that I saw sense. Nothing but the most life-threatening danger could have summoned Huxley into the open before so many people. Then there was this." Reaching into his pocket, he pulls out the braid end, laying it carefully on the stone wall, still without looking at me. "I hated that thing," he says, "but I couldn't bring myself to throw it out. And then suddenly it was gleaming gold. I touched it, and I saw you, lying on the ground, Feivel leaning over you."

His boot kicks the wall with a brutal thud.

"I thought you were dead." He turns slowly to face me, his eyes burning caverns in his face. "I was an arrogant Fool," he says bitterly. "And you nearly paid for it with your life."

Shaking my head, I start toward him. "It's not your fault, Harken—"

"Yes," he says bluntly. "It is."

We face each other across the terrace. I want to touch him, reassure him, but the implacable expression on his face warns me against it. Instead, I pour two glasses of Weald whiskey. Harken shakes his head in curt refusal. He stands with his back to the valley, hands thrust in his breeches, head down.

"I should have stopped the Race the moment I realized Arkady had Pathfinder's silver in his veins. I didn't, though." Harken delivers each word starkly, without any apology. "I cared more about uncovering those who were using Arkady than about the danger he might pose." His mouth curls in what I realize is self-contempt. "Later, I was so angry with you that I took a savage pleasure in the thought of a Pathfinder winning their sacred Race."

His voice cracks. He looks away, his mouth working, every aspect of his stance warning against approach of any kind. When he looks back, his face is hard-set once more.

"The visions you saw when you touched the braid," he says roughly. "Did they show you how Torsten and I met?"

I nod mutely, color firing my face. It seems that I can feel nauseating shame in my new, immortal form just as viscerally as I did in my old. Then I remember what I saw, the moment before I was sucked into the Woven Tower.

"Torsten." I can barely say the name. "He knew what Leo was going to do, at the Race. You were right about him all along."

"No, I wasn't." Harken's mouth is a hard line. "Whatever Torsten might have been—might still be, for all I know—he wasn't behind the plot to send Arkady into that Tower. It was Torsten who ransacked Feivel's belongings, searching for the Familiar."

"But isn't that proof of his guilt?"

"No," says Harken shortly. "Torsten went through Feivel's belongings not to find something, but rather to see what might be missing. It seems that Leo dropped his tool roll, the day you and Feivel met him at the library. Torsten noticed Jaxan's name inside it. He also noticed this." He holds up the twisted, stunted remains of a small herb knife.

I stare at it, thinking of Leo's nervous blushes, his shaking hands, then of Anahita's insidious voice: *It needed only the barest fraction, melted into the Cup, to create a crack . . .*

"It was Feivel himself who gave Leo his Familiar," Harken says. "Unknowingly, of course. But Torsten studied herb lore under Feivel, long ago, in the Lotus Palaces. He knew what that knife was. It didn't take long for him to discover that Leo was Jaxan's son."

"Surely everyone knew they were related? Leo openly called Saxan his uncle."

"Divines do not marry. And they do not father children." A muscle tics in Harken's jaw. "Nobody ever suspected Leo was Jaxan's child. Why would they? Leo had been raised by Saxan's sister. It's possible even Saxan himself thought the boy was hers. After she was killed in the fighting, Saxan saw to it that Leo was adopted by the abbey, which offers a certain anonymity." Harken shrugs. "Nobody checked into the boy's background, certainly not after Leo disappeared into the Seam. Nobody, that is, until Torsten."

Striding forward, Harken picks up the glass he previously refused and takes a deep swallow, grimacing as the whiskey hits his throat. "And who was he going to tell of his suspicions?" Harken stares hollowly into the depths of the glass. "His own sister had likely orchestrated the plot. The Comitas was, at the very least, sympathetic to Sereia's ambitions, and like as not complicit in the plan itself. The Northern Alliance hate Torsten almost more than I do; most of them have never understood why I allowed him to live." His hand draws down his face like a shadow of old pain. He raises his eyes to mine. "What was he going to do," he says bitterly, "come to me?"

I think of Harken's fury in the vision I saw: *Be gone, and pray to all the twelve knots of your broken faith that you never see my face again . . .*

Harken sees the awareness in my eyes and snorts in self-contempt. "Exactly," he mutters. "But at least, when that Rip opened, Torsten was ready. He captured Leo, and the knife—though not before Arkady turned to silver and escaped through the Rip."

"Leo always seemed so incompetent." I shake my head, trying to reconcile the nervous boy I knew with the deranged master-mind he appears to have been.

"It was a good act." Harken pours us both another glass.

"Leo, in fact, was top of his class in alchemy. It wasn't nepotism that brought him back to Astria. Leo spent all that time in the Seam not as punishment, but by choice. He was searching the slave records, looking for one very specific slave."

"The exiled Pathfinder." I remember Leo's obsession with the slave records, think of how we all admired his kindness and charity. *And all that time*, I think furiously, *he was trying to find a way to get inside that Tower. To finish his father's dark work.* I remember Arkady's grim intent, the kraken wrapped around his face. "Arkady knew all along, didn't he? What he'd been brought here to do?"

"I believe so." Harken nods. "I imagine he was raised knowing of the Shadow Bargain his mother had made to get them to safety. He may not have known he was doomed to die— but he certainly knew he would be summoned, and called on to fulfill a debt. And there's no doubt he'd been told you presented a threat. He really was trying to kill you, from that first day. They couldn't risk you winning the Braid Race, nor later, the Maverick's. That's why Leo opened the Rip at the very time he knew you'd be there. Your death would have been quickly dismissed as the result of a Dark Rip." His mouth tightens. "The only wonder is that he didn't poison your Race Cup before the Braid Race."

"He may well have." I'm unable to suppress a shudder. "I tossed the Cup instead of drinking it." I shake my head. "He pretended to be my friend."

"It was never about you. Leo had his own reasons." Harken's face seems carved in stone. "He was barely six years old when I hung Jaxan on the abbey gate. Throughout Leo's formative years, he was forced to pass beneath his father's rotting corpse every day, with none knowing the man was his father. If such torture wasn't enough to make Leo crave revenge, it seems he himself was born as the result of one of Jaxan's dark experiments with priestesses. Jaxan told his son he had been born to a divine mission: find the golden needle, raise Anahita, and become her servant. He even left Leo several gifts to help him see that mission fulfilled."

Opening Leo's leather tool roll on the table between us, he withdraws a knife. It's small and unassuming, with a blunt blade and wooden handle. Harken passes his hand over it, and suddenly it gleams with the sick, potent gold I saw in the Tower.

"I searched high and low for Jaxan's tool roll." He shakes his head. "I never suspected it had been given away before I ever caught him—nor to whom." He stares at the knife, his eyes distant. "All of this is my fault. Jaxan's death, Leo's sick ambitions, Arkady's presence here. All of it the result of my arrogance and pride."

CHAPTER 70

STARLIGHT

*H*arken walks to the wall of the terrace, placing the glass carefully atop it, not looking at me.

"Does this mean," I say tentatively, "that you have reconciled with Torsten?"

"No, I haven't *reconciled with Torsten.*" His scathing contempt silences me. "I doubt I will ever be able to so much as look at him without loathing. But the Woven Court is my responsibility to guard, and I can't do that from behind these mists. Not anymore. Even if that means sitting at a table with a man who betrayed me."

My fingers tighten into fists, then slowly release. I take a deep breath. "I betrayed you."

Harken's face twists toward me. He frowns, opens his mouth to speak.

"No." I hold up my hand. "You've told me how I ended up in that Tower. Now there are things I need to say."

Harken drops his eyes, shaking his head slowly, as if already resolved not to hear me.

"The first vision I ever saw through that braid," I say quietly, "was when we went through the Nexus."

Harken tenses.

"I drank the Darkwine you gave me, and suddenly I saw you, standing amid the wreckage of the Lotus Court." Harken's head snaps up. "You were newly Woven." I meet his eyes. "You were the most beautiful being I had ever seen."

He stares at me, his face like water under moonlight, every shadow changing it.

"I watched you bury all those people." I hold his eyes. "Bring flowers forth from their bodies. Save a man who would surely have died without your help, and nurse him back to health."

Harken makes a hard noise, his eyes glittering.

"I didn't know who it was. I never saw his face. I had no idea —" My voice cracks, and I force myself to halt, to breathe. "You offered me the braid knot, but I told you to keep it. I told myself that was because I wanted to use the connection to spy on you, to gain an advantage." Harken's eyes are haunted. I hate myself for every word. "But that was a lie." I shake my head, almost violently. "I knew I could trust you. From the moment you offered me that knot, I knew, even if I hadn't known earlier, when you healed me. I wanted you to keep that braid because I wanted to know you." I close my eyes, grimacing with regret. "I knew it was wrong. I knew it was spying. And I did it anyway."

"What did you see?" Harken's voice is ripped from somewhere inside him, rough and harsh.

"I saw it all." I stare past him, remembering. "I saw you walk through the streets and learn the savagery of men. I saw you watch the carnage of the Isle of Nine. I watched the old Lord of Goath give you his son, and Gemory ask you to save Huxley." Tears I can't fight well up in my eyes. "I saw you save Darien from the dungeons," I whisper, "and then I watched you bid him farewell." The tears spill down my face, and I can't look at him any longer, can't see the betrayal on his face.

"It was only after the council meeting," I say, the words so painful I can barely get them out, "that I saw a vision of your fight with the man you had saved and saw his face. That was when I recognized Torsten, and understood why you hate him so much."

I want to explain myself, but to do so would be seeking absolution, and I won't do that.

"I forced you to that table." I say it grimly, my tears drying on my face. "I forced you to sit with the man who betrayed you in the worst way any person could. I don't blame you for casting me out of your home, Harken." I raise my eyes to his. "What astonishes me is that you would ever bring me back in."

The silence between us is laden with the weight of betrayal and my own regrets. It draws on for a long moment, Harken's face shadowy in the starlight.

"You say you wanted to know me." His voice is low, pained rather than rough. "Yet I told you more of my life than I ever have anyone, even Darien." His voice falters slightly. "Why wasn't that enough?"

The stark pain behind his question pierces me deeper than any spear ever could.

"It should have been." Words swirl inside me, each more terrifying than the last. Confession is one thing, emotional exposure quite another. The thought of Harken rejecting the innermost part of my soul fills me with dread that makes facing Anahita seem almost insignificant.

But the innermost part of his soul is exactly what you took from him, I think, *without so much as asking.*

He watches me from the shadows, still as one of them. I take a deep breath.

"You changed me, that first night we met in the Seam." The words come reluctantly, like water from a disused well. "After you healed me, I could feel you, like some kind of talisman inside, shielding me from the world beyond. It seemed impossible that the one person who made me feel that way could be the Savage King others described. Then you claimed me."

Harken flinches.

"No." My hand goes up instinctively to touch the braid that is no longer there. "What I'm trying to say is that up until the moment you tied that braid to the ring, a part of me had always felt utterly alone. But suddenly, there you were. I could feel you. Against my skin. Inside my body." I stare at him across the dark void that separates us. "It felt like someone had turned on a light, one that grew brighter with every vision. I understood you better each time I woke, and trusted you more because of it. The visions made me feel less alone. They kept the darkness at bay." I take a half step toward him, then halt. The words have to be brought to the surface, laid bare, no matter how difficult it feels. "I was afraid that if I told you about the connection, you would take the braid off—and then the darkness would come back.

"The simple truth is that I betrayed you because I couldn't face losing you." I swallow hard. "And my greatest regret, for the rest of my life, will be making that choice."

In the silence that follows, I feel both the profound peace of having finally spoken my truth, and the devastation of losing the very thing I risked it for.

Then Harken comes out of the shadows, taking the terrace in long strides, his face blazing fiercely. "What other choice did I give you?" His hands capture my face. "For twenty years I have told myself that the world beyond these mists isn't important. That I am an observer who exists beyond it, removed from emotional entanglement or obligation. I've guarded my past as selfishly as I have the Woven Court—but what I was really guarding was my own heart." His eyes search mine. "You don't know what it was like, here, after you left," he says hoarsely. "You speak of darkness. Without you, my court felt darker than any Rip, filled with memories of the terrible things I have done —and the knowledge that you had seen them." His thumbs stroke my jaw, his hands trembling slightly. "I told myself you must have had some ulterior motive, some endgame that I hadn't seen. It didn't seem possible that you could truly love me, not after knowing the truth of what I have been, and all I have done. I tried to convince myself you were best forgotten, and I better without you.

"It wasn't until I saw Huxley fly off through the mists, and realized the danger you must be in, that I knew myself for a Fool. And then, when I touched the braid end and realized that I could no longer feel you—" He shudders. "I thought I was too late, that I had lost you forever."

"But that was what saved me." My hands cover his. "When you touched the braid end, I felt it. Felt you call me home. You might have untied the knot." A laugh chokes in my throat. "But you never said the words. I may no longer be enslaved—but I'm still yours."

"Body and soul," he rasps.

I nod in his hands. "Body and soul," I whisper.

His mouth takes mine, and I am lost, in starlight and Darkwine.

A LONG TIME LATER, the blazing moon shines down on the orchards.

"You do know," Harken says, trailing his fingers over the curve of my breasts, "that your own Revel is underway as we speak."

"I don't care." I turn toward him, my leg over his hip drawing him toward me.

"You should." He smiles, tracing my mouth with his finger. "You deserve that prize," he says quietly. "You won it."

"Wait." I pull back from him, studying his face. "Are you, of all people, telling me I should attend an Indigold Revel? That I should care what they think?"

"I didn't say you had to care what they think." His mouth quirks with a hint of his customary cynicism. I find it oddly reassuring. "But that prize is yours. Go and collect it." He gives a soft huff of laughter. "For the street urchins," he says dryly, "if nobody else."

I search his eyes in the moonlight. "Do you really mean that?"

He kisses me. "I mean it so much," he murmurs, "that I had your dress brought here." He tugs one of my curls. "But you have to promise to leave this unbound." He rolls onto his back, an arm flung over his head. "Just once," he says softly, "I want to see you wear it down."

IT TAKES HARDLY any time for us to stand beneath the waterfall again, then change, Harken into dark breeches and gleaming boots, topped by a rich coat of deep Darkwine, his shirt open, as ever, at the neck.

My dress is an extension of my dragon costume, burgundy silk that fades to rose as it climbs up my body. A storm dragon wraps sleek silver and indigo coils around me, from the hemline of the burgundy skirt to the scooped top of the bodice.

Harken stands behind me as I look in the mirror, feeling the odd sensation of my hair touching my back.

"Like a storm dragon's mane," he murmurs, his lips on my neck. I shiver as I turn to him.

"You know," he says, grinning crookedly, "the first time we went to one of these damned things, I told you I was taking you into a place more dangerous than Huxley's chamber."

"I remember." I think how much it suits him, to smile.

"Tonight, it is you who will be the most dangerous thing at the ball." The humor fades from his eyes. "I think the facts of your transformation are best kept between us. I can keep the council at bay, for one night, at least. Do you agree?"

I press myself closer to him. "Are you asking me," I murmur, "to play another game with the Indigold nobility?"

His eyes flare, his mouth curling. "I suppose I am, yes."

I put my lips to his ear. "Savage."

His silent breath of laughter thrills my skin. "Criminal."

When he pulls away, his eyes are glittering, and the desire there makes my breath catch. "This is one ball," he murmurs, "that I wouldn't miss for all the threads in the Interweave."

He casts a scye, and we step through it together.

CHAPTER 71

UNWOVEN

"*D*ragon! Dragon!"

The first thing I hear, as Harken and I land in front of the entrance to the Indigo Palace, are the street urchins chanting my name. They line the rooftops, waving their dragon banners.

"They can't have been waiting here all evening," I say, horrified.

"Oh, they have, my lady." The footman bows as Harken and I approach. "And loudly," he says, in a rather disapproving tone.

"They must be starving." I turn to Harken, but he's already murmuring to a footman, handing him a purse.

At the entrance, Harken stands aside, gesturing me ahead. "It's not me they're here to see," he says with a slight smirk. Nudging him, I start to move forward, but the footman halts me. He nods to someone over my head, and there is a great drumroll. The crowd falls silent, and every face turns to me.

"It is my honor," says the footman sonorously, "to present this year's winner of the Maverick's Race: Zaria, henceforth known as the Lady of Caer Helfrach."

A great roar goes up. For a moment I stand there, rather

stunned, trying to process the fact that it is me he's talking about.

They aren't looking at me because of my braid, I think dazedly. I no longer have a braid. I'm not a slave.

I'm Zaria, Lady of Caer Helfrach.

"Move, Lady Zaria," Harken murmurs in my ear, "or they'll all think you Darkwine soaked." I cast him a chiding glance, and he grins.

Then it is a jumble of faces and bubbling voices, one shouting over the other. "I thought you were gone for a moment there," Everett says, his eyes flaming with Weald whiskey.

"We saw you bleeding," adds Brooks, stumbling slightly, "and thought it was all over."

"Then you were dead on the landing!" Everett swallows the contents of his glass and holds it out to the footman. "Dreaver's knot, Zaria. They'll be talking about you for years."

Amid the tumult of their raucous reliving of the Race, I'm aware of Harken stiffening beside me. Following the direction of his gaze, I see Torsten's tall figure, head inclined slightly as he listens to Kendrick. His eyes lift, meeting Harken's, just as they did long ago, at that first Revel, as if drawn by a thread only the two can sense. Harken's mouth tightens, all trace of wry humor fleeing his face.

Then he nods. It is barely a civility, but Torsten returns it, his own head dipping in clear acknowledgment.

The moment is gone as briefly as it occurs, a mere flicker of connection amid a sea of humanity. *But still*, I think, as Harken turns away, *a beginning*. And if Harken is right, about Anahita being more dangerous than ever, then we will soon need every ally we can get—even if that means dealing with Torsten.

A little further on I meet Tanwen, her face pale, but drinking Weald whiskey, nonetheless. "I'm so glad you're safe," she says.

I kiss her cheek. "Thank you." I pull back, still holding her hands. "You saved me today," I say honestly.

"Ha!" Tanwen raises her glass to me. "From what I saw, it's everyone else that needs saving from you." She winks at me. "Take care of Harken, now," she whispers. I laugh softly and move on into the ballroom, which is a mass of heaving bodies.

Feivel finds me somewhere amid the crush. "Zaria!" Drawing my face down, he kisses my cheeks, his eyes sparkling. "Thank you, firstly, for not dying," he says in heartfelt relief, casting his eyes skyward. "Harken never would have forgiven me that. And secondly, for bringing my needle back. I know it can't have been easy."

"Has it helped?" I touch his cheek. "Are your memories back now?"

"Sadly, no." Feivel's mouth twists ruefully. "Although I suspect Sereia would like to see me in a dungeon, to be sure."

I know he means me to laugh, but I can't. "It's Sereia who should be in a dungeon."

"Possibly." He lifts a resigned shoulder. "But politics, you know." His eyes flicker to Harken, for once without their customary shadow of reproach, which makes me wonder what hand Harken has had in Sereia's fate. I'm also confused by what Feivel has said.

"I thought your memories were held in your needle?"

"I thought so too." He smiles sadly. "But some things, it seems, can't be mended. I am not the man I was when I went into that Tower, nor is my needle the same tool it once was. It no longer knows me, and I cannot connect with it. Then there is the matter of Leo having melted down a good portion of my Familiar." Feivel's mouth twists. "Quite the alchemical achievement," he says dryly, "considering we all thought him a quivering idiot." Shaking his head, he covers my hand with his own. "Forgive me, Zaria," he says gently, "for not seeing it earlier. It is my fault there was ever a way into that Tower."

"You saved me in there." I embrace his rotund, comforting form, his familiar tapest scent like a sweet memory. "You Wove

Darkberry around the Tower," I murmur. "I could feel you in the berries. You protected me, helped me when I couldn't help myself, as you always have." I draw back to find Feivel's eyes glistening, his hands shaking. "I think you Wove almost all the strength you had into those Darkberries," I say, "and that Darien cast you from the Tower with the last of his. He wanted to save you, even if it meant leaving a vulnerability in the Tower." I hold his hands. "And I'm so very grateful," I whisper. "I don't want to imagine this world without you."

The glance we exchange holds the potent memory of the life we knew in the Seam, and the darker, more recent threads of the foe we have both faced and miraculously survived. "My child." Feivel squeezes my hands. "Thank you." He looks more closely at me, his eyes narrowing curiously. "But you are changed," he murmurs. "Quite changed."

It is at that moment the drums roll once more. Feivel's hands slip from mine, and I feel Harken's heat at my back.

"Ladies and gentleman," the footman intones. "Prudence, the Queen of Revels."

The audience applauds as Prudence mounts the dais. Harken's lips touch my shoulder. "Here we go."

Prudence is as exquisitely clad as ever, her silver and indigo ballgown an ethereal mist. "Ladies and gentlemen," she says, with her quiet dignity. She waits until the most raucous of the Indigold cries have died to silence.

"I wish it was my place to grant the winner her prize." Her eyes rest on me, her smile a slow curve. "But it is not. That honor goes to Lady Fearach, who donated it, and who championed an unknown slave when our own council would have forbidden her race." Silence falls over the crowd, every eye straining to the dais. "I may be only an honorary queen," Prudence says with quiet dignity. "But I have lived long enough to know true honor. Lady Fearach." She turns to Lupa and curtsies gracefully. "Please," she says, her head bent, "present our winner with her prize."

Lupa mounts the dais. Taking Prudence's hand, she raises her up and kisses her on both cheeks. "My queen," she says, with as genuine a smile as I've ever seen her give.

Lupa turns to me. "Zaria."

I mount the dais, the crowd a blur before me, not one face making any sense.

"You fought today." Lupa turns me to face the crowd, her voice ringing out across the ballroom. "You found your fire. You found your dragon. And even when all was lost"—she raises her glass with blazing eyes—"still you raced!"

The crowd roars, but I'm not looking at them. I'm watching Harken, who is leaning against a nearby pillar, watching these proceedings with a wry smile.

"It is my greatest honor," Lupa says, beaming as she presses a huge key ring into my hand, "to give you the keys to Caer Helfrach—along with this chest of gold." I don't miss her wink as the footmen bring the chest forward. Lupa raises my hand high in triumph. "Lady Zaria!" she calls.

"Lady Zaria!" the crowd cries back. They repeat it, over and again, and I'm relieved when finally the cries subside. I'm about to step down when Harken comes up beside me, instantly silencing the crowd.

"I believe," he says, in his customary sardonic drawl, "that our honorable Comitas has another announcement." Turning to the stairs, Harken makes an elaborate gesture. "Comitas Ormond. If you would."

The Comitas, looking extremely strained, mounts the stairs, barely glancing at me. He coughs uneasily, looking around at the crowd.

"Get on with it, Dirk," hisses Lupa from behind me.

Comitas Ormond's eyes flicker resentfully to Harken, who says nothing, but merely folds his arms, raises one eyebrow, and gives him a lazy smile. The Comitas colors, then clears his throat.

"In light of recent events," he begins pompously.

"You mean in light of your son having his arse whipped," yells a Maverick from the rear of the crowd, to a chorus of hoots.

"In light of recent events," the Comitas says again, glaring into the crowd, "and in recognition of the Woven Lord's permanent return to our council—"

But the crowd's shocked gasp cuts off whatever he is about to say, every eye turning to Harken, who gives a slight, ironic bow that makes the braver of them titter. I'm too stunned to speak at all.

Permanent return?

"Compromise," Harken murmurs, his lips curving against my ear. "The price of me taking my seat at their table—and Sereia keeping hers." He casts me the merest ghost of a wink. I'm still trying to process this startling revelation when Comitas Ormond continues.

"As a sign of goodwill to the Race winner," he says irritably, raising his voice over the hubbub, "the council members have agreed to make a rare exception to the laws on Shadow Braids. Lord Halvard, if you will."

The crowd parts to reveal Kendrick, his grim face strangely softened as he steps up to the dais and kisses my cheek. "I can never thank you for bringing Harken back to us," he murmurs. "But I do hope this is a beginning."

As he steps aside to reveal those behind him, my heart slows, then begins to thud again, heavy with a hope I barely dare allow myself to feel.

"The council," the Comitas continues ponderously, "hereby orders the unweaving of three Shadow Braids: those belonging to the ladies Shimi and Neoma and the Candidate Paladin, Levin."

I'm dimly aware of his words, but I don't truly hear them. There is nothing anymore but the roaring in my ears and the three figures standing before me.

Shimi's face is hard with disbelief. She holds Neoma by the arm. For once, Neoma's eyes sparkle with life that has nothing to do with the Sight or Darkwine. Levin, taller and stronger than I might ever have imagined, holds Neoma's other arm. His curls are gone, and his jaw is set hard, but the hand holding Neoma is gentle, and the eyes he turns to me hold such a wealth of understanding that I want to weep.

"Feivel thought," Harken says quietly in my ear, "that you might wish to do the honors."

Feivel comes onto the dais. "It isn't mine anymore," he says, holding out his needle. "But I think it already knows its new owner."

I stare at it dumbly. "I don't know how to Work."

He places the needle in my hand and closes my fingers over it. "Yes," he says, smiling at me. "You do."

I feel it, the moment the needle finds its place in my palm. I feel it as if it has always been there and as if I have come home.

I hold the needle out toward Shimi. "Unwoven," I say, my voice not entirely steady.

Shimi stands frozen as her braid slowly unwinds, the threads falling away.

"Unwoven," I murmur again, directing it at Neoma. She stumbles forward as the braid unravels, her entire body heaving. Tears blur my eyes.

"Unwoven," I manage, my needle feeling Levin's braid. He falls forward, coughing, his eyes shining with unshed tears.

I stare at them, my three siblings, and I know all of us are thinking only of the fourth.

"Wait."

I can't bear to look in the direction of that gruff voice. I think it must be an imagining, born of the moment. It's only when I see the others turn that I dare raise my eyes to the door.

The crowd parts to reveal a tough, grizzled Stitched Man, his gray uniform stiff with salt and his body lean with hardship. Garrick stares at me across the ballroom, disbelief and pride warring on his face as he comes toward me.

"Lass," he says roughly as he nears the dais. "Look who I found." He steps aside.

Striding through the crowd, looking neither right nor left, his lean face blazing in a smile that takes my breath away, is Doron. His harelip scar is a jagged tear the length of his face, gleaming like a subterranean channel where the light catches it. The hard, glittering silver is gone from his eyes, which shimmer now with a joy so deep it warms my soul. He pulls each of our siblings into a hard embrace as he reaches them, holding Levin the longest of them all. Then he turns to me.

"Zaria." He says my name as he halts in front of the dais.

Tears fall unchecked down my face as I come slowly down the stairs to stand in front of him. "You came back." I can barely whisper. "You came home."

Doron takes my hands. "Actually," he says quietly, "I found my home." I look over his shoulder, to where a tall girl with vivid red hair and deep emerald eyes stands somewhat nervously behind him, smiling tentatively. "It's a long story," Doron says, seeing my eyes go to her. "Marguerite's was the voice I heard coming from the Dark Rip, back in Hiraeth."

His smile isn't twisted anymore, I find myself thinking, just as his face is no longer wary and grim. His smile is real, from a place inside him that is no longer woven in darkness, but rather wreathed in light.

My eyes fall to the braid at his neck. It's black, just as the braid end was, and seems almost seared into his flesh, a horrific bind that speaks of unendurable suffering.

Doron grimaces. "Ugly," he says lightly, "isn't it?"

"Oh, I don't know." My light tone matches his, and I glance back to where Harken is watching us, a slight smile on his face. "I've learned a little," I say, "about darkness and savagery."

Doron's eyes widen as they follow mine. To my surprise, he strides past me, halting before Harken. "I believe," Doron says, holding out his hand, "that I have you to thank for the ship that came looking for me."

"For the ship, perhaps." Harken takes Doron's hand with genuine courtesy. He doesn't look at me as he speaks, holding Doron's eyes instead. "But it was Garrick and your friends in the Seam Guard who came to ask for it. Your rescue is their doing. Not mine." Doron's eyes narrow slightly, as if he's taking Harken's measure. He looks between Harken and me, then nods, a faint smile on his face, and releases Harken's hand.

My eyes fly to Garrick, who tilts his head in acknowledgment at my surprise. "I told you we had orders," he says, grinning at me. "I didn't say from whom."

My heart twists as I think of Harken's long-ago words, in Hiraeth: *The Seam Guard tell me your brother was bound for the Stitched Men. His fate is their responsibility now.*

Doron turns to me. "I did hear," he says, a gleam of our old dark humor in his eyes, "that you might be able to do something about this." He gestures to the braid.

Glancing over at Garrick, barely able to see his beaming face through my tears, I raise my needle.

"Go on, then, lass," he says gruffly. "Show the bastards what you can do."

THERE ARE MORE WOVEN books coming! LINKS AND FREE DOWNLOADS BELOW.

But first, if you loved this book, please tell others by leaving a review. It helps so much.

Order Woven in Savagery, Book Two in the saga, on my website, www.lucyholden.com.

Download your free prequel to Woven at www.paulaconstant.com/fleur-de-lis. THIS WILL ADD YOU TO THE MAILING LIST.

Would you like to advance read the rest of the series? Sign up to the ARC team.

Doron's story, Seam of Gold, the first in the Waterpaths saga, is also available on Amazon now. It links the Woven and Nightgarden Sagas.

Read an excerpt of the Nightgarden Saga on the pages FOLLOWING THE ENDNOTES.

The Nightgarden Saga Prequel is also free on my website: https://www.paulaconstant.com/the-nightgarden-saga.

I love hearing from you. Get in touch on my socials or by email: lucyholden@lucyholden.com.

I LOVE TIK TOK, so if you review there, please tag me @lucyholdenparanormal.

I'm on insta @lucyholdenauthor, and there is also a street team you can join on facebook, Lucy Holden Street Team, where you can meet other readers.

THANKYOU so much for reading Woven in Darkness!

Lucy

ENDNOTES

THE WOVEN WORLD

The following pages are a glossary of commonly used terms, included at the request of my advance readers. There are four sections:

1. Places
2. People (Races, not characters)
3. Institutions
4. Lore, objects and substances.

I hope you find it useful.

PLACES

Interweave

The fabric between the worlds, a dark and terrifying place most cannot enter or navigate.

Dark Rip

A tear in the Interweave which opens up a link between worlds. Unstable and dangerous, Dark Rips are opened by fragments of Anahita's Gold, either accidentally or by Dark Weavers who don't wish to use normal pathways.

Seam

A small fold of land made by Weavers many centuries ago to protect the Woven World from the Interweave and the Dark Rips that open there. Now a place of slaves and the downtrodden who have no knowledge of how to work Indigo, or skill to do so.

Hiraeth Forest

An ancient and dangerous forest that exists in multiple

worlds. The Interweave has many holes here, and creatures often use the forest to move from one world to the next.

The Woven World

The world on the other side of the Seam. All here are still connected to the Indigo and are raised with it. The Woven World is made up of six countries:

- Astria
- Tabellar (north of Astria)
- Basetana (South, across the sea)
- Sjollin (Far north east of Astria)
- Songlands (Far distant south east, a land wrapped in legend that few know)
- Sherimah (the lost kingdom of the First Woven)

Astria

Arguably the most powerful country in the Woven World, Astria is home to the legendary Woven Court, where the Weavers once had their Lotus Council. It is where all of this book takes place.

The Drop

A hole made in the Interweave during the fall of Sherimah. Located south west of Astria, amid the sea, the Drop leads directly into the Interweave itself.

The Nexus

Located at the border of the Seam and Astria, the Nexus is a turbulent labyrinth amid the Interweave where paths from many worlds meet. Passing through the Nexus was traditionally only done by Weavers, and then with care. Pathfinders can also navigate it, but are rarely permitted to do so and are carefully monitored when they do.

The Foolish World

The mortal world in which you and I live.

The Indigo City

The capital city of Astria, from where the Council of Twelve rule.

Wolf Weald

Court in the far north west of Astria, mountainous, heavily forested, and including the Astrian side of Hiraeth Forest and the Kept lands, which border the Foolish World. Those born in the Weald are ruled by fire and trained to use that element. Many have the ability to shift into wolf form. Home to the Fire Guard, who patrol Hiraeth and monitor it for breaches in the Interweave.

Goath

Court in the north eastern mountains symbolised by the Eagle. Ruled by air, many from Goath can shift into avian form and control flying beasts. Goath monitors 'breezes', the means by which messages are sent. It also controls Pathfinders.

Waterlands

Court in the warm south west, set around the canals of the Indigo River, and the Indigo City. Ruled by water, those born of water can often work with aquatic creatures or turn into them.

Dencover

Underground court in the arid, dry south east, governed by earth and notorious for its mines and jewellery. Dencover natives can work with creatures that burrow underground, or which have hooves.

(Woven Court)

Long hidden behind Woven Mists, the Woven Court is the ancient heart of Astria, the place where Weavers were raised and trained, before the War. It was also home to the Lotus Council, tasked with disciplining and managing Weavers.

(Sherimah)

Ancient city of the First Woven. It was blasted into oblivion during the fall of Anahita some two thousand years ago, and the Drop now exists where it once stood.

Woven Tower

Created especially to hold Anahita, the Woven Tower cannot be entered by any. It is shrouded in Shadow mists, which not even Harken can penetrate.

PEOPLE

Fool/Foolish

Human beings like you and I, rarely seen in the Seam or Astria. Fools usually have little or no ability to work with Indigo, but sometimes the worlds connect and Fools possess stronger doses of Indigo, which bestow them with supernatural/paranormal abilities.

Seamish

Once Indigold themselves, after years of interbreeding with Fools and monsters, the Seamish no longer remember how to work Indigo in any way. They are downtrodden and poverty stricken. Many are slaves. They cannot survive for long in Astria as their bodies have changed after so long in the Seam.

Indigold

The people of the Woven World. They live longer than Fools or Seamish, around a century to a century and a half, but are NOT immortal. They are, however, born with both Silver and Indigo in their bodies which they can be taught to Work with, using a needle. They heal quickly, possess many skills to help them heal, and have elements in their appearance that would appear supernatural to a Fool or Seamish person.

Weorpan

Rejected by the Woven World, Weorpan are commonly considered to be half breeds, part Indigold and part something else, be that demon, Seamish, Fool, Pathfinder, or monster. In reality, most of them are simply Indigold who were born into unfortunate circumstances - illegitimate, for example. They are usually slaves in the Seam, where they are mistrusted. In Astria they are considered as lowly creatures, and mistrusted for what mysteries may hide in their blood.

Weaver

Immortal beings, Weavers are born on the Isle of Nine in a Great Ceremony that is shrouded in secrecy. They are born with a needle inside their body, unlike the Indigold, who are given a needle at age nineteen. The extraction of the Weaver's needle is a closely guarded secret. They Weave Indigo rather than Work it as Indigold do. Weavers belong to Astria, and exist to serve the Woven World as teachers and guides. They should not have allegiance to countries or families, but only to the Woven Court.

Priestess

Women with gifts of a particular type who live on the Isle of Nine, known as the pomegranate Isle. They can be Sylphs, Seers, Shifters or Salvers. They are guarded by the Sabers, an all female band of warriors.

Shadow

Extremely mysterious people, Shadows can unthread and rethread themselves, ultimately rendering them able to be invisible. They are spies, assassins, and can grant favours, known as

Shadow Bargains (see later entry). Their Work is untraceable. If they Work a mist, or a slave braid, none can tell who made it. They listen to conversations through Shadowscyes, and can also travel through them (see later entry).

Pathfinder

Pathfinders are made up of Silver, which looks like Foolish mercury. They can travel the pathways of the Interweave at will, but because nobody trusts them, they are closely monitored and forced to move through registered silverscyes that lead directly from one place to another (see later entry).

Demons

A rather broad term for a race that can appear a variety of ways. Demons usually come through Dark Rips by accident from other worlds. They aren't inherently bad, though they can be very ugly, and put to dark uses. Many Indigold have traces of demon blood, and although this is looked down on in some circles, they are often strong warriors.

INSTITUTIONS

Seam Guards and Stitched Men

Founded by Caspian the Sailor, the Seam Guards patrol the places where the Interweave is most porous. The elite of their force are the Stitched Men, found at the headquarters of the Seam Guard, which is a floating fortress on the edge of The Drop. The Stitched Men are able to sail their ships over the Drop and enter the Interweave itself, mending the tears that open there.

The Paladins - symbol is the Cup and Serpent

Originally a monastic order of alchemists, an offshoot of the central Coronastrian religion, established to guard the sacred fountain, the water from which is used in the sacred Cups of Coronastrian ceremonies. The water can heal any ailment and has mystical properties. The Paladins are now a very powerful, secretive institution centred in the Paladin's Abbey. They have their own military arm and consider themselves an alternative religion to Coronastrianism.

- **Paladin's Water** - *the healing water from the fountain, rumoured to grant immortality if used correctly*
- **Blade** - *a warrior from the Paladins military ranks*
- **Divine** - *an alchemist trained to mix the sacred Cups*
- **Saber** - *female warriors trained to guard the Isle of Nine. Since the war the Sabers have broken with the Paladin Abbey and train with the Weald instead.*
- **Consul** - *represents the Paladin Abbey on the Council of Twelve*

Coronastrian Tapest - symbol is the twelve pointed Astris

The central religion of Astria, the Tapest worked closely with the Woven Court for centuries, and is the only institution inducted into the secrets of the Great Ceremony. The Taspest ran all the educational institutions, hospitals, etc, in Astria before the war, but has lost a lot of power since the War to the ambitious Paladins.

- **Astrid** - *much like a parish priest*
- **Astar** - *head of the Coronastrian Tapest, sits on the Council of Twelve*

Isle of Nine/Pomegranate Isle - symbol is a pomegranate

Home to the female spiritual arm of the Coronastrian Tapest, and keepers of the secrets of the Great Ceremony. They use Darkwine to give them visions. The head priestess is called the Sybil.

The Great Ceremony is held on the Isle (or was before the War) and all Weavers are born here, under the legendary Songtree. The Isle is located off the north western shore, beyond the Wolf Weald.

The Woven Court - symbol a twelve pointed lotus

The ancient heart of the Woven World, the last remnant of

the First Woven. Before the War, home to the Lotus Council of Weavers. Now shut away behind the Woven Mists, and known as the Savage Court.

- **Darkwine** - *produced in concentrated form in the Woven Court, it is a highly hallucinatory drink if taken in strong quantities.*
- **Darkberry** - *a potent berry that grows only in the Woven Court. It is considered to be made of pure Indigo and is both deadly and highly powerful depending on how it is distilled.*

Council of Twelve
The governing body of Astria since the War. Made up of:

- Four Indigold members drawn from the four most powerful courts (Goath, the Weald, Dencover, and the Waterlands)
- The Paladin Consul
- The Paladin Weaver
- The Coronastrian Astar
- The Coronastrian Weaver
- The head priestess (the Sybil) from the Isle of Nine
- A Weaver from the Woven Court
- The Indigold Comitas, who leads the Council
- The Comitas's Weaver of choice.

The House of Thread and Shadows (HOTAR)
Wreathed in mystery, the HOTAR has been located on the Isle of Jezarah, near the Drop, since the days of Sherimah. Said to be established by Jezarah, a powerful Weaver who was one of Anahita's associates, and who allegedly stole a golden needle and ran to the Isle. Nobody enters the HOTAR except Stitched Men, and those chosen to train there. The HOTAR is wreathed

in Shadow Mists and so can't be discovered by any not inducted into its mysteries.

- **Shadows** - *trained in the HOTAR, they are so called because they cast no shadow, and can move without detection. Feared and distrusted, they listen from the shadows, and so if someone asks for a Shadow Favour, they will appear to make the bargain.*
- **Shadowscye** - *a portal that is created and opened by Shadows, and can only be detected by them. The portals enable Shadows to see/hear what is happening in the room where they have placed a Shadowscye. They can also travel through the Shadowscyes from one place to another, though Shadows can also disappear and reappear seemingly at will (this is a mystery of the HOTAR training.)*
- **Shadow Bargains and Shadow Favours** - *the words of the Shadow Bargain are 'take what you want, and pay for it'. A bargain is made when someone asks a Shadow for a favour. The favour will be granted on the understanding that the debt will be called in at some undisclosed point in the future. The favour collected will be of equal value, but not necessarily the same. Such bargains are bound by silence - they cannot physically be spoken of, or written about, and they can be collected many generations down the family tree, which makes people treat them very warily. The man who asks for riches may find his grandson impoverished in return. The debt cannot be avoided, nor traded away. The Bargains are binding. People often put down to 'fate', or 'luck', what is actually a Shadow Bargain, a Favour being collected. Shadow Favours are just another way of speaking about Shadow Bargains. One asks for a Favour, and when it is granted, a Shadow Bargain is made to bind the deal.*
- **Shadow Braid** - *a slave braid Woven by a Shadow, which means it is anonymous - the slave will never know who*

ordered them enslaved, nor who Wove the braid. Shadow
bound slaves are considered with suspicion by everyone,
even other slaves, since a Shadow Braid is a costly favour,
and usually implies some very dark, dangerous secret.
Possibly tainted bloodlines, the use of Dark Weaving.
Shadow Braids can only be unwoven by approval from the
Council of Twelve, whereas a normal slave braid can be
unwoven by the Indigold lord who wove it.

LORE, OBJECTS AND SUBSTANCES

Indigo

A potent form of matter that is considered the threads of life itself. A mysterious, almost ephemeral stuff that lives inside every Indigold, and in the earth, air and water of the Woven World itself. Indigold train to use their needles to Work with Indigo, but although their powers can be considerable, they do not rival the Weavers in their skill.

Silver

A substance that lives inside every Indigold (in varying quantities), Silver is the means by which Indigold are able to shapeshift.

Pathfinder's Silver

A concentrated form of Silver. A Pathfinder is more Silver than they are Indigo or flesh, meaning that they can dissolve and reform. Even though their Silver is actually the same as the Shifter's Silver in the Indigold form, Pathfinder's Silver is considered deceitful, dangerous, and very much not to be trusted.

Silverscye

A portal through which Pathfinders travel from one place to the next. Indigold can also travel through a silverscye, if they go with Pathfinders or Weavers.

Golden needles

After the fall of Sherimah six golden needles were made from a central dagger. They are mysterious and magical, but most have been lost or stolen in the intervening years. The most important one, from the Coronastrian Tapest, was lost during the War, which is why there are no longer any Great Ceremonies.

Anahita's gold/Serpent's gold

When Anahita was blown into the Interweave during the Fall of Sherimah, with her went the last of the gold used to make the golden needles. The origin of that gold is shrouded in myth and legend, though it is said to come from another world. This is the gold floating in the Interweave and harvested by Dark Weavers to make tools that open Dark Rips. Anahita herself was almost totally made up of this gold by the time she was originally defeated. It is highly sought after by Paladins and alchemists, who believe it can help create an immortal form.

Weaving

The term used for what Weavers do with their needles, manipulating the threads of life, silver, indigo, and gold, to create wonders.

Work

The term used for the way Indigold use their needles and Indigo.

RED MAGNOLIA EXCERPT

PROLOGUE

*D*ear Tessa,

It's a year today since I watched you die. If one more person tells me not to feel guilty, I might actually lose it. As long as we were still the Ellory twins, somehow it didn't seem so bad that it was just us and Connor. But me alone is different.

Alone, I am an orphan.

I never felt like one before, though technically I guess we both were after Mom died.

Connor misses you. He doesn't say much, but I can tell. He's my legal guardian now, which is actually just weird, since he's barely twenty-one. Someone had to do the job, I guess. We changed his name to Ellory before we moved. We both know his dad is never coming back. And although he never said anything, I know he hated having to explain who he was to teachers or doctors, every time there was a legal form to sign.

There've been way too many forms lately.

I'm starting a new school today. I couldn't face going back to the old one after you died. I did homeschooling for the rest of the school year, and we moved over the summer. Connor made me go to that camp you and I applied to for two weeks, I think just to get me out of the house while he packed up your things. I sure couldn't face doing it. I didn't tell anyone at camp you were dead, just that you changed your mind about coming. It seemed easier. I actually talked about you the whole time as if you were still alive, which is pretty messed up, I know, but a whole lot easier than telling people your twin sister died. Nobody knows what to say to that, including me.

I know I should have written all this earlier. But today is the first day I've felt like I can talk to you directly. Or write, at least. I can't stand the idea of "journaling," as the grief therapist called it. It feels self-indulgent and pretentious. But writing to you is easy. You always knew what I thought before I ever said it anyway.

My new school is in Deepwater Hollow, Mississippi. It's a little town an hour or so upriver from Baton Rouge, no more than a dot on the map. I'm glad to be leaving the city. To be leaving Louisiana. Everything about our old place reminded me of you.

I want Connor to feel good about this. There are more old plantation ruins here than anywhere else in the continental US, and plenty of grants to restore them, apparently. We used Mom's insurance money to buy a huge, decaying antebellum house on the Mississippi after Connor designed a winning proposal for it. If he makes good on his plans, and I know he will, he'll be able to bid for more. He says it's a new beginning for us. I want to believe that, even if the ruins of the past are a strange place to look for a new beginning.

This place is insane, truly. You would love it. Big old oaks hung with Spanish moss hide the house from the road, and down back a little wood dock juts out onto the river. The red magnolia trees you loved so much grow by the porch and run the length of the back lawn. Their scent reminds me of you.

Plaster is crumbling from the ceiling, and we're using

kerosene lanterns and an icebox until Connor fixes the wiring. It feels as if Miss Haversham might live in the attic, though so far, it's just been the bugs and us.

I'm writing this from the school parking lot on the first day of senior year. I'm still driving the old pink Mustang convertible you and I bought together. When the crystal you put on the rearview mirror catches the light, the turquoise in it reminds me of your eyes. Which is weird when you think about it, because actually, I see your eyes every time I look into a mirror. But that's the thing about being an identical twin. Almost everything about us looks the same, but no matter how hard I try, I can't make my eyes look like yours. Some days I stare into the mirror at them until I ache, just hoping I catch a glimpse of you inside them.

Because I miss you, Tessa. And the truth is, missing you is the reason I haven't written. Because if I let myself think about how much I miss you, everything in me starts to crumble, and I think that if I let even one piece fall, the whole of me will come tumbling down in a way even Connor's DIY cannot fix.

A new school might not be able to bring you back. But maybe, if I try hard enough, it might bring me back.

The bell is ringing. I have to go.

Wish me luck.

Your twin,

Harper

CHAPTER ONE

CURSED

*D*eepwater High has fewer faces in the entire student body than the senior-year class at my old school, but I'm pretty sure every single one of them is staring at me in the corridor. I was expecting the usual first day once-over, but this feels next-level, and by the time I clear the registrar and find my new English class, I'm starting to miss Baton Rouge. Everyone else is seated already.

"Ah," says Mr. Corbin, making a mock bow. "Miss Ellory. The new tenant of Deepwater's favorite Gothic mansion graces us with her presence." I have to do the awkward newbie walk of shame through another barrage of curious eyes, to a desk crammed between a tall, pale boy with floppy brown hair falling over his face and a dark-haired girl who has her head down writing notes. I slide into my seat, face burning.

"Mr. Marigny," Mr. Corbin addresses the pale boy, who looks up warily. "Perhaps you could show your new neighbor where we are in the textbook." He turns back to the board. The boy leans across the aisle and flips my book open.

"There," he says, pointing to the page. He doesn't look at me when he speaks. When he turns back to his book, I see the flush rising on his neck, and I realize he's not rude, just shy. I know how he feels. I glance at his paper and see his name at the top: Jeremiah Marigny.

I can almost hear Tessa beside me, giggling at the name. Our mom loved old rock songs, and when we were kids she'd play one song on loop whenever we were driving around. There's a line in it that goes around in my head: *Jeremiah was a bullfrog.* I write it on the side of my page, making swirling patterns out of the letters, getting lost in the finer points so Mr. Corbin's voice fades away. The words become a vine down the margin of my book. The vine becomes the frame for a window. I sketch the wood dock at the back of our new home as if I were sitting inside the window looking out and then add a full moon blazing down. I'm so lost in my drawing that I'm startled when the clatter of chairs signals the end of class. I scramble for my bag and realize, too late, that Jeremiah has seen the words in the margin. Even made into a vine, they are unmistakable. His eyes meet mine, wide and dark and deep somehow, as if he already knows how much the world is going to hurt him.

"I'm sorry," I mutter. It's all I can think of. He tilts his head and shrugs, almost smiling, then slings his bag over his shoulder and is gone. For a lanky boy, he moves fast. He's out of the room before I've even stood up.

"Don't worry about Jeremiah," says the girl who was sitting on the other side of me. "He's shy, is all." Her skin is tawny in the morning sun, eyes dark over slanted cheekbones. She's so beautiful it's like standing in a gallery just looking at her. My fingers itch to sketch her face. "I'm Avery."

"Hey, Avery." I gesture at the offending words on the page before me. "I didn't mean anything by it. It's just the name, you know? I couldn't help but think of the song."

"Like I said, don't worry." She gives me a friendly smile that I could literally hug her for about now. "We've been ragging on Jeremiah about that name since grade school. He won't mind."

She glances at my class schedule and map. "I can walk you to the art hall if you like. My class isn't far away."

"Thank you," I say gratefully. Map reading has never been my strong point. We head out along the breezeway, and I try to ignore all the curious stares. "So Mr. Corbin mentioned that Jeremiah is our neighbor," I say, more to make conversation than anything else. "I hadn't noticed anyone living nearby."

"He's not your neighbor anymore. I'm not sure that he ever really was." There's something in the way she says it that makes me look sideways at her. "The house you bought is the Marigny mansion. It belonged to his family."

It takes me a moment to digest that. Connor handled the documents for the house. I never looked hard at the names involved. Besides, the mansion is so decayed it hadn't occurred to me that anyone could have tried to actually live in it in recent years. Connor worked all summer while I was away at camp just to make it safe to step inside.

"You mean he used to live there?" I imagine a lifetime amid the crumbling plaster, lack of electricity, and rusted bathtub and think it's no wonder Jeremiah looks so sad.

"Not exactly. He and his parents lived in a trailer. They parked on the grounds there, sometimes." Avery chews her lip, clearly holding back.

Normally I'd be far too shy to ask further. But my natural introversion is overpowered by the memory of Jeremiah's hurt eyes and the fear that I'll inadvertently do or say something else hurtful.

"Um, Avery?" We're nearly across the sloping lawn to the art hall. "If there's some kind of story about our house, it would really help to know about it so I don't do anything else stupid that might upset someone."

Avery shrugs. "It's nothing, really. All the old places around here have a story, you know?" Her eyes slide away.

"So, what's the story with mine?"

She gives me a look like she'd rather not say but knows I won't let it go. "Your house has been in the Marigny family for as long as anyone can remember, but it's been a ruin for decades now, and even longer since anyone actually lived in it." She looks around as if to make sure nobody is in earshot, then leans in and lowers her voice. "Thing is, a few months ago Jeremiah's parents both died in a car crash. It was awful. My aunt is a nurse at the hospital, and she said the bodies were so messed up you could barely recognize them. Jeremiah doesn't have any brothers or sisters, and his parents never had a lot of money. The sale of the Marigny mansion is all the money he was left with."

I feel humiliation crawl up my spine like a roly-poly bug. "So I just made fun of the boy with dead parents whose house I stole."

She stares at me a moment and then bursts out laughing. "Well," she says, "when you put it like that, I guess."

"At least that explains why everyone is looking at me. Thanks for telling me, Avery." I give her a smile and turn toward the art hall.

"Harper, wait." When I turn back, she's shifting her feet, like she's trying to decide whether to speak or not. "You should know. It's not just the car crash or dead parents that's the story with the Marigny mansion."

"Then what is?"

She tilts her head awkwardly and does her feet-shifting thing again. "You know that Deepwater is real old country, right? Like, that mansion you bought—it's so old, nobody around here even knows the truth about it anymore."

"Sure." I look at her, waiting.

"So, the story is just something everyone hears, you know, growing up. They say that something bad happened there, a long time ago. People died. And that afterwards, there was a curse put on the house, like an old voodoo thing."

My eyes bug a little. "An old voodoo thing? Seriously?"

She nods. "The story went that so long as the Marigny mansion stayed in the family, the curse would be contained, and nobody else would die. But if it was sold . . ." Her voice trails off and she gives me an apologetic shrug.

"Oh, great." I try to keep a flippant tone, but I'd be lying if I said my heart didn't stop a little at that. I've had about enough of death to last me forever. "Well, I guess every old place around here has a story, like you said."

"Maybe."

I don't really want to hear any more stories, but we've come this far, and there's something in her voice that says she isn't quite done. "Go on, then. Give me the rest." Avery meets my eyes, and now there is no hint of laughter in her face.

"It wasn't Jeremiah who chose to sell the house. It was his parents. They were real happy about it, too. The night they signed the papers, they went to the local roadhouse. Bought a round for the whole bar. They told everyone they were putting a down payment on a place down in Biloxi. Time to leave the past behind, they said, and move on."

I feel a cold sensation in my spine.

"They never even made it home." Avery's words drop into the day like the first cold touch of winter. "They left the roadhouse and crashed the car, not a mile up the road. It happened the very same day they signed the Marigny mansion over to your family. That's it, Harper. That's the story. That's why everyone is looking at you. They think you're living in a cursed house, and they're all wondering what happens next."

CHAPTER TWO

VEILS

*I*t's a relief to go into the quiet art hall. The teacher has a sweet face and a funky, bohemian look, and she thankfully doesn't remark on my newbie status. "I'm Miss Calhoun," she says in a low voice, steering me past the other students toward an easel. "We're working on a layering technique that will be the background for a new piece. Choose a watercolor and apply it in layers, like veils." She demonstrates then gives me a once-over. "You might want to tie that hair up." I flush and scrabble through my bag for a hair tie. Tessa and I had the same copper hair, so thick and curly Mom gave up trying to tame it when we were kids and just let it grow. It's been down to my waist for as long as I can remember. I wrap it up in a big knot and pull the hair tie around it. I know it makes me look like I'm the beehive queen, but I'm already embarrassed enough, and I figure there isn't any point trying to pretend to an elegance I definitely don't possess. Mom always said our hair and coloring were a gift from a distant ancestor. Maybe if we lived in Europe, she'd be right, but I feel like ivory skin and deep copper ringlets aren't much of an advantage in southern Mississippi.

I get to work, welcoming the soothing strokes of my paintbrush and the dreamy music she has going in the background. There are only a few of us in the class. One of them is Jeremiah. I glance at him once, but he seems immersed in his painting and doesn't look at me.

My brush rolls over the page and gradually the layers form the same scene I sketched earlier, with a ghostly moon reflecting in the water. I like the way the veils make the image emerge, as if the scene creates itself, rather than me painting it. I'm surprised when the class comes to an end. Miss Calhoun stands behind me as I pack up.

"I know that view," she says, smiling. "Looking out over the river from behind the Marigny place." As soon as she speaks, she goes red and glances at Jeremiah, but he is already out the door, walking up over the hill. "Oh, dear," she sighs. "That was clumsy of me."

"Don't worry." I can feel the curious eyes of the rest of the class on me. "At least you aren't the one living in it."

"Oh!" Miss Calhoun waves a hand in a not-entirely-reassuring effort at dismissal. "Never mind those old stories."

I give her what I hope seems like a convincing smile. "I'm more worried about whether or not my stepbrother Connor will actually make the water tap work, to be honest." That at least gets a rumble of laughter.

At lunch I sit with Avery and her friends and try to remember their names. Jeremiah Marigny, I notice, is sitting on his own at a table a little distant from ours.

"Should we ask him to eat with us?" I ask Avery under cover of conversation.

"You could try," she says, equally quietly. "But Jeremiah isn't really one for chat, especially now, since his parents died."

I know how that feels. It hadn't mattered so much after Mom died. There was Tessa and me, and because we were our own little friendship bubble, people weren't scared to talk to us.

And Tessa was always bubbly. People were drawn to her. Mom used to say that Tessa did the talking for us both, while I did the listening. I know she said it because she worried I felt overshadowed by Tessa, but the truth is, I never did. I could easily listen to her chatter on all day and never get bored. It was only after she died that I realized I didn't really know how to talk at all— and by then, nobody knew how to talk to me either. In the end, it was easier to be homeschooled and communicate in monosyllabic peace with Connor.

The rest of the day passes in a blur of faces, names, and embarrassing class entrances. When the final bell rings, I spot Jeremiah leaving the building and walk faster to catch up to him. He's really tall and moves so fast I almost have to run. "Hey," I say, puffing slightly as we near the parking lot. "Jeremiah. I just wanted to say I'm really sorry for making fun of your name this morning." I smile, but he doesn't look at me, and it might be my imagination, but he seems to have upped his pace even more. He's looking uneasily toward the parking lot, like he's expecting someone. "I wasn't actually making fun of it," I say. "I draw a lot."

"I know." He stops and turns to face me. "I saw you in art hall."

"I didn't realize it was your house we bought." He's looking at something over my shoulder and couldn't be less welcoming, but I plow on regardless. "Or about your parents." This is awkward as hell, but if anyone has experience in awkward, dead-family conversations, it's me, so I push on. "My parents are both dead, too." I can't quite bring myself to mention Tessa. "So, I guess I just wanted to say that I'm sorry."

He nods but still doesn't smile.

"Anyway." I'm definitely embarrassed now. "I just wanted to say that." I start walking away, feeling like a prize idiot, when he takes my arm and stops me. His face is pained, as if he's already regretting his decision to talk to me. "If you really are sorry about the house," he says, "maybe you could ask your brother to sell it back to me."

"Sell it back to you?" I stare at him. "Why? And it's my name on the deed, not Connor's."

His eyes widen. "You own it?"

I nod. "My brother has power of attorney because I'm underage, but it's in my name. Connor won a grant to renovate it. I'm really sorry, Jeremiah. I know it must mean a lot to you, but I can't just sell it back."

"No. You don't understand." If his agitation wasn't already clear enough, he grips my arm hard enough to hurt. "You need to sell that house, Harper. It isn't safe there, for you or your brother." He looks over my shoulder again and his face tightens, like he's afraid.

"Ow, Jeremiah. You're hurting me." I pull my arm away and look around. There's an old teal-colored Chevy truck pulling into the lot, the kind guys always say they want to buy and restore but never do. I can't see who's driving it, but Jeremiah is watching it like it's coming for him. I lower my voice. "Avery told me the story about the house, but surely you don't believe it's actually cursed?" I feel stupid even saying the word.

He laughs, but not in amusement. It's more the kind of laugh someone makes when they know something you don't, a little wild and out of control. I don't like how tense he is, and I step aside as he pushes past me toward the Chevy. "You don't know anything about the curse," he says, and now he just sounds tired, almost despairing. "Please, Harper. I've already sent a lawyer's letter to the house. It should be there when you get home today. At least look at it and consider the offer."

"Okay," I say. "I'll look. But I have to tell you, Jeremiah—even if I wanted to sell the house, I don't think my brother would be very happy giving up a grant he worked all summer to get. I'm sorry, truly I am, especially about your parents. I just can't see that selling you back the house is going to help anything."

www.ingramcontent.com/pod-product-compliance
Lightning Source LLC
Chambersburg PA
CBHW020246030726
47499CB00001B/82

* 9 7 8 1 9 2 2 6 6 6 1 3 0 *

He's already walking toward the lot and doesn't answer. There's a man leaning against the grill of the Chevy, arms folded, watching us. He looks Connor's age, maybe a little older, early twenties. He's wearing faded jeans that look like he was born in them and a V-neck a shade darker than his truck. He's taller even than Jeremiah, but lean and hard rather than lanky, and outdoor-adventure tanned. There's a three-day stubble on his face that looks like it's a way of life rather than an accident. His tousled dark hair has nothing to do with product, and his features seem carved from polished wood, unyielding and time-less. Then his eyes hit mine, and despite the distance between us, they are as clear as if he stood right in front of me.

They're an intense slate color, like dark thunderheads rolling in over the water. But it's the way they're looking at me, rather than their startling depth, that stops me right in my tracks. He is unnervingly still, his face unsmiling. Even from across the lot, hostility comes at me, as if the tropical storm in his eyes is about to make landfall.

Jeremiah opens the door of the truck and glances back, his eyes shifting between the man and me, and I realize it wasn't dislike I saw on his face earlier.

It was fear.

The man's eyes shift away from me and I feel them go, as if an invisible cord is released. I must have glanced away for a moment, because when I look back, the Chevy is already reversing.

Jeremiah glances at me through the window, and I can't tell if he is more angry or afraid. The Chevy pulls out and I watch it go, feeling even more disturbed than I did when Avery first told me about the curse on my house.

SAVE $15 WHEN YOU BUY THE COMPLETE Nightgarden Saga BUNDLE!